GUARDIANS

Book 6: The Lyris

GUARDIANS

Book 5, Part 2: The Lyris

NEW YORK TIMES BESTSELLING AUTHOR

Lola StVil

GUARDIANS: THE LYRIS

By Lola St.Vil

Formatting by Dallas Hodge, dalhodge56@gmail.com

Cover design by Renu Sharma

TABLE OF CONTENTS

*This book is dedicated to all the readers
who lovingly stalked me online
and wouldn't let me give in to the void of heartbreak.
I sincerely hope it was worth the wait.*

*This book is also dedicated to Shanna Bellingham
for her friendship and endless patience.*

BOOK 1: MARCUS CANE

"Nothing is worth doing unless the consequences may be serious—"

—George Bernard Shaw

(Submitted by contest winner, Shannon Liskowycz)

We have a deal: sl

almost ready, I look up at the door as if she will come bursting through it.

Nothing happens.

For the first time in her life, Emmy is following my instructions; she is staying away. I wish to Omnis I could see her, even if it's just for a few minutes. But I know it's not what's best for her. It's bad enough I have to go through with this; why should she have to watch this wedding take place?

"Marcus!" Ameana shouts in a tone that lets me know this isn't the first time she's called my name.

"What?"

"It's time," Miku says gently.

"Oh…yeah," I reply, unable to move towards the exit.

We're at St. Katharine's Church in Scotland. The vast, beautiful structure now holds thousands of angels and Quo. I'm in a little room off to the side, where grooms get ready for their big day. Miku and Ameana fuss over things I couldn't care less about.

Is my tie straight enough? Does my hair fall to the side that is most complimentary to my face? Should the red rose be pinned to the right or left side of my lapel?

"You look great," Ameana says, breaking the silence.

"It's my wedding day, so I guess I better."

"Well, mission accomplished," Miku says, forcing a smile.

"Am I doing the right thing?" I ask them.

"Time will tell," Miku replies.

Ameana nods in agreement, adding, "You're doing what's best for a race of angels who depend on you. I would do the same."

"The hell you would," Rage says as he enters the room. "Thomas—" "You would really marry someone else?" "To save an entire race? Yes," she replies. Miku and I exchange a quick glance. Once again, Rage and Ameana aren't on the same page. We had all hoped this "love affair" would burn out, but it just flames on. Who knows how many victims it will leave in its wake?

"Can you two take it outside?" I order.

The two of them walk away, eager to continue their argument.

"Can you believe that's still going on?" Pretty says.

"Huh? Oh, yeah," I reply, clearly distracted.

"Marcus, Emmy knows this isn't what you want. She knows you love her and that you're only doing this to save us. That's why she gave you her per mission."

"She gave me her permission because she's used to getting screwed by me."

"Okay, you have done some really questionable things that have ended up hurting Emmy, but this isn't your fault. You didn't know what Bianca was up to. None of us did."

"I made love to her, asked her to be mine, and then I signed a contract to marry a stranger."

"She knows why you're doing this. She knows where your heart really belongs. She understands."

"That's just it, Pretty. Understanding why someone is breaking your heart again doesn't make it hurt less."

I recount to Miku the conversation Emmy and I had once we were alone after Dalce gave me the ultimatum. I had sent the team away, and it was just Emmy and I alone in the room.

It was strange because we were desperate to be alone after Dalce made his announcement. But when we were, neither of us spoke. She leaned against the wall and looked up at the ceiling. I stood a few feet away studying her.

Finally, it wasn't a sound that broke the thick silence, but a gesture, one that nearly tore my soul to shreds; Emmy handed me back the engagement ring.

"C'mon, don't do that," I implored.

"I have to; bigamy is illegal in the state of New York," she replied.

"I'm not going to marry Bianca," I assured her.

"Then what are you going to do?"

"I'm gonna go talk to her. I have to reason with her and get her to understand that this can't happen."

"You think Bianca lacks understanding? Marcus, that bitch knows exactly what she's doing. She wants power, fame, and recognition. And she's right —marrying you is the best way to get that. That girl is brilliant."

"It doesn't matter, because I will not marry her."

She laughed a joyless laugh.

"What's so funny?" I demanded.

"If you don't marry her, the blood of thousands of angels will be on your hands. She has you right where she wants you."

"I'm not gonna enter a marriage just for politics."

"Yeah, you will, if it means saving lives."

"What about us? You think I could just give up on us and take another girl? I'm not gonna do that. I'm not gonna break your heart like before. We just got back together; I'm not losing you again. I'm not marrying Bianca. That's final."

"We both know who you are. It may be an hour from now or a few days, but in the end, you will do what a leader does—save your people."

"Emmy—"

"I know, you love me. I love you, too. And it's only now I'm realizing how little that matters."

"Emmy, that's not true. Our love matters."

"No, it doesn't. It should, but it doesn't. Look at your team—you all loved your families, and most of you were killed by them. Love doesn't matter; power does. And Bianca has all of it. The only thing you and I can do is brace ourselves…"

She handed me the ring again. I shook my head "no." I refused to take it from her. She walked over to me and placed the ring on the small table beside me. She kissed my cheek lightly and whispered in my ear.

"We tried…"

She walked through the door and didn't look back.

Now, standing before Miku, I find myself clearing my throat, trying to maintain some kind of composure. Miku looks at me with sad eyes.

"That was the last time you saw her?" she asks.

"Yeah, that was three days ago."

"I'm sorry. I know how you feel about Emmy. I know how hard you've tried to make it work."

"I thought I could talk Bianca out of this. I thought I could find some way where this didn't have to happen. I mean, there had to be a mixture, potion, something…but no, there's nothing."

"Bianca covered all her tracks. Including the Exchange clause."

"I couldn't believe she had them put it in there."

"Well, a lot of Quo marriages have them."

"Yeah, but it's not a real marriage, so why is that clause there?"

"I can't even begin to guess. Does Emmy know about the clause?"

"No. I was going to tell her, but what would it matter? I mean, all it would do is hurt her even more."

"You promised you wouldn't keep things from her."

"I always promised to marry her and spend my life with her. All my promises have added up to nothing. She knows that by now."

Miku gently places her hand on top of mine.

"Do you think she regrets it?" I ask.

"Regrets what?"

"Loving me…"

"You'd have to ask her."

"I can't."

"Why?"

"She might answer me."

Chapter One: I Speak To Angels

Pretty hugs me tightly. I wrap my arms around her and wonder how things got this bad. How did the mission go so far off course?

Stop wasting your time wondering, Marcus; just deal with what's in front of you.

"Seeing how things are with me and Emmy, does it make you want to run from you and Jay?" I ask her as we pull apart.

"There is no 'Miku and Jay,'" she reminds me.

"So, you talked to him and he doesn't feel the same?" I ask.

"No, we haven't talked, but the 'no talking' is coming through loud and clear. It's telling me, 'Jay doesn't like me.' So, it's whatever."

"You know he just lost someone. It's not easy for him to…"

"Yeah, I get that. But I just had this crazy picture in my head that when he found out, he'd be…"

"Happy?"

"Yeah, and relieved because secretly our hooks began to mean something. I was hoping…never mind. I'm starting to sound like Emmy: full of wishful thinking."

"You should try talking to him."

"Jay has never had any issues telling anyone what he thought. If he liked me, he would have said so."

"I'm sorry, Pretty."

"It's okay. It's just a little crush. It'll go away. Not every couple is 'Marcus and Emmy.'"

"Given the way things are going between us, you should be grateful not to be like us."

Just then, someone opens the door. Even before I can look up, I hope to Omnis it is her. I know it's selfish, but I need her.

Jay enters the room. The rest of the team, including Rage, is behind him. Jay looks alarmed.

"What is it?" I ask.

"It's nothing too bad…," he says.

"Is it Emmy? Is she okay?"

"Well…yeah…no…yeah—"

"Jay! What. Is. It?"

"Emmy's in jail."

As I race out of the church, I hear someone say they will stall the wedding for as long as they can. I'm not sure who says what because I am already in the air. Rio and Jay are right behind me. Jay takes us to the 17th Precinct on East Fifty-first Street in Manhattan.

Once there, Jay uses his powers to Convince the cop at the front desk to let us see her. She sits alone, in a cell, on a dirty cot. She has her knees drawn up to her chest and her arms around her legs. She bows her head. I think she's crying.

"Emmy?" I call out as the officer allows me into the cell.

She looks up at me slowly. She isn't crying. In fact, she's smiling. Actually, she's grinning from ear to ear. She has dark circles under her eyes and her hair looks like it hasn't been washed in days.

"Hey, it's my fiancé. Hi, baby. How's the wife?" she calls out.

I look over at Jay.

"Baby girl is *baked*," he says, confirming my suspicion.

My jaw drops, and Jay shakes his head.

"Emmy, let's go," I order.

"No. I like it here," she replies.

"You can't stay."

"You are always so serious," she mocks.

I turn to Jay. He tells me to reason with her while he tries to keep the arresting officer under his power.

Emmy tells me to sit beside her. Reluctantly, I do as she asks.

"How did you get here?" I ask, forcing myself to remain calm.

"I'm so hungry," she says.

"How did you get arrested?" I ask again.

"I know this guy at school, he's a weed head. But there are no weeds growing from his actual head. Weird, right?"

Dear Omnis, what have I done to this girl?

"Anyway, he gave me some weed. But I couldn't smoke it. Marcus, it was sooooooo nasty."

"But I'm guessing you got past that?"

"Nope. He gave me a brownie. So. Good. Chocolate with little walnuts. I *love* walnuts."

"How many did you have?"

"A lot. They had walnuts. I *love* walnuts."

"You said that already."

"I did?"

"Yeah…"

"Well, I was walking home and the fire hydrant made a joke; I started laughing along and the cop pulled me over. Lame."

"The hydrant was speaking to you?"

"Yup."

"You don't find that strange?"

"I speak to angels, why not a fire hydrant?" She laughs.

I take her hand in mine and look into her glossy eyes.

"Baby, you need to get out of here and get some rest, okay?"

"Will you come with me?"

"I can't. Not now."

"Because you're getting married today, right?"

"Right."

"To me?"

"No, Em. To Bianca."

"The mean girl?"

"Yes, the mean girl. Now c'mon, we have to go."

"If you give me another brownie, I'll go."

"No more brownies. Ever."

"Why?"

"They're not good for you, Em."

"No, they are. They make me giggle, and they make me see things in slow motion."

"Yeah, I get that, but you can't have any more."

"I have to keep eating them because they make you go away."

"What do you mean?"

"When I don't eat them, all I see is you. *You* holding me, *you* making love to me, *you* giving me a ring… Then, I see you marrying her. And everything goes dark. Then, I want to do something I have never wanted to do in my life…"

"What?"

"Die."

CHAPTER TWO:
WHAT YOU DESERVE

I'm the first thing

"Hey…," Emmy whispers.

She looks at her surroundings. She doesn't recognize the loft-style cabin we're in. She finds herself in bed surrounded by a quilt and pillows. She looks over my shoulders and sees the living room and kitchen below.

I sit beside her and patiently wait for the onslaught of questions she will ask.

"Marcus, what's going on?"

"Breakfast."

She looks up at me once again, totally confused. I quickly assure her that everything will be explained once she has eaten.

"Wait, where are we?"

"Cabin in the Green Mountains."

"Okay, but—"

"Eat first, questions later."

"How did I get here?"

I knew this wouldn't be easy.

"After we picked you up from jail, I had Jay Convince you to sleep—for a long time."

"How long?"

"Day and a half."

"What?!"

"You needed it, Em; you were exhausted."

"Yeah, I was, but—"

"I know you have a lot of questions, but can it wait until after breakfast?"

"Okay…"

I quickly take her hand and walk her downstairs before she changes her mind.

"Is that bacon?" she asks, sniffing the air.

"Yeah."

"Wait, when you said breakfast, you meant like homemade and not something from 7-Eleven?"

"Yes, it's all homemade," I say proudly.

"Is Jay here?"

"Hey, he's not the only one who knows how to cook."

She looks at me suspiciously.

"Okay, okay. He was here earlier and cooked up a few things. But I diced the tomatoes."

"I'm impressed."

"Wait until you see the toast, only halfway burned," I vow.

"Wow; all that and bacon. I'm a happy girl," she jokes.

She takes a seat at the round wooden table. I'm about to place the food in front of her, but then I remember something very important and I race up the stairs.

"Where are you going?" she asks.

"Be right back."

I come back down seconds later with my cell in hand.

"Jay made me write down the names of every dish on my cell because he said it was the only way to do his food justice."

She laughs despite herself.

"Okay, I'm ready."

"Today, Ms. Baxter, you will be having smoked applewood bacon and egg crepe squares, sliced tomatoes with a hint of basil, and garlic and herb home fries. That will be followed by raspberry swirl scones. In addition to fruit, fresh squeezed orange juice, and coffee."

She laughs at me.

"How'd I do?" I ask.

"Jay would be very proud."

"Thank you," I reply as I start to serve her.

"The thing is, I'm really not hungry," she confesses once the food is in front of her. She must have seen my face fall because she picks up her fork and begins to eat.

I watch her, and for the first time in what seems like forever, I'm content. I know the feeling won't last, but I pray to Omnis to get as much out of it as I can.

Emmy must have sensed how much I don't want to talk because she waits until she's taken at least two bites out of everything before she starts with the questions again.

"Marcus, what's going on?"

"We're having breakfast."

"Okay. Where is it?"

"What?"

"Your wedding ring? Don't the Quo exchange rings when they get mar ried?"

"Yeah, they do."

"So where's yours?"

"I didn't get married."

"I don't understand…"

"When I went to see you in jail, you said you got high because you wanted to die."

"Oh, Marcus, I'm sorry. I didn't mean to worry you—"

"Emmy, when we first came to Earth, you were this happy, kind human who had a mom and peace of mind. Now your mom is gone, you're getting high and wishing you were dead. I did that to you."

"Marcus, it's not that simple."

"Yes, it is. I looked in your eyes, and high or not, you meant what you said. And if you were to do something to yourself and I wasn't there to stop you…"

"I'm not gonna do anything. It was just the weed talking."

"Really?"

"Yes."

"So you have never wanted to die?"

She avoids my eyes.

Chapter Two: What You Deserve

"That's what I thought. I'm done hurting you, Emmy. I'm not gonna marry Bianca."

"So what are you going to do?"

"The dishes."

"Marcus, be serious," she scolds.

I don't reply. I just start to clear the table.

"What's going on with the team? What's happening with the Sage?"

"I don't know."

"Did he find the underground city yet? Are they coming for the ang els?"

"I don't know."

"How long do we have until the Sage finds them—"

"I DON'T KNOW!!!" I scream, hurling the plate in my hand at the wall.

I place my hands on the side of the wooden island that divides the living room from the kitchen and lower my head. I speak because I think I'm more composed now. But I'm wrong. My voice is filled with agonfEmmy, two days ago you looked at me and said you wanted to die. Do you know what that *did* to me?"

Defeated, I sit down on the floor, head in my hands.

"I know," she says softly.

I shake my head. "No, Emmy, you don't."

She gets up and sits on the floor beside me.

"Tell me," she pleads.

"After watching you being tortured and hunted time and time again, I prayed that you would survive this mission. But sitting there in that cell, I realized it's not the mission you need to survive; it's me. You need to survive loving me."

"Marcus, I shouldn't have said what I said. I'm sorry."

"No; stop being sorry. Anyone else would have lost it by now. Emmy, you have gone through so much because of me."

"You didn't put my name as the clue. You didn't tell Lucy to kill my mom, and you didn't make me love you. Things happen; awful, dreadful things. But you are not to blame for all of it."

"I'm not leaving you ever again," I promise her.

"What about the Sage?"

"We'll fight him as best we can. I sent Jay and the rest of the team to find as many Paras as they can to help us fight. They've texted me; they have gathered nearly three hundred Paras."

"Is that enough?"

From my silence, she gathers that the answer is no.

"What about Bianca and Dalce?"

"They have given me until sunrise to reconsider. If not, the deal is off the table."

"Marcus—"

"I don't care. We'll handle the Sage. We'll stay here until morning. Then, we'll go back to the underground city and help them gather as much reinforcement as we can. Maybe we can make up for the lack of numbers with strategy."

"Really?"

"We have a meeting with Wolf in the morning. He's bringing the Omari."

"The Para assassins?"

"Yeah, they're brilliant fighters, and they can help train others."

"So, you really think we can do this with the army?" she asks, filled with hope.

"Yes, I do."

Tears of joy spring to her eyes as she embraces me tightly.

"I love you so much. I didn't know how I was going to deal with you and Bianca together," she confesses.

"You won't ever have to think about that," I promise her.

"Wait; did you already give Bianca your Rah?"

"No."

"So that means we can…"

"Hell yeah," I say, taking her into my arms and up the stairs…

Chapter Two: What You Deserve

A little while later, she lies on her stomach as I kiss between her shoulder blades. I make my way down to her lower back. She laughs and shakes her head.

"Marcus, we just made love; you're ready to go again?" she asks.

"First Guardians are never satisfied."

"You mean First Guardians are greedy," she corrects me.

"That too."

"Can I ask you a really personal question?"

"Instead of going again?"

"Before we go again."

"Then, yes."

She turns so that she is now on her back, looking up at me. I have known Emmy for a while now, and it stills surprises me how much I crave her.

"Have you forgiven your mother for killing you?"

"Wow, we really have to work on your pillow talk," I reply.

"Sorry, I didn't mean to break the mood. I was just wondering."

"What made you think of that?"

"Julian's been calling me and coming by the apartment looking for me."

"You're avoiding him."

"Trying…"

"You know, I don't really like Julian, but the truth is, he really tries to look after you."

"How, by raping my mother and abandoning me?" "He says it wasn't rape, and I kind of believe him." "Well, that's not the way my mom remembered it." "You sound like you don't want anything to do with him." "But every now and then…" "You wonder what it would be like to know him?" "Yeah. I mean, he knows a part of my mom I will never know. What was she like on the bridge? Why did she fall for him? And if he loved her so much, how could he just walk away from…her?"

"You mean how could he walk away from you," I say gently.
She avoids my eyes.

"Look, I don't know why Julian made the choices he made. But honestly, since being on this mission, I've done things I never thought I would ever do," I confess.

"What are you saying?" "I'm saying angels suck sometimes; just like humans." "You think I should forgive him after everything he's done?" "I think you should hear him out." "He tried to ruin our relationship." "He tried to protect you from evil." She doesn't answer. She's deep in thought. "Hey, where'd you go?" I ask. "Oh, just thinking what it would have been like to have him around." "He's not dead; just talk to him." "Marcus, he hates you." "No, he just dislikes me, greatly," I kid her. "You didn't answer the question. Do you forgive your mom?" "Most days." "And other days?" I look off to the side and suddenly I'm the one deep in thought. I replay my last day on Earth, and ask myself questions I know I have no answers to.

Could I have done anything to help her before things got so bad? If I had known what my mom was going to do, would I still have tried to stop her? What would I have done differently when I woke up that morning if I knew that day was my last day?

"Hey, it's okay if you don't wanna talk," she says, placing her hand on the side of my face.

"No, it's fine. It's just most of the time I can accept it. But every once in a while…"

"You went to all this trouble to be with me, and I'm ruining the moment."

"No, you're not. Emmy, you deserve a time-out. I just wish I could give you more than a few days."

"I don't care how long you give me. I just want to be with you. That's all that matters to me. And now, I'm done overthinking things. And I am ready for round two."

Chapter Two: What You Deserve

"Oh, really?"

"Yeah, and this time you won't have to remind me to breathe."

"You're getting much better at remembering. But I think round two will have to wait."

"Why?"

"We have company."

"Who?"

"The team."

She looks out the window and finds the team and Rage standing outside the door.

She quickly wraps the sheets around her.

"Oh, no! Are they here because they're pissed we took some time to ourselves?"

"No, after I told them about the weed, everyone agreed you need a time-out."

"Everyone?"

"Yes, even Ameana. We're supposed to meet them in the underground city in the morning."

"So, what are they doing here?" she asks.

"I don't know. But I'm guessing it's not good."

A few minutes later, both Emmy and I are dressed and standing in the living room with the team. Emmy hugs everyone (everyone except Ameana and Rage).

"I'm so glad you're better," Miku says, looking her over.

"Me too," Emmy replies.

"So, the perfect human got wasted. Awesome," Rage says.

"Why are you here?" I ask, unable to keep the harshness out of my voice.

"Because my girl is here and I don't trust your team to keep her safe."

"Ameana can take care of herself," I reply.

"Damn right she can, but she's into saving people, and I don't want her to get hurt trying to save your pathetic team."

"Yo, man, what the hell is your problem? You're a damn demon. You're lucky we let you live," Jay counters, pissed.

"You want it, 'Speedy,' come get it. I'm right here," Rage says darkly. The two exchange glares.

"At least the demon is decent enough not to screw his friend's sister," Rio says snidely.

"Really, Rio? That's really where you want to take it?" Jay asks.

"You can't tell me who to be with," Miku shouts to her twin.

"Since when are you 'with' Jay?" Rio asks.

"Yo, we ain't together," Jay adds.

"Why do you have to say it like that?" Miku says, clearly offended.

"I'm just say'n—" Jay starts.

"You say'n you think you could do better than me?" Miku accuses.

"It's not about that," Jay replies.

"Sounds like it is," Rage says to Ameana as an aside.

"Can you stay out of it?" Ameana warns Rage.

"So, now you want to tell me what to do?" Rage asks.

"I just don't want us to get involved. We have enough issues of our own," Ameana says, almost to herself.

"What the hell does that mean?" Rage asks.

"It means you don't have to say every thought you have out loud," Ameana informs him.

"You asked me how your hair looked and I said I didn't like it up. What's the big deal?" Rage inquires.

"The big deal is you're being—"

"Like what, Ameana, a demon?" Rage asks.

"I was gonna say, 'a jerk,'" Ameana protests.

"You ask for my opinion and when I give it, you get mad. When I say anything, you automatically dismiss it because I'm a demon; if demons are so bad, why did you spend last night with one?" Rage roars furiously.

"Stop putting my business out in front of the team!" Ameana shouts.

"We're not just a team, Mimi, we're friends, and since when have you two started sleeping together?" Miku says, clearly hurt.

"She doesn't want you to know because she knows you don't like me," Rage replies.

Miku shouts back at him, "Shut up, Rage! I didn't ask for your—"

"His name is Thomas. That's why I can't tell you anything—because you won't give him a chance. No matter what he does, he'll always be Rage to you," Ameana replies.

"At least Redd understands that I'm a demon, and she's not trying to change me," Rage replies.

"My name is not—" Miku begins.

"ENOUGH!!!" I yell. The silence is instantaneous. I look around the room and wonder how things got to be the way they are. But now is no time to ponder.

"I know you guys didn't come here so that Emmy and I could have a ringside seat to this petty crap. So what is it?" I demand.

"We know we said we could handle things for a few days but something's come up," Rio says.

"Did the Omari back out?" I ask.

"No, they're ready and willing to help," Miku replies.

"Has the Sage gotten closer to finding our location?" Emmy asks.

"Yeah, but that's not why we're here," Jay says.

"Okay, well, what is it?" I push.

"The Foundation is pissed about you changing your mind about the marriage," Ameana reports.

"Well, it doesn't matter. I'm not marrying Bianca and that's final."

Ameana answers me using her "second-in-command" voice; it's calm but deadly serious.

"Dalce says if you don't marry Bianca, the Foundation will join forces with the Sage."

CHAPTER THREE: REMEMBER ME

I can't bring myself to look at her. I know what she's going to ask. Rage and the rest of the team wisely remain quiet.

"What does that mean for us?" Emmy inquires reluctantly.

"Winning the battle without the Foundation will be difficult. But if they join the Sage, failure is guaranteed," Rio replies.

I'm pretty sure it's not enough that Rio says it. She will need to hear it from me. And sure enough, she calls out my name, her voice made frail with desperation.

I search my mind for the words that will cause her the least amount of pain. That's like trying to choose which knife will hurt the least when you plunge it into the person you love. It doesn't matter which one you choose, it's going to hurt them—badly.

"Marcus, answer me. Is Rio right? Will we lose this battle if the Foundation joins the Sage?"

"Yes."

She turns away from us; from me. She looks out the window at the mountains surrounding us. When she speaks again her voice is stronger, more resolved. Still, she doesn't face us.

"Then you have no choice; you have to marry her," she says.

"Emmy, I'm so sorry—"

"I know. Let's just go and get this done," she says, running upstairs.

The rest of us look on as Emmy packs her things and prepares to leave.

"Is she okay?" I ask Rio.

"Really, Marcus? You need my powers to tell you she's dying inside?"

"I don't have a choice. She knows that," I say, mostly to myself.

Chapter Three: Remember Me

"You have to tell her everything," Ameana cautions.

"Wait, she doesn't know about the Exchange clause?" Jay asks, shaking his head.

"No," I reply.

"And you're really gonna tell? Man, that chick is gonna cry herself to death on the spot," Rage adds.

"Yeah, the human is good at crying. Actually, it's her superpower," Ameana jokes with her boyfriend. They exchange a quick look of amusement. I turn and address Jay.

"When this is all over, remind me to kill Rage."

"No doubt," Jay replies, glaring at him.

"You have to tell her," Miku says.

"I know, it's just…it's only going to hurt her even more."

"You know what happens when you try to hide things from Emmy, Marcus? It blows up in your face. And you end up hurting her anyway. Please, for once, can you just be upfront with her?" Miku encourages.

I run my hand through my hair and look down at the ground. I'm hoping, somehow, a massive hole will appear in the floor and suck me out of this awful situation.

"Miku's right. You need to keep it one hundred percent with her. She's stronger than we give her credit for," Jay says.

"She got high and went to jail. How is that strong?" I remind them.

"She had a few brownies. It was stupid. But any other person would have done much worse by now. I'm tell'n you, baby girl can handle it," Jay counters.

I order the team to wait outside, place my hands in my pockets, and head up the stairs to hurt the girl I love (again).

"I'm almost ready," she says as she sits on the bed, lacing up her sneakers.

"Emmy, we need to talk."

"I know, I know. It sucks and yeah it hurts—a lot. But we're gonna survive this. Bianca, Lucy, the Sage, no one is going to stop us from being together."

"I hope not."

"Marcus, I know this isn't what you want either. But look, it's just a marriage on paper. So, who cares, right?"

"That's what I wanted to talk to you about."

"Okay, what is it?" she asks.

"You know how angels can't kiss others when someone else has their Rah?"

"Yeah."

"Well, that's a way of assuring that both parties have let go of the relationship. The Quo don't have that rule. But what they do have is a way to ensure that the couples who marry are truly happy."

"How would they assure happiness?"

"They have an Exchange clause."

"I don't understand…?"

"The couple getting married has to make love to each other. Not only that, but they have to have an Exchange. In human terms, if they both don't have an orgasm, the marriage is then nullified."

"Marcus, are saying you have to have sex with Bianca in order for the marriage to count?"

"Not every night; just the first night."

"You're telling me that you're gonna have sex with Bianca?"

"Yes."

The scream comes from outside. I turn my head towards the door and see Rio doubled over on the ground. Miku and Jay tend to him, but whatever they are doing is not helping. He cries out in excruciating pain.

In between screams, Rio shouts out to me with a tortured voice.

"It's Emmy… she's… killing me."

That's when I understand: whatever Emmy is feeling is so strong, it's overpowering Rio's ability. This has happened before, but normally, when Rio is overwhelmed by one person's emotions, he can fly away. But this time it's different. Rio can't fly. In fact, Rio can't do anything but lie on the ground and wail.

Chapter Three: Remember Me

I go to Emmy to fly her away from here and save Rio in the process. She's shaking and crying on the edge of the bed. I place my hand on her shoulder—Rio cries out.

"NO, NOT MARCUS!!!"

I see why Rio protests. My touching Emmy only causes her body to be rocked by violent sobs. I want to hold her. I want to make everything better, but Rio is dying and Emmy can't even bear to look at me.

I call out to Jay; he runs into the cabin and up the stairs.

He scoops her up from the bed; she wraps her arms around his neck.

"I got you, baby girl," Jay says as he flies away with my girl.

It takes a full hour before Rio is able to fly again. Jay calls my cell and tells me he's taken Emmy home. He also tells me to give her some time because this is hard on her.

"You really think I need you to tell me that?" I snap.

"Yo, be easy. I'm just telling you she isn't doing well with this."

"You said she was strong enough for this!"

"Yeah, but that doesn't mean it's not going to hurt. C'mon, Marcus. She just learned you gonna be do'n some Quo chick!"

"I'm coming over there."

"Fine, but we need to be back in the underground city today. Or we're screwed," he reminds me.

"I know."

"Marcus?"

"What?"

"Emmy may not be as strong as I thought. In fact, there's very little keeping her together."

"I'll take care of her."

I hang up and tell the team to go ahead and I'll catch up. I fly to her apartment in Manhattan.

The door is unlocked. Jay waits for me to enter, then leaves the two of us alone.

She's sitting on the sofa with her legs tucked beneath her.

"You okay?" I ask her.

No, Marcus, she's not okay, you idiot!

She nods and apologizes for causing a scene. She asks if Rio is okay and begs me to tell him how sorry she is that she caused him such pain.

"He knows," I assure her. She nods but is facing away from me. I go over to the sofa and sit next to her. "Can you look at me please?" I request.

She turns to face me. The whites of her eyes are red. When you add that to the usual purple of her irises, her eyes look bizarre and intense. She's wearing the same thing she wore in the cabin but she's added a gray button-down sweater that looks to be twice her size. I'm guessing it was her mom's. She wraps herself inside it as if it can somehow shield her from what's happening.

"Can we talk?" "No." "Please? We really need to." "I don't wanna talk to you." "Why?" "BECAUSE YOU'RE ALWAYS BREAKING MY FUCKING

HEART AND I HATE YOU!"

Her words tear into my chest, rip out my insides, and hurl them to the ground. But while her words hurt, the thing that's even more painful is where those words came from: the deepest part of her soul.

Emmy's not just angry and lashing out. She's being completely honest. And it's that brutal honesty that causes a crippling sadness in me. Suddenly, I'm embarrassed to be here with her, knowing that she hates me so much. I open my mouth but there are no words. Since we met, I've been hurting her. Since the day I landed in her life, she's faced unimaginable losses and inhumane torture.

But I didn't think she actually hated me…

"I didn't realize… I'm sorry… I'll go," I whisper as I get up from the sofa and head to the door.

"Good, go! Get out! I hate you!" she shouts. And without warning, she hurls the nearby lamp at my head.

I duck just in time; it hits the door and shatters.

"Emmy!"

Chapter Three: Remember Me

"Shut up. Don't say my name. I hate you, I hate you, I hate you!"

By now she is literally throwing anything she can find at me. I'm dodging picture frames, books, and tons of miniature statues. When I finally get close enough to stop her, I take her hands in mine. She screams at the top of her lungs.

"Let me go, I hate you!"

She repeats it over and over again, each time with more venom. She twists and turns her arms to get out of my grip. I have no choice but to let her go, fearing she will end up breaking her own arm. Once she is free, she gives up on throwing things and attacks me.

She lands punch after punch into the center of my chest. She's hurting herself and causing no harm to me whatsoever. But that doesn't stop her. She continues to attack and yell how much she hates me.

Finally, fearful of the damage she will cause to herself, I effortlessly lift her several feet into the air and gently back her against the wall, with her arms folded. She screams and cries, but I don't let her go.

She doesn't stop wailing over and over again that she hates me. Angry tears stream down her red, puffy face. Her legs bang against the wall as she tries to break free of my hold. I call out to her to calm down but that just makes her fight me harder.

I want to make eye contact so that she knows I get it; I know she hates me. I know she's had enough and that it's over. I don't know how I will deal with losing her, yet again. But that comes later. Right now, all that matters is her safety and well-being.

I gently take her face in my hand. I try to prepare myself; the girl I love will be looking back at me with bitterness and loathing. But when I look into her tear-filled eyes, that's not what I see. The hardened, pissed-off girl who's been attacking me isn't hardened, or even pissed.

She's scared it's over between us for real this time…

"Baby, I love you," I assure her.

"I hate you," she says, trying to convince herself.

"I know."

"I do. I hate you," she says, refusing let the anger die.

"I know," I reply softly as I put her back down on the living room floor.

"I'm not in love with you, Marcus. I don't care what happens to you. You can do whatever you want with Bianca because I don't care," she lies as she sobs into my chest. We are only a whisper apart; trying not to kiss takes up all our energy.

"You want me to leave?" I ask.

"Yes," she says firmly.

I stay where I am.

"Marcus, I'm serious. Get out," she orders.

I stay where I am.

"Because you hate me?" I ask.

"Yes."

"Emmy?"

"What?"

"I hate you, too."

She stands on the tips of her toes, places my face between her hands, and kisses me hungrily. I growl and eagerly receive her lips and tongue. She leaps into my arms and wraps her legs around me. I carefully navigate the ransacked living room and take her to her bedroom.

By the time we land on her bed, our kisses go from seeking to out-right demanding. She pulls off my shirt and throws it to the floor. She then gets on top of me and takes off her shirt. She quickly unhooks her bra and begins to kiss my bare chest.

She's like a tornado: powerful and unpredictable. As I stroke her beautiful hair and she kisses my neck, I can't help but think something is wrong. Then, she whispers in my ear. "This is so you won't forget." I lift her off of me and gently place her on the bed. I gather her clothes

and give them to her.

"What's wrong?" she asks, confused.

I kneel in front of her and take her hand in mine.

"Emmy, I don't have to have sex with you to remember how much I love you."

"You're gonna be with Bianca and there's nothing I can do about it. I want the memory of us to stay with you."

"'Us' is never far from my mind or my heart."

"You're gonna make love to her and I won't matter anymore," she cries.

"We're not making love. We're just…having sex," I remind her.

"So? You and I had sex and it got us back together."

"That's different."

"How?"

"We didn't fall in love because we had sex; we had sex because we were in love. One night with Bianca won't change that."

"You're gonna hold her…caress her…you're gonna be inside her. Marcus, how do I make myself okay with that?" she begs.

A sharp pain crosses my chest. I know she's picturing Bianca and me together. I know what it's doing to her is worse than any torture she's ever faced.

"When I kissed you, held you, made love to you, I did those things because I wanted to. Bianca can make me marry her, but I will never want her the way I want you."

"Marcus, I don't think I can handle this," she pleads.

"You can. Please, don't give up on us; I can't lose you again."

"How are we supposed to do this?" she asks.

"We'll make vows to each other. I vow not to let Bianca near my heart because it belongs to you."

"I vow to remember our love is stronger than any Exchange clause and not to give up on us."

"You promise?" I ask desperately.

"I do."

"Seriously, Emmy, things can get…crazy… once Bianca and I are married. Promise you won't forget how much I love you. Promise me."

"I promise."

I embrace her tightly and whisper in her ear.

"We're going to get our happy ending, baby. I swear to Omnis, we are."

Emmy and I stan

to proceed. Emmy seems to be taking it well. That is, as well as anyone can take something like this.

Before we left, she took a quick shower. Her hair is still wet and smells like jasmine, thanks to her shampoo. She's wearing a simple summer dress with little flowers on it. She's the kind of girl who doesn't have to try to be beautiful; she just is. I want more than anything to marry her. In a perfect world, Emerson Hope Baxter would be the last girl I kiss.

"Hey, you okay?" she asks.

"Yeah, I was just thinking how beautiful you are."

"Yeah, well, the wet look is in this year; even among the Quo," she says, smiling.

I take her hand in mine.

"Thank you for understanding why I have to do this. No other girl would get it," I share with her.

"When we finally beat the Sage, find the Alphas, and a new council is formed, you're gonna owe me big."

"How big?"

"Big," she assures me.

"You mean, I'm going to have to buy you something from Tiffany's?"

"Something? No, everything," she jokes.

"Done. Now, is there anything else I can do to make this easier?"

"Yeah, actually there is. I don't want to know about the night you two spend together."

"Are you sure?" I ask.

"Yes. I don't ever want to hear about it."

"Okay."

"Are you ready?" she asks.

"No, I want a last kiss. I mean our last kiss for a while. And you better make it good," I tease.

She smiles with her eyes and closes the gap between us. She stands on the tips of her toes; I lean in and close my eyes as our lips touch.

The blinding light appears quickly and expands between us. Before I can do anything about it, the light lifts Emmy up in the air and hurls her across the canyon. I take off into the air and find where she has been thrown. She's on the ground, groaning and rubbing the back of her head.

"Baby, are you okay?"

"So, I'm guessing Bianca has your Rah now?" Emmy asks as she winces.

"Yeah, normally the two of us would put it in the mountain together, but I guess we're so pressed for time, Bianca did it herself."

"Wow, that wife of yours sure is thoughtful," she counters.

I frown at her remark.

"Sorry, it's just…I thought we'd get a last kiss," she confides.

"Me too. But we did kiss back at the apartment."

"Yeah, that was nice," she says, touching my cheek with her hand.

"How's your head?"

"Hey, any time I don't land in a dumpster, I consider it a good day," she jokes.

"I love how you do that."

"What?"

"Find something good in everything."

"We better get in there," she says quietly. The smile in her voice is gone. I can understand that. It's enough that she has to endure this, I can't ask her to smile about it. We head back to the entrance of Cree. "Marcus?" she calls to me.

"Yeah?"

"Let go."

I look down and realize I'm still holding her hand. We can't enter the city of Cree holding hands. The Quo have to believe that Emmy and I are over. They have to feel that I am genuinely into this union. In order for that to happen, I have to do what I never wanted to do again: let go of Emmy's hand.

Cree is only a few miles long. We can see the entire city from the entrance of the Whirlwind. I actually like Cree because while it's simple, it's also very inviting. The rooms are carved into the side of the mountains. The rust-colored earth gives the whole city a soft golden glow. Normally there are a few Quo and angels milling among each other, talking politics and doing the chores needed to keep the city running.

However, the small city of Cree is different today; it has been turned into wedding central. There's a tent with four pillars standing in the middle of the city. The pillars have silver ribbons that coil around and unravel into silver shadows.

"When did they have time to get Shadow Servants?" I wonder out loud.

"I've never seen so many," Emmy replies.

We watch in awe as dozens of Shadow Servants set up a dining area a few yards from the tent. I don't even notice Tony-Tone until I hear his voice.

"Beautiful, isn't it?" he asks.

We turn to face him. He gives us a big 'salesman' smile.

"You had something to do with this?" I ask.

"I recommended the decorator, Tonya; we had a thing once. Actually, she still has a thing for me," he brags shamelessly.

"Nice to know, Tony," I reply.

"Doesn't this place look spectacular?" Tony asks.

"Yeah, everything looks nice," Emmy says, almost to herself.

"Nice? C'mon, this setup is amazing! Bianca has excellent taste. She chose exquisite colors to combine: jade, champagne, and silver. The tablecloths are champagne with jade table runners and silver-rimmed dining plates."

We both look at him strangely.

"Tonya's been teaching me. Who knows, I might have a second career; Seller by night, decorator by day. I am a man of many talents."

"That's nice," Emmy says, avoiding my eyes.

Anyone could tell she didn't really want to hear the wedding details.

Well, anyone but Tony-Tone. He continued as if he was hosting his own version of the Martha Stewart show.

"Now the trick was to sit a hundred or so guests but not make it seem crowded. Tonya and I managed that with the lighting," he says, pointing to the champagne and silver orbs floating throughout the city.

"But the best thing about this has to be what Bianca's wearing. Her wedding dress is even better than the original one she chose. It's a champagne colored, strapless princess gown."

Tony, shut up…

"Oh, and your suit is in your room. It's muted silver with a jade tie to match the bouquet Bianca will carry."

"I'm gonna go find Miku," Emmy says as she walks away.

"No, don't go," I reply, reaching out to stop her.

"You have to get ready," she says, giving me her best fake smile.

"Maybe it was wrong to bring you back here."

"No, Marcus, I want to be here. I know it's crazy, but I don't really think I can stay away."

"This will be over soon," I assure her.

"Wait; Emmy, you're not okay with this?" Tony asks.

I roll my eyes and Emmy shrugs.

"The story is that you two have been over for a while. I thought that was strange since I helped you get a ring. But then I heard you have a new boyfriend and everything. I thought maybe the ring scared you away. Hey, it's okay to be afraid of commitment. I mean, Tonya keeps trying to tie me down. That's why it never works with us," Tony confides in us.

"Um... Lucas and I broke up," she explains.

"Oh, well, I have a potion that makes serpents come out of his eyes or a powder that can cause him excruciating pain every time he crosses your mind. It's yours if you want it; half off. You know, because you're family."

"Thanks, but I'm okay," Emmy replies.

Tony looks at each of us and a light bulb goes off in his head.

"You two are still in love!" he shouts.

I pull him aside and threaten to dismember him if he doesn't lower his voice.

"I'm so glad. I love you two together. You know, Marcus, she's your softer, caring side," Tony replies.

"I thought you liked Bianca?" Emmy asks.

"Well, yeah, she's high class and elegant. But you saved my life. And we all know you two belong together," Tony informs her.

"Maybe, but for now, we need to make this happen," I reply.

"Okay, so your team is just going to act like you two aren't together?" Tony asks.

"Until we can figure a way out of it," I tell him.

"Okay, but you two might want to work on the longing glances; I mean, even a demon can pick up on that," Tony tells us.

Emmy and I look at each other. He's right. Not only that, I don't look like a guy who's about to get married. I look like someone who's been sentenced to death.

"Marcus, may I see you, please?" Dalce orders from the Foundation entrance a few yards away. I walk over to him and he takes me inside his headquarters. Standing there is Bianca and her cousin, Eta. Bianca had not yet gotten into her wedding dress. She's wearing dark slacks and an expensive looking blouse. Honestly, she is very striking.

"What is it?" I ask.

Dalce brings out a single earth-colored parchment and places it at the center of the table. The words are handwritten in a gold font. The text on the page moves in swirls that form the Foundation's initials. Dalce places his hand on the paper and instantly the words come together to form our ag reement.

Chapter Four: The Advisor

"Once you two have the Exchange, the contract will go from words on paper to carvings in stone. Each member of the army has been instructed to wait for their Rush."

"Rush?" I ask.

"It's a symbol that will carve itself into their skin. In this case, the Foundation's initials will appear on each member of the army. That is when they will march on the Sage."

"Where is the army now?" I ask.

"Nearby. They are waiting for the Rush. It'll only appear after the Exchange. So, if you run out on my daughter again, things will be very difficult for you," he warns me.

"Father, you can't blame Marcus. He was worried about the human," Bianca says in my defense. That catches me off guard.

"Nevertheless, we had to do a lot of damage control. If our people don't believe that you and Bianca are really united, they will side with the Sage. This marriage is worth more than just a piece of paper. This has to look like the real thing."

"I'm already supposed to have sex with her, how much more real can we get?" I ask bitterly.

"Come now, Marcus, my daughter is gorgeous. You could do a lot worse, like the scrawny human back there."

"Uncle…," Eta says quietly.

"My niece loves the human. She thinks you and her are meant to be together. My niece is a romantic—that is why she will never rule," Dalce says.

Eta puts her head down. Dalce addresses me with a cocky smile.

"Actually, I was okay with a human marriage, but my advisor convinced me that I should ensure that things are official by marrying you two the Quo way. And thus, inserting an Exchange clause."

"I thought Bianca did that," I reply.

"I agree that it's best to do a traditional Quo ceremony. But it was the advisor who pushed for the Exchange."

"Where is your advisor? I'd like to thank him," I spit out bitterly.

"Right here," a voice says.

I turn and find Julian in the corner, glaring at me.

"Seriously?" I bark at him.

"What? Are you shocked, because I'm shocked too. I didn't think you would go through with this," Julian says, sounding disappointed.

"You put thousands of lives on the line all so that Emmy would be mad about the Exchange and leave me."

"Yes."

"You really hate me that much, Julian? Seriously, what is your problem with me?"

"You took my child to Difi and now she's Lucy's new target. You get her kidnapped, tortured, and brutalized. Now, you stand there and ask me what my problem is with you?"

"I didn't take Emmy to Difi, she came on her own."

"She did that for you."

"ARGH!" I scream as I smash the tables into pieces.

"DO YOU KNOW HOW MUCH THIS EXCHANGE IS GOING TO HURT HER?" I shout.

"I'm not hurting her. That's you. You could have chosen not to go through with this," Julian rants.

"I can't let my people die!"

"And I can't let my daughter stay in a relationship with you; you are a cancer to her. She's too young to see it, but I will not let you ruin her life."

"If the Sage has his way, humans will suffer too. It's not just the angels," I remind him.

"I'll protect her from him. Right now, the biggest threat to her is you."

"Well, your plan didn't work because Emmy and I are still together," I snap.

"So, now you've turned my daughter into the other woman; you cold bastard. You said you love her," Julian accuses.

"I do love her, that's why I'm not splitting her father in two with my bare hands right now."

"You can carry on with Emmy so long as the world doesn't know about it. If you should be seen with the human doing anything inappropriate, if you should change your mind about marrying Bianca after the Exchange, the contract states you will give up your soul. So please, Marcus, be smart and play the good little husband," Dalce advises me.

"So, there is no way I can get out of this?"

"Well, if Bianca decides, for whatever reason, to give you your Rah back, it would be her making that choice. So, the contract would then be broken. Or if she dies."

"Should I worry that you're going to kill me, Marcus?" she asks sincerely.

I glare at her.

"No, he's an angel. He wouldn't kill someone with a soul; now would you, Marcus?"

I don't reply. Dalce smiles at me.

"You're really going to subject Emmy to this?" Julian asks.

I shake my head and walk towards the door. As I pass by Julian, I whisper to him.

"You failed at loving Femi, and now you're failing at loving your own child…"

He winces but doesn't say a word as I storm out of the room.

Once outside, I see Emmy with Miku. I want to tell her what her father has done, but I'm too angry to do anything but shout; and what would it help?

I run up to my room and change. It's time for me to make vows I plan to somehow break; although right now, I don't know how I can do that without suffering the consequences.

An hour later, the entire city of Cree gathers to watch the wedding. There's limited seating, so many just stand and others watch from their balconies. Jay stands beside me as the best man. Bianca has Eta and a few other family members as her bridesmaids. Her father, Dalce, is presiding over the vows. Much of the ceremony reminds me of a human wedding; once the bride comes down the aisle, the guests stand up.

I make a conscious effort not to look for Emmy. I hope she's missing this, somehow. But I know she's watching somewhere. Only a few days ago I asked her to marry me. I had no idea it would turn out like this. Standing here, watching Bianca come down the aisle gracefully, I want nothing more than for it to be Emmy.

We don't even have to be getting married. I would settle for just sitting next to her, watching her feed Ms. Charlotte. Watching her love and care for something so intensely always gives me a window to her heart. She has a capacity for love and kindness not found in most Paras.

"Marcus, repeat after me," Dalce calls out.

I repeat what he says, but I'm a thousand miles away, thinking about the first time I laid eyes on Emmy. She was so mad at me for telling her what to do. No matter what I tried, I couldn't get her to follow my orders. Sometimes, I would say things just to piss her off so that she'd get mad. She's sexy when she's mad. Her eyes light up, her nostrils flare, and she bites her lip to keep from cursing. Honestly, I have no idea what the vows I just spoke are; something about loving forever and being faithful and protective. Luckily that part is over quickly. Then I'm told to walk around Bianca; she does the same to me. That signifies we are each other's world.

Then Dalce says it's time to kiss the bride.

Damn it!

I completely forgot about that.

Please, Emmy, tell me you're not seeing this…

I lean in and give her a quick kiss. Then someone in the crowd boos and everyone chimes in. Bianca shrugs her shoulders. I lean in again, part her lips with mine, and kiss her deeply. Her lips are soft. Her touch is war m.

I miss Emmy.

The crowd stands up and cheers. That's when I feel some kind of powder falling on my shoulders. I turn and look. There's a small stream of dust falling from the ceiling above. I lunge at Dalce; he falls to the ground just as gigantic rock comes crashing down where he once stood.

Suddenly, the ground begins to shake, and the rooms embedded in the side of the city start to crumble. The walls crack and the ceiling of earth above us begins to split. The crowd screams and runs for cover. The city of Cree is under attack.

"Take everyone to the tunnel at the back," I order the team.

Days before we had planned an escape route, for use when we were under attack. While the tunnel is a great escape, some can't get to it because of the massive earthquake being caused by the Sage's army, determined to destroy Cree.

The twins and Jay rush over to help the others stop the entrance from opening, but there are cracks forming every second. It's only a matter of time before the Sage's army enters. I spot a small crowd of kids, too scared to move. I swoop in and grab them just as the earth beneath their feet gives way.

I'm thankful when I spot Wolf and the rest of the Omari. They hold hands and form a barrier of light to protect the city. Over by what's left of the tent, Bianca tends to her father while Emmy guides the kids towards the tunnel.

Ameana tries to help a Quo woman who has injured her foot. Rage shouts at her to move as another piece of earth falls down on them. Ameana can't get out of the way in time. Just before the rock falls on them, a soft breeze blows by them. Ameana and the Quo woman look up and find Jay smiling back at them. Rage rushes to check on his girl.

I shout for Emmy to get inside the tunnel but she refuses until she gets all the kids to safety. I look across the tunnel and spot a family with two children. The mother is trapped between two boulders and can't get free.

The kids cry uncontrollably while the father uses his power to self-multiply to try and rescue his wife. But none of the multiples are strong enough to pull the woman out. I fly over to them and help them free the woman. Emmy is right behind me; she helps them get to the tunnel.

As hard as the angels and the members of the Foundation are trying, they can't stop the cracks in the city from widening. The Sage will soon be inside.

"Dalce, you have to call for the army, now!" I order.

"If the contract isn't fulfilled, the Rush will not appear."

"Damn it, Dalce, people are dying!" Ameana shouts.

"He's right. The army can't do anything without the Rush even if they wanted to. They are bound by the contract," Eta yells as she helps Emmy with the kids.

"You want to save them, take your wife and go. NOW!" Dalce orders me as he points the way to the only entrance that has yet to crack.
I look around, and the city is filled with cries for help, mangled bodies, and bloody chaos. Without thinking, I grab Bianca, head for the exit, and take off into the sky. I glance back and see Emmy watching us take off. Soon, she grows smaller and smaller in the distance. Until eventually, she disappears completely.

CHAPTER FIVE:
FRIENDSHIP

We make two qui

sour, but it's a Quo thing.

Then, finally, we head to the place she reserved for us. I'm surprised she had time to reserve anything. Everything has happened so quickly. But then again, she had the wedding put together in a matter of hours, so I shouldn't be surprised. It turns out she not only made reservations, she made impressive ones. She has booked us into the Four Seasons in Bora Bora, a small island in the South Pacific.

The high-end resort is surrounded by the ocean and its gentle waves. The night air is still, aside from the occasional soft breeze that passes by us. The sky is full of stars; they dance and shimmer on the surface of the ocean. This place is almost too perfect to be real.

Emmy would love this…

The staff take us to our bungalow, located directly above the water. We enter and find the bungalow has modern décor with an island touch. There are flowers on the end tables, a basket of fresh fruit, and schools of tropical fish are visible below the glass floor.

Yeah, Emmy would really love this. Maybe I can take her here after the mission.

Marcus, she isn't going to come here knowing you were here with Bianca.

Bianca…

I haven't so much as looked at her. I've been off somewhere else, and given what we have to do, I need to stay focused. She looks at me with a strange expression I can't read.

"What?" I ask.

"Oh, you see me now?" Bianca scolds.

"Look, I have a lot on my mind. We were just under attack—"

"Don't act like you were thinking about the attack. Your team texted you a half hour ago and told you they were able to stop the Sage's army from entering, at least for now. What you were doing was thinking about her."

"Okay, yeah I was. She's my fiancée. I love her and I am not gonna pretend like I don't."

"Good, you shouldn't," she replies.

"You're actually agreeing with me?"

"I'm not upset that she's on your mind. But I do need you to be present. Your team needs you to be present. So, can you come back from 'Emmy Land'?"

I sigh and pace up and down the bungalow. The pacing upsets the fish; they swim away. Even they can sense the tension in the room.

"Okay, you know what, I'll just say it—I have no freaking idea how to do this," I snap.

"Marcus, is this your first time?" she replies.

Is this girl serious?

"No, I'm not talking about sex. I mean, I don't know how to make this happen when we both know we don't even like each other."

"You don't like me?" she asks, sounding like a wounded little girl. Something about her tone causes a pain to shoot across my chest. She looks at me with these big beautiful puppy dog eyes and she looks like she's about to cry.

"No, it's not that," I say, scrambling for words.

"I know you don't love me. I didn't know you didn't like me."

"I do like you. I just mean, we don't know each other," I insist.

"We can fix that," she offers.

"How?"

"Let me Frame you."

"What is that?"

"Framing is the ability to sort through someone's past using their memories."

Chapter Five: Friendship

"I'm not sure…"

"Marcus, it may help."

She signals for me to put my hand in hers. I do as she says. She tells me to close my eyes. I follow her instructions and suddenly a series of bright flashes appear. They only last seconds. I open my eyes and find Bianca on the other side of the room, crying. I rush over to her.

"What's wrong? What happened?" I ask.

"I'm sorry, Marcus. I just, I've Framed a lot of people, and I've never felt as much pain as I did when I saw you realized your mother killed you. You were so hurt. It wasn't just pain from your injury, it was your heart; your mother broke your heart."

It's like standing in the room with a stranger and finding yourself suddenly naked. I'm embarrassed, uneasy, and have no idea what to do. I didn't think she could dig that deeply into my mind. People tend to think the worst thing is that we Guardians died so young. But actually, the worst part isn't that we died, but who killed us. It's usually a loved one. That betrayal never really goes away.

"Bianca, don't cry, okay. Just, it happened a long time ago. Really, I'm over it," I lie as I walk back to my corner of the room. She follows me and gently places her hand on my shoulder.

"That's not the only thing that made me react the way I did. Yes, your mother killing you was hard to watch but the worst part was being inside the memory of how you felt."

"I didn't feel anything," I lie again.

"Marcus, it's not your fault."

I shrug the whole thing off as if I don't care.

"Marcus, really, it wasn't your job to take care of your mother; it was her job to take care of you."

I turn away from her. Then I cross my arms over my chest like that will somehow stop her from getting closer to my feelings, to me.

"So what's in the sippy cup?" she asks.

I turned to her, confused. She reads my face and smiles.

"I saw a flash of your mom sick in bed with what I'm guessing was the flu. You were about four. You climbed into the bed and handed her a sippy cup. Then you said 'Drink, Mommy, feel good juice.'"

I smile at the memory. It was so many lifetimes ago, I didn't even know I had it inside my head.

"Dish soap," I reply.

"What?" she exclaims with a big smile.

"My dad said she got sick because of germs. I knew germs were dirty so…I tried to clean it."

We both burst out laughing.

"I haven't thought about that in forever," I admit, still laughing.

What the hell am I doing? I can't laugh and talk with this girl. I can't betray Emmy any more than I already am.

I stop laughing. My face hardens. She notices instantly.

She leans into me; there is only a small gap between us. Suddenly, a little vial filled with liquid appears in the air. Although I had thought to bring Tam, I'm not ready to sleep with Bianca. I don't think I can do this. Still, thank Omnis for angel condoms.

"Bianca, I don't think I can—"

"Marcus, I'm not the bad guy," she whispers softly in my ear.

"This is…wrong," I whisper to her.

"If she didn't exist, would this be right?"

"I don't know…"

"Marcus, I would have married whoever could ensure my people a place in society. We've been oppressed and held down for far too long. But I feel like Omnis loves me because he made it so that the guy I have to be with is truly an angel. Not just because of your wings but because of your actions. You're selfless, kind, and genuine."

I avoid her eyes. She takes my face in her hand and gently lowers it so that we now have full-on eye contact.

"Can I tell you a secret?"

I nod. She leans in even closer.

"I knew an angel once; his name was Jackson. We were together for a year. I finally got the courage to tell him I loved him. He said our time together was fun, but he didn't love me because I'm Quo. And Quo don't matter."

"That must have been hard to hear. I'm sorry."

Chapter Five: Friendship

"Marcus, I know I'm not Emmy. I know you belong to her. But if it's okay with you, since we have to do this anyway, can I pretend like you care about me? Just for a few moments, can you pretend like I matter?"

"Bianca—"

"I know you hate this. And I'm sorry if I'm supposed to hate it too. I just want to know what it feels like to matter to someone like she does to you. Show me, Marcus, show me…"

Dear Omnis, please, please give Emmy the strength to forgive me…

I drink the Tam, lean in, part her lips, and kiss her lightly. Her lips are tender and her tongue is warm inside my mouth. She moves it expertly around, darts it in and out, giving me just enough to make me want more. But I don't want more. I desperately want to stop.

I want to be holding Emmy. I miss the way her lips taste. I miss how her skin feels beneath my hands. I miss the way she inhales sharply when my lips brush a sensitive spot on her body she didn't know she had. I crave the sound of her moans and long to feel her nails digging into my skin when the pleasure is too much for her to take.

It's not just my mind that misses her; it's my body. My fingers unbutton Bianca's blouse in search of Emmy's breasts. My tongue seeks out their familiar slopes, only to find Bianca's. While hers are perfect, they are not what my tongue craves.

She guides my lips down her perfect body and they lick, suck, and nibble every inch of her in hopes of finding some part of her that feels or tastes like the girl I love.

Emmy is not here. She's not here…

The thought causes a sadness in me that renders me still. Bianca looks up at me in wonder. She's naked now; we both are. She extends her hand to take me over to the bed. I try to remember what's at stake. I try to remember all the lives at stake if this doesn't happen.

I can't move.

I'm going to fail this mission…

The thought paralyzes me even more.

Then, I see her.

She's in front of me. She's standing where Bianca once stood.

"Emmy, you're here?"

She shakes her head "no."

Then I understand it's just my mind playing games. The person in front of me is Bianca, and she's waiting for me.

I can't do this.

As soon as I think that thought, my mind's eye changes from Bianca to Emmy once again. It's okay to make love to her now because Bianca's face has officially morphed into Emmy's.

I take her hand and we go over to the bed. We kiss fervently. She moans and kisses my chest repeatedly. I inhale her lavender scent and kiss every inch of her: from her impossibly purple eyes to her belly button and down to her toes. Emmy sighs and moans in utter delight.

She returns the favor by whipping me into a frenzy with her fingers and lips. She makes patterns on my chest until I'm shaking in ecstasy. She grabs my hair roughly and guides me once again to my favorite path: the contours of her breasts. Once I reintroduce my lips to her nipples, she calls out my name.

She arches her back and opens her legs. My fingers, overjoyed at having found Emmy again, eagerly play between her legs until she is so far gone, she can no longer control her breathing and her eyes roll to the back to her head. She begs me to enter her, and since there is nowhere I'd rather be than inside Emmy, I sink into her gently but firmly.

"Oh shit," she cries out.

Her body is rocked by waves of orgasms, or in the Angel world, the Inner Arc. The sheer pleasure of being inside her is all I need to achieve my Inner Arc a few short minutes later. My wings expand in the air and flap wildly. I glow and shake for several minutes.

The Outer Arc begins to form outside our bodies. The orb starts out the size of a tennis ball, then expands to fill nearly half the room when Emmy gets on top and starts to ride me. She teases me by going so slow it feels like delicious torture. Then she speeds up until I'm dizzy with lust and wanting.

She embeds me even deeper into her, then she slowly, skillfully turns her body a full 360 degrees, never once losing contact. The elation of making "wall to wall" contact inside her causes me to bolt upright.

"EMMY! YES! YES!" I groan helplessly.

Just then Emmy grows massive wings. I close my eyes and collapse back onto the bed. The Exchange is happening; we are taking on each other's traits. Emmy tells me my skin color now matches hers. I'm too exhausted to open my eyes.

I just lie there as she places her head on my chest. I stroke Emmy's hair for a few moments, and then finally open my eyes. I find Bianca looking back at me.

Damn…

The disappointment I feel is so profound it becomes a physical pain. It travels up and down my body. I feel like someone is carving a hole in me. It's like I've been tossed out of the light and into a bitter reality. I knew Emmy was just in my head but at one point it just felt so real…

I get off the bed, causing Bianca's head to slide off my chest. I hurriedly put on my clothes.

"We gotta get going. I need to prepare the army before the Sage gets inside the city," I tell her.

"It didn't happen until now…," she says quietly.

I look over at her; she's using the sheets to cover her bare breasts. I feel odd that she's all but naked. I know it's strange given what we just did, but still…

"What didn't happen until now?" I ask.

"I never hated the thought of being with you because I knew it had to be done and because I knew you were a nice guy. But right now, I really hate this," Bianca replies.

"I don't know what you mean?"

"Marcus, I know this situation is tough, but it didn't have to be like this. We could have had sex as friends; you didn't have to make me a whore."

"What? How did I do that?"

"You yelled out her name."

"Look, I—"

"The worst part is when you opened your eyes and realized you were back with me; all of a sudden, you leap off the bed like you're ashamed."

"I didn't do that."

"The hell you didn't."

"Look, this wasn't my choice; we had to do this," I remind her.

"This is the only way to ensure a future for my people where they actually have a voice. So I didn't have a choice either. But when it's all over, I put my head on your chest because we shared an experience. And good or bad, it was just the two of us. We could have done this as friends," I—"

"I thought, 'yeah, he's thinking about her, but he knows I'm here. And when the Exchange is over, he'll hold me like a friend.' I didn't think you'd push me away like I get paid by the hour."

"ARGH!!!" I scream as I hurl the lamp across the room. "What is it you want from me? I can't stop loving her. I tried. I can't. I won't," I vow.

"I'm not asking you to stop seeing Emmy. I'm asking you to start seeing me," she says as tears fill her eyes.

She wraps the blanket around her. She looks lost. I run my hands through my hair and clench my jaw.

I hate Julian. I hate Julian. I hate Julian…

She remains seated on the bed across from me. I hear her crying softly.

I can't begin to think of the appropriate thing to say. I walk over to her and hope something will come to mind. I sit on the floor below her.

She looks down at me with fresh tears. I feel like crap. This is the second girl I've made cry in less than twenty-four hours.

Some angel you are, Marcus…

"I'm sorry. I should have been…" I can't think of the word.

"You made me feel like trash," she says.

Damn.

"I didn't mean to."

"Maybe that's what you think of me; maybe that's what I am," she says as her lips tremble. Before I can reply, she's sobbing again. I reach up and embrace her; her whole body trembles.

"It's okay. This is weird and strange for both of us. But you're right; I should've been a gentleman. It's just that there's a lot going on. And I don't want to hurt Emmy at all."

"I understand. But does 'not hurting' Emmy have to mean hurting me?"

Ouch.

"No. I shouldn't have pushed you away like that," I admit.

"I know we have to go, but can we just stay and you hold me for a few minutes?"

"Yeah, sure," I reply.

She wraps herself in the blanket and sits on the floor beside me. She leans her head on my shoulder.

"Marcus?" she calls out softly.

"Yeah?"

"I think you and I are going to become really good friends…"

CHAPTER SIX:
ANYTHING I CAN GET

The battleground

It looks like there is nothing to separate our mountain range from the
Sage's, but there is a shield that prevents both sides from entering. While
each mountain range is filled with well-armored Quo and angels, no one
has breached the shields yet.

I inform the team that Bianca and I are ready to enter the mountain
range. They arrange for a section of the shield to be lifted. There are
meters everywhere to make sure the being going past the shield is an angel,
or at the very least, has a soul.

As we enter the makeshift command center, I find the Foundation's
army standing at attention, waiting for my orders. There are a few thousand
of them. They're dressed in hooded robes that are the same earth tones
as the mountain range that surrounds us. "The Foundation is pleased to
have you lead our army," Dalce says with an official tone. He looks at his
daughter beside me and they exchange a quick hug. My team appears by
my side and report the latest news on the Sage's army.

"For one thing, we hear from our inside source, they are calling
themselves the Believers," Ameana informs me.

"What is it they believe in?" I ask.

"The Sage; they think he will make their lives better and that angels are
basically evil," Rio replies.

"Great. Do we know how many Believers there are?" I ask my team.

"They roll'n real deep. The source says as far as Quos are concerned, they outnumber us two to one," Jay says.

"That's in terms of Quo. What about demons?" I ask.

"For every angel we have, they have three demons," Miku says.

"Okay, and I'm assuming they have Fire Swans," I reply.

"Maybe two dozen or so, according to the source," Ameana says.

"What about us, how many in our army?"

"Five thousand," Dalce replies.

"Send a few hundred to look after the children, injured angels, and Quo that are without active powers," I instruct.

"I don't have an active power, but I can be useful in this," Bianca reminds me.

"Looking into someone's past doesn't help during an attack. We only need Quo with abilities that can harm. Otherwise, they're just a liability," I inform her.

"We can't spare any soldiers. The ones who can't fight we left back in base camp. They'll be fine," Dalce counters.

"I was under the impression this army was mine to do with what I wanted," I reply.

"Yes, but I think—"

"I don't care what you think. The people of Cree can't be left defenseless. If the Believers should get past us, they'll head straight for base camp."

"If that's the way you want to do it," he says, clearly unhappy with my decision.

"Is there anyone here who has the ability to quickly survey what powers someone has?" I ask.

A few soldiers raise their hands. I call them out and instruct them to survey the crowd for Quo soldiers with powers that can help during an evacuation. They step out of the line and begin to pick out the best Quos for the job. Meanwhile, the team and I take Dalce aside.

"What do I need to know about your army?" I ask Dalce. "Every soldier has, at the very least, the ability to shoot Powerballs. That's a minimum requirement. Some can tear into flesh without touching it. I have soldiers who can lift nearly ten times their weight and others can manipulate their surroundings," Dalce replies.

"But the Believers are Quo and they too have similar, if not the same, powers," I remind him.

"That is correct. But Quos have powers to different degrees. They may share the same ability; it doesn't mean they have the same skill level," Bianca answers.

"How well trained is your army, Dalce?" Ameana inquires.

"They've waited years for a battle like this. They are ready."

I survey the group of ominous looking men and women in hoods.

Dalce informs me that their robes are made of special material that helps them fend off most minor Powerball attacks. In addition, a few of them have the power to disappear for a short time and reappear again. Dalce reminds me what a great power that is, but I'm betting that a few Believers share that same power.

"The source told us one last thing you should know, Marcus," Ameana says in a tone that tells me whatever she is about to say, it won't be to my liking.

"What is it?"

"They have Death Stalkers."

"What are Death Stalkers?" Dalce asks.

"They're four legged beasts with poisonous fangs that can run at inhuman speeds. But they an only eat human flesh; they can't process soul. So they won't be able to kill angels. And since the Quo are half angel, they may cause injury but they can't kill your kind," I reply.

"I would think that's good, right?" Miku asks.

"Yeah, but why would the Sage use beasts that couldn't kill angels or Quo?" Dalce asks, reading my mind.

Oh no...

"Emmy's at base camp with the others, right?" I ask, fearing the answer.

The team avoids my eyes. Rage suppresses a smile, but wisely says nothing.

"Emmy's at base camp, *right?*" I challenge.

"No, she's here," Rio replies.

Chapter Six: Anything I Can Get

"WHY THE HELL IS SHE HERE?" I shout. My voice causes everyone to stop moving. I force myself to regain control and lower my voice.

"She refused to leave," Miku replies.

"So, what? You guys just let her stay?" I ask, furious.

"Let her? Have you met this girl? Since when does she follow anyone's orders?!" Ameana shouts, clearly ticked off.

"You guys should have made her go," I snap.

"C'mon, man, be real. Emmy would have just found a way to escape and come back here," Jay says.

He's right, but it still pisses me off that they let her stay.

"Where is she?" I ask.

"Wolf is teaching her some basic moves so she can defend herself," Miku says.

"Does she know I'm—I mean—we're back?" I ask.

"Yeah," Rio says.

He's reading my disappointment. He knows I'm slightly hurt that Emmy was here the whole time and didn't come to see me.

Maybe she didn't miss me…

Really, Marcus, what did you expect? She can't just come up and embrace you and your new wife. She's probably just going along with the plan by giving me and Bianca space.

I shake my head and clear my throat in an attempt to stay focused.

"So Lucy sent the Death Stalkers just for Emmy," I conclude.

"Yes. We don't know how she knew Emmy would be here," Miku says.

"The Sage knows her. He knows she won't be too far from the action. She has this thing where she has to help, no matter how many times her 'help' ends up being more of a pain," Ameana says.

"C'mon, Mimi. Emmy has saved us a few times," Miku reminds her.

"Here and there, but we work better when we don't have to babysit," Ameana counters.

"This wouldn't be a problem if you guys had let me kill her all those times," Rage says as an aside.

"None of that matters. She needs to be back in base camp," I order.

"She's earned a right to be here, Marcus," Miku says.

"What part about Death Stalkers don't you get, Pretty?" I ask her.
"You don't let her stay and you will spend this whole time wondering
if she has, yet again, found another way to disobey your orders. And it's
good to have her close since she's Lucy's most wanted," Miku responds.

"Fine, we'll just have to make sure we take out the Death Stalkers
before they even get a chance to seek her out."

"Yeah, let's center every move we make around Emmy," Ameana says
bitterly.

"Yo, what's your issue, son? We've been going crazy turning meters on
and off for your boy toy. So, be easy," Jay scolds Ameana.
"What do you mean turning meters on and off?" I ask.
"Well, the alarms go off when the meter registers something without
a soul has breached the perimeters. So every time Rage gets near there, the
alarms go crazy. The soldiers have been running to and from the perimeter
all morning," Miku tells me.

"We could just recalibrate the meters so they don't go off," Ameana
offers.
"We don't have time for that. I say we throw Rage out into the middle of
the battlefield and take bets to see how long before his wings are ripped
off," Rio offers.

"Really, Rio, that's the most angel-like thing you could say right now?"
Ameana says defensively.

"I'm being an angel by not killing him," Rio offers.

"Oh, and how would you kill me? Read me to death?" Rage mocks.

Rio's wings spread in the air and flap furiously.

"We have made an exception to include the human in the meter; I
don't see why we can't include Thomas," Ameana counters.

"Because Emmy has a soul. She has a heart. That reminds me: how do
you love a guy who can't love you back?" Jay asks.

"Who said he can't?" Ameana snaps.

"How could he? He doesn't have a heart. I mean, maybe after this
battle, we should go see the wizard about getting him a heart," Jay mocks.

Rio looks over at him and smiles. It's the first thing the two of them
have agreed on in days.

"You're right, Speedy; I don't have a heart. But at least I can protect my girl from getting blown up into a million pieces. Tell me, when the explosion ripped her soul into shreds, do you think she just blacked out? Or did she feel *every* slow, agonizing moment?"

I knew Jay was going to do it even before I turned towards him. He tackles Rage, and soon the two are in the air, fireballs flying everywhere. Jay skillfully dodges them and gets the upper hand on Rage.

Jay's advantage quickly goes away as Rage hurls a fireball at his head. Jay ducks it just in time, but Rage grabs him by his foot and hurls him to the ground. Rage looms over Jay with a fireball in hand. Rage underestimates Jay's speed; before he can throw down the fireball, Jay is up and standing behind Rage. Ameana places herself between the two of them and shouts at them to stop.

"We don't have time for this. The Sage is getting ready to attack. So, either kill each other quickly or shut the hell up and let me figure this out," I shout at them.

They stop attacking each other but they continue to throw evil stares each other's way. Miku shakes her head at Ameana. She is clearly irate that the 'Rage thing' is lasting this long. She isn't the only one, but now is not the time to address that.

The truth is, while I do not trust Rage, Emmy has yet to see him doing anything wrong in the Tracker she wears.

"We're going to need help with the Fire Swans. We can't take on them, the Quo, and the Death Stalkers. We need more reinforcement," I inform them.

"I have a Keeper friend of mine—he might let us use some of his animals," Bianca offers kindly.

"Perfect; give him a call and see if he has anything that can take on Fire Swans. Tell him we'll pay whatever."

"Sure, honey." She smiles, kisses me on the lips quickly, and goes off. The team stops and looks at me.

"We have to keep up appearances or the Quo won't back us," I remind them.

They all avoid my eyes. I clear my throat and head back to the soldiers. Dalce hands me a map of the territory and we plot out the best places to position the soldiers.

Soon, Wolf joins us, along with the rest of the Omari. Wolf keeps throwing evil glances at Rage. Rage, in turn, sneers at him. Ameana places a hand on Rage's shoulders in an attempt to keep him from doing anything stupid.

Rage attacking Wolf would be just that: stupid. Wolf is an expert fighter and although not a fan of taking a life, he seems more than willing to make an exception for Rage. There is also the matter of Wolf being a Kon. The Omari would follow him into Difi if they had to. He is their leader, and they will protect him no matter what.

Wolf tries to stay focused on the battle ahead, but the more glances he steals at Ameana, the more it angers Rage. Sensing it is only a matter of seconds before one of them attacks the other, Ameana wisely suggests that she and Rage inspect the shield for any possible weak points.

After Wolf and I come to a decision regarding the placement of the Omari, I address the army and thank them for fighting alongside us. I promise them that they won't be forgotten and discarded like they were before by the council. They shout and cheer.

One of them calls out, "How was she?"

Dalce tells me they are referring to my night with Bianca. I nod reluctantly, and they respond with a series of profane noises. Even the female soldiers find the subject of Bianca and me worth cheering for.

When the crowd finally calms down, I dispatch them to various points along the perimeters, and throughout the mountain range.

After addressing the soldiers, I spot Emmy a few yards away with Eta. She excitedly shows Eta the basic moves that Wolf has taught her. She beams with excitement as she shows off her new right hook jab. She's not going to kill any demons with her new skills. In fact, I'm not sure she can even land a punch at all.

But the thing that has me completely captivated isn't her newfound "moves," it's her face. Emmy is beaming. She's never really been taught to fight. I think she's really enjoying it.

She's happy, so that means she and I are okay, right?

Chapter Six: Anything I Can Get

When our eyes meet, I smile at her. She quickly turns her face back to Eta. She says something to her, and the two of them quickly take off. *She can't even look at me…*

I order the twins to head to the Market and seek out any weapons that might give us an edge. Although most Sellers are in hiding, fearing that they will be killed in the crossfire, I'm certain Tony and a few others have stuck around, knowing that because it's wartime, they can charge three times as much for weapons.

I turn to Jay and order him to send a few lookouts ahead so we know exactly when the Believers are coming.

"Don't let our lookouts breach the Sage's shield. We don't want to be the ones who start this. Once there are enough Fire Swans circling, we can get the soldiers ready; when the Swans attack the shield, that's the signal."

"Won't that be too late?" he asks.

"One Fire Swan can't break the shield. It will take at least six of them. Tell the others—once there are six Swans in the air…we engage."

"Okay, I'm on it," he says, about to rush off.

"Jay, where was Emmy when the contract was fulfilled and turned into stone?"

"She was in the room with Dalce and Eta."

"She saw the whole thing?"

"Yeah, Miku offered to go for a walk with her, but she said she didn't want to go."

"She knew exactly when Bianca and I had our…"

"Exchange? Yeah, everyone does."

He pats my shoulder and Glides away.

Through the afternoon, Emmy and I make eye contact—or at least I do. She always avoids me. I make myself focus on the battle ahead. I want to make sure we are ready for whatever the Sage has in store for us.

Finally, night falls. We are waiting for the Sage to make the first move by sending the Fire Swans into the air. The soldiers are ready and the perimeter is secure.

Emmy hasn't said a word to me, much less looked at me. I have to admit it hurts. I've missed her so much. I want to hold her more than I have ever wanted anything in this world. But I doubt I will be able to get her to hug me. In fact, it'll be a miracle if she ever looks directly at me again.

Emmy has chosen to sleep in the opening of the cave, furthest away from my sleeping area. I'm sharing the space in a small opening in the side of the mountain with Bianca. Well, I'm supposed to, anyway. I have yet to leave the command center. And even if I were to leave, I would Recharge somewhere alone. Right now, I'm too tired and miserable to care what the Quo think about where I do or don't Recharge.

Ameana tells me to go Recharge since it's been days since I had some rest. She assures me that she will take my place and oversee everything.

"No, I'm good. I want to be here," I promise her.

"Marcus, you're going to have to face her sometime," she points out.

"She hates me."

"She should; you betrayed her."

"I had no choice. I didn't—"

"Marcus, I didn't say you didn't have your reasons. I'm saying it's still a betrayal. You still slept with another girl. That's only a few weeks after you kissed another girl. No offense, but if I were Emmy, I would've kicked your ass a hundred battles ago."

"Wow, thanks," I say dryly.

"I'm just telling you the truth," she replies sweetly.

I shake my head and let her stand watch over the shield for a while. So far, there is one Fire Swan in the air. It swoops around in a circle but has yet to attack. No doubt it's waiting for others to arrive.

I look all over for her. Finally, I find her sitting alone, at the side of a small rocky hill. She looks out into the black sky. The sun should be out soon, judging from the bright orange hue on the horizon. I walk to her and sit a few feet away. I want to touch her, but the Sage and I aren't the only ones with our shields up.

"Hey," I say softly, looking out into the sky.

I think it's easier to look out than directly at her. That way I don't see the immense pain in her beautiful eyes. I can pretend I didn't put it there. I continue to speak without looking at her. She sits so still it's like she's barely breathing. She looks straight ahead, out into nothing.

Chapter Six: Anything I Can Get

"I'm not gonna ask you to look at me, because I've already asked too much of you. It seems like whenever there's a sacrifice to be made, you're the one who is forced to make it."

She remains perfectly still. I can't tell what's going on in her head. Normally, I would have some indication, but she's keeping me out of her thoughts, out of her heart.

"I know it's asking too much to expect you to run into my arms after I come back from spending the night with someone else."

The second Fire Swan appears in the sky. I'm on alert, but I know two Fire Swans aren't enough to break our shields.

"When you were going out with Lucas, I was in Hell. I pictured him holding and kissing you. I lost it. I knocked down an entire building. Actually, a few buildings," I admit.

My girl doesn't respond, so I continue, in the hope that my words will be enough, but fearing they won't be. I pause and fight the urge to pull her close to me and feel her against me.

Damn, it still amazes me just how strongly I need her...

"Emmy, I know you were there the moment the Exchange happened. I can't imagine what it was like to have everyone in the room look at you. So, you don't have to look at me. But I have never loved any one being the way I love you. And while I won't ask for the embrace that I so desperately want..." I finally look over at her and see tears falling down her cheeks and onto her shirt. My first and only instinct is to reach out for her. But her shields are far from down. I keep trying to reach her with my words since my touching her isn't an option.

"You don't have to say anything at all if you're not ready to talk to me. But, Emmy, put your hand in mine, let me know I haven't lost you."

I look over at my hand, only about a foot or so away from her. But I know my reaching out to her won't tell me what I need to know; is she still with me? Or was the reality of knowing I was with Bianca too much for her to take? I wait for Emmy to place her hand on mine. It doesn't happen. A wave of pure dread creeps down my body, causing me to feel weak. I can't turn to face her now because I fear what I will see in her eyes.

Has she finally had enough? Is this really truly the end for us?

"Emmy, you can hate me if that's what you need to do right now; just give me some indication that we'll get past this. Emmy, take my hand," I say, finally turning to her.

I hold my hand out to her. She does not take it. Her tears have dried now. In her eyes there is a wariness I have never seen before.

She's been attacked one time too many. She's been disappointed and hurt by me one time too many. And no matter what the reasons were, like Ameana said, I still betrayed her yet again.

It's been less than a minute but it feels like my hand has been held out forever. Emmy does not budge. I put my hand down on the jagged rocks we're sitting on. As a leader, to prepare myself for the battle, I tried to hone my strength and certainty. It has been replaced with crippling sadness and anxiety.

I flash back to all the times I loved her from afar.

When she stood there in her Piglet T-shirt and messy hair and still looked more stunning than any girl I had ever seen in or out of the light…

When she berated me for calling Ms. Charlotte "just" a cat…

When she brazenly marched down the stadium steps at the Runner Ball game to scold the official because I got hurt…

Now, it's over.

Please, please don't let it end like this.

I turn towards her; I try one final time.

"I know I haven't loved you the way you deserved to be loved, but I would give the last feather from my wings, the last drop of soul from my blood, if it means you would let me try again."

She sits still.

"I don't remember how to live without you; I don't remember how not to want you…"

She is unmoved.

This is the end.

Despair weighs heavy on me and causes me to bow my head as yet another memory flashes in my head.

It was our first date. She was so nervous, she wrapped her hand around the doorknob and wouldn't let go. I helped her by kissing each and every one of her fingers and assuring them that everything was going to be okay.

Chapter Six: Anything I Can Get

But it's not; Emmy and I are over…

Something softly grazes my finger. The touch is slight; I'm not sure it's anything more than the wind. I look over to where I placed my hand.

It's her! She moved her hand just a little. Now her pinky finger grazes me lightly, or at least I think it does. It may all be in my head.

Please…

There's no further movement.

Damn.

Then she curls her finger around mine.

Thank you, Omnis.

She still can't bring herself to look at me, but that's okay. I'll take anything I get, so long as I get to be in her life.

CHAPTER SEVEN:
THE VIEW FROM HERE

would like to stay with her until everything is okay between us. But I think it will take a lot more than a few hours. I would also like to walk her to her makeshift home, but the Quo are everywhere. It wouldn't look right. I think she knows that too, because she heads home without asking me to join her.

I walk back to the command center to relieve Ameana. I'm about to enter when I hear her and Rage talking. Again, as her ex-boyfriend, I have no desire to know what the two of them talk about. But as the leader, it would be foolish not to keep an eye on the lead Akon.

I cross over to the side of the opening that allows me to see the two of them better. Ameana and Rage are alone. She's holding a plate, a flat circular crystal the size of a golf ball. Something appears inside it when she touches it. I can't make out what is says from here.

"Where'd you get that from?" Rage asks her.

"It's a souvenir from the wedding. It was in the small boxes."

"Oh, that's what was in it? I thought the boxes contained what was left of the human's dignity."

She laughs softly.

"I can't believe Emmy is okay with it."

"Humans are stupid."

"I can actually see her heart breaking. Dear Omnis, that girl is weak," she says with a sigh.

He laughs and shakes his head.

"If you were in Emmy's position, what would you do?" he asks.

"Thomas, I would *never* be in Emmy's position."

"Why?"

"Because the minute Dalce opened his mouth and said you had to marry Bianca, father and daughter would have matching headstones."

"I love when you talk like a demon. It does things to me," he says, pulling her into his arms.

They kiss passionately. I ask Omnis to please blind me because I definitely do not want to be seeing this. Thankfully, they pull apart a few moments later.

"What's inside the plate?" he asks her.

"It says "Marcus & Bianca. Always.""

"Let me see it."

She hands it to him; he studies it closely.

"It's crap. Why do you still have it?" he wonders.

"Why would I throw it away?"

"It's from your ex's wedding. Why would you keep it?"

"I don't know. It's…nice," she says carefully as she walks away from him. She is looking at the maps, but even from this distance I can tell she's faking interest.

"Why is the plate important to you?" Rage asks, not fooled for a minute.

"It's not," she lies.

"Cree was being destroyed, you sought out a freaking plate and saved it. Why?"

"What's the difference?"

"Wait; are you still in love with the Tic?"

"He's not a Tic anymore."

"I ask you if you are still in love with another guy and that's your answer?"

"I'm not in love with him anymore. You know that."

"The only thing I know is that not one but two of your exes are here. It takes everything in me not to drown them in an ocean of flames and dance on their ashes."

"I know it's hard, Thomas; I appreciate you trying."

"I don't need your appreciation; I need to know what's so special about the stupid plate."

"NOTHING!"

"Good," he says, snatching it from her.

"Give it back, Thomas. I'm not in the mood to play."

"I'm not playing either. If this isn't important, then I can break it."

"Thomas, why are you being such an ass?"

"Why are you lying to me?"

"You want to throw it away, fine. Whatever," she says, clearly irritated. She puts all her attention on the maps once again. Rage hands it back to her. He starts to head towards the entrance, but before he gets there, she calls out after him.

"It's not about Marcus," she swears.

"Then what the hell is it about? You know I can't do the mind reading crap you chicks dig so much."

"I just like the design; it's nice. It's like what I would choose for my…" She falls silent.

"For your what?"

"Nothing," she replies.

"I FREAKING HATE THAT CRAP! JUST SAY WHAT'S IN YOUR HEAD, DAMN IT!"

"Fine; it's how I pictured my wedding ceremony. Marcus and I never got to have one because we had to prepare for the mission. Then, I was with Wolf but we didn't get that far. And now…"

"Now you're in love with a demon who doesn't have a Rah and can't marry you."

She lowers her head. He looks over at her and his face darkens.

"You said you were okay with that," he reminds her.

"I don't—what? I am okay with it… I don't care… It doesn't matter… I am…?"

"Then why the hell are we having this conversation?" he says in a serious tone.

She shrugs. He shakes his head, clearly pissed. She goes over to him and tries to touch his shoulder but he shrugs her off.

"Thomas, it's just a stupid plate. It doesn't mean anything," she says. Then, to show her sincerity, she drops the plate on the ground and steps on it. Some plates are unbreakable; this one is not. It smashes into pieces.

"See; means nothing," she says casually as she stands on her toes and embraces Rage.

He holds her, but all of his attention is the on the now shattered wedding plate.

"Hey, can I talk to you?"

I turn around and find Rio standing a few feet away. I head over to him, glad to have a reason to turn from the bizarre scene of a Guardian and an Akon interaction.

"What is it?" I ask.

"The soldiers have a lot of Waves. Excitement, nervousness, worry…"

"That's normal. They're about to go to war," I reply.

"Yeah, but there's this Quo—he's scared."

"They all are, to some extent," I reason.

"Not like this. Marcus, this kid is petrified. Having him in the field is a bad idea," Rio warns me.

"Where is he?"

Rio points to a small boy who looks to be about thirteen. He pulls nervously at the robe he's wearing. He summons a Powerball. It's the size of a lemon. He tries again. It's now the size of a grape. He does this a few times with very little success.

"Why did Dalce let him in?" I ask.

"If they're eleven and can summon up a Powerball, they have the right to join the army if they wish."

"You're right, we have to pull him out," I reply, in agreement with Rio.

"He looks like he's going to wet himself."

"Is there anyone else feeling this way?"

"Everyone is nervous, but they've managed to keep it under control. Actually, some are even cocky."

"Well, that's a lot better than scared."

"Yeah. I'll tell him he's out so he can relax and head back to base camp," Rio offers.

"No, I'll talk to him."

I head over to the frail beanpole of a soldier.

"What's your name?" I ask.

He turns to answer me, but once he realizes who I am, he freezes.

"What's your name?" I ask again.

"Marcus Cane."

I look at him, perplexed.

"I mean…you're Marcus Cane. Like, *the* Marcus Cane…Marcus… Cane…leader…Guardians…," he says breathlessly.

I'm about to reply when I realize this kid is literally breathless. He begins to hyperventilate.

"Kid, calm down," I order as I help him bend down to his knees, still struggling for air.

"Big…fan…me…you," he mumbles.

"Yeah, I get that. But right now, I need you to stay calm. I'm gonna count backwards from ten and when I get to one, you're going to stop acting like a groupie and start acting like a soldier, got it?"

He nods his head "yes," and I begin to count. I have no idea if this will work but it's worth a shot. Luckily, as I begin to count, he starts to let in some air. By the time I'm down to three, he's standing once again.

"Two…one."

"Thank you, sir. Sorry about that. Sometimes I get too excited," he says, still looking at me like I'm wearing a cape of some kind.

"Are you sure you're okay?" I ask.

"Um…yeah, I mean, yes."

"Good. What's your name?"

"Ty, sir," he says, unable to keep his voice from shaking.

"Ty, you look like you might not be ready for this."

"No, sir; I'm ready. My whole family is back at base camp, and they are so excited I made the cut."

"What did you have to do to qualify?"

"I had to summon up a Powerball and show them my other power."

"What's your other power?"

He disappears instantly before my eyes. Then, a few moments later, he reappears.

"Good; what about the Powerballs?"

"I can make big ones with a force that could knock out an entire block," he says proudly.

"I was just watching you…"

"Yeah, it turns out, when I'm…about to do battle, they kind of shrink."

"Why?"

"I don't know. But it's not because of fear. I'm Quo. We don't fear things," he says, mostly to reassure himself.

"How old are you?" "Twelve and a half." "Why did you want to be here?" "My dad told me all about your adventures. How you took on a bunch of evil dudes like Akons, the Hun, and even Kairo. I want to fight alongside you guys."

"You're not afraid of angels, given what the Sage has said about us and what the council has done to your kind?"

"My dad said not all angels are bad. And since you killed all those evil guys, it means you and your team are the good guys, right?"

"Right."

"Well, I joined the army because I want help you guys. Actually, I want be a Guardian. But I heard you have to be human, suffer, and die in a horrible way so…I guess that's out."

"I guess it is."

"But you guys let other beings into the team, like the First Akon. He's on the team, so I figure I have a shot."

"Rage isn't really—never mind. Look, Ty, you seem like a good kid, but you're not ready. There's no shame in wanting to go back to base camp."

"Back? Why would I go back—I'm not scared."

"I didn't say you were."

"Sir, I can do this," he says, eagerly looking up at me.

"Your Powerballs couldn't harm a fly."

"I'm working on it. They just get small when I'm—"

"When you're 'not' scared?"

He shakes his head. Shakes or nods?

"Ty, we can't use you."

"Sir, I'm the only one in my family with an active power. Ever since my dad found out I could form Powerballs, he's talked about me joining the army. I can't let him down. He's my dad."

Damn this kid. The second he talks about his dad, I flash back to mine. I remember wanting to prove to him that I was tough. I was in pee wee football and this kid who weighed about four hundred pounds ran into me. I hit the ground hard. The pain was intense.

Everyone ran over to see if I was okay, including my dad. As soon as I saw him, I somehow willed the tears to stay back. I forced my body to understand that boys don't cry. Looking back, I'm sure I didn't fool anyone because my lips were trembling uncontrollably and my face was twisted in agony.

I tried to hold back the crying for as long as I could. But once I got up from the ground, the pain intensified and the tears came. I was sure my dad was ashamed of me. I had let him down and now he wished he had a better son, a stronger son.

Later that night, my dad told me about falling off a tree once and crying so loud the whole neighborhood knew about it. He said crying wasn't a big deal as long as I didn't allow it to stop me from playing again. I was so relieved to still be worthy in his eyes.

I look over at the kid as he summons up yet another mini Powerball. The smaller they are, the more frustrated he gets. The more frustrated he gets, the smaller the Powerballs. It's a vicious cycle.

"I'm glad you're not scared. But if you were scared, I'd tell you that it's okay because the other guy is scared too."

"Really?" he asks incredulously.

"Everyone in a battle is scared. No one wants to die. So, what the other guy does is focus on something else to keep from being scared."

"Like what?"

"Like what he's fighting for. That's why you have to make sure you're in a fight that's worth it," I reply.

"This is worth it. My dad says we can have a future with the angels."

"Ty, don't fight because of your dad; fight because you think it's the right thing to do. I know your dad believes in us, but what do you believe in?"

"I like the humans. I don't think they should be forced to worship the Sage. And maybe some angels are bad but not all of you guys. So, he shouldn't be allowed to kill you all. I mean, yeah, the council treated us like we were accidents and locked us away, but you guys aren't like them. I know the Guardians like us. I mean, for Omnis' sake, you fell in love and married one of us."

"Yeah, I did…," I say, almost to myself.

"So that's what I'm fighting for."

"You're fighting for the humans and the lives of thousands of angels. That's a good reason, Ty."

"Yeah, them too, but mostly I'm doing it for you and Bianca. I can't believe you married a Quo. For so long we were told we were insignificant, but now…you and Bianca…that's what I'm fighting for."

Damn…

I clear my throat like it will somehow take the guilt away.

"Hold out your hand," I instruct. He does as I say.

"Now, when you summon the Powerball, it will be big and powerful because you, Ty, are powerful. Got it?"

He summons the Powerball. It's the same baby Powerball as the other ones. He shakes his head, frustrated. I order him to try again. He does, and this time the Powerball is bigger, but not by much.

"ARGH!" he shouts.

"Ty, focus."

He closes his eyes and when he opens them up again, a massive Powerball forms in his hands. His eyes widen in shock.

"It's never been this big, ever!" Ty declares.

"Keep practicing and remember: focus."

"So, you'll let me stay?" he asks, filled with hope.

"For now."

"Okay, thank you. Thank you."

I smile reluctantly and hope I haven't condemned a little boy to his death. As I walk away, he calls after me.

"Sir?"

"Yeah?"

"Do you think a Quo could ever, somehow, become part of your team? I mean, if he worked really hard and practiced all the time?"

"Um…yeah, I guess. Maybe one day," I reply, unable to think of a better answer.

He grins broadly and goes back to practicing.

"How did it go?" Rio asks from a few feet away.

"You weren't reading my Waves?" I ask as we head back.

"Yeah, saw a few interesting colors. So I take it you're not sending him home?" Rio inquires.

"He really wants to be here," I reply.

"And that's all it takes?"

"Rio, the Quo allow children to fight. That's not my rule, it's theirs."

"I'm just saying, he's a kid. He thinks this is a video game or something."

"He's gonna be fine."

"How can you guarantee that?"

"I'll look after him."

"How? You're leading the team," he says, as if I need reminding.

"Yes, I am leading this team. And since that's the case, maybe you could have a little faith in me then and not question me every five minutes. Can you do that?" I ask bitterly.

"I don't think I'm asking anything unreasonable. That kid needs to go home."

"If we lose this, everyone will be affected, including Ty. So if he wants to fight, let him."

"He's fighting for something that's not even real. He thinks you and Bianca are some type of symbol of angel and Quo harmony, but you're not."

"Just because the two of us aren't…it doesn't mean that we can't get along with the Quo."

"I know that. But you guys are perpetrating a lie. And that kid is putting his life on the line for that lie!" he shouts.

"Keep your voice down!" I scold.

"This kid is being lied to," he says in a lower tone.

"This isn't about Ty. It's about you."

"Me?"

"Yes, you. No matter what happens, you always find a reason to be pissed at me."

"That's not true."

"Rio, I don't need your powers to know you're lying. Ever since we were in the light and Ameana rejected you, you've hated me."

"Ameana has nothing to do with this."

"She has everything to do with this. But what I don't get is why you're still hating because, in case you didn't notice, I'm not with her anymore."

"I told you this isn't about her," he says tightly.

"Then what the hell is it about?"

"This is about a kid who's gonna get himself killed because he believes in you."

"If I tell him the truth about us, I might as well tell the whole army. Then what? Who will help us then?" I snap.

"I think it's wrong for you to let him stay," he replies, shaking his head.

"So you're just gonna keep pretending this is about Ty?"

"I'm not pretending. I'm doing what you should have been doing: looking out for these people."

"You always act like you know better than me."

"It's not an act," he sneers.

I stop walking and turn to face him. My face is stone and my voice is steel.

"Rio, you wanna run this team? You wanna lead this war? Fine. I will relinquish complete control of this team if you answer one question."

"Marcus, you're being crazy."

"No, I'm not. For the longest time I knew you felt Omnis was wrong to make me First Guardian. Maybe he was, but it's done. The only way you can lead the team now is if both Ameana and Miku die. Or if I willingly relinquish my title to you."

"Why would you risk your leadership like that?"

"It's not a risk. I'm certain you won't have the balls to answer the question."

"And if I do?"

"You won't."

"But if I do?"

"Then I will step down as First Guardian. Ameana will remain the second-in-command but you... will lead."

He studies me to see if I'm serious. I remain perfectly still and never break eye contact.

"Rio, I've been trying to steer this team down the right path and all you've been doing is judging and condemning me from the backseat. Come on up to the front; see if you like the view from here."

"This is crazy," he replies, still studying me.

"You wanna lead so badly, fine. You answer the question I ask, and you will be the new First Guardian."

"You're serious?"

"Read. My. Waves."

"If I give you an answer to this question, I'm in charge?" he restates.

"Did I stutter?"

"What's the question?"

"Why did you try to kill me?"

CHAPTER EIGHT:
STEEL & PAPER

I've never seen Ri

"Yes, Rio, I know it was you that night on the New River Bridge in

West Virginia."

He turns away, but I don't let that stop me.

"It was a few days after we came to Earth. You went out of your way to make sure I knew what an awful boyfriend I was being to Ameana. You read my Wave and you knew I had feelings for Emmy. I was trying to fight those feelings, and instead of helping me, you just condemned me every chance you got.

"I was chasing a demon who we thought could lead us to Julian. I caught up to him somewhere around West Virginia. He led me into a trap. He had called for backup, and they ambushed me. There were at least half a dozen of them. I had dropped my cell and there was no way to contact you guys.

"They ganged up on me. Everywhere I went there were Powerballs headed straight for me. One of them managed to hit my left wing and that sent me flying to the other side of the bridge. Seeing that I was hurt, one of them rushed over to me to finish the job. He made the mistake of getting too close to me; I reflected his fear back to him. He cried like a baby. He was so distraught he didn't even realize he was falling off the bridge. The others came after me. I managed to take all of them out. But in the final moments of the last demon's life, he somehow latched on to me as he was going over the side of the bridge.

"That's when I realized my wings were more damaged than I thought. I was able to shake the demon loose, but I couldn't pull myself up. Then, from the corner of my eye, I saw a being take flight and land a few yards away.

"The being was too far away for me to make out anything but the outline of their wings. I couldn't even tell what color they were. The being just stood there, watching me. I was confused. If it was a demon, he would have killed me. If it was an angel, he would have saved me. So, who would just stand there, looking at me clinging on for dear life?

"The figure watched for several minutes, then flew away. It took me nearly an hour to pull myself up. When I finally did, I had this sick feeling that I knew the being that had appeared on the bridge.

"That night I got back to the house, everyone had had their hands full with Emmy and the Akons. But you were off somewhere, hunting down demons you said. I asked if you didn't read my Wave, and you said you were having trouble with your powers that night. Then you said you wanted some alone time and you flew away.

"Every angel moves their wings in a different pattern. The difference is slight, but it's there. I had several minutes to watch the being on the bridge. I was sure I had seen it before but I couldn't place it. Then back at the house, I watched you take to the sky. That's when I remembered where I had seen that pattern before. It was you, out on the bridge.

"I tried to come up with an explanation. I even made myself believe that I had somehow dreamed the stranger on the bridge. I lied to myself because I needed to know that no matter how much you disagreed with me, we were still family. Friends. Teammates."

"Marcus, we are," he replies.

"YOU LEFT ME TO DIE!!!" I roar, unable to stop myself.

I force myself to lower my voice. But what my tone is lacking in sound, it makes up for in firmness. I look at Rio and ask what I have dreaded asking him since that night.

"I know it was you. You saw I was going to lose my life and you did nothing. Just tell me, why? Why were okay with me dying?"

"How do you know it—"

"Don't!" I caution him.

"Marcus, it's…"

"I just want to know why," I push.

He still can't bring himself to look me in the eye.

"You tell me why you did that in the next sixty seconds and you can lead this team."

Silence.

I wait. I know he won't tell me. But for some reason, I need him to try. I need him to explain what I have never been able to figure out.

This couldn't just be about Ameana. If Rio felt so strongly about her, then he would have gone after Ameana when we broke up.

Silence.

Somewhere in the back of my mind, I'm hoping it's an excuse I couldn't think of. Like some kind of Rio clone. Or, maybe I was mistaken and what looked like Rio standing still was really him thinking of the best way to help me.

Yeah, I know that makes no sense. But when one of your closest friends decides to let you dangle off of a bridge, very little makes sense at all.

Silence.

Furious, I shake my head and address him in an irate whisper.

"That's what I thought. You want to lead but you can't do that with 'paper' wings. You need to be willing to grow a set of steel wings. That means if you wanted me to die you should have pushed me. Or sucked up whatever schoolboy emotions you had and saved me.

"Instead you just stood there like a punk and did nothing. You can never lead this team. You don't have what it takes. But don't worry; I'll call on you when I have a job that suits your capabilities, like helping schoolchildren cross a busy intersection."

"Marcus—"

"I swear if we didn't need you to help fight this war and put the Shoma back together…"

"Look, you don't understand—"

"Save it! Our friendship is done. As far as this team is concerned, you question even so much as the color of my shirt and you're out!" I glare at him bitterly and storm off.

"Your wings are gonna snap off if you keep flapping them so hard," she cautions me.

I turn around and find her looking at me.

"Emmy, I thought you went to sleep."

"Yeah, it turns out when you're only four Fire Swans away from war, sleep isn't an option."

"Three Fire Swans away from war," I correct her.

She looks up the sky and finds that another Fire Sawn has begun circling our shield.

"Oh, is that what's causing your wings to go into overdrive?"

"No, everyone has instructions. They know where they are supposed to be when the last Fire Swan takes to the air."

"Then what is it?"

"I just ran into Rio and of course he wanted to chew me out about something. Never mind that, I'm glad you're here," I confide to her.

I look into her eyes and she looks down towards the ground.

"Are you ever gonna look me in the eye again?" I ask.

She shrugs. I step towards her, she steps back. I didn't expect that after the interaction we had earlier.

"Okay, I know this is hard, but I've had the worst night. Emmy, I really need you right now."

"I'm trying," she whispers.

"Well, *try* looking in my eyes."

"I can't."

"So, that's it? We're done?"

"No, I just…"

"You just, what? Emmy, we talked about this. You knew what was gonna happen. You were okay with it," I remind her.

"I was never okay with you making love to someone else!"

"Fine, but you agreed."

"Yes, I did."

"And you also vowed not to let that come between us."

"Yeah, I know but—"

"But what?"

"I need time."

"Emmy, the only people who can stop us from being together are you and I. I hated what I had to do to get the army. I hated what it did to you, and to us. But it's done. And we need to get past it."

"You say that like it's easy. Like you and Bianca split an ice cream sundae or something. You slept with her. The two of you had an orgasm. Or maybe it was more than one. I don't know."

I hope to Omnis I'm wrong about the direction this conversation is going to take…

"How many orgasms did you have with her?"

I hate being right.

"Emmy, I'm really not in the mood to do this with you right now," I warn her.

"It's a simple question. I can handle it," she lies.

"Don't do this; not tonight, okay?" I say in the calmest voice I can summon.

"That means you two had, like, multiple ones, right? You guys were just having orgasms left and right, huh?" she accuses bitterly.

"We had what was needed to make the Exchange."

"Don't do that. Don't try to be diplomatic with me. Tell me the truth: who had the first orgasm, her or you?" she asks.

"Are you serious?"

"I need to know."

"Need to know what?"

"I need to know what happened that night."

"You said you didn't want to know. You made me promise not to tell you."

"Well, I changed my mind. I want to know what the two of you did."

"Trust me, you don't," I snap.

"Why don't you want to tell me? Is it because you enjoyed it so much? Of course you enjoyed it; she's gorgeous. She's probably highly skilled and limber. So, how limber is she?"

I'm trembling with anger. I know whatever I say to her next will make things worse. So, I wisely shake my head and start to walk away.

"Marcus, wait!" she calls after me.

"What?"

"You're right. I did say I didn't want to know, but that was before…"

"Before what?"

"Before I had to stand there and watch the contract turn to stone. Marcus, I knew the exact moment you two…how am I supposed to be okay with that?"

"You know why the Exchange *had* to happen."

"Yes, but what I don't know is how was it for you? I mean, did you even think about me?"

"No, Emmy, I didn't think about you at all. I just went in there and screwed her brains out. You never even occurred to me," I reply with disdain.

"Marcus, this is serious."

"No, what's serious is the fact that we are outnumbered, even with the Foundation by our side. What's serious is the fact that in a few hours, there will be dead bodies sprawled out all over this mountain range."

"You want me to be happy and to swallow this situation up whole. But it's hard. I want you to give me some time."

"Okay, take it."

"You're mad at me?"

"I'm not mad, I'm exhausted. No matter what I do, it's not good enough. I'm not a good enough boyfriend for you. I'm damn sure not going to be a good husband, and as far as being a leader…maybe if I had stayed focused, we wouldn't be in this war."

"What do you mean stayed focused? Are you talking about us?"

"I gotta get back…"

"Are you regretting that we're together?"

"Are we together? Because back at your apartment we talked about this and we vowed we'd get through this and now you 'need time.'"

"What's wrong with needing some time?"

"WE DON'T HAVE IT!!!" I snap.

"Fiancé," she replies softly.

"What?"

"You called yourself my boyfriend. You're my fiancé," she corrects me.

Chapter Eight: Steel & Paper

"Wow, really? That's all you got from what I just said to you?"

She's about to reply when something in the air catches her eye. I follow her stare.

"There's another Fire Swan. I've never seen a silver one before," she says, looking up at the sky.

"That's not a Fire Swan," I inform her.

"Then what is it?"

At that precise moment, Miku runs out and shouts from the top of her lungs. Her voice is overflowing with excitement.

"Oh my Omnis, it's an Alexi!"

Miku jumps up and down like a kid. Soon, angels, Quo, and the team all come out to see what's going on. They look up and see the incredibly beautiful silver glowing bird in the sky. The Alexi cuts through the air with the precision of the Omari and the grace of a Para. The sight of the Alexi causes some of the angels to clap and cheer.

"Okay, can we pause for a moment to do a Q&A with the human please?" Emmy begs, unable to take her eyes off the Alexi.

"Alexis are immortal. It can't be hurt or killed," I inform her.

"Okay; is it on our side?" she asks, fearful of the answer.

"It's not like that," I try to explain.

"What Marcus means is that when you see Alexi appear, it means only one thing," Miku explains.

"What?" she asks.

"Someone is pregnant."

CHAPTER NINE:
THE HANDOVER

know there will be a ton of questions coming from Emmy, so I try to get ahead of it and inform her because I know she hates being left in the dark.

"An Alexi will fly over to the female who's expecting."

"You mean like a stork?" she asks, laughing.

"Yeah, except this stork seeks out the mother and nearly kills her," Rage says.

"Okay, wait. Start from the beginning. How does the Alexi know someone is pregnant?"

"A baby angel is called a Sib. When the Sib forms inside the angel, it emanates a series of sounds that can only heard by an Alexi. The bird will then seek out the Sib," Rio replies.

"Okay, so the bird knows where the Sib or baby angel is—then what?"

"Then, the Alexi will swoop down and land next to the female that's pregnant."

I don't need to be Rio to know that Emmy is panicking. Her eyes widen with terror and anger. She looks at me, and I'm fairly certain if she had wings, they would be causing a giant twister right now. She leans in and whispers to me in a deadly, ominous tone.

"Marcus Cane, I swear to Omnis, if the Alexi lands ANYWHERE near Bianca—"

"Emmy, the Alexi is not going looking for Bianca," I assure her.

"Well then, who is she looking for?"

"I don't know, but it's not looking for her."

"How do you know?" she says, refusing to let the issue go.

"I used a Tam. So relax, okay?" I whisper back.

Chapter Nine: The Handover

Finally, Emmy takes a breath and starts to blink again. I have never seen her so on edge before. We look up at the sky, and the Alexi is headed straight for us.

"Can it get past our shield?" Emmy wonders.

"Alexis are immortal. They can get through anything: Fire, Holders, Shields…they're unstoppable," Rio tells her.

"They just spring up out of nowhere?" she asks as we watch the bird make graceful loops up and down the sky.

"What happens when the Alexi lands?" Emmy asks him.

"Then the female has only a few minutes to get comfortable and try to handle what will be the most painful moments of her life," Ameana replies.

"What does the Alexi do to her?"

"The angel lies flat on the ground with her arms out on either side of her. The Alexi lands on top of her chest, and then it opens its beak and emanates a laser beam right into the center of her chest. Although the pain starts with the cutting, the agony really begins after the Sib has been pulled out. That's when the Alexi will suck up nearly all of the angel's soul. That process is called the Handover."

"Can't that kill the angel?"

"Yes, some have died."

"So, why does the Alexi have to suck out the angel's soul?"

"It's what the Sib needs in order to survive the journey to Noni."

"What's Noni?"

"It's a field of crystal cocoon on the outskirts of Daraquin. The Alexis take all the Sibs there. They drop them into an empty cocoon and they begin to feed off the mother's soul, since the Sib and the mother are then connected."

"So, she just lies down and lets a bird peck her soul out?"

"It's more than that, baby girl; Alexis are nicknamed 'Surgeons.' They cut you open with precision and never make mistakes," Jay tells her.

"Then, why do some angels die?" she challenges Jay.

"Because they can't stop until the Sib has had its fill. Even if the mother is dying, the Alexi will continue."

"That sounds so crazy," she replies, filled with concern.

"Actually, it's kind of like humans. But instead of being connected to the newborn by an umbilical cord, it's connected by an invisible thread they share. The more the angel's soul gets replenished, the bigger and happier the Sib will be in the cocoon," Miku tells her as she studies the Alexi's every move.

"What happens if the mother dies during the Handover?" Emmy asks.

"The Alexi will go to Noni and drop off the newborn. But since the mother has died, the baby will have nothing to feed from. It, too, will eventually disappear."

"Baby angels just disappear and go away forever?"

"Yes, if the soul has nothing to feed on, it will perish. Every once in, like, a thousand cycles there are stories of Sib feeding on the father's soul, but it's rare since the father's soul is not as potent as the mother's. So, the Sib dies anyway."

"How do they know it died?"

"There are symbols that appear on the mother's hand during the time the baby is in Noni. It's called Kaiden. When the Kaiden is complete, it will glow—that means the Sib is ready to be out in the world."

"Then the Alexi brings the baby to them?"

"No, the mother and father will then go to Noni, where the mother would then place her hand on the crystal cocoon. That pattern in her hand will then match up with the one on the cocoon and the Sib will fly to the mother."

"That's just like when Tony-Tone makes a key out of a pattern?"

"Exactly. When the pattern, or Kaiden, is done, it glows. The more complicated the pattern, the more powerful the child will be. Some beings are so powerful that their Kaiden runs from the mother's fingers to her forear m."

"So, no matter what species, childbirth is always complicated and painful?"

"It's more than just that. The mother has to preserve as much of her soul as possible since she is sharing her soul with another being. That is why angels generally don't come to Earth when they have a Sib in Noni. Earth can deteriorate our souls after a while," Miku explains.

"Wait, what happens now there is no light to go to?" Emmy asks her.

Chapter Nine: The Handover

"That's why not everyone is happy seeing the Alexi take flight. There is nowhere for the mother to recuperate, since the light is all but gone. She has to stay here and hope she can maintain enough soul to keep both her and the Sib alive."

"So even if she survives the Handover, she could lack the soul she needs to nourish the baby?"

"That's why having sex without a Tam is a very bad idea," I say, trying to keep the irritation from my voice.

"Okay, so who is it? Who's pregnant?" Emmy asks impatiently.

She doesn't have to wait long for the answer. The Alexi swoops down to us and lands in the middle of our camp. The shield did not slow it down at all.

Everyone waits as the Alexi walks around the camp. It has a melodic chirp that every female angel I know loves. The Alexi flaps its wings and moves a few yards away, to the opening of Bianca's makeshift home.

I force myself to remain calm. Three hellish minutes later, the Alexi moves onto an opening on the other side of the command center. I clear my throat to cover the relief I'm feeling. A few moments later, the Alexi flies into the nearest opening and stays there.

A young woman comes out of the opening with the Alexi by her side and a male angel beside her; I'm guessing he's her husband. She is beaming with happiness. All the angels cheer and congratulate them. Suddenly her smile is replaced by fear.

She just now realizes how risky it is to have a Sib without being able to take refuge in the light. So, if she survives the Handover, there will be another huge hurdle: how to generate enough soul to feed both mother and Sib with no access to the light.

She cries out to Omnis, and her husband holds her. The team and I run over to walk her back inside.

"It won't survive. My baby won't survive while I'm here. Oh no, oh no…" She wails in agony.

Emmy goes over to her, takes her hand, and asks her name.

"Angela."

"Okay, Angela, everything is going to be fine."

"How do you know? You're a human."

"I know because I've seen what you angels can do. I know you guys are capable of amazing things. And this baby will be too."

"No, it's not gonna survive. It's not." She moans again.

I look over at the husband and he looks almost as scared as Angela does. I take him off to the side and try to calm him down.

"Look, having a baby now is dangerous and foolish. But it's here, so you better get it together because she needs you."

"Yeah, yeah, yeah, okay. Okay."

"Go over there, help her get on the ground, and make her as calm as possible for the Handover."

"Okay, okay." But I know I'm not getting through to him, because as many times as he says okay, he has yet to move.

"HEY, SHE'S ABOUT TO HAVE YOUR KID, MOVE YOUR ASS!" Rage bellows from across the room.

Strangely enough, it works. He runs over to her and takes Angela's hand. She calls out his name over and over again, saying she's scared.

"Everyone, clear the room!" someone yells from the doorway. We look over and find Wolf standing in front of the opening.

"I mean it, everyone out," he says, sounding more official than I have ever heard him.

"You've done this before?" I ask.

"Yes, a few times. It's nothing to worry about, Angela. It's just nature, doing her thing. The Alexi is here to help guide your Sib to Noni," he tells the stricken woman.

"We'll leave the three of you alone," I announce as we start to head out.

"Marcus, I need you to stay and keep her body still while I try to keep her calm. The more upset she is, the more difficult the Handover."

"Okay, I'll stay."

"We'll be outside if you need us," the twins say in unison.

Ameana reassures her that things will be okay. Rage takes her hand and they head out. Before they can make it to the opening, Angela calls out for Emmy.

"Human, you were tortured once before, right?"

"Um…once or twice," she replies.

"Then you can stay. You know what this will feel like," Angela tells her.

"This is not torture; this is a beautiful moment that transcends nature. It's righteous," Wolf reminds her.

"Screw that; this will be torture," she shouts.

"Okay, I'll stay with you," Emmy swears. Angela nods gratefully and she calls out for her husband.

"Uri!"

"Angie, I'm here. I promise everything will be alright," he says.

But his voice is shaking so much, it's hard for anyone in the room to believe him.

Wolf and I exchange a concerned glance. Judging by the shaky voice and hands, not to mention the terror in his eyes, Uri is not doing well. He keeps pacing around, looking at the Alexi as if willing her to come back at another time. But once a female is pregnant, there is no getting rid of the Alexi. She will stay there until the Handover is complete.

"Uri, I want you to go get a vial of Mist. It's a liquid that produces synthetic soul. It'll help her regain some strength after the Handover. Go to the market, our source says it's in Puerto Rico today. Find Tony-Tone, he should have some," Wolf says.

"Okay," he says, too panic-stricken to move.

"Uri, go now!" I order.

He gives his wife a quick kiss, looks over at the Alexi with a mix of excitement and fear, then he runs out and takes to the air.

"Why don't you guys use Mist to protect against Soul Chasers?" Emmy asks me in a whisper as Wolf tries to calm Angela.

"It's only for pregnant women. It doesn't have any effect otherwise," I inform her.

"How will the Sib survive in Noni? I won't have enough soul for it to grow," Angela cries as she is helped to the ground.

We help her place her arms out to her side and straighten her legs. The Alexi, a bird who's not known for patience, flies around the room, signaling she's ready for the Handover.

Emmy gets down on the ground and takes Angela's hand. Wolf goes over and takes her other hand. He instructs me to hold Angela's legs and make sure she doesn't move so that the Alexi is not thrown from her chest. If that happens, the Handover will be unsuccessful and the Sib will die.

As the bird lands on Angela's chest, panic and horror spread across her face. Wolf reminds her that she needs to stay calm in order for the Handover to go as smoothly as possible. The Alexi opens its beak and emanates a white laser beam right into Angela's chest. Angela was right; the Handover is nothing less than torture.

As soon as the Alexi's beam hits Angela's skin, she unleashes a cry so chilling, everyone in the room winces, even Wolf. As the Alexi continues to carve a line, about six inches long, down Angela's chest, Angela screams like she is being set on fire. Emmy tries to reassure her and convince her that everything will be okay.

For the next fifteen minutes, the room is filled with heart-wrenching screams and moans. Wolf tells Angela not to focus on what the Alexi is doing. But the young woman is in so much pain, I don't think she can focus on anything other than the agony.

Once the Alexi is done carving the line down her chest, Angela begins to calm down. I look at Wolf as if to ask if the worst is over. He looks back at us and shakes his head "no."

Wolf explains to us that the Alexi is now searching for the Sib. Once it finds it, the beam will disappear and the Alexi will inhale as much of Angela's soul as the Sib needs. We're hoping it's not more than Angela has to give.

The beam disappears. The Alexi begins to suck from the open cavity in Angela's chest. It sucks in a light blue speck the size of a pearl—the Alexi has found the Sib. Wolf tells her that she needs to brace herself because this is the hard part; the Alexi starts sucking out Angela's soul.

"OMNIS, KILL ME! KILL ME!" she begs repeatedly.

Her body shakes violently as though she is being electrocuted. Emmy and I exchange a look of fear. We're both thinking the same thing: Angela might not make it.

Wolf scolds me for not holding her down hard enough. I put more weight on her so that she doesn't move. Still, I can't put all of my weight or I'll break her legs. I try to find the right amount of pressure but no matter what we do, Angela is in agony.

Chapter Nine: The Handover

"PLEASE, PLEASE, PLEASE, PLEASE, KILL ME, KILL ME, KILL ME!!!"

She manages to wrangle out of my grip and sit up slightly. The sudden movement causes the Alexi to lose its balance. We all watch in horror as the Alexi is about to be thrown from Angela's torso.

This baby is going to die…

"No!" Emmy shouts as the Alexi starts to fall sideways.

Thankfully, at the last second, the Alexi is able to use its wings to regain balance and remain on Angela.

"Angela, you have to stay still. If the Alexi falls off again, your Sib will die," Wolf tells her with great alarm in his voice.

"I can't do this…I can't do this," she moans desperately.

The Alexi continues to suck even more soul from Angela's chest cavity.

"ARGHHHHHHHHHHHHHHH!!!"

She is in too much pain to make words anymore, and she's shaking just as violently as before.

Wolf looks at us and shakes his head. This isn't going well. At this rate, Angela will throw the Alexi off again, and this time, it may not be able regain its balance. I have her legs, but again, any more pressure and I will snap them in two.

"Angela!" Emmy calls out.

She doesn't stop wailing.

"Angela, I know it hurts. I know death would be better than anything right now. But you have to do this for your baby. You have to stop moving!"

Angela tries to stop but she can't. She shakes her head and keeps begging for death.

"You know how I survived all the torture? I was never really there. I just left and went somewhere else in my head. Let's go somewhere, Angie."

"I can't, I can't, I can't…" She moans.

"Where did you meet Uri?"

She doesn't answer right away. She groans as the Alexi continues to suck her soul from her.

"Where did you meet Uri?!" Emmy shouts.

"New Zealand…challenged me…soul diving contest," she manages to tell Emmy between moans.

"Did he win?" she asks.

"OMNIS! PLEASE...MAKE IT STOP!!!" She writhes in pain. Emmy calls out to her again.

"Angela, you're not here. You're in New Zealand with Uri. Tell me about the contest."

"Loser...buys...bottle...Coy."

"Who won?"

"Me....cheated...kissed him before we jumped...he lost control... injured on his way back up. He said make it up to him...exchange Rah..."

"He gave you his Rah on the first day you met?"

"Yeah...crazy..." She forms what looks to be the beginning of a very small smile.

It's working. While Angela is still in pain, she's moving less. The Alexi hasn't lost its balance at all since Emmy has been talking to Angela. "The Alexi is nearly done," Wolf tells me.

Angela bites her lips as she talks to Emmy. She squeezes her eyes shut and moans between words. The pain of having her soul sucked out hasn't lessened but the distraction is helping. I signal to Emmy to keep talking to her.

"How was the kiss?" she asks Angela. She can't answer; she's starting to shake again.

"Angela, was he a good kisser?" she pushes.

"No. I had to teach him...his ex was...Traveler...used too much... tongue."

Emmy laughs despite herself.

"Well, I guess you taught him well," Emmy replies.

"I'm a great...kisser," she says.

And against all hope, Angela manages a real smile, all the while keeping her eyes closed.

"Angela," Wolf calls.

"I can't take it anymore. I'm sorry...I can't," she cries.

"Angela, open your eyes," Wolf instructs.

She opens her eyes to find the Alexi has flown off her chest and is now a glowing, sparkling blue.

Chapter Nine: The Handover

"Did the Handover take?" Angela asks in a weak voice as she watches the bird.

"Yes, the blue glow means she has cargo," Wolf replies.

Angela's eyes fill with what looks like silver tears.

"Is she crying? I thought angels couldn't do that?" Emmy asks Wolf.

"It's called Weigh. It's like afterbirth. It seeps out of the new mom's eyes. It's a good release. It's really the closest an angel gets to tears."

The Weigh slowly seeps from Angela's eyes. The cut made by the Alexi starts to close itself as Angela tries to get up.

"You are very weak. You need to rest," Wolf orders her.

"I want to see the Alexi. I need to make sure it has my Sib," Angela says, unable to hold her head up. Emmy takes off the sweater she is wearing, uses it as a makeshift pillow, and places it under Angela's head.

Wolf tells Angela that she is connected to the Alexi because the Handover was successful. All she has to do is call the Alexi over to her.

"Alexi, Alexi…come here, pretty girl; come close," she whispers, sounding exhausted.

The bird walks over to her. She strokes it and speaks in a loving tone.

"You have all my happiness inside you. Please, be good to him," Angela asks of the bird.

The Alexi makes a soft singsong like sound and takes off into the sky.

"How do you know it's a boy?" Emmy asks her.

"Just a feeling I have," Angela says, then closes her eyes.

Emmy calls out her name, fearing she lost too much soul and has passed away.

"She's Recharging," Wolf assures her.

"How long will it take for the Alexi to get to Noni?" Emmy asks me.

"It depends on the flying conditions. But when the Sib does get to Noni, markings will start to appear on Angela."

"We should let her Recharge in peace," Wolf says. We follow him outside, where numerous angels and Quo are watching the sky. The Alexi has taken flight. It gets smaller and smaller until it disappears from our sight.

I take Emmy off to the side for a few moments.

"Thank you for helping out," I say, lovingly touching the side of her face.

"Wow, that was unbelievable," she says.

"I know."

"A Handover is pure agony."

"You humans don't have it any better," I remind her.

"I guess not. The crazy thing is, as soon as it was over, all Angela could think about was her Sib. She looked so happy… Like she'd do it all over ag ain."

"Most angels feel that way from what I've been told. And most humans," I reply.

"I still can't believe the whole Handover thing."

"You ever…think about it?" I venture.

"What—like, babies?"

"Yeah."

"Marcus, I'm only seventeen."

"Believe me, life is short."

"Okay, then let's go have a few Sibs and then catch a movie," she says sardonically.

"I didn't mean now. I just meant…forget it."

"What?"

"I like making plans with you, Emmy. You're my tomorrow. Why can't there be a Sib? I mean, when you're like twenty something?"

"Marcus, I love that you factor me into your life, but let's not lie to ourselves. You could be Bianca's husband for a long time."

"I won't let that happen."

"When the Alexi landed near the opening of Bianca's cave…," she replies.

"I know. But I promise you, I was safe when we were together," I assure her.

"I just want a problem-free moment with you for five seconds."

"Hey, we're gonna have an entire lifetime together. It won't always be like this."

She reaches out and embraces me. I hold her tightly as I scout the area to make sure we're alone.

"Emmy, I gotta go."
"Wait, I just need a few more seconds in your arms."
"No. We have to go."
"Why?"
"The sixth Fire Swan is airborne; we are now at war."

Emmy's eyes wid

need to be taken to the hideout near the back of the camp, because it's the safest place for them.

"After you get them there, you'll stay there too. Got it?" I order.

"Okay. What about Bianca? She doesn't have an active power."

"Dalce will take care of her. You go help Angela."

"Okay," she replies.

She starts to take off; I take her gently by the arm.

"Emmy, I mean it. There are Death Stalkers here—beasts that feed only on human flesh. You have to go to the hideout and stay there."

"Okay, I got it."

"Don't pull an 'Emmy' and show up out of nowhere. I'm serious."

"I won't leave the hideout."

"Promise?"

"Marcus, do I really have to—"

I give her a stone cold, serious stare.

"Marcus—"

"Emerson, I'm serious. I need to be completely focused on this battle and this battle alone. I can't do that if I have to worry about you. Promise me you will not leave the hideout, no matter what."

"I promise."

Chapter Ten: The One Day

I squeeze her and she takes off to get Angela and Uri. I turn towards the command center, where Ameana signals to me that the team is ready and everyone is in position.

Moments later, Bianca runs up to me, breathless with excitement.

"My Keeper friend sent us a dozen Tallies."

I look up to the sky within our shield and find twelve Tallies: "flash freezing" falcons. Their massive wings spread wide as they skillfully soar in the sky. I've heard of Tallies but have never seen them in the flesh.

Tallies are the natural enemy of the Fire Swans. A beam of light emerges from a Tally's eyes, and when it hits its target, the target is instantly crystallized. It then falls from the sky and shatters. The two natural enemies face each other from opposing sides.

"That's perfect, but you need to get to the hideout—now," I tell her.

"You're right; I'm going. Marcus?"

"What?" I ask impatiently.

"Good luck," she says, giving me a sweet quick kiss on the cheek.

"Thanks," I reply, uncertain. She smiles sweetly and rushes off.

Meanwhile, as the six Fire Swans blast our shields, a fleet of demons take to the air behind them, ready to attack. On the ground, the army of Believers gathers around our shield, eager to destroy the Foundation soldiers.

We don't have one angel in the air. The Foundation soldiers are hidden along the mountain range. All we have out in the open are the Tallies and me. That is exactly the way I planned it. We don't want to show our hand just yet.

We don't want them to know how many soldiers and angels we have or where they are located. The Sage is arrogant and thinks that he will win based on the sheer numbers, but what we lack in numbers, we will make up for in tactics, as I said before.

Finally, the last of the shield is down. Immediately, the birds begin attacking each other. A Fire Swan opens its mouth and lets out a river of flames at a nearby Tally. The Tally cries out and bursts into flames on the side of the mountain.

The other Tallies counter by attacking that Fire Swan from both sides. The Swan is instantly rendered into a solid crystal. It crashes on the mountain top and the pieces shatter to the ground below.

Meanwhile, all the demons in the air are hurling Powerballs at me and the Believers run towards our camp, hell-bent on killing us. I dive and cut through the air to dodge their attacks. There are at least three close calls where I almost have my wings ripped off.

The entire army of Believers and demons are after me. I lead them to the exact spot I need them to be: the center of the camp. Once I've got as many of them to gather as possible, I give Wolf the signal.

Without warning, the Omari and other Paras gather in the air and hold hands. They form a circle of illumination that expands. The demons, knowing what's about to happen, shout for the others to go back, but it's too late.

The ball of illumination explodes. The blast takes out hundreds of demons and Believers. Their bodies drop lifelessly from the sky. The demons that are still alive on the ground race for cover.

"Now!" I roar.

Suddenly, the Foundation soldiers come from everywhere and attack the demons and Quo that didn't make it out of the blast zone. Unfortunately, the Paras can't summon up another massive surge of power since it drains them. But the blast they created was powerful enough to help us take out hundreds of Quo and demons.

Once the Foundation soldiers have the upper hand, my team and I take to the sky, along with Rage. Two demons gang up on Rio; he uses his shield to block their attacks. He then waits for the right moment to retaliate.

Rio snaps one demon's neck and pulls the wings off the other. I have never seen him this violent before. I'm guessing he's pissed, but not just at the demons.

"Marcus, move!" Miku calls out frantically.

I turn in time to see death coming for me in the form of a giant Powerball. There is no time to duck or outrun it. Just as I brace for impact, Ameana redirects it back to the demon, who then explodes on impact.

Seeing this, a demon near Ameana tackles her and wraps his hand around her throat. The demon doesn't see Rage approaching. He doesn't even realize he is in flames until his flesh starts melting. The demon is reduced to ash and blows away with the wind.

"I'm not human—stop rescuing me," Ameana demands.

"Most chicks would say 'thank you,'" Rage counters.

"I'm not most chicks," she reminds him.

"That's why I like you."

"Damn right," she says playfully.

Flirting, even in a battle, seriously?

I shake my head and fly over to Miku, who is pinned by a demon to the side of the mountain. I know she's afraid to sing because there are too many Foundation soldiers around. I snatch the demon off her and toss him across the mountain range. The force and speed I throw him causes an imprint of the demon's body to be left in the mountain.

Miku spots a group of demons far enough away that she can sing to. She flashes me her best deadly smile.

"Go get 'em, Pretty," I encourage.

Miku swiftly flies over to the demons and holds a little concert, where she sings softly to them. Within two minutes, they are begging for death in several different languages. Miku kindly complies.

Jay Glides over, snatches three demons, and beats the hell of out them before they even realize he's there. He then places them inside a Holder and kicks them across the mountain range. The Holder opens and spills out what's left of the demons' remains.

"Any angel can kill a demon; but ya got to have skillz to make it look this good. I mean, am I right?" He asks me as he Glides away, looking pleased with himself.

Without warning, a demon tackles me. We both tumble awkwardly in the air. We grab each other by the neck, both refusing to let go. Off to the side of us, I spot a Fire Swan about to blast an unsuspecting Tally. I drag the demon so that he is forced to switch positions in order to maintain his balance. The demon is now in the line of fire, and when the Fire Swan sprays, the demon is charred.

Furious, the Fire Swan aims at me. Fortunately, a Tally shoots a beam, freezing the Fire Swan mid-flame. Another Fire Swan a few yards away, clearly pissed, sends a whirl of flame across the sky in retaliation. The

Tally is set on fire and nose-dives to his death. While the battle between the birds rages on, down below, the battle between the Foundation soldiers and Believers has turned vicious.

A Believer effortlessly waves her hand and the ground splits open. Dozens of Foundation soldiers fall into the gaping hole. Before I or any other angel can fly down to get them, the Believer closes the ground back up. Many of our soldiers have been swallowed whole by the earth. The Believer waves her hand to do it again, but a Foundation solider nearby attacks her. He does this without even touching her. He opens his palms and two shadows shaped like snakes spring to life. The shadows wrap themselves around the Believer's neck. The soldier controls the shadow snakes with a slight movement of his hand. The Believer dies within minutes.

We aren't winning every battle. In fact, a few feet away, a Foundation soldier is being skinned alive by a Believer who makes a motion in the air like she's peeling a banana. I'm too far away to help; I call on Jay, but it's too late. The Foundation soldier dies in a pool of his own blood.

A Foundation soldier quickly attacks the Believer with the peeling power. Judging from the anger with which the soldier tackles the Believer, I'm guessing the slain soldier was somehow related. The soldier tackles the Believer to the ground. They throw Powerballs at each other and fight to get the upper hand.

A Foundation soldier watches the two of them wrestle to the ground. She stands a few yards away and mumbles something. Suddenly the Believer with the peeling power is screaming for dear life.

"That's Tracy, 'Bone Collector,'" Eta shouts up to me.

At first, I can't see why they would call her that but then I watch as a bone in the Believer's arm rips itself from her body and flies over to Tracy.

Tracy calls for yet another bone from the Believer's body. By that time the Believer is in so much pain, she passes out for good.

So glad the bone collector is on our side. From the corner of my eye, I spot a blur of red. I look down below and see a river of blood. I follow the river to get to its source. A Believer has mind controlled a group of Foundation soldiers into hacking each other to death with blunt instruments and various powers. They are like possessed zombies carving into each other and, in some cases, themselves.

"Where's the mind controller?" I ask Ameana.

"I can't see who's doing it," she replies.

"Ask Rio whose Waves are reading 'extreme concentration.' Hurry!"

Ameana takes off towards Rio. I scan the crowd but can't find the Believer that's in control. I touch down in the bloodbath and try to stop them from mutilating each other any further. Other angels join in to help me, but it's useless without taking down the Believer controlling them.

In the sky, Rio waves feverishly to get my attention. He then points me to a Believer a few miles away. She's only about five four. She's slim and so unassuming, she's easy to miss. I take to the air to go after her.

"I'm on it," Miku vows, popping up out of nowhere.

"Pretty, don't sing too loud," I warn her.

"I'll try."

The next thing I know, the Believer with the mind control is ripping the skin from her chest. She's in too much pain to concentrate on her powers. I can actually see her exposed heart pumping. Or at least it was. Miku snatches it from its chest cavity and smells it like she would a rose.

Sometimes, I really worry about that girl…

Once the mind controller is dead, the Foundation soldiers stop attacking each other; but the damage is already done. Some have lost hands, legs, and entire arms, while others lost their lives. The carnage is made worse by the endless screaming coming from the victims who, just out from the haze of mind control, find themselves disfigured.

The other angels and I carry as many of them towards the back of the camp as we can. We then place them in the cave that serves as a makeshift infirmary, near the hideout. I head back to the battlefield littered with blood, bones, and broken wings. To make matters worse, Powerballs are zooming through the air, traveling at unnatural speeds.

In the center of all the chaos, I spot a small beanpole of a soldier trying to summon up a Powerball to take on a Believer who has electricity between her palms.

Ty!

I run to Ty, who has managed to summon up a Powerball. The Believer laughs at him, takes the micro ball inside her hands, and crushes it. The Believer raises her arms to strike and put an end to Ty's short life.

I tackle her; we fall to the ground, and she quickly gets on top of me. She is surprisingly strong. She's enjoying the fact that she's much stronger than I anticipated. She raises her hand to electrocute me, but I grab both of her wrists to keep her hands from touching, knowing that will result in a blast of electricity.

"What's wrong, Guardian? Did you think you were the only one with super strength?" she mocks.

"No, but I'm the only one that can do this," I reply venomously.

I reflect her fear back to her. She begs for me to stop. Her body shakes violently. I double my efforts. She dies with fear frozen on her face. I throw her corpse off of me.

"Marcus, why'd you do that? I had her!" Ty says confidently.

"I know you did, but we need you to look after the soldiers in the infirmary," I reply.

"Aw, c'mon, I have to be on the front lines. That's where the action is!" Ty protests.

"You can always come back; but right now I really need you in the infirmary, protecting the wounded in case the Believers or demons attack."

"You really think they'd get that far?"

"Yeah, and there's only one person I trust to stop them."

"Okay, I'm on it!"

"Good," I reply as I watch Ty head towards safety. I signal a nearby angel to watch him.

Once back in the air, I spot two of the four Death Stalkers. They charge through Believers and Foundation soldiers alike, leaving a trail of injured Quo. They gallop up and down the battlefield, growling and snarling. Hungrily they search for human flesh. I'm relieved that Emmy is nowhere near here.

However, I still need to take care of the Death Stalkers. I call out to Wolf, who is closer. He hurls two illuminated Powerballs at them at the same time. It kills both beasts on the spot. I look around and find the third one not far from me.

Chapter Ten: The One Day

As my team tackle demons in the air, I fly down to kill the second-to-last beast. Once I land, it charges towards me. It picks me up off the ground and sends me flying into the air. I manage to hop onto its back and ride it.

The Death Stalker is furious and tries to throw me off like a raging bull. I stay on him until I spot a weapon I can use on the ground. I pick up a jagged, discarded human bone and plunge it between the beast's eyes. It jerks itself around uncontrollably and roars as a geyser of black blood gushes out from its skull. Only when I stab it again and again does it finally die.

I look around for the final Death Stalker but can't seem to find it. Just then, Eta frantically calls out to me. I turn to see what she's pointing at and I find the last Death Stalker. It's standing a few feet away from its next meal: Emmy.

Damn that girl!

Without even thinking, I race into the air to go get her. I'm fast, but not fast enough. The beast races after her. Emmy screams and takes off running. She will never be able to outrun it. I cut through the air at unheard of speed.

The Death Stalker has chased Emmy down the road to the now fallen city of Cree. I follow them but I can't see them well enough from the sky. I land in hopes of finding her. Fearing calling out her name will alert the beast, I quietly scour through the small city.

I hear the Death Stalker growl and Emmy's screaming right after. I follow the sound and find the beast has her cornered along the walls of what was once someone's home. Emmy searches for some kind of weapon, but there is nothing useful around her.

The Death Stalker is toying with her, moving in and then backing off. It's like a twisted cat and mouse game. Finally, the animal has had enough. It roars and Emmy makes this soul-shaking scream that cuts right through me. Then she does something that only Emmy would think to do: she tries to reason with the beast. Her voice is shaky and her eyes fill with tears. But apart from that, she tries hard to stay in control.

"Look, you think I'm grade 'A' flesh but I'm not…I'm on the track team, so I'm all muscle. That's tough to chew. And I didn't get a chance to moisturize this morning, so my skin is really dry. I'm tough and dry—I'm human jerky. I wouldn't taste good at all."

The beast has had enough; it lunges at her with all its fury. She screams again and covers her eyes. When she opens her eyes again, she realizes she is in the air and in my arms. She is shaking with relief.

She thanks me repeatedly. I remain silent.

"I couldn't find anything to hit him with. And then I saw his teeth… thank you so much," she says breathlessly once we land a few yards from the hideout.

Again, I remain silent. She nervously fixes her clothes and addresses me.

"Marcus, I know I promised I wouldn't—"

I take off without hearing the rest.

A little while later, I head to the infirmary to look in on Ty, the wounded angels, and the Foundation soldiers. They are being looked after by Paras with healing knowledge and Quo with similar powers.

There are about two hundred wounded men and women. Although the other side had more deaths due to the power blast from the Paras, we too have casualties. They number in the hundreds.

The second Ty spots me, he comes up and asks if it's time to go back to the front lines. I tell him we still need his help, and a Para angel calls him to fill up a pitcher of water. That's when I look over and find Emmy among the helpers.

I ignore her and focus on my job: making sure the wounded stay positive. I stop and talk to each of them. I tell them that they will be fine. In some cases, I am lying. Ameana uses her x-ray powers and points out at least fifty of them who won't survive.

Still, I try to keep their hopes up. It's better to die with a little hope than live without any at all. By the time I get to the last patient who is likely to die, I seriously feel like I'm about to lose it. But I know I don't have that option. I can't just fly off the handle. They need to know that I am in control and that I have faith in what we are doing.

Chapter Ten: The One Day

Emmy tries to catch my eye again and again, but I avoid her. She had no business on the battlefield. And yet, as usual, she showed up. I'm glad that there are others around us because I really don't want to be alone with her. I'm way too upset with her right now.

Unfortunately, the Paras and Ty go off to get supplies. Then the Quo helpers go to collect wounded soldiers from the field. And Ameana is long gone, leaving the two of us alone. I focus on the wounded and cover them with blankets. Most, if not all of them, are asleep by now.

"So, how mad are you that I went out into the field?" she asks hesitantly. I don't make eye contact.

"I'm not mad at you; I'm mad at myself."

"For what?" she asks.

"For thinking you would keep your promise."

I can tell my comment hurts her. She lowers her eyes.

Whatever.

"Marcus, I'm sorry. I just had to go get—"

"Emmy, don't."

"I'm trying to explain to you why I was out there."

"I don't care. You promised that you would stay in the hideout. And you didn't. Your reasons don't matter."

"You're not even gonna hear me out?"

"Why? This is nothing new. This is classic 'Marcus and Emmy.' I tell you not to do something for your own safety. You say okay, then you turn around and do it anyway," I snap.

"It's not like that."

"It's *always* like that. It's our thing; it's what we do. You put yourself in danger; I put everything aside to save you, only to have you put yourself in danger, like, ten seconds later."

"Hey, I've saved you a few times too," she protests hotly.

"So, what is this, a contest for you?"

"No, I'm just saying we have saved each other—that's what you do for people you love."

"No, what you do for people you love is take care of yourself. But you're not doing that. You're just running out into danger like some demented, attention hungry thrill seeker. And you know what, I really can't deal with it."

"Well you know what, Marcus, I don't really give a damn what you can and can't deal with. I'm too busy losing people I love, getting tortured, and attending your wedding."

"This isn't about me and Bianca; this is about you *always* putting your life in danger for stupid reasons."

"You didn't hear me out."

"What possible reason could you have for going into a battle with no damn powers?"

"I dropped my necklace."

"Oh, well, you're right; that's a good reason. You put your life on the line for jewelry. Awesome," I spit bitterly.

"It was the cross my mother gave me."

"Your mother wanted you to be safe; just like I do."

"My mother wanted me to be happy. And I'm not. I haven't been happy since…"

"Since what?" I ask.

"Never mind," she mumbles.

"You were gonna say you haven't been happy since we met," I accuse.

"That's not what I was gonna say."

"Yes, it was."

"So, what, now you have the Sage's power? You can tell what I'm thinking?" she asks, irate.

"I don't have the Sage's power to read minds. But I swear to Omnis, I wish I did because I have no idea why you do half the things you do."

"Well, we have something in common because I can't understand some of the things I do either. Like, why I'm watching you and Bianca kiss and play house. Or why I haven't lost it completely and said to hell with you and this mission."

"Is that what you want?"

"Is that what I said?" she snaps.

"You know damn well you're wrong for going out there and you're trying to turn it around on me. But this isn't about me. It's about you always giving me more to deal with than I need!"

Chapter Ten: The One Day

When she speaks, her tone is unyielding and harsh. Her hands are folded across her chest and she is turning beet red with anger. "Listen, Guardian, I can run naked through the House of Fire, throw myself inside a Soul Chaser, or dance naked in front of a Fire Swan if I want to. Why? Because nothing I do will compare to the crap I've had to deal with since I met you!"

She marches up to me, hands on her hips, lips white with fury and eyes practically glowing "purple" rage.

"SO WHAT IF YOU HAVE TO RESCUE ME ONCE IN A WHILE? MARCUS JASON CANE, YOU BETTER JUST SUCK IT UP AND DEAL! BECAUSE THAT'S *EXACTLY* WHAT I HAVE HAD TO DO!"

I nod slowly and sit down at the edge of an empty cot; in the background, the war outside rages on. I put my head in my hands and massage my temples to ward off the migraine that I didn't know angels could get. I remain silent.

"Okay, well…say something," she says.

Her tone has softened but not completely. She's reserving her anger until I argue back. But no argument comes from me; that worries her. When I speak, it's in a low whisper. My voice is too soft for a Guardian; let alone a First Guardian. It's filled with uncertainty, doubt, and fear. It's a voice I can only reveal to the girl next to me. But even then, I'm too vulnerable to look her in the eye.

"Emmy, I'm not worried about the days I have to rescue you. I'm worried about the one day I can't…"

Since the team ar

minutes asking if he can go back to the front lines.

The team agrees with each other on most, if not all, matters having to do with the war. But on the personal front, we aren't on the same page at all. The twins are friends just enough so their powers aren't affected. Rio is still pissed at Miku and Jay for hooking up.

Miku, on the other hand, is too busy trying to act indifferent to Jay's rejection to really care that Rio is mad at her. Jay's been trying to stay out of Miku's way so that Rio will stop being mad, but it's not really working. Emmy, fresh from telling me off, isn't really sure she's done being mad yet. I can tell by the way she bites her nails. As for me and Rio, well, I try to stay official with him. I don't want to let my feelings get in the way. Sometimes, though, I can't help it.

Ironically enough, Rage and Ameana are the only ones really getting along. That is, if they can avoid Wolf, who is having a seriously hard time with the sight of the two of them together. I know we can't go on this way. We're going to have to fix things, but now is certainly not the time. Our first priority is ending this war and going after the Shoma.

We pore over the maps and find the best points to strike the Sage's Believers and demons. Just as the meeting is about to end, someone pops in on a Port.

"War or no war, that is no reason for this lack of glam," she says.

Chapter Eleven: Anything You Say

We all turn to see the official Para party girl, Arden. As usual, she looks like a sexy Judy Jetson meets Lady Gaga. Her body-hugging, skintight jumpsuit emphasizes her perfect curves. Her rose-red lips are highlighted with sparkling gloss.

"Yo, son, that's my girl, right there!" Jay exclaims, running to give her a hug.

She jumps off the Port and embraces him.

"I've been without chocolate for too long. I'm having withdrawal pains. Can you help me?" She flirts.

"C'mon now, girl, you *know* how I get down," he replies, looking her over. They both laugh and hug each other again.

"Moody, it's been too long. I'm starting to take it personally," she says to Rio.

"Hi, Arden," he says, suddenly shy.

She pulls him towards her and plants a big, quick kiss on his lips. She then turns her attention to the other twin.

"Merry melody of death, how are you?" she asks Miku.

"Ya know, killing them softly," Miku says with pride and a sweet smile.

"The last I heard, you turned 'Redd' and killed tons of people."

The smile fades from Miku's face. She still carries a lot of guilt from when she turned evil. That's why she hasn't been able to get rid of the red-colored feathers on the tips of her wings. The only way for her wings to go back to being all white is for her to forgive herself.

"Don't feel bad, the whole time you were killing people, both your hair and your outfit—stellar. And the red wing tips, so on tend. Promise."

Miku smiles despite herself. Arden looks over at Ameana, then down at her stylish black high leather boots.

"Manolo?" she asks.

"Naturally."

"Nice."

They smile at each other like they are in some secret club. She turns her attention to Rage.

"So, it's true? You and the second-in-command, huh?" she asks him.

Rage shifts his weight uncomfortably.

"I know everyone is giving you heat for it, Ameana, but yeah, I can understand why."

"Really?" the twins ask in unison.

"Yeah, well, demons have big—wingspan."

Every guy in the room wishes they were not hearing this conversation. Angel and demon alike, we really don't want to be here.

Arden turns to me and Emmy.

"Human. Rough road, huh?"

"Keeps getting rougher every day," Emmy says, almost to herself.

"Now you're a free agent. You can get another guy…or three," she offers.

Emmy smiles politely but turns her down.

"C'mon, I know a Traveler who's six two, hot, and loves to go—"

"Arden," Rio warns her.

"What?" she replies innocently.

Emmy starts blushing, as do all the girls in the room.

"I was gonna say Soul diving," she lies.

Then she whispers to Emmy.

"He can dive for hours…"

"What did you want, Arden?" I ask.

"For starters, how about a hug for your favorite Para? Just because I don't carry dead bodies to Difi like Rahell doesn't mean I don't need any love," she says dramatically.

I know the only way to get to the bottom of why she's here is to play along. I go over and embrace her. She holds on tightly and inhales my scent.

"Argh, why do heroes always smell so damn good? Guess that's why we can never get together: you're always taken," she teases.

"It's really my loss, Arden," I reply sheepishly.

"That it is," she says with a killer grin.

"How can we help you?" I ask.

"My stupid sister, Rahell, is insisting I come help you guys since she's still recuperating. So, I'm here."

"You're gonna go out in the field?" Emmy asks.

"With these heels? No."

"Then how are you supposed to help?" Miku asks.

"I don't know. Does anyone need a makeover?"

"Maybe later. Right now, we could use your help in the infirmary," I reply, shaking my head.

"Sick people…I don't know. Is there blood, because this is couture," she says as she whirls around to give us a view from all sides.

"Wow…," someone says as they walk in.

It's Ty.

He enters the command center and the sight of Arden renders him nearly speechless. His eyes are wide with preteen desire and wishful thinking. Judging from his reaction, no one else is in the room but him and Arden. The team and I exchange a look of bemusement.

"Ty, this is Arden, she's a Para," I say slowly, trying to give him time to recover.

"Arden, this is Ty."

"Well, aren't you a cup of cute," Arden says.

She extends her hand. Ty manages to get out from under the shock of Arden's appeal and shake her hand. Knowing Arden, she is enjoying the effect that she's having on Ty.

"You're so…wow," he says, unable to take his eyes off her curves.

"Yeah, I kind of am," Arden replies.

"Ty, what did you need?" I ask.

"Wow…," he says again, not hearing me at all.

"Ty wants to be on the battlefield. I've been trying to convince him to stay and help at the infirmary but he won't."

"No, I have to be on the front lines. I'm just that kind of man," he says to Arden as he lowers the register of his voice.

"In addition to Powerballs, Ty can disappear," I say, hoping he takes the hint and disappears back to the infirmary.

No such luck.

He speaks again in his fake "manly" voice. It's all we can do not to laugh.

"It's a shame you didn't come earlier, Arden. I just shaved my 'tash."

That statement is too much for Miku. She starts to giggle; the team stops her from breaking down completely.

"I like your new look. Clean-shaven is kind of hot," Arden replies.

Ty is so excited he loses his "man" voice and squeaks his reply.

"Really?"

Omnis, help this crazy little boy…

"Ty, it's too bad you're going to the front line. I'm helping out in the infirmary. It would be nice to have someone walk me through everything," Arden says.

"You know, the most important part of war is keeping the soldiers in the fight. So, I think I'll keep working in the infirmary. You know, help them get better. And that way I could show you around."

"That sounds great, Ty; thanks," Arden says sweetly.

"But, Ty, the team needs you on the front lines," Jay says, faking urgency.

"Yeah, man, how can we win this without you?" Rio says, playing along.

"If you're not out there protecting us, I won't feel safe," Miku teases.

Ty walks up to Miku and strokes her cheeks lovingly.

"Be strong," Ty says, talking like a bad actor in a telenovela.

"I'll try," Miku says as if the love of her life were leaving her.

He extends his hand out to Arden. She takes it and smiles at me. I mouth a "thank you" to her. She was able to do in three minutes what I could not do all day: get Ty to agree to stay out of harm's way.

"You know, since the 'Marcus and Bianca' thing, it's fairly common for angels and Quo to be together," Ty points out as they exit.

We can't hold it anymore. As soon as they go, we all start laughing. Even Rage has a smile on his face. The best part is that I can finally relax now that that kid is out of immediate danger.

A demon has just nearly ripped Miku's arm clean off her body. She cries out in immense agony. Rio flies down to the ground where his sister lies bleeding out. The rest of us fly down to her, but Rio assures us he can heal her and tells us to go back to the battle.

I take to the sky, find the demon that hurt Pretty, and reflect his fear back to him. I didn't know demons could make tears but apparently, they can. He cries like a newborn and begs for death. I give it to him, but I make sure it's slow.

I head back to the ground, where Miku is still not fully healed yet. Wolf flies down and informs me that Dalce wants to see me. I order Rio to keep me informed about Miku's condition. Then, I head to the command center to meet Dalce.

"What is it?" I ask him once we're face-to-face.

"I thought you might like to meet the source who feeds us the information we need about the Sage," he says.

"Yeah, where is he?" I ask.

"He? Um…sexist much?" a voice replies.

I turn and find a girl standing in the corner. She is about Miku's height, with light blue spiky hair and combat boots.

"Marcus, this is Winter."

"Hi, sorry about that," I reply as I shake her hand.

"No worries," she says with a big smile.

There's something very carefree and easygoing about her smile. Given that she's a spy, I thought she'd be more…serious. Sinister.

"Thank you for everything you've done. Your information has really helped us," I tell her.

"All good; where's the Coy?" she asks Dalce.

He goes over to the corner where the food supply is kept and tosses her a bottle of Coy. She takes the cap off with her teeth and flings the bottle cap onto the floor. She then knocks back the entire bottle in one swallow.

"Oh, Omnis, I've missed this. Do you know what demons drink?" she asks us.

"No."

"Kool Aid and Red Bull," she says disapprovingly.

"Why?"

"Something about the sugar content. Anyway, it's disgusting but I drink to play along."

"Do you have news for us?" Dalce asks her.

"Yes and no. There is something coming but I don't know what it is yet," she replies.

"What makes you think that?" Dalce asks her.

"The Sage has been on edge ever since the Paras blasted nearly his entire army. But today, his mood has changed. His spirits are lifted, somehow. None of the Believers or demons know why. He left the camp early this morning—he never leaves."

"Where did he go?" I ask.

"Not sure. I couldn't follow him without blowing my cover," she says as she heads over to the supply area and drains another bottle of Coy.

"You have to find out what the Sage is planning. We can't let our guard down just because we're winning," I inform her.

"Hey, you said you wanted to know about Miku; she's healed, totally. But Ameana had her sit out of the battle for now," Rio says as he enters.

"Got it. You can get back to the field," I reply.

Rio doesn't move. Instead he stands there studying Winter from head to toe.

"I can't read you," Rio tells her.

"Yeah, that happens," she says casually.

"No, it doesn't. I can read almost everyone. What are you?" Rio says, dumbfounded.

"Winter is a neutralizer," Dalce explains.

"I thought only Cravens could do that," I reply.

"Winter is the exception," Dalce replies.

"I can't make out anything at all," Rio says, almost to himself.

"I told you, Rio, she's a neutralizer. When she's around, only your wings will work," Dalce insists.

"Sorry, I didn't mean to stare, it's just…aside from the Sage, I can read everyone," Rio tell her.

"It's nice, right?" she asks.

"What's nice?" Rio replies.

"Getting some time off from your powers."

"People would kill for my power," he says defensively.

"You're one of the twins, right? You read what people are feeling?"

"Yeah."

"Sounds exhausting. Who wants to know what everyone feels all the time?"

"It's helped this mission a great deal," he says.

"Has it helped you?" she asks.

"What do you mean?"

"I mean, I'm sure your girlfriend hates that you can tell what she's thinking. I'm sure sometimes she wants to tell you to shut up, but she doesn't want you to know she's feeling that way," Winter says.

"Why would she tell me to shut up?"

"I don't know, you seem kind of like a know-it-all. And since you basically 'know' everything people feel, I'm guessing you can kind of suck to be around sometimes." Winter turns to me to see if I agree.

I *try* not to nod, but she picks up on what I mean.

"See, your leader agrees," she says to Rio.

"My powers are a gift," he spits.

"Or a mislabeled curse," she says, still very casual in tone.

"A curse?" Rio says, clearly offended.

"Wow, sensitive. Didn't think you would be," she says to herself.

"I'm not sensitive and I'm not cursed. I think the curse is taking someone's powers away, like you're able to do."

"You only feel that way because you're a Tic."

"What?! I've never done drugs in my life: as an angel or a human," he counters.

"I'm not saying you're addicted to drugs; you're addicted to your powers. You're like a 'power Tic.' You couldn't last one day without using them."

"I don't choose to use them, I just see what people feel," he informs her.

"Yeah, but look what happened when you can't see their feelings—you get upset."

"I'M NOT UPSET!"

"I'm glad you're not upset; otherwise you might start screaming," she quips.

"Whatever," he says as he stomps out.

"What's his problem?" she asks.

"He's…complicated. Never mind that, can you find out where the Sage went?" I ask.

"Do my best, but try and prepare because something is coming," she warns as she jumps onto the Port.

"We'll be on the lookout. Thanks," I reply.

"Hey, does he have a girl?"

"Who?" I ask.

"Dark and brooding."

"No, Rio isn't seeing anyone."

"No wonder; she'd have to be nuts."

I can't for the life of me figure out what wicked plan the Sage may be making, but I figure I should talk to the one person who can think evil while still being good. I head to the infirmary to talk to Miku. No one knows evil like she does. She may have some idea what the Sage's next step will be.

Inside the infirmary, Arden plays nurse to some very happy male Quo and Ty follows her every move. As soon as he sees me, he comes my way.

"How do you do it?" he asks.

"Do what?"

"Make Bianca go out with you."

"Well…it just…happened."

"C'mon, I need to know. I need to ask Arden out before the rest of these guys."

"She's a little too old for you," I caution him.

"No, she's perfect. And we could be just like you and Bianca."

"Ty—"

"Think about it. You looked at Bianca and you didn't care that she was a Quo. Arden could feel the same way about me."

"I know, but—"

"She could take me into her heart the same way you took Bianca. Yeah, Bianca's hot but she's still a Quo. You looked past that."

"There is nothing to look past. There's nothing wrong with being a Quo," I try to impress upon him.

Chapter Eleven: Anything You Say

"Well, I know that now, because of you and Bianca. Nothing is off-limits to me now. That includes super hot 'spacey' chicks."

"Ty, I don't think—"

"Who says Arden can't love me like the way you love Bianca?"

I take him off to the furthest part of the infirmary so that we won't be overheard.

"Ty, I have to tell you something."

"What is it?" he replies innocently.

"It's about me and Bianca…"

"Okay," he says, waiting for me to continue.

"Bianca and I are…we're not…Bianca is…"

Damn it!

"Bianca and you are what, Marcus?" he asks, growing more and more curious.

"We're glad that our union inspires you. But you should just speak from your heart when you talk to a girl. Just be honest."

He smiles broadly and tells me he's going off to prepare his opening line to Arden. I rub my eye sockets with the heel of my hand and feel yet another headache coming on. I should have told him the truth but looking into his eyes, I just couldn't hurt him. So instead, I've allowed him to believe a lie.

Some angel I am.

I make myself focus on why I came to the infirmary. I find Miku a few cots away from the entrance. Her arm is as good as new. Judging from her expression, she is not a fan of being laid up.

"How are you?" I ask her.

"Why am I here, Marcus? I'm fine."

"Yeah, but rest can't hurt."

She rolls her eyes and turns away.

"C'mon, Pretty. Just another hour, then you can do a mega mix of death songs, okay?"

"I guess," she says like a stubborn child.

"I met the source and she says the Sage is planning something. She doesn't know what yet, and I was hoping you had an idea."

"Well, if I was him, I'd find a way to change the state of this war. We're winning because we have more soldiers. What would change that fact?" she asks.

"There's no more Quo for them to recruit, so how would the Sage turn things in his favor?" I ask.

"I'm not sure. But whatever it is, I'm sure it's going to be on a grand scale. The Sage went to a lot of trouble to get the Quo to have faith in him and become Believers. In order to keep the Believers on his side, he's going to have to renew their faith in him."

"In order to do that, he's gonna have to do something big."

"Exactly."

"Hey, can I talk to you?"

I look up and find Emmy standing behind me.

"Miku, how's your arm?" she asks.

"Better, thanks. You can have Marcus. I'm gonna go back into the field," she says as she hops off the bed.

"I thought I said you should stay here for another hour," I remind her.

"Marcus, you can't stop the music, or the death toll," she says, smiling as she heads out.

Emmy asks if we can go somewhere. I follow her to the side of the mountain where she touched my hand and gave me hope that we would be okay. Why does that feel like forever ago?

"What's up?" I ask when it's clear we're alone.

"I'm not saying sorry for blowing up at you before because I'm not… sorry."

"Okay."

W hat???

"But, I am sorry that I worried you. I know it sucks to see the person you love in pain, and I didn't mean for you to have to go through that," she says softly.

"Come here," I whisper in her ear.

She leans in and embraces me tightly. Somehow, feeling her against me makes everything better. And for the first time, the sound of Powerballs, screaming, and death go silent.

Emmy: my peace in the madness.

Chapter Eleven: Anything You Say

"I know this is hard, but it won't be this way forever," I remind her.

"It's just…that necklace meant a lot to me. And since you're with Bianca, it's all I have."

"Emmy, you know that's not true. Bianca is just a lie we need to live in order to win this war. I don't love her. I don't want her. She's just a means to an end. The person I want and love is you. Baby, it's always you."

I gently pull Emmy out of the embrace so I can see her face. I find an expression I didn't think would be there—shock. She is looking at something over my shoulder, and it is causing her to panic. I turn to see what she's looking at.

Ty.

He looks at us with a mixture of loathing, surprise, and confusion. His face is like that of someone who has been stabbed in the heart by a friend.

Ty immediately runs off.

"Ty, wait!" I shout as Emmy and I take off after him.

He doesn't stop. He walks past the hideout, the infirmary, and the command center.

"Ty, wait, let us explain," I call out to him again.

He turns to Emmy and me.

"LIAR!" he accuses.

"Ty, keep your voice down," I implore him.

"We can explain, if you just listen," Emmy tells him.

"NO!!! YOU LIED! THE SAGE WAS RIGHT, THERE ARE NO GOOD ANGELS. YOU'RE JUST USING US SO YOU CAN GET WHAT YOU WANT. I HATE YOU, MARCUS. I HATE ALL OF YOUR KIND!"

As he speaks, a Powerball starts forming in his hand.

"Ty, calm down and listen," I order him.

"I DON'T HAVE TO DO ANYTHING YOU SAY, LIAR!!!"

The Powerball has grown to a normal size and is thus very dangerous.

"Ty, you can hurt someone with that. You have to destroy it," I warn him.

"YOU'RE JUST LIKE THE SAGE SAYS—EVIL. THIS WHOLE TIME YOU'VE BEEN PRETENDING TO LIKE US—TO LIKE ME."

"I wasn't pretending, Ty. I do like you."

"WHAT ABOUT BIANCA?"

"Ty, it's complicated…"

"YOU USED US JUST TO GET YOUR ARMY!"

The Powerball is now among the biggest I've ever seen. He's getting angrier and angrier with each passing moment. He's going to throw it at me. I should attack him and force him to put down the Powerball, but I don't want Ty to get hurt in the process.

"Ty, please, put down the Powerball," I beg.

"WE BELIEVED IN YOU, WE DIED FOR YOU, AND YOU BETRAYED US FOR HER!"

Without any warning, Ty hurls the massive Powerball. But he doesn't throw it at me; he throws it at Emmy.

There's no time to block it.

No time to duck.

No time to intercept.

Today is the one day…

The Powerball hits Emmy center mass.

She collapses to the ground, lifeless.

CHAPTER TWELVE:
SNAKES & EX-GIRLFRIENDS

kneel over her but I can't see her face, there's too much blood in the way. I call out her name repeatedly, each time more and more desperate. She is dead silent.

"Marcus, move!" someone shouts behind me as they yank me away from Emmy's body. It happens so fast, it's hard to keep up. I hear people talking but I'm too fixed on Emmy to make out who is saying what.

I swear to Omnis, I don't know how I got to the hospital. I don't remember flying there. I don't remember lifting Emmy off the ground or carrying her in my arms. But I know it happened because I'm here in the hospital, giving her over to the ER doctor. The staff quickly place her on a gurney and race down to the operating room.

I don't notice them until I feel Miku's hand on my shoulder. I look and the whole team is in the hallway with me, along with Rage. Nothing makes sense. I'm trembling and I can't seem to steady myself. I need answers. I need to understand what just happened.

"Why is she here? She needs to be healed by a Healer. Why is she here?" I ask them frantically.

"Emmy's body is weaker than that of a Quo. They didn't have anything that would help her in the infirmary. And the mixtures that could have helped her were blown up in the blast with the rest of Daraquin," Miku explains slowly.

From the tone in her voice, I'm guessing this isn't the first time she's told me that. But for the life of me, I can't recall her explaining it to me.

"She wasn't breathing, so we brought her here because nothing can be done until she gets air in her lungs," Jay says sympathetically.

"Oh, yeah…," I reply, still in a daze.

"Marcus, sit down," Ameana says softly.

"She's gonna be okay, right, Rio?"

"I still see a Wave, so she's alive," he replies.

"Okay, okay, that's good. She's alive," I announce to them. But when they look back at me, it's not with joy or relief. They look at me with sorrow and concern.

"What? What is it?" I ask.

"Marcus, she's alive but that's the only Wave I'm getting from her," Rio says sadly.

"So?"

"It's like when you were a Tic, I only got a faint 'ghost' of a Wave."

"But I'm alive. So Emmy's gonna live too. Everything is going to be fine."

"Marcus—"

"SHE'S GONNA LIVE!" I shout. The whole hospital staff stops and stares at us.

"You're right, she's gonna be fine," Ameana says.

"She will," I vow.

Everyone looks at me sadly. I don't pay attention to them. There's no reason to be sad. Emmy will be just fine. How many times has she been injured and come out okay? This is just like the other times.

They'll see, she'll be just fine...

It's only then that I notice her blood seeping through my fingers. My hands shake even worse now. I can't make it stop. I feel like someone is cutting me open with a dull blade. The thought that today could be her last day on Earth makes an acute, violent pain travel up my chest and spread through my body.

My legs start to give way. I lean on the wall for support and slide down onto the floor. My bloody hands leave a morbid maroon trail on the once white painted hallway. I hold my head in my bloody hands and pray. The team sits on the floor alongside me. Rage stands not too far away.

It seems like an eternity before the surgeon comes out of the operating room. Once he's out, we anxiously stand up. He says he can't tell us anything because we're teens and more importantly, we're not family. Jay Convinces him quickly and he begins to talk.

"She was bleeding into her brain. We operated and were able to relieve some of the pressure."

"But, she's gonna be okay, right?" I ask.

"People with head injuries this bad have a very small survival rate. We'll monitor her for the next few hours and we'll know more then."

The doctor tells us how sorry he is once again and heads down the hallway.

"Okay, this isn't bad. I mean, it is, but we can find a mixture of something to cure her, right? Maybe the Healer that helped me when I was a Tic? We can find him," I tell the team.

"He died in battle on the first day. I saw his body. And the Healers that were comparable to him died in the blast set off by the Sage," Ameana says.

"FIND SOMEONE ELSE!!!" I order.

"Marcus—"

"I AM NOT LETTING HER DIE!"

"Alright, Marcus, what do you want us to do?" Ameana asks.

"FIND SOMEONE TO HELP HER!"

"Everyone who could help is dead," Rio says softly.

"Are you saying that with all the Paras and mixtures we have, we're still powerless?" I ask.

"Healing an injury this bad in a human is something that could be taken care of in Daraquin. But it's gone. There are no Healers left who are that advanced," Miku reminds me.

"Pretty, if her only chance is human medicine, she'll die," I reply.

She looks back at me with sorrow, and that's when the reality of the situation begins to sink in.

"I might know someone…," Rage says reluctantly.

"Who?" I ask.

"My ex-girl."

"Your ex-girlfriend is a Healer?" Jay asks, stunned.

"Angels aren't the only ones that get hurt and need healing," he says defensively.

"Well, is she any good?" I ask desperately.

"Yeah, she's the best. Little crazy though," he says, almost to himself.

"You never mentioned an ex-girlfriend," Ameana says suspiciously.

We all turn to look at her.

"Sorry," she says, realizing this maybe wasn't the right time to grill Rag e.

"Where is she?" I ask.

"I'd have to look around; she's rarely in one place for too long," Rage replies.

"Okay, go get her," I instruct.

"I'm coming with you," Ameana says.

"Um…she doesn't like…"

"She doesn't like angels. Big shock," Ameana says.

"Well, no she doesn't. But she also doesn't like *you*, especially," Rage says, clearing his throat.

"How does she even know me?" Ameana replies incredulously.

"Yo, on the real, Emmy has saved our ass a million times. So you two need to squash whatever this is here and now. Rage, go find this Healer demon."

Rage looks at Ameana. She signals she's okay with it, although I doubt she's being honest. Rage takes off to find his ex.

I lean against the wall and start laughing. It's a sad laughter: the kind that comes from knowing you're almost certainly damned. I say the words out loud and they sound even more hopeless than they did in my head.

"The survival of the girl I love is in the hands of the First Akon…"

The members of the team are talking amongst themselves in the waiting room. They sit a few seats away from me, leaving me alone. They sense that's what I need. Still, they won't go away completely. They insist on being there for me and for Emmy. I overhear them talking, but since I feel like I'm in a dark hole, their voices seem to be floating around me.

"You know I love Marcus, but really, Emmy never should have been on that field," Jay says to Miku.

"Jay, you know he wouldn't have been able to stop her from coming along."

"Yeah, Baby Girl is an action junkie."

"You are so dense. You really think Emmy comes along on our mission for the action?"

"Hell, yeah."

"She comes along because she'd rather spend an hour with him in the face of danger than years safely without him. She comes with us because she loves him."

"Look how she's paying for that now," Jay says, shaking his head.

"How can you be this way? Since when was love a bad thing? You're being a jerk," Miku accuses.

"Yo, you do'n a lot right now."

"What does that mean?"

"That means I'm not the bad guy just cuz I don't want to be in a relationship-type situation."

"You're just scared."

"Why you trying so hard to be with me? Did you see what happened to the last girl that was with me? They still haven't found all her body parts."

"The Sage did that. It wasn't you, Jay."

"Doesn't matter. Marcus is in hell right now because he loved someone. Now he's losing it and Baby Girl may not make it."

"Emmy is gonna be okay."

"Before the light blew up, yes. But now that we can't find good Healers, there's no telling if she'll make it or not."

"Shhh, I don't want Marcus to hear you. And say what you want, but Marcus doesn't regret loving Emmy."

"No, but when Baby Girl took that Powerball to the chest, I'm sure she started regretting."

"Is it that you don't want to be in relationship or don't want to be in one with me?" she asks with a small voice.

"Miku, I love you. You're my home girl, why isn't that enough?"

"I'm not asking for your Rah, Jay. I'm just saying, maybe we could try and see if this goes somewhere. Unless you don't feel anything for me at all, then it's fine—whatever."

"Yo, why you so down with ending our thing?"

"What thing? Oh, you mean the meaningless sex?"

"Meaningless? So what, if we don't become a couple, then all the times we spent together was worthless?"

"I want something more. I want it with you. But I'm not gonna beg you. I'm smart, I'm kind, and I'm hot. I mean, really. Look at me."

"You know I dig you. Why does it have to be something more? Why do I have to make it official?"

"I deserve official. If you can't see that, maybe I was wrong about you," Miku says.

She doesn't give Jay a chance to reply. She storms off and joins Rio. The two of them head back to the battlefield. The team decided to take turns going to the battle and coming back so that I'm never alone. While I appreciate the support, I would give anything to be by myself.

The doctors aren't letting anyone in to see Emmy yet. Jay offered to Convince them, but I said no. I want to see Emmy, more than anything, but something in me needs to believe she's not really hurt. Something in me needs her to be at home reading her thoroughly worn-through romance novel and feeding Ms. Charlotte. If I walk into her hospital room and see her lying there with tubes coming out of her...

I can't...

Just a few minutes after the twins leave for the battlefield, we spot Dalce coming towards us.

"How is the human?" he asks.

"It's bad, but we're hoping we can find the Healer we need in time," Ameana replies.

"Bianca wanted to be here, but I convinced her to stay on the field. After all, we can't have it look like both the leader and his wife have abandoned the soldiers," Dalce says.

"That's not what's happening," Ameana assures him.

"Well, I know but it does *look* a lot like that; especially after the episode that happened with Ty."

"What do you mean, man?" Jay wonders. "I mean more than a few soldiers overheard Ty. They're wondering if what he said was truth: Did Marcus marry Bianca just for the army? I've spent hours smoothing things over. Convincing them that Ty was an overemotional kid and mistook a friendship between Marcus and the human for something else. I promised them that you two are, in fact, very much in love."

"Lying comes very easy to you," I reply.

"I'm a leader, Marcus. I do what needs to be done."

"Yeah, and look what it's cost us," I reply.

"Excuse me?" Dalce counters.

"If we're weren't pretending and lying to the Quo, Emmy wouldn't be in some hospital bed fighting to live," I snap.

"I know you're upset, Marcus, but come now, let's be fair. The reason Emmy is fighting for her life is because of you."

Ameana puts a hand on my shoulder in an attempt to keep me from losing my temper. It doesn't work.

"What the hell do you mean, it's my fault?"

"Well, Marcus, you weren't supposed to be having private meetings with the human. You were supposed to be leading the army and being by your wife's side. That was your duty. You did not do that."

"What is wrong with you? You put everything aside just so you can have some semblance of power? You pimp out your own child just so you can, what, get an invite to a council dinner? Or have your name in the paper?"

"I do what I do because I know the pain that comes with being unseen. And cycle after cycle, we have been ignored. That will NEVER happen again. And I will not let some human girl make you lose focus on what's important—winning this war and placing us where we belong: at the top."

"Damn, you're an asshole," Jay says, studying Dalce.

"Maybe, but at least I'm smart enough not to devote my life to a Guardian who can't ever be with me. Honestly, the human isn't all that bright."

Before the team can stop me, I grab Dalce by his neck, raise him several feet in the air, and slam him so hard against the wall, it starts to crumble.

"You say anything bad about her again and I'll rip out your fucking vocal cords," I vow.

"Marcus, put him down," Ameana says firmly.

I can feel the life draining out of him; I squeeze his throat even harder. He makes a horrible choking sound as his air supply is completely cut off.

"Marcus, now!" Ameana orders.

I drop the snake and he falls to the floor, gasping for air.

I stomp out of the waiting area and head outside. The team tries to follow me and I tell them to stop where they are.

"We want to make sure you're okay," Jay says.

"I'm not. Dalce is right; I shouldn't have been sneaking around with Emmy."

"Marcus, this isn't your fault; you didn't know what Ty was going to do," Ameana reassures me.

"It doesn't matter. I should have sent him home like Rio suggested. But I said no. If I just listened to him…"

"Marcus, she's gonna be okay," Ameana says, trying to sound upbeat.

"Listen, I know you guys want to help, but…I just wanna be alone."

I don't wait for them to reply. I just start walking out of the hospital. I decide to go by Emmy's apartment. There's something comforting about being around the thing the person you love cares about, it brings a strange peace. Unfortunately, I can't stay more than a few minutes before I have to get back to the battle and to Emmy.

I head across the street, but someone calls out my name. I turn and see a frantic Quo girl. She calls me back towards the hospital entrance.

"Eta, what is it?" I ask.

"Marcus, I know this is a bad time but I need to tell you something," she says, sobbing.

"Okay, okay, calm down. What is it?"

"I think Dalce killed my grandmother."

It takes a few min

"My grandmother, Nipoe, and Dalce have always fought about whose side the Foundation should be on. He hated that she wanted to build a relationship with the angels. He thought the only way that Quo can have a say is to force the hand of the council. It was a really big issue that divided my grandmother and my uncle for years.

"When the Sage blasted the light, Uncle Dalce thought it was the perfect chance to bring the angels to their knees and force you guys to make us part of your world. But Nipoe wouldn't do that. She insisted we help the angels, regardless of how we would or would not be rewarded. They fought about it heatedly, and I once heard him say that her time leading the Foundation would soon end," Eta concludes.

"It sounds like they disagreed, or even hated each other, but what makes you think Dalce had anything to do with Nipoe's death? She died of a heart attack," I remind her.

"I had an autopsy done, as soon as her body was found. The medical examiner contacted me today; he thinks her pacemaker malfunctioned," Eta replies.

"Eta, that happens. Granted, not often, but it does happen," Rio says gently.

"A witness saw Uncle Dalce coming out of Nipoe's room just before she died."

"They could have been having a meeting of some kind," I reply.

"No. The person who saw him said that Dalce had just used his powers."

"I'm sorry, I'm missing your point," Miku says, confused.

"Do you know what Dalce's power is?" Eta asks.

"No," I reply.

"He controls devices, like pacemakers."

"Hold up, you think your uncle used his power to speed up Nipoe's pacemaker?" Jay asks.

"Speed it up or slow it down. Either way, he is responsible for her death."

"Who saw him coming out of her room that night?" I ask.

"He really doesn't want to be involved in this," Eta says carefully.

"He doesn't have a choice. He can't just accuse Dalce without proof," I counter.

"Marcus, he did it. He killed my grandmother. She was a kind person who loved the Foundation and gave her life to it. She didn't need to die," she says as a fresh stream of tears comes down her face.

Miku goes over to comfort her. The team and I exchange a look of concern. I signal for Miku to take Eta away so the team can talk. Miku takes her to the ladies' room. As soon as they disappear around the corner, we begin to discuss what to do about Dalce.

"We have to make him step down as the leader of the Foundation," Ameana says.

"We can't do that on the word of an emotional granddaughter," I reply.

"Rio, was she telling the truth?" Ameana asks.

"She's telling what she believes is the truth. There's no way to know if it's what really happened," Rio informs us.

"If he did do this, he has to step down," Ameana reiterates.

"Right now, we're leading an army that still has reservations about us. Getting rid of their leader could make them turn on us," I caution her.

"So, what, we just let Dalce get away with murder?" Jay asks.

"We don't know that he did it," I remind him.

"Please, that guy is all types of shady. You saw how he was with you just now. Do you doubt for a second he's capable of killing an old lady to take her place as leader?" Jay adds.

Chapter Thirteen: Out Of Sight

"The sad truth is, even if he did it, we still need him in order to keep the Foundation soldiers on our side," I reply.

"So, we're okay working with murderers?" Ameana wonders.

"We're good working with demons; really, are murderers such a big leap?" Rio quips.

"C'mon, he's helping us with the human. Why don't you cut him a break?" she asks Rio.

"Because demons don't do well with second chances."

"Whatever, Rio," Ameana replies, shaking her head.

"I don't like this either, but we need Dalce to keep the soldiers together," I interject.

"So, he's gonna get away with murder?" Eta asks as she heads towards us.

She's washed her face but the sadness remains in her eyes. Miku takes her hand and assures her that we would never do that.

"Fine, then what are you guys going to do about it?" she asks, getting angry.

"Eta, we know how important Nipoe was to you. But Dalce isn't an angel. We can't just come in and impose our rules on him," I tell her.

"What do Quo do when they suspect someone of taking a life?" Miku asks.

"We do as the humans do: we have a trial. If he's found guilty, there is process called Rue. It strips the Quo of his power. It can be for a few months, years, or a lifetime depending on how bad the offense."

"Fine, then you guys can hold a trial, but that will have to be when this is over," I reply.

"Marcus, he's a killer and you're just gonna let him loose!" she shouts.

"I don't know if you know this or not, but we're actually in the middle of a war. Not to mention having to go on a mission to find the three missing pieces to put the council back together. I can't take on Dalce right now," I snap.

The others explain to her about the Shoma. They tell her it's the only chance we have to set things right and rebuild the light again.

"How much time do you have?" she asks us.

"We had months and now…days," Jay says.

"Look, I know you guys have a lot going on and I'm sorry, but this can't wait," Eta says.

"We just can't fix this right now. First of all, we don't even know who this witness is," I reply.

"Fine, I'll tell you but you have to promise Dalce will pay for what he did."

"If he did it, he will. Now who is this witness?" I reply.

"It's Uri; Angela's husband."

"He knew all this time?" Ameana asks.

"No, he only remembered having seen Dalce last night. That's when I started to put it together in my head," Eta says.

"Okay, I'll go talk to Uri."

"Thank you, Marcus," Eta says, embracing me.

"We can talk to Uri for you. The doctor said you can go see Emmy now," Miku tells me.

"She's awake?" I ask.

"No, but you can go in," Ameana says.

"Later; right now I need to talk to Uri. Then we need to take out the rest of the Sage's army and end this war for good."

"Wait, you don't want to go inside and see Emmy?" Ameana asks, puzzled.

"I said later," I snap.

I send the twins and Jay back to the front line of the battle. Eta and I get on a Port and head back to base camp. Ameana stays in the hospital, waiting on Rage's return.

Once back at base camp, I send Eta to find Uri. While she's gone, I attend to something I have been avoiding: Ty.

"Where is he?" I ask one of the Foundation soldiers.

"He ran away."

"What? Find him!"

"Are you going to kill him?" the soldier asks.

"He's a kid."

"Not anymore. Now, he's a traitor," Dalce says, standing at the entrance.

"What do you mean?" I ask.

"He's on the other side now. He's been attacking our soldiers."

"We have to get him back here. He doesn't know what he's doing."

"Yes, he does. He's chosen to join the Believers. We have to treat him exactly like what he is: the enemy. If the chance comes to take him down—"

"Anyone touches that kid and I will kill them myself. Ty isn't the enemy. He's a scared kid. And we are not gonna hurt him. Got it?"

The soldiers around me reluctantly agree. I send them out to find Ty and bring him back safely. Dalce glares at me.

"You are so much weaker than I first thought," he says, disgusted.

"Why? Because killing doesn't come so easy to me?"

"I keep telling you, Guardian: I do what needs to be done."

"Really, and what needed to be done to Nipoe?"

"What are you talking about?"

"You better hope it's all a misunderstanding," I vow.

"I have no idea what it is you are referring to."

"Nipoe was all Eta had. She loved that old lady and just like that she was gone."

"Marcus, Nipoe's passing hurt us all. In fact, I'm still grieving."

"Are you?"

"Can't you tell by the look of my face?"

I look right at him and I swear there's a slight smile. That bastard murdered the old lady. And he enjoyed it.

"You're not as smart as you think you are, Dalce. I promise you that."

"Marcus, if there's something you want to accuse me of, don't beat around the bush."

"Did you have anything to do with Nipoe's death?"

"Me? No, that would make me a monster."

There's the smile again.

"The two men in my life, in one room," Bianca says from the entrance.

Dalce and I continue to glare at each other. Bianca enters and asks if everything is okay.

"Yes, I was just catching up with your husband. He thinks I killed Nipoe."

"What? Why would you kill your own mother?"

"Marcus is just overtired. I guess leading an army is far more taxing than he thought," he says pointedly as he heads out.

I would love to end this guy's life. Seriously, it would be a pleasure.

"Speaking of which, how is the human? Is she going to make it?" Bianca asks, concerned.

"We don't know yet," I reply.

"I should go visit her and give her my best."

"Ameana is with her now," I reply.

"Maybe later, then. Now, what's this about my father?"

"There's a witness who says he saw your father coming from Nipoe's room the night she died."

"That doesn't mean anything," Bianca counters.

"The medical examiner said Nipoe's pacemaker failed. And you know your father can control devices."

"Marcus, my father would never do such a thing. He loved Nipoe. They didn't agree on much, but murder…that's ridiculous. Who is this witness?" she asks.

"It's me," Uri says as he enters with Eta.

Uri explains that he can tell who has what power and when it was used. And according to him, Dalce used his power in Nipoe's room. And moments after he came out, Nipoe was found dead.

"I'm sorry, Bianca, but there has to be a trial," I warn her.

"It's fine, Marcus. I'm not worried. I'm sure Uri is just remembering wrong," she says, smiling politely.

"No, I'm not. It was your father, Bianca," Uri swears.

"Well, whatever, I'm sure we'll clear this up soon," she replies.

"When the war is over, Uncle Dalce will pay for what he did," Eta says.

"My baby cousin has always been one for theatrics. It's okay, Eta. I know you're only acting out of grief."

"You father has always wanted to lead the Foundation. I just didn't know how far he'd go to make it happen."

Bianca ignores Eta's outburst and turns her attention to Uri.

Chapter Thirteen: Out Of Sight

"How is Angela feeling?" she asks him.

"She's doing okay. The patterns on her hands are forming, so the baby is alive and well, so far."

"We Quo give birth the human way. So, I'm not all that familiar with the angel way. Am I to understand that any stress or sorrow can cause her to lose the baby?"

"Yes, that's why she's in the hideout: to make sure her soul isn't affected by all the death around us."

"And it is true that heartbreak can cause her to lose the baby, too?"

"Yes, but there's no chance of that. I'm keeping her happy and focused on positive things. Like us winning this war. Rumor has it that it should only be a few days now, right, Marcus?"

"Yeah, it should be over soon," I reply.

"Good, then I can get Angela back to camp safely. How's Emmy?"

"It's too early to tell," I reply, trying very hard to keep the emotion from my voice.

"Well, she's in our thoughts," Uri says as he and Eta head out.

Uri turns around and addresses Bianca.

"I'm really sorry I saw what I saw. I wish I didn't, Bianca. I really do." Bianca walks up to him and touches the side of his face lovingly. She closes her eyes for a brief second, then opens them up again and smiles radiantly.

"Don't worry about it, Uri. I have a feeling this will work out."

He smiles and walks out with Eta.

"You're not the least bit concerned that your father did this?" I ask her once we are alone.

"No, because it's all a big misunderstanding. What I am concerned about is you."

"What about me?"

"How are you doing with Emmy getting hurt?"

"You called her by her name," I point out.

"I didn't realize how much she meant to you until I saw the look on your face when you had to carry her broken body in your arms. You really love her."

I can't look into her eyes. Just like back in Bora Bora, it feels like she knows too much about me. Things I'm not willing or ready to share. Luckily, I get a call from Ameana that interrupts me and Bianca. But that's where my luck stops. Rage has been in touch with her and he has not found his ex. I tell her to make sure he keeps looking.

"Marcus, there's something else," Ameana says on the other line.

Dear Omnis, what now?

"I'm listening," I say, bracing myself.

"The doctor said…"

"The doctor said what?"

"He said we should come back to the hospital to say our good-byes."

"What the hell are you doing?" Rio shouts as he lands on the ground a few seconds after me.

"What's the problem?" I ask.

"Your wings are damaged and you fly into a freaking nest of Powerballs just to get one demon?"

"I got him."

"Marcus, you're being reckless."

"I'm doing my job. We are almost done with this thing. All we need to do is take out the last of the Fire Swans and a few hundred Believers."

"What about the demons, Marcus? They don't die as easily as Believers, you know that."

"That's why I'm doing everything to kill them."

"You can't kill them all by yourself. We had a plan. The Paras would attack from the west and we'd attack from the east. What happened to that?"

"Look, I saw a demon and I attacked him. What is the big deal?"

"Risking your life won't make Emmy better. That's not what she would want for you."

Chapter Thirteen: Out Of Sight

"This has nothing to do with Emmy."

"Yes, it does. Ameana called me. I know how bad things have gotten. I know they don't think she'll live, but that doesn't mean you can go off and get yourself killed!"

"Hey, what's with all the effort for one demon?" Miku asks as she lands.

"He's a demon. He should die," I reply simply.

Rio then tells her about Ameana's call.

"I'll get the rest of the team; we should go see her," Miku says, filled with sorrow.

"You guys can go, I'm not done fighting," I reply.

The twins look at each other with an uneasy stare.

"What?" I ask impatiently.

"You should go see Emmy with us," the twins say in union.

"I have work to do," I snap.

I take off into the sky. My wings are slightly slower than I'm used to, as a result of the blast from several dozen Powerballs. None of them got me directly, but they were close enough to slow me down. But what I lack in speed, I make up for in fury.

I grab a demon just as he's about to strike and hurl him to the side of the mountains, where he collides with a Fire Swan. The two of them explode in the sky like fireworks.

Die. Die. Die. Die.

The demons attack me back with Powerballs and brute strength. One demon gets the upper hand and rains down blow after blow to my face and chest. He grabs me by the neck, takes out his knife, and slashes me from my chest to my belly button.

I cry out as my blood drips down onto the ground below. The demon laughs and tells me how much he's wanted to be the one that kills me.

"Before you do, just one thing," I reply between gritted teeth.

"What is it?"

"Your song's playing."

As soon as I say that, Miku gets up close to the demon and sings right into his ear. The demon is in agony from that moment on. So much so that he has no choice but to let me go. But my wings are far more injured than I first thought. I'm falling, not flying.

Jay pulls me back up at the last minute and gets on me about not being carful. He then scolds me for not agreeing to go see Emmy in the hospital. I'm about to argue with him when one of the soldiers announces he spotted Ty half a mile from here. He warns me that Ty isn't alone; he's accompanied by dozens of Believers. I take off after him, broken wing and all.

Ty shoots at us with big Powerballs that are meant to kill. It appears the source of his power is anger. I try to fly over to him but with my wings, I can only hover in the air. I call out his name but he ignores me.

He shoots at the soldiers, and they begin to shoot back. I shout at them to stop, but they are under fire and their natural instinct is to protect themselves.

"No, stop!" I roar as I try to make it over to them.

It infuriates me that the more I try to fly, the less I am able. Ty hurls a Powerball at a Foundation soldier on the ground. The Powerball hits the soldier and sends him flying in the air. When he lands, he's missing a leg. The soldier looks up at the face of the being that attacked him.

"No, don't do it!" I shout.

It's too late. The soldier launches six blades, three from each palm, right into Ty.

"NO!!!"

I land on the ground and race over to Ty. He caught two blades in the leg, two in his shoulders and two in the heart. His shirt is drenched in blood. His breathing is shallow. I place his head in my lap and tell him everything will be fine.

Tears fall from his eyes. He takes a quick breath. Then I feel his body relax in my arms. He looks up at me with a blank stare.

"Ty? Ty? C'mon, don't do this, wake up!" I look off into the direction I came from and I see him standing there. "Rio, read his Wave. Then help me take him to the infirmary," I demand. "Marcus, he's gone."

"FUUUUUUUUUUUUUUUUUUUUUUUUUUUUUUUUUCK!!!"

Chapter Thirteen: Out Of Sight

I don't know how long I sat there with Ty's corpse on my lap. They tried to get me off the field but I wouldn't budge. They tried to tend to the gash across my chest but I wouldn't let them. Rio placed his shield around us. But it didn't stop the demons from trying to attack.

Night begins to fall. Someone comes and takes Ty's body. I would have stopped them but I was losing a lot of blood and was weak. The person promised me they would take good care of him. I think it was Miku but I'm in a daze and can't be sure.

Somehow, I end up in someone's makeshift room, sitting on the edge of a cot, with my shirt off. She stands over me and goes to administer a sticky blue liquid to the wound to my chest. I stop her.

"What am I doing here?"

"I had your team bring you to me," Bianca replies.

"Why?"

"I just wanted to help," she says earnestly.

I release her hand, and she dabs the liquid up and down my chest. My wound starts healing on contact.

"What is it?" I ask.

"A paste of healing herbs. It's already worked on your wings. Now we just need to take care of that nasty cut."

"Could it help—"

"No, it doesn't work on humans."

"Oh."

When she's done, she puts the vial away.

"You should be better soon," she promises.

"Ty…"

"I heard. I'm so sorry," she replies.

"I said I would protect him…"

"You did the best you could."

I look up at her and make a confession.

"I abandoned her; I abandoned Emmy."

"How?"

"They said I could go to her hospital room and see her because she might not…but I couldn't. I couldn't face her; she's in this situation because she loves me."

"I think your wound should heal nicely," she says.

"Thank you," I whisper, looking off into the distance.

She takes my face in her hand and gently turns my head so that I'm facing her.

"I can heal your other scars. The ones you get from trying to make love work when it's clearly not meant to."

She kneels on the floor before me, leans in, and caresses my face with her fingers. That's when exhaustion begins to set in. The battling, the killing, the blood, the sacrifices…

I haven't Recharged in what feels like weeks. And it's just now hitting me. I look at her, wary and worn. She studies my face.

"Emmy's not gonna make it through the night. It's okay to let her go; let everything go because I'm here."

She looks up at me. Bianca is truly beautiful. Her piercing eyes could start wars. Her caramel skin dares you not to taste it. The shape of her supple breasts promises a night of inconceivable pleasure. No guy in his right mind would push this girl away.

"Marcus, it's okay to let her go…," Bianca whispers again, as if reading my mind.

I look down at her: true perfection. She begins to unbutton her blouse slowly.

"There's so much pain in your eyes, so much weighing on your soul. I can take that pain away. I can lift the weight off of you. Marcus, let me make it better…"

Her blouse slides off her shoulders and onto the floor behind her. She sits before me, half naked and willing. Her body is undeniably a weapon.
I reach out towards her. She eagerly awaits my lips on hers. I lean in even closer. My face is only inches away from her. She closes her eyes and awaits my lips. I reach past her, pick up her blouse, and cover her back up.
Like I said, a guy would have to be out of his mind to pass up a girl like Bianca. And that's what I am: out of my mind, in love with Emmy. She somehow manages to make the other girls fade to the background.

It may be that she is out of my sight, but Emmy is never out of my mind. And yes, Bianca is insanely hot, but she's not Emmy.

I apologize to her, put my shirt back on, and head outside. Bianca calls after me.

"Marcus, where are you going?"

"I'm going to see the girl who went to Hell for me."

CHAPTER FOURTEEN:
TRICKS OF THE WICKED

I arrive at the hospital a short while later. I find the team in the waiting area. They've already gone inside to see Emmy. The only person who has yet to show his face is me. They ask if I need them to come with me; I tell them I am fine going on my own.

I head down the hallway and stop in front of her room. I see her through the window in the door. She looks small, frail. There are several tubes attached to her and the machines keeping her alive hum quietly in the background.

I try again; this time I get as far as the door handle. And still, I can't get myself to go in. I sink down to the floor with my head in my hands.

Omnis, if you need to take someone, take me. Take me a million times. Just don't take her. The only thing she ever did wrong was love me; don't make her pay for that mistake with her life.

Pretty comes to sit beside me on the floor. I look into her eyes and confess that I can't do it. I can't handle seeing her this way.

"When my mom got cancer, Rio and I had to go see her in the hospital. I couldn't go in. I just sat outside her room. I kept waiting for the courage to see her. Then, I remembered what she said to me my first day of kindergarten, when I was scared to go inside the classroom. She said courage doesn't wander. It is with you always, you just need to find it."

"I don't even know what to say to her."

"You don't need to say anything. You just need to show up. That's what you do for people you love: you show up."

She takes my hand and we get up together. I place my hand on the cold doorknob. My fingers are shaking but I manage to steady them enough to open the door. I look at Miku, and she smiles reassuringly. I walk into Emmy's room.

My chest feels like it's going to explode from the pain of seeing her so broken. Her skin is pale, her head is bandaged, and she lies so still, the bed is more like a coffin. The thought of her being six feet under causes a chill to run down my whole body. I slowly walk up to her bed and take her frail hand in mine.

"I'm here, Em."

I pause as if she will somehow respond to me. Her only response is more silence.

"I'm sorry I didn't come sooner. I was being selfish. I do that a lot. I should have been here with you but I couldn't face it. The funny thing is, I know if it was the other way around, you would have been there for me. "That's the thing I could never get you to understand; you're the strongest person I know. You think my powers make me strong, but the truth is, it takes more courage to be human."

I kiss her hand and place it between mine. She is unmoved.

"Baby, ever since we met, I've asked you to do impossible things. And I know you're tired. I know you're ready to give in. But I need you to do just one more impossible thing for me. I need you to fight to come back to me. Emmy, please come back to me…"

The knock on the door jolts me out of my thoughts. I place Emmy's hand gently back to her side and open the door. Rio stands there, looking distressed.

"What is it?" I ask.

"It's Uri. His life is in danger."

"What? He's not even supposed to be in battle," I reply.

"I know, but that's what I'm reading."

"If something happens to him in battle…," I begin.

"Then Angela will freak and lose the baby. I know. That's why we need to get Uri, now."

I look back at Emmy and hope she understands why I have to leave so abruptly. Rio and I rush out of the hospital, then head for the camp.

Once there, I find the rest of the team looking at each other, unsure what to do.

"What's the problem?" I ask.

That's when I hear a girl screaming profanity from the top of her lungs. Angela is a few yards away, throwing everything in sight at her husband, Uri.

"I FREAKING HATE YOU!!!"

She hurls the nearest rock at his head, he dodges it at the last minute.

But she keeps coming and the third attempt is successful. The rock hits Uri in the head and bursts open his forehead. A stream of blood runs from his forehead down his face and onto his shirt. We all rush over to them.

Angela is absolutely unwilling to settle down. She charges towards her husband with full strength. Jay has to hold her back to keep her from beating the hell out of him.

"Yo, son, chill," Jay shouts as Angela furiously fights to break free from his hold.

"I'm sorry, Angie, I'm so sorry," Uri begs.

"I'M GONNA KILL YOU!!!" she vows.

Then, without warning, she opens her mouth and sinks her teeth into Jay's flesh.

"Yo, she bit me," Jay says, more shocked than in pain.

By now the entire camp has gathered and everyone is watching this insane scene play out.

"Uri, what's going on?" I demand.

"TELL THEM, TELL THEM HOW YOU CHEATED ON ME, YOU BASTARD!" Angela yells at the top of her lungs.

"I'm sorry, Angie. I'm so sorry."

"FUCK YOU!"

"Try to understand, I gave you my Rah so quickly…I panicked. But I love you. Please find it in your heart to forgive me."

"GET FORGIVENESS FROM YOUR QUO WHORE—"

"Okay, this needs to end right now!" I order.

"JUST LET ME KILL HIM!" Angela says, gritting her teeth.

Chapter Fourteen: Tricks of the Wicked

Once again she leaps out and aims to murder her husband.

I snatch Uri and pull him out of her reach. He begs me to let him stay and talk to his wife.

"Right now, what you need to do is be gone," I order.

"I'm not leaving her."

"Did you cheat on her?" I ask.

"Yes."

"Then you need to leave," I reply.

"It can't be over. She's my life," he swears.

"Look, I'm not saying it's over but right now, for the sake of your Sib, you need to go so that Angela can calm down. So long as you're here, she's gonna be upset. You know what that will mean for your child. You need to go to hide out and give her some space."

"But—"

"Uri, go!"

"Okay, okay," he says as he reluctantly flies away.

I head back to Angela, who is now whimpering loudly. Miku and Ameana take her back to her makeshift room. They signal to the rest of the team not to come in. We all agree it would be best to let the girls go in and find out what happened.

While we wait on them to return, Jay sticks his arm out for us to see.

"You see this?" he whines.

"It's a small bite," Rio says dismissively.

"Yo, son, she took some of my flesh."

Out of nowhere, I do something I haven't in awhile—laugh. Rio joins me.

"Oh, so y'all just gonna laugh? Really? You guys are gonna do me like that?" Jay replies.

We try to contain our laughter, but fail.

"That's not funny, this is gonna scar. Damn you!" Jay says as he studies his arm.

"Just go to the infirmary and have them fix you up," I say once I finally manage to control my laughter.

"Your teammate is suffering and what you do: laugh? Yo, that cold, son," Jay says, shaking his head dramatically.

Rio rolls his eyes and flashes a bemused smile. But the smile quickly turns into concern.

"What is it?" Jay asks.

"Angela, she's devastated," Rio replies.

"Yeah, we saw that—" I begin.

"It's not about Uri," Rio says as he runs in to see Angela. The rest of us follow.

"What's going on?" he asks.

"The patterns on Angela's hands are fading," Ameana says, on high alert.

Angela studies her hands and, sure enough, the complex pattern begins to fade from her fingertips. Her rage and sorrow are affecting her soul. And if she doesn't calm down, she's going to lose the Sib.

"Angela, what happened?" I ask.

She shakes her head and looks down. She's too shaken up to talk, so the girls fill us in.

"Bianca came by to congratulate her on the baby. She hugged Angela and accidentally passed on a few memories in the process. The first one was some little boys playing, the other was a soul diving contest and the last one was of Uri and another girl… in bed," Miku says gently.

We look at her and see silver tears coming from her eyes. That's bad. Only pregnant angels can cry. But that's normally during the Handover. The fact that she's able to cry right now means something is going terribly wrong with her pregnancy.

"Angela, you have to stop crying," I urge her.

"How could he do this to me?" she asks no one in particular.

"How could Uri even kiss another girl if you had his Rah? It's not possible," Jay says.

"There's a mixture on the black market, it's called Trickk. You get something that belongs to your spouse: a hair, fingernails, anything. You place it into the mixture and the person you're cheating with drinks it. Trickk then 'fools' your Rah into thinking it's with the spouse," Angela explains.

"I've never heard of it," Rio replies.

"The council banned it. But if you want it bad enough, like Uri, I guess you find a way," she says bitterly as she starts to sob again.

"Okay, I know this is hard for you, Angela, but you need to stay focused. You need to stop letting the rage eat away at your soul," Rio warns her.

"I loved him and I thought he loved me. How could he do it? I hate him. I hate him so much," she wails.

"Angela, guys are much weaker than us. We are the strong ones. And that's what you need to be right now: strong," Ameana tells her.

"I don't ever want to see him again," she cries into Miku's chest.

Miku strokes her hair and signals to us to look at Angela's hand. We look and, sure enough, the pattern in her palm is disappearing. Once the pattern just above her wrist disappears, the Sib will be gone.

"Don't think about Uri. Think about your beautiful baby, who can't wait to meet you," Ameana says.

"It just keeps playing over and over in my mind," Angela says.

"You have to forgive him. Or, at least, let some of the anger go," Rio informs her.

"Just think about how much you love him," Jay suggests.

It was the wrong suggestion. The thought of even saying she loved Uri out loud causes Angela to lose it all over again.

"Love him? I hate him. I wish that Omnis would douse him and his Quo bitch in gasoline and set them on fire!"

That did it. The pattern disappears completely from both of Angela's arms.

Angela looks at her hands, realizing what has just happened, and she freaks out.

"No, no, no, no, no, no…" she begs Omnis.

The pattern does not return.

"Please, I'm sorry. I won't say anything bad again. Please." She lies down on the ground and begs Omnis once again to return her child.

Miku places her hand on her mouth. She can't believe Angela's baby is gone. The guys can't face the broken woman on the floor. Ameana covers her up with her jacket.

Suddenly, Angela remembers that in some rare cases, the father's soul is strong enough to take over. She gets up and flies over to the hideout to see if the Sib latched on to Uri's soul.

She doesn't even bother explaining it to him. She just pulls up his shirt sleeves and studies his arms. There are no patterns. She looks again and again. There is nothing. Their baby is dead.

Angela was so distraught she needed a mixture to help her calm down. The mixture doesn't work on pregnant women. But since she's no longer pregnant, it helped her relax. The twins then took her back to her makeshift room to Recharge.

Shortly afterwards, Bianca appears in the entrance of the hideout, looking frantic.

"Is it true what I heard? Did your wife miscarry?" Bianca says, beside herself.

"You should know, you gave her the memory!" Uri spits.

"Why would you do that, Bianca?" I ask.

"I'm so sorry, Uri. It's my powers. Sometimes, when I make contact with people, some of their memories stay with me. Then later on, that memory accidentally gets transferred to other people. I'm deeply, deeply sorry. I didn't even know I had transferred anything at all."

"Well, you did, and now our baby…" Uri is too upset to finish.

"Uri, if I could, I would do anything to take this hurt away from you. I'm so sorry," she says as her eyes fill with tears.

"I'm gonna go look in on her," Uri says as he heads out the door. Bianca catches up to him. She then looks deeply into his eyes and addresses him with a sweet tone.

"Oh, that poor girl, she must be on the edge. Right now, I'd imagine any little thing could set her off. Well, it's a good thing my power didn't do any more damage. It could have been much worse. Sometimes, with my powers, I can dig so deeply into someone's past, it completely *demolishes* their future."

Uri nods slowly. I could swear there's a hint of fear in his eyes.

Chapter Fourteen: Tricks of the Wicked

"I should go," Uri replies with a shaky voice.

"Okay, but you be sure to tell Angela how sorry I am. And that she's *never* too far from my mind."

Uri hurries away as if something wicked is chasing him.

The next morning, Ameana tells me that Rage has once again struck out with finding the Healer. To make matters worse, Emmy's doctor tells she is showing no sign of improvement. I go to check on Emmy for an hour or so. I then force myself to go back to the battlefield and join Wolf and the others. On my way to the front lines, Eta approaches me looking very upset.

"I know you want the trial, Eta, but now is not—"

"There's not gonna be a trial," she corrects me.

"Why?" I reply.

"Uri ran off with Angela. He left this behind," she says, handing me a slip of paper.

"I was mistaken about Dalce.

I'm sorry…"

CHAPTER FIFTEEN: THOMAS CASE IS DEAD

The news about U

and then throwing her over when he was done.

The fact that no one knew who the mystery Quo girl was didn't stop everyone from speculating. Some thought the Quo girl was Bianca and that she passed on the memory out of spite because she was still in love with Uri. A few suspected the Quo was Eta, since she had been seen around the camp with Uri. From there, the theories got more and more absurd. Some are supportive of Uri, given what he has just lost, while others want to skin him alive for cheating. What's more, now that the mixture called Trickk is known to everyone and not just a few people, couples argue over whether their mates have ever used it.

The gossip didn't really hold my attention at first. But as the chatter grows more and more, Quo and angel start to turn on each other. "The angels claim they had never heard of us Quo, but they knew us well enough to carry on affairs with our kind," a Quo woman says to a friend as they use their powers to airlift water to the infirmary.

"You're right. Uri knew we existed; who's to say the Guardians didn't?"

"And they only acknowledge us because they need our help," a soldier chimes in.

When they see that I'm within earshot, they stop talking and walk away.

"This is bad," Miku says, standing behind me.

"I know. We only need one more major attack to reduce the Believers and demons to nothing. But that won't happen if the Quo start doubting our intentions," I reply.

"That's exactly what I was thinking," Bianca says as she walks up to us.

"You shouldn't be this close to the battle," I remind her.

"I'm here because you need my help. If my people keep thinking the way they are, they will pull out of this war just as we're about to claim victory," Bianca adds.

"So, what do you suggest?" I ask.

"I think that we should remind them that Quo and angels are on the same side. And that we won't let some girl's bad judgment ruin the solidarity between our people. If only I had gotten a look at her face in the memor y…"

"Why are you blaming the girl? What about Uri?" Miku says, disgusted.

"Males lack self-control. We don't. She should never have cheated with him, or should have done a better job of hiding it," Bianca counters.

"You can riffle through memories; how were they supposed to hide it?" Miku asks, clearly annoyed.

"Well, I guess you're right. There really is no escaping your past. But, then again, looking at your red-laced wings, I guess you know better than anyone."

Miku glares at her. Bianca turns her attention back to me.

"So, later tonight, we can stand together in front of everyone and make the announcement. Agreed?"

"Yeah," I reply reluctantly.

Bianca smiles and walks away.

"You really think Bianca used her powers on Angela by accident?" Miku asks.

"I don't know, Pretty. I admit it's really convenient. But I've asked around and people with Bianca's powers can sometimes pass on a memory without meaning to."

"Think what you want, but that girl is evil on a stick," she mocks.

"She's definitely…strong willed."

"Are you really gonna make that stupid speech with her?"

"Pretty, like it or not, she's right. The Quo feel like we may not be on the same side. We're so close to winning this thing…if I have to stand up and play 'nice' with Bianca, then…that's what I have to do."

"Where is the limit with you, Marcus?"

Before I can answer her, an argument breaks out a few yards away from us. A group of Quo versus a group of angels. They are hurling accusations at each other, each side claiming the other is untrustworthy.

The Quo accuse the angels of using them, like Uri used the mystery girl. Meanwhile, the angels accuse the Quo of plotting to break angel families apart. Miku and I try to stop them from bickering, but both sides are too angry to hear us out.

In the midst of the chaos, the rest of my team shows up, along with Winter. I'm eager to see if she has an update, but I can't leave the crowd right now because someone has just thrown a Powerball. The team joins in and tries to stop them from fighting but, at this point, some of them have already gotten hurt.

"This is crazy; calm down!" Rio shouts.

"Of course you would side with them, you're one of them. Angels can't be trusted. Look what they did to that poor Quo girl," someone shouts from the crowd.

"Yeah, they used her up and then went back to their angel family. We won't be used and thrown away any longer!"

All the Quo in the crowd cheer.

"Whoever the Quo girl is, she's a damn home-wrecker and we angels won't stand for it!"

The angels in the crowd cheer, and the madness escalates once again.

"Why are we risking our lives for the winged ones?" a Quo asks.

"We never needed your help!" a pissed off Traveler angel replies.

"Death to the Quo!"

"Death to the winged ones!"

I can't make out who is shouting what. It's a free-for-all.

"Uri probably killed the Quo girl to shut her up!" someone roars from the crowd.

"We *should* have killed her, she's a disease," an Angel shouts back.

"Uri seduced her!" a Quo woman suggests.

Chapter Fifteen: Thomas Case Is Dead

"She's a whore!" an Angel counters.

"She's a victim!" a Quo replies.

"Everyone, stay calm," Miku pleads.

"No, we want to see the Quo girl and make sure she's okay!" a Quo soldier says.

"We don't have her," an Angel shouts.

"Liar!"

"I won't be disrespected by a damn Quo!" an Angel vows.

"Screw you. Where's the girl?" a Quo woman asks.

"The angels killed her!" a Quo nearby responds.

"She was a whore!" the angels counter once again.

"Victim," the Quo insist.

"Whore!"

"Victim!"

"Whore!"

The two sides go back and fourth for several rounds. Suddenly the chaos is interrupted by a piercing whistling sound that cuts through the crowd. It so sharp and painful, it causes everyone to put their hands on their ears.

Mercifully, a few seconds later, the sound stops. We look over at where the noise came from and find Winter standing a few yards away. I guess she is more than a neutralizer. Her power is very effective. Each one falls silent and looks at her. Out of everyone, Rio looks the most concerned by what she's about to say.

"The Quo girl who had the affair with Uri is not dead. She's not a victim and she's not a whore. She is standing right here. And she doesn't owe any of you an explanation."

Winter turns on her heel and walks away.

The crowd falls silent. It takes a few minutes but, eventually, everyone goes back to their duties. I look through the crowd and find the team. Just as Rio runs off after Winter, I get a text from Ameana. I quickly catch up to Rio.

"I have to talk to Winter. The crowd isn't done with her," he yells to me.

"Rage found the Healer, but he needs our help," I reply.

Rio looks torn.

"You can talk to her when we get back," I promise him.

He pauses for a brief moment, then takes to the air with the rest of us.

We meet Rage in the parking lot of a dive bar. He tells us his ex-girlfriend, Elle, is being held captive.

"Who's holding her?" I ask.

"This lower-level demon loser who calls himself 'the Boss,'" Rage replies.

"Why?" Miku asks.

"She lost a major bet and she couldn't pay."

"She sounds charming," Ameana quips.

Rage wisely decides not to get into it with Ameana and to stick with the topic at hand.

"The Boss has her on a contract. The only way she can leave is for him to let her go of his own free will."

"What happens if we rescue her?" Jay asks.

"She dies. Her life is linked to the contract. If it's broken…"

"Yeah, I know all about contracts like that," I reply bitterly.

"What do you want to do, Guardian?" Rage asks.

"Let's go in and see if we can't work something out with the Boss," I say as we head inside.

The bar is far bigger than I thought at first. There's a makeshift boxing ring where Pawns are beating the hell out of each other while demons look on and cheer. Judging from the excitement, there's a lot of money riding on the fight.

Over at the bar, a fat demon with red eyes and a scar across his face studies us. He speaks to the waitress behind the bar and she comes over to us.

"The Boss doesn't allow angels on the premises," she informs us.

Chapter Fifteen: Thomas Case Is Dead

"What about Guardians?" I shout loud enough for the whole bar to hear.

It works—all of the patrons rush out the door, fearing for their lives. The only being left aside from the Boss and his guards is a figure in the corner. She's chained to the floor by the Samson string around her neck. She has long black hair, Goth makeup, and red lips. She looks small and vulnerable but something in her eyes tells me it would be a mistake to underestimate her.

As soon as Elle spots Rage, all her attention goes to him. Ameana glares at Rage's former girlfriend in a way only a current girlfriend can.

"We're here for the Healer," I demand.

"She's mine. I bought her," the Boss says, never once taking his eyes off his TV above the bar.

"We'd like to buy her back," Rio says.

"She's not for sale."

"Name your price," Miku adds.

"I hate repeating myself, Redd."

"It's Miku. If Redd were here, you wouldn't have a tongue to speak with," she says pointedly.

That's when he finally looks at us.

"She's important to us; we need her to heal a human," Rio says carefully.

"I don't care what you need her for," he counters.

"I'm trying not to kill you. It would be great if you helped me with that," I warn him.

"Killing me is the same as killing her. The contract is written that way. You want her, you would have to give me what I want."

"What do you want?" Ameana asks.

"Nothing. My dog and I are happy. Aren't we?" he asks Elle.

She doesn't answer, she just focuses on Rage.

"We'll pay whatever you want for her," Rage replies.

"Go away. I have more than enough money," he gloats.

"Who are you so angry with?" Rio asks.

"What?" the Boss replies, confused.

"You are wishing for someone's death. I can read the violence in your Wave. If it's another demon, we can take care of them for you," Rio replies.

"You make an interesting point. There is someone I would like you to take care of for me. I've been looking for him but have had no luck finding him."

"What did this demon do that you want him dead?" Jay asks.

"He stole from me. I ordered five hundred vials of weeping oil and he switched it with baby oil. He walked away with fifty thousand coats. That's a lot of money. I want him to pay. You find him, kill him, and bring his body here. Then I will release the Healer to you."

"Fine, what's the demon's name?" I ask.

"It's not a demon, it's a Seller—Tony-Tone."

"Why, Tony, why does your name *always* come up?" I bark at him.

It's a half hour later and we're a few miles from the bar. Tony appeared on a Port after I called him on his cell and demanded he meet us.

"I'm a popular guy. I try not to let it go to my head, but you know how it is…," he says proudly.

"Tony, this 'Boss' guy wants you dead!" Jay informs him.

"The guy's always so dramatic. I mean, so I relieved him of a few coats. Big deal," Tony says defensively.

"It is a big deal. He has a Healer we need and he won't let her go until we kill you," Rio replies.

"Oh, that's bad," Tony says to himself.

"It won't be too bad. You're a Seller, you'll just come back, right?" Miku asks.

"Normally, yes. But with the light being destroyed and the council being gone…there's no guarantee. I could end up in limbo like all the souls that have died during these past few months."

"Well, then, you have a problem because if it comes down to choosing between your life and Emmy's…," I reply.

"Okay, okay, but just so we're clear, this isn't my fault. Baby oil for weeping oil? Man, that guy's such an idiot! I wish I could have seen his face when he opened the boxes." Tony laughs so hard, he can't catch his breath.

"I don't think you understand what's happening. If we don't kill you, we can't save Emmy's life. And I'm not sacrificing my girl for a sneaky, lying, cheating Seller!" I tell him honestly.

"You know, Marcus, words hurt," he says as if I've just broken his hear t.

"TONY!" I shout as I grab him by the neck and lift him up in the air with one hand.

"Okay, okay, I have an idea," he says, trying to catch his breath. I put him down.

"Let's hear it," Miku says.

"I'm assuming he has you under contract, right?" Tony asks.

"Yes, and according to the contract, you have to be dead," Rio replies.

"I have the perfect thing. See 'death' is tricky. You have to get specific. If my heart stops, then yeah, I'm dead but that doesn't mean I'm not alive," he brags.

We all look at him, confused.

"You don't get it?" he asks.

"No and we're running out of patience," I warn him.

"I have a mixture here that can stop your heart for five minutes. Then start it back up again. So, I drink the mixture, you show my body to the Boss, and he gives you the Healer. Then, you tell him you're going to discard the body and you take me out of the building; minutes later, I come back to life. Easy, right?"

"Or we could just kill you," Ameana says.

"Mimi, that hurts," Tony says.

"Don't call me that," she warns him.

"She likes me, the 'hostility' thing is just a thing we do," he says to Rag e.

"Okay, you're sure this mixture will make your heart stop for five full minutes?" Miku asks.

"Yup, I'm ready when you are," he says, smiling.

I don't know why I haven't killed Tony. He's helped us in the past but often he's more trouble than he's worth.

He drinks the mixture, his eyes close, and his heartbeat slows down until it stops. Ameana uses her powers to lift him into the air and over to the Boss's bar.

When he sees Tony's body, he's delighted. So much so, he offers us Coy to celebrate.

"Thanks, but we're pressed for time. Release the Healer," I order him.

"Of course," he says, smiling.

He unties the Samson string from around her neck. Elle runs towards us. The Boss looks down at Tony's body, kicks it a few times, and spits into Tony's face.

"We'll get rid of the body for you," I offer.

"That won't be necessary," the Boss says.

"Why?"

"I'm gonna send a message to Sellers who dare try to cheat the Boss. We're gonna Bar-B-Cue Tony-Tone," the Boss relays smugly.

The team and I exchange a quick look of panic as the Boss takes Tony's body out back.

We follow him in hopes of stopping him.

"That's messy; we'll just get rid of him for you," Miku replies.

"It's already been decided. Light 'em up!" the Boss instructs his bodyguard.

One of them goes into the bar and comes back with a gallon of gasoline. He pours it all over Tony. He then flicks open his lighter and throws it directly onto the body. I catch Ameana's eye just in time to signal her.

She waves her hand and redirects the lighter away from Tony. The Boss's guards quickly hurl Powerballs at us. Rage sets half of them on fire. The other half quickly take cover. The Boss takes out his own lighter and throws it at Tony's lifeless body. Ameana is too busy with the other bodyguards to stop the lighter from making contact. Tony is going to be burned alive.

Luckily, Rio throws himself on top of Tony just in time to block the flames with his shield. The two of them are under a sea of flames. Jay Glides over to the Boss and takes him out with a swift blow to the head.

Chapter Fifteen: Thomas Case Is Dead

All the demons have been killed, but the fire on Rio's shield rages on. Elle walks up to the flames and sucks the fire up into her mouth.

"She inhales fire?" Jay asks Rage.

"Yeah, and that's not all," he replies.

We look on as Elle spits the blaze back out a few feet away from us. Rage looks at her with admiration. That is, until he spots Ameana looking at him. He turns away from Elle and acts as if she doesn't exist.

Tony wakes up and smiles brightly.

"See, what did I tell you? No big deal, right?" he says.

I resist the urge to strangle him. Tony asks if Emmy has woken up yet.

"No, but the Healer will help her," I inform him.

"The Healer that's flying away?" Rio asks me.

We look up and, sure enough, Elle has taken to the sky.

"I'm so sick of this," I swear as I take off after her.

Her massive raven-colored wings allow her to skillfully dodge me. I signal to the team; they take to the sky and block her from every direction.

"I don't have to help if I don't want to," she demands.

"We saved your life," I remind her.

"I'll send you a thank-you note, Boy Scout. Right now, I got places to be," she says, looking for an opening to escape.

"We'll give you whatever you want. So long as it doesn't involve harming anyone," I inform her.

"Fine. I want money. Lots of it," she demands.

"I'm sure we can arrange something," I assure her.

She smiles and heads back down to the ground. We land right beside her, fearing she may try and get away again.

"I want more than just money. I want protection the whole time I'm working on the human. If Lucy finds out that I was helping you—"

"We won't let anything happen to you," Rio assures her.

"One last thing; this is the deal breaker. I don't get this and your human dies," she vows.

"What is it, and keep in mind, I'm quickly losing my sense of humor," I warn her.

She looks at Rage as if they are the only two people on Earth.

"Elle, don't," Rage warns her.

"You owe it to me," she spits bitterly at him.

"What is it?" I ask again.

"I want Rage to answer my question. The same question I asked months ago. The same question he's been avoiding," she says, never taking her eyes off of him.

"See, that's what pisses me off about you. You always force me to be the asshole," Rage replies.

"I don't have to force you, 'handcuffs.' Being an asshole is what you do naturally," Elle counters.

"Handcuffs?" Ameana says, addressing her boyfriend.

"It's a long story," Rage responses, avoiding Ameana's eyes.

"You guys want my help, then you better get the *former* First Akon to answer my question."

"What's the question?" Miku asks.

"This is gonna be bad…," Rio says, mostly to himself.

"The question is—"

"Elle, don't," Rage warns her.

"Remember when this mission was just about getting a little map?" Jay quips.

The former couple stare at each other. Ameana watches the exchange carefully.

"Elle, seriously close to killing both you and Rage," I promise her.

"What do you want Rage to tell you?" Jay says, sensing how serious I am about killing them both.

She looks at Rage and speaks as if they were alone. There's pain in her eyes, and her voice shakes slightly.

"Why her and not me?"

It isn't just the question that catches us off guard. It's the tone of Elle's voice. Since meeting her, she has been flippant and snide. But this time, her voice was soft, uncertain…human.

Wow…

Chapter Fifteen: Thomas Case Is Dead

We all turn to Rage. His jaw is clenched and he balls his hands into fists.

"We'll find another way to save the human," he tells us.

"What? No. Just answer the damn question," I order.

"No!" he replies.

"Thomas, we don't have a lot of time. Just tell the bitter little demon what she wants to know," Ameana says.

"C'mon, Rage, stop be'n a punk 'n say something, damn!" Jay swears.

"ANSWER, DAMN IT! WHY HER AND NOT—"

"BECAUSE I DIDN'T LOVE YOU!!!"

The fury in his words causes fireballs to spring up in both his palms. He hurls them angrily towards the surrounding trees. When he speaks again, the anger gives way to brute honesty.

"I tried. I couldn't," he confesses.

"Then, I'm the stupid one because I did, Rage. I loved you," she admits fearlessly.

"Elle, you loved Rage; Ameana loves Thomas," he replies simply.

"I hope I get to be there when your little angel realizes the truth: Thomas is dead. He's been dead for a long time," she says to Rage.

She walks up to Ameana. Their faces are inches apart.

"Sooner, rather than later, Rage's true nature will resurface. And in more ways than one, he'll burn you."

Tony meets us at the hospital with all the items Elle asks for. We head to Emmy's room, where Elle skillfully prepares the mixture.

I remind her that if she messes up in any way, I will have no issue taking her out.

"Relax, Boy Scout, I know what I'm doing. I'm great with my hands. Isn't that right, Rage?" she teases.

I can feel Ameana starting to lose it. I signal to Miku to take her out of the room, but Ameana refuses to budge.

Hours later, the mixture is complete. It's a sticky blue color with flecks of gold in it. Elle explains the process to us as she coats Emmy's chest with the mixture.

"Right now, it's searching for her soul. It should take about an hour or so. Once it finds it, the mixture will glow bright silver. When it latches on, it will change to violet. That means she's on her way back to the living."

After Elle's done, we look on helplessly. An hour passes and the color has not changed. Elle tells me some souls take longer to find than others.

C'mon, this has to work…

We wait another hour. There is no change in color.

I warn Elle that if she somehow did something to Emmy, she'll pay for it.

"I need the money you're giving me. Killing the human doesn't get me anything," she tells me.

"Can she be trusted?" I ask Rage.

Wait, did I just ask the First Akon who I could trust?

"She knows how to heal," Rage assures me.

"What else can she do, 'handcuffs'?" Rio asks, suppressing a smile. Jay and Miku laugh at Rio's comment.

"CAN WE PLEASE FOCUS FOR ONE MINUTE? THIS GIRL IS NOT WAKING UP. SHE'S THE ONLY THING I LOVE, AND SHE IS NOT WAKING UP!"

The room falls silent, instantly.

"C'mon, man, let's take a walk," Jay says.

"No, I'm gonna stay here."

"It's all good, son. We'll just step outside," he assures me.

I follow him down the hallway. When we get to the end, I lean up against it and hang my head.

"She can't die, Jay. She can't…"

"Remember who you're talking about; Emmy is a ride or die chick. She NEVER gives up. She's like the Energizer Bunny on, like, extra crack and CP," he jokes.

"If this doesn't work…"

"This'll work," he says with certainty.

"It has to, because…I'm all out of moves."

Chapter Fifteen: Thomas Case Is Dead

Just as we are about to head back to her room, someone exits the elevator across from us and bashes me in the head. It happens so quickly, neither Jay nor I have time to process it.

I look up and find Julian aiming to hit me again. Jay Glides over to him and stops him.

"What the hell is your problem?" I shout.

"You dirty, selfish piece of Guardian crap!" he roars as he tries to attack me again.

"Julian, be easy," Jay orders.

"Get off me. Your useless, infantile leader almost gets my child killed, yet again. This time she's in a coma and he doesn't even tell me about it. I'm her father!" Julian screams.

"I didn't have time to tell you," I counter.

"That's bull and you know it! You are a plague on Emmy's life, Marcus, and I swear to Omnis I will be the last thing you see before you die."

"You're the one who keeps hurting her, Julian, not me!"

"How many times do you plan on taking my daughter to the edge of death?!"

"Oh, just shut the hell up!"

He leaps on top of me and knocks me to the ground. I can't kill Emmy's father, but I'll be damned if I don't knock him out. I tackle him and pin him down.

"HEY!" someone yells.

We all look up and find Elle looking down on us.

"The color's changed. It's silver. Meaning, it found her soul," she says.

"So, she's gonna be okay?" I ask.

"Like I said before, after silver, it's supposed to change to violet. That means she's getting better. But that's not what's happening. Instead of violet, it's turning gray with dark patches," she replies.

"What does that mean?" Julian asks.

"It means the human doesn't want to come back…"

CHAPTER SIXTEEN:
THE CITY UNDER GLASS

pull up a chair and sit beside her bed. Her face is still completely drained of color and she manages to look frailer than before.

"You came into my life with a Piglet T-shirt, tangled hair, and a wicked stubborn streak. Yet somehow, you made it impossible for me to live without you. I fought my way back from being a Tic so I could be with you, so you better not leave me. Do you hear me, Emerson Hope Baxter? You are not allowed to die."

My cell vibrates. I step away from her bedside to answer it.

"Yeah?...Tony, what is it?...Okay, calm down, we'll be right there." I hang up and go back over to her bed.

"I have to take care of something. I'll be back as soon as I can. Emmy, I'm not gonna give up on you. Ever." I kiss her forehead and make her a promise.

"Emmy, you better wake up or I'm coming after you because our love doesn't stop when our lives end. I'll find you in the light, in darkness, or in Hell itself. I will not be without you."

I look lovingly at her one last time, then head out to the waiting room.

"Tony called; there's something at the shop he wants us to look at," I inform the team.

"What is it?" Miku asks.

"He won't say," I reply.

"What kind of trouble could he have gotten himself in? He just left us a little while ago," Rio says.

"I don't know, but he says it's urgent," I add.

I turn my attention to Elle.

Chapter Sixteen: The City Under Glass

"I'm leaving Emmy with you. Look after her as if your life depends on it, because trust me, it does. Let me know as soon as something changes."

"What if nothing changes?" she asks.

"Emmy can't give up; she doesn't know how," I promise her.

A short while later, we land in an alley off Times Square where Tony has moved his shop. If you don't know it's there, it's easy to miss. It's a small "hole in the wall" type shop, with bad lighting. As soon as we land, Tony lets us in.

"This better be important," Rio snaps.

The team and I exchange a glance. That's when I remember he wanted to talk to Winter and make sure she was okay after admitting she was Uri's mistress.

"This is very important," Tony swears.

"Well, what is it?" Ameana asks.

"I've been working on something to help you guys," Tony replies.

"Working on what?" I ask.

"I've been trying to create a master key. One that could open any and every lock ever made," he informs us.

"That sounds difficult," Miku says.

"It is. There are millions of patterns to copy and mixtures to configure. But I did it! I made a master key. I call it Prim. After the first girl I kissed," Tony says proudly.

"It sounds dangerous, if it falls into the wrong hands," I comment.

"Well…," Tony begins.

"Who did you sell it to?" I ask, not bothering to hold my temper.

"Hey, I wasn't going to sell it," Tony replies.

"So you just made a master key to have a hobby?" Rage says.

"Look, First Akon, the Guardians and I have a long history. They know who I really am in my heart," Tony says, eyeing us.

"We do know. How much were you selling it for?" Rio asks.

"See, I'm hurt," Tony replies.

We all look at him with growing suspicion.

"Okay, half a million, but I was gonna come to you guys first. And I was gonna give your team the Friends and Family discount. That's fifteen percent off."

"You said you *were* gonna sell it. Did something happen to the Prim?" Miku asks.

"Well…kind of."

"Go on," Rio pushes.

"Well, here's the thing…"

I don't know what he's about to say but I have a feeling I'm not gonna like it. And judging from the expression of the faces of the others, I'm not alone.

"Tony, spit it out," Ameana orders.

"A couple of demons and a Pawn broke in here and took it. I came in just as they were leaving."

"The Prim is gone?" Miku says incredulously.

"Yeah."

"How did they even know about it?" I ask.

"The Pawn must have told them," Tony concludes.

"And who told the Pawn?" Ameana snaps.

"That would be me. I told some people at the market. He overheard," Tony confesses.

"Why would you do that?" Rage asks.

"It's not every day a Seller makes a working master key. Prim is my legacy. This is the stuff that makes history. I want credit for my creation."

"Does this mean the Sage has it?" I ask, fearing the reply.

"Yeah, I'm pretty sure he sent them to come and get it."

"What could he do with it?" Rio wonders.

"Every single gate, shield, or lock in the Angel world uses some kind of pattern. So he would be able to unlock just about anything," Tony adds remorsefully.

"So, if he wanted to, he could use the Prim and unlock the shields that protect the entrances of our camp?" Jay asks.

"If he has the Prim, your camp is an open door for him."

"That's great, Tony. Good job," I snap bitterly.

"Hey, I have done some good," he says, sounding very hurt.

Chapter Sixteen: The City Under Glass

"We have to stop the Sage from getting his hands on it," Ameana tells me.

"How do we know he hasn't already?" Rage asks.

"You can ask the Pawn that came in the shop with them," Tony sug gests.

"You know where he is?" Ameana asks.

"That's what I called you over to see. I caught him. The others got away but I caught the Pawn with a Holder," Tony brags.

"Where is he?" I ask.

"He's in the back," Tony replies.

We head towards the back room and find a kid of about sixteen held captive under the bubble-like prison. He has dark eyes and a scar above his right eye.

As we walk into the room, Tony looks up at me and smiles smugly.

"See, helpful," he says proudly.

I shake my head and free the Pawn from the Holder.

"Yeah, you better let me go," he says venomously.

He looks around the room to see if he could somehow escape.

"Does the Sage have the Prim by now?" I ask.

"Screw you!" he says as he spits on the floor.

"Why would the Sage send you? You're just a Pawn," Ameana asks.

"Yeah, that's just like you angel bastards. You look at me and all you see is a lousy human. But things won't be that way for long. Godfather welcomes and loves us all. He didn't send me; I wanted to serve him. I'm not just a Pawn, I'm a Believer."

"You really think the Sage is going to look out for you?" I ask.

"Better than you guys ever did. I overheard Tony-Tone bragging at the market about the master key he created. I told some demons, and the Godfather set this up. I came along so that he knows how dedicated I am."

"You're an idiot; he doesn't care about you," Miku replies.

"Your words have no effect on Believers. We know the truth: we owe everything to Godfather and his version of an angel-free world."

"You're going to tell us what he plans to do with the master key," I instruct him.

"You wish, Guardian," he says confidently.

"Okay…," I reply.

I signal to Ameana and she lifts him into the air and slams him back onto the ground, hard. He cries out as his body hits the floor. I go over to him, look in his eyes, and reflect his fear back to him.

He screams and wiggles around in pain for several seconds. I ask him if he's ready to talk and he says no. I reflect back to him a few more times, but as much pain as the Pawn is in, he refuses to give us any information.

This is why I really hate Pawns: it takes twice as long to get anything out of them because they know we can't take their lives. If I reflect any harder on him, it'll kill him. And while the council is no longer here, killing someone with a soul is still wrong.

Jay Glides over to him and warns him that things are about to get worse. The Pawn just laughs. Jay grabs his left arm and snaps it out of its socket. The cry that comes from the Pawn sounds very much like a wounded animal.

"Are you ready to talk?" I ask.

"Fuck you."

Jay puts more pressure to the already pain-filled arm. The screaming continues. Rage asks Ameana why Jay can't Convince the Pawn to tell us what he knows. She informs him that Jay can't make people give away their secrets.

Finally, I tell Jay to let the Pawn go when he's shaking and bleeding on the ground. I look down at him and ask him why he's willing to suffer for the Sage.

"Godfather promised all of us a better life. All we have to do is get rid of you angels and we can have all the power we want."

"You really think the Sage is going to share his power with you? He's just using you."

"There's a reason for all he does. Believers don't question. We just have faith and we do as he says."

"You guys aren't gonna win. We've already gotten rid of more than half of the Sage's army," Jay reminds him.

"You will never truly be rid of us. Believers aren't all out in the open. We move covertly. You'll never know where Godfather has placed us. We are everywhere. An army of Believers that are determined to eradicate you winged mistakes."

"We can torture you to death. Is that what you want?" I bluff.

He laughs despite the pain.

"You think I became a Pawn yesterday? You can't kill me, Guardian. I have a soul," he says with smug satisfaction.

"You're right. We can't kill you," I reply.

I look over to the back of the room where Rage stands in the shadows.

"But he can," I say, signaling for Rage to come forth.

As soon as he sees Rage's ink-colored wings flap in the air, the Pawn urinates on himself.

"You can't let him…no, that's not fair," the Pawn pleads.

"I'm only going to ask you this once more. Then, I'm gonna let the Akon have some fun," I reply.

The Pawn can't take his eyes away from Rage.

"How is the Sage planning to use the Prim? Is he going to use it to try and unlock the shields that lead into our camp?"

The Pawn tries to talk but no words come out of his mouth. Rage summons up a Powerball in the palm of his hand. It dances dangerously close to the Pawn's face. I signal to Rage that he can kill the Pawn. Rage raises his flame-filled hand high in the air.

"Okay, okay," the Pawn says.

"How is he planning to get into our camp?" Rage shouts.

"H-h-he's n-n-not using the Prim to get in; he's using it to get something out."

"What?" Rage orders him to reply.

"I don't know. I swear," the Pawn cries.

"We need to go back to the field. Winter might know what the Sage is planning," Ameana replies.

"You'll never be able to stop us. Long live Godfath—"

The Pawn never gets to finish the sentence because Rage's Powerball engulfs his face and sets him on fire. In a matter of seconds, the Pawn has been reduced to ash.

"Yo, for real, did you have to kill him?" Jay asks.

"Um…yeah, I kind of did," Rage replies.

"Yo, you sure know how to pick 'em," Jay quips as he walks by Ameana.
"Tony, you're coming with us," I order.
I now see that we have to watch him. Who knows what other kinds
of trouble he can get into. And we may need him to help us keep the Sage
out of our camp.

"Okay, and because this was my fault, you guys get up to twenty percent
off anything in the store," he announces.

"We don't need to buy anything from you, Tony," I remind him.

"Some of you have already," he mumbles. "What?" I ask, not
sure I heard him right. "Nothing, nothing. I'm ready. Let's go."

Once we get back to the battlefield, Rio goes to find Winter and the rest
of us head straight for the command center. There, we find Dalce and his
daughter, in addition to a Quo soldier who's gathering supplies to restock
the infirmary.

"We need to talk," I declare as soon as I see him.

"What is it?" Dalce replies.

"According to a Pawn, the Sage is planning to set something free. Do
you have any idea what it could be?"

"No."

"Look, Dalce, we are too close to winning this thing to drop the ball
now. So if you know something, now is the time," Ameana warns him.
"You have no reason to distrust me."
"Funny, it feels like all I have are reasons," I quip.
Frustrated, I order Tony to the infirmary to help and send others back
to the battlefield. Then I head off in search of Winter. She may know what
the Sage is planning.

I find Winter and Rio sitting on the edge of a cliff together. Judging
from Winter's body language, she's having a hard time.

I want to interrupt them, but I know Rio wanted to get some time
alone with her. And I know all about wanting time with someone and not

being able to get it. I think in the time that I've known Emmy, we've been alone a total of five minutes.

Great, I have to be nice to the guy who tried to kill me. Sometimes I hate this job…

"I have info about the Sage, but it's not much," Winter says, looking out across the mountain range.

"Then, it can wait," Rio replies.

"Does Marcus think so?"

"I don't know what he thinks. I came to check on you."

"Why?" she asks.

"I thought you might need…I don't know."

"I don't need anything, thank you," she says curtly.

"Look, don't listen to what everyone says. Uri is the one who lied; you just fell for him. Then, when you found out he was taken, it was too late. You were already head over heels. It happens."

"Wow, that's a nice little story you've written for me. Do I get the final edit?"

"What do you mean?"

"Your story is fiction, Rio."

"What part?" he wonders.

"The part where I didn't know he was married."

"Oh."

"I'm sorry I couldn't help you find a way to justify my behavior."

"You don't have to be so snippy. I came here to help you," he responds.

"You came here because you needed something to make you feel better about falling for a girl who could commit such a hideous act."

"Wait a minute. Why are you jumping on my case?"

"You came here to make yourself feel better," she challenges.

"That's not true."

"Yes, it is. Well, I can't help you. Because the truth is, the girl you're starting to have feelings for is an awful person."

"Who said I have feelings for you?"

"I don't need powers to see when a guy likes me."

"You're delusional."

"Maybe, but I'm not wrong about this," she maintains.

"Fine, maybe I do have feelings for you. So what?"

"So stop."

"Just like that?" he asks.

"Yes."

"Because you're an awful person?"

"Exactly."

"You think you're the only one who's done stupid, unforgivable things?" he counters.

"What are you saying, Guardian? You've broken up a marriage before?"

"No, but I've done things that were awful," he confesses.

"Like what? Crossed against the light? Had a few too many bottles of Coy?"

"I left my friend alone to die."

She looks at him, shocked.

"That's not true," she concludes, looking into his eyes.

He meets her stare. She can tell he's being serious.

"What happened?" she asks.

He tells her what happened in West Virginia on the bridge.

"Wow…why did you leave him there?" she asks.

"I thought I did it because he took away the girl I loved. Or because I resented him being chosen as leader. But those aren't really the reasons. The real reason I left Marcus to die is far darker…"

"Tell me," she says.

"I can't. Then you'll know."

"Know what?" she wonders.

"How broken I really am."

"Rio, I pursued Uri because of the way he made Angela smile. I wanted that smile. Angela's smile seemed to be almost magical. And I thought if he could make me smile like that, maybe it would be enough to fend off the loneliness."

"Did it?" "The first few times, yes. But when you're with someone's love, you're on borrowed time. I knew he was starting to regret cheating on her; our time was nearly done. But I fought to keep him because he was the only thing that stood between me and the abyss." "Why didn't you get someone else?"

"Somewhere along the way, he became more than a weapon to ward off isolation. I started to love him. He, on the other hand, was with me because he was deathly afraid he'd committed to Angela too soon. But the more time passed, the more certain he was that he only wanted her. So, while he was falling for his wife, I was falling for him."

"How did it end?" Rio asks.

"He started to enjoy the hold he had on me. It was an ego boost, I guess. In a weird way, I think he needed me to need him. We were both playing games. And one day…he stopped playing."

"Are you still lonely?"

"It's better now," she replies.

"Why?"

"Because I don't fight it anymore."

"Winter, the last guy in your life can't be the *last* guy in your life. You should make room for…someone new."

"And who wants to date the broken?"

"I left Marcus to die because I wanted to teach the girl I loved a lesson. I wanted her to grieve, to be inconsolable. I wanted to make her hurt just like she hurt me."

"Wow, you are a horrible person," she confirms.

"I regretted my actions instantly, but I did it, so I guess we're both… broken," he says miserably.

"I guess so," she says, smiling warmly.

A few moments later, Winter turns to Rio and speaks with a forced casual tone.

"So, you still feel something for this girl?"

"No, not anymore."

"Oh."

"What about you and Uri?" he asks.

"No, it's…over."

"Oh, that's good."

They exchange a heated gaze.

Finding out why Rio left me on the bridge didn't have the effect I thought it would. Instead of being pissed, I'm actually feeling sorry for him. I didn't think he loved Ameana to that extent. When Emmy was with Lucas, it was brief but I planned many ways to kill him in my head. They were all painful and very un-angel like.

Yes, but I didn't actually do it. Rio actually left me on the bridge to die…

No matter what I feel about the situation with Rio, once again, we don't have time to get into it. I interrupt the two and we head back to the command center, where Dalce and Bianca are waiting. I summon the rest of the team from the battle lines.

Miku comes in, soaked in blood, wearing a goofy smile. I'm guessing she really enjoyed her last kill. Jay looks worn out, but he assures me that he's fine. Ameana doesn't have a hair out of place, although I'm sure she's been fighting. Rage watches protectively over her. I call Elle to check on Emmy before we start; there is no change.

C'mon, baby, please wake up…

I force myself to keep it together and stay focused. We ask Winter for an update.

"I really don't have a lot, I'm sorry to say. Sage continues to act strangely. Like I said before, it's like he knows something we don't. Something that will somehow swing things back in his favor."

"Winter, we need more. He sent demons to go to Tony-Tone's shop to get Prim, a master key that can open any gate or lock. A Pawn told us he wanted to set something free. Do you have any idea what that thing is?" I ask.

"No, but last night he did send his best demons on an errand. I couldn't follow without being noticed. But I was able to hear some of their conversation. He's sent them to the Black Sea."

"What? Are you sure?" Dalce asks, clearly frightened.

"Yeah, I'm positive."

"What is it?" I ask.

"No, no, no, Sage is not crazy. He wouldn't do it. He just wouldn't do it," Dalce says, muttering to himself as he paces back and forth.

"He wouldn't do what?" Ameana asks.

"No, no, no… It can't be. It just can't." Dalce continues to mutter.

"Daddy, is the Sage going to set them free?" Bianca asks, terrified.

"No, he's not crazy," Dalce replies.

"Yes, he is. He wants all the power he can get and he will do anything to get it. Now, what is going on?" Jay demands.

"The only thing in the Black Sea that's of any importance is the City of Tess," Dalce replies, once again going into his own thoughts.

"Hey! What's so special about the City of Tess?" I bark.

"It's a city we built, but kept under glass. You can't see it unless you know it's there. But it is. And is holds them prisoner."

"It holds who prisoner?"

"The Goumy."

As soon as the words come out of Dalce's mouth, Rage turns to me with an emotion I've never seen on his face: fear.

"Wait, the what?" I ask.

"It's pronounced 'Goo-My.'"

"Okay, and who or what are they?" I push.

"They're a group of Quo that were so evil, they were sent directly to Lucy," Dalce replies.

"And?"

"And she sent them back," Rage says, looking at Ameana with grave concern.

"Why?" Miku asks.

"She was afraid of them."

CHAPTER SEVENTEEN: EVIL THAT EVIL FEARS

"**Y**OU DIDN'T THINK WE NEEDED TO KNOW ABOUT THE GOUMY?" I shout angrily at Dalce.

"Sage won't do that. He knows he can't control them; no one can," Dalce counters.

"Everyone, just calm down," Rio says.

"You calm down, rainbow boy. I'm taking my girl and we're leaving," Rage says as he takes Ameana's hand.

"Thomas, stop," she replies.

"Ameana, we can't fight the Goumy. That's why, cycles ago, both good and evil got together to imprison them. They are an aberration: evil that evil fears," he pleads.

"Yes, but we can't just leave. We have to do something."

"No, we don't. Maybe a few angels and demons will survive this. But as for humanity, they are done."

"'I won't let that happen," she replies.

"You're gonna risk your life for the humans? You're not tired of doing that yet?" he snaps.

"Are you tired of protecting me?"

He's taken off guard by the question. She presses the issue by repeating it.

"No," he says softly.

"That thing that keeps you wanting to protect me is the same thing that keeps us on this mission. Thomas, we have to help," she begs him.

"Great, we're gonna die. Again," he says, shaking his head.

"Tell us everything we need to know about the Goumy, and don't leave anything out," I order.

Chapter Seventeen: Evil That Evil Fears

"There are forty of them. And, individually, they have exceptional powers. But a few cycles ago, they banded together. And what was once a few powerful beings, became a gang of gods."

"How powerful are they?" the twins ask.

"They were responsible for the Yellow River flood in China, 1931. It killed four million people. They also caused the Chilean earthquake in Valdivia. It was the most powerful earthquake in recorded history. Then, there's the mega tsunami in Lituaya Bay in 1958. The Goumy moved ninety million tons of rock and glacial ice in the water. It caused the biggest wave in the history of humanity."

"The Goumy did all that? Why?" Rio asks.

"Because they could," Dalce replies.

"How were you guys able to get them inside the City of Tess in the first place?" Ameana asks.

"It was a massive undertaking. It required the power of both good and evil. It was the first and only time in history that Omnis and Lucy worked together. You have to understand, like Rage said, the Goumy are an aberration. Something neither side planned for."

"You were pissed the council locked you up in Adam City. Then you go and lock up your own kind?" Miku asks.

"You don't understand the kind of power they wield. Yes, technically, they are Quo. But there is a major difference between us and them. When we use our powers, a few people could get hurt. But when the Goumy use their powers…let's just say, humanity remembers," Dalce replies.

"How come we don't know about this?" Jay asks.

"Humans call it the wrath of Mother Nature; they just don't know that Mother Nature is really forty pissed-off Quo," Bianca replies.

"But, there has to be another reason for the Sage to send demons to the Black Sea, because there's no way he could unlock the City of Tess. There are measures in place to prevent it."

"Measures, such as?"

"The City of Tess is locked by more than just a 'traditional' pattern lock. Good and evil also placed a Three Condition lock at the gate. That means, three events have to take place in the world before the lock can be opened. Master key or not," Dalce informs us.

"What are the three events?" Ameana asks before I can.

"We Quo feared, one day, the council would just do away with us. So in order to protect ourselves from extinction, we wrote the first condition: the Goumy could break free if twenty-five percent of our population died at the same time."

"Dalce, we killed more than twenty-five percent of the Believers at the start of this war," I remind him.

"He did it on purpose. The Sage wanted us to take out a large portion of his army so that one of the three conditions could be met," Ameana concludes.

"She's right. He knew we were setting a trap for his army, and he let them walk right into it," Jay adds.

"That would explain why he didn't send his best demons to the front," Winter confirms.

"Damn it!" I shout.

"Calm down, Marcus; there are two other conditions that have to be in place for the city to open."

"Well, c'mon, old man, what are they?" Rage asks.

"Whoever leads the most Quo would have to be killed. And since that's me, you can rest easy," Dalce replies.

"I guess. What's the final condition?" I ask.

"There has to be a powerful Para there to place her hand on the lock. The Sage will have a hard time finding a high-ranking Para, because all of them are here in this camp," Dalce replies.

"Not all of them," someone says from the entryway.

We turn towards the person who just spoke and find Arden looking very scared. Her eyes are wide with apprehension.

"Arden, what's wrong?" Ameana asks.

I understand Ameana's concern. We've never seen the party girl look so serious. The sadness in her eyes looks out of place with her normal fun demeanor.

"The Sage has my sister. He has Rahell, Marcus!" Arden says frantically.

"How did that happen?" Ameana asks.

"She was helping some injured Paras get to one of our hideouts when demons ambushed them. They took her."

Chapter Seventeen: Evil That Evil Fears

"It fits. Arden and Rahell are the daughters of an Original Para," Rio replies.

"Yes, Rahell is ranking high enough to fit the second condition," says Dalce, growing more concerned.

"Dalce, we're gonna have to hide you," I order.

"No, I'm fine right here."

"The Pawn said we don't know who is and isn't a Believer. You're the only thing that stands between us and the Goumy," I remind him.

"Rio can read everyone's Wave and tell us who is and who isn't a Believer," Dalce suggests.

"The Waves will only tell me if they are hiding things, and I get the feeling that everyone here, Believer or not, is hiding something. That doesn't make them a Believer," Rio replies.

"We need to move you to a safer location," Ameana says.

"They're right, Daddy. You need to be careful," Bianca responds, concer ned.

"Wait a minute, why does the condition call for your death?" I ask.

"Although the Goumy are evil incarnate, they are still Quo. If thousands of Quo are killed and the leader is killed as well, that means our existence is in danger. That's when the Goumy can be set free."

"Set free to protect the Quo?" Miku asks.

"Ideally, but the truth is, they can't be controlled," Dalce replies.

"So, how does the Sage plan to control them?" Ameana asks Dalce.

"I don't think he—" Dalce's voice dies midsentence.

His face is twisted in horror. We look down and find a knife protruding from his stomach. The person holding the knife is the Foundation soldier who was taking supplies to the infirmary.

"Long live Godfather!" he roars.

He lifts the knife high above his head and lunges at us. I tackle him before he can strike and break his neck. I look down at the soldier's twisted corpse and make an announcement.

"He's dead."

"So is Dalce," Rio replies.

Bianca rushes over to her father. She calls out his name. She places her hand in the center of Dalce's chest where the wound is, as if she could somehow take it away.

"Daddy, no, no!" She sobs deeply and won't let any of us touch him.

"Bianca, I'm so sorry," I say, kneeling beside her.

Her cries send chills down my spine. Her body shakes uncontrollably as she looks into her father's lifeless face.

I pick her up from the floor. She's shaking so much in my arms I have to hold her tighter to stop her from slipping from my grip.

"Get the team ready, we need to go to the Black Sea. And make sure no one knows about Dalce yet," I tell Ameana.

"Marcus, you have to find Rahell, please," Arden begs.

"We'll get Rahell back, don't worry. Go get Wolf and tell him what's happened," I instruct Arden.

She looks like she wants to say something, but I assure her once again we will bring her sister back. She takes off to find Wolf.

"I'm sorry I couldn't read that was going to happen," Rio replies.

"Even if you could read who was and wasn't a Believer, with Winter here, it's not possible," I remind him.

"Marcus, we can't let that maniac set the Goumy free. It's the one thing both good and evil agree on," Rage says.

"I know. I'll take Bianca back to her room. Then, we head to the City of Tess."

Miku grabs two blankets from the supplies in the corner. She hands her brother one to cover Dalce and she drapes the other around Bianca. I take her to her room, careful not to be spotted by the soldiers.

Once inside her makeshift room, I place her on the edge of the bed. She's still shaking. Her hands are soaked in her father's blood and tears run silently down her face. I get a towel and try to remove the blood from her hands.

"Bianca, can you look at me?" I ask.

She can't. She's frozen somehow. It's like she's not sure where she is or what really just happened.

"Bianca, everything is going to be fine. Do you hear me?"

She looks down as if she sees me for the first time. She nods.

"Okay, I have to go, but I'm gonna send someone to look after you, okay?"

She looks back at me, and once again she looks lost in some void of some kind.

"I know it's a shock and everything is crazy right now, but you can't zone out. You have to stay with us. There's a chance there are more Believers among us, so you have to stay alert."

She has no idea what I just said. She's in her own world. I go over to the jug and pour her some water. She can't hold the glass, so I put the cup to her lips. She takes a few sips then pulls back.

"Bianca, your father would want you to be strong. He loved you and he raised you to lead. I know that because he made sure you were in the position to take charge. So take charge now. Don't fall into this abyss, because you need to stay focused."

She nods. I think, finally, she's back to her senses. Relieved, I have her lie down on the cot. I cover her with the blanket and tell her to close her eyes. I know she won't sleep but at least she can get some rest.

"I'll be back soon," I say as I squeeze her hand and exit.

I head back to the command center, where the team is ready to go. Arden wants to come along but I convince her to stay behind. If the Sage has tortured Rahell or killed her, it wouldn't help Arden to see it in person. I also don't know what her fighting skills are like. Although she is powerful, she spends more time drinking Coy and dancing than battling. She could be more of a liability than anything.

Before we go, I give Wolf last-minute instructions for the army.

"The most important thing is that they don't know Dalce is gone," I remind him.

"Death is a part of life, but I see where you're coming from," he replies.

"Also, I need Winter to head back to the Sage's camp and see what else she can find."

"Wait, she'll be in danger," Rio objects.

"That's part of the job," she reminds him.

The others look on suspiciously.

"I think you should stay here and help out. What if you go back and they find you out?" Rio insists.

"I've been doing this for a long time. I can handle it," Winter assures him.

"No, you're not going!" he orders her. We all turn to him. It's so unlike Rio to have an outburst. "Sorry, I just think she should stay," he tells us.

"Do you want to stay here?" I ask Winter.

"No, I want to go do my job," she says, glaring at Rio.

"Then go, report back as soon as you know something," I reply.

"Winter, can I talk to you for a second?" Rio asks impatiently.

"I guess," she replies, uncertain.

Jay looks over at me and I shrug my shoulders.

I'm not sure what the point of them speaking alone was because things get loud enough for us all to hear.

"You can't tell me what to do," Winter informs Rio.

"You're putting your life in danger."

"So are you," she reminds him.

"That's different," he replies.

"Why, because I'm a girl? Argh! I should have known you'd be sexist. All of you are. Uri was the same way."

"Hey, stop comparing me to him," he warns her.

"Well, stop acting like him," she says.

"I just want to make sure that you are okay. What's so wrong with that?"

"What's wrong is if I were a guy, you wouldn't think twice about me going. Well, I'll have you know that women can do anything you guys can," she says, getting upset.

"This isn't a war of the sexes. It's serious."

"Rio, I know that. But I'm good at my job and I'm not gonna stop doing it, so get over it."

"I have enough people in my life I have to worry about. I don't need another," Rio cautions her.

"So, what are you saying?" she asks.

Chapter Seventeen: Evil That Evil Fears

"I'm saying stay here."

"If you think I'm the kind of girl you can give orders to, then you really are useless without your powers," she replies.

"I just…I'm trying to look out for you," he whispers.

"Okay. But if I stay here then you have to stay too," she demands.

"What? I can't do that."

"Why?"

"Because I'm a Guardian, it's my job,"

"And what do you think this is for me? A hobby?" she replies.

"Fine, then go. But you're being impossible. I don't know why you—"

She kisses him with the intensity of a girl who's fallen helplessly in love. When it's over, Rio is speechless.

"Yo, son! It's go'n *down!*" Jay says, enjoying the scene before him.

When Winter is done kissing Rio, she looks over at me.

"Keep him safe, Guardian. I'm not done with him yet," she says as she gets on her Port and disappears.

"Yo, that chick is my favorite Quo right now!" Jay announces.

"What the hell was that about?" Miku asks her twin.

Rio says nothing and avoids her eyes. But he doesn't really need to say anything. His goofy crooked smile tells us everything.

"I think they're…cute together," Ameana says approvingly.

"Mood Ring found love and just a few hours before the world ends. He's got great timing," Rage says sardonically.

Ameana taps me on the shoulder as we're about to take off.

A few yards away from us, Bianca stands looking dazed and confused.

"Go, I'll catch up," I order them.

"No, we leave as a team. Well, a team and that guy," Jay says, referring to Rage.

I run over to Bianca.

"You're supposed to be resting, Bianca. What are you doing out here?" I ask her.

"I'm looking for my father; I haven't seen him all day."

CHAPTER EIGHTEEN:
I HAVE SEEN IT

"We can't leave her like this," Miku says, looking at Bianca.

"I thought you didn't trust her?" Ameana says.

"Yeah, she's a grade A bitch, but she just lost her father and she needs help."

"Miku's right. Jay, can you come with me?" I ask. He follows me as I take Bianca back to her room.

"I have to go see my father," she tells us.

"I saw him a few minutes ago, and he said he'll speak with you later," I reply.

"Oh, okay."

Jay and I exchange a worried look. I have Bianca sit down on the cot.

"Jay, I need you to Convince her."

"Sure, what do want me to say?" he asks.

"Convince her that everything is okay and that she should rest."

"I can get her to rest, but Convincing her that she's not grieving is tricky. It's in her subconscious, Marcus. Sooner or later, it will come out," he warns me.

"I know that. But right now, she needs to rest. When we come back, we can find a better way to deal with things."

"Alright, I got you," he replies.

He goes over to Bianca and whispers softly in her ear.

As Jay works his powers on her, I step outside, where Tony rushes to address me.

"What do you want?" I ask curtly.

"I know you're still upset with me," Tony replies.

"You think?" I snap.

"I want to make it up to you."

"How?"

"Well, there are a few things Dalce didn't get to tell you before he died. I thought I would fill you in."

"I'm listening."

"The Goumy have been to the House of Fire before. That journey completely destroyed their bodies."

"They have no bodies?"

"No, it's like Difi stripped them of it. They are no more than spirits. They float wrathfully in the air, leaving no trail. When you go to Tess, you will see what looks like a series of dark twisters whipping through the town."

"That's the Goumy?"

"Yes; dark, uncontrollable spirits that destroy everything in their paths."

"Okay, got it. What else?"

"The lock is about fifty inches on all sides. It's got a pattern embedded in it. The Prim is a silvery flat layer that looks like a screen protector. Once the Prim and the pattern on the lock are perfectly aligned, the Prim will start to configure."

"How will we know if it configures?"

"It will glow. And since the other two conditions have been met, the only thing left after the Prim is configured is Rahell's handprint. You can't let Rahell's hand get on that lock, Marcus," Tony warns.

He's about to give me more information, but we are interrupted by a text from, of all people, the Sage.

I gather the team and read it to them.

"If you don't interfere with my plans,
I will spare your team. Onetime offer."

"Wow, he has really lost it," Miku says.

"Write him back and tell him to go screw himself," Rio says.

"Wait, why don't we make a deal?" Rage asks.

"What about the millions of people who stand to die?" I ask.

"How is that our problem?" Rage replies.

"The fact that you need to ask that is why she deserves someone better," Wolf says as he walks towards us.

Wolf offers to come with us, but I tell him we need him here in the field.

"What do we say to Sage?" Miku asks.

I text him back and ask him how he plans on controlling the Goumy. He replies shortly.

"Control? No. Want to unleash the Goumy.
Kill all humans & angels.
Start over."

I text him back that we're not interested in a deal. Just then, Jay comes out of Bianca's room and says she's sleeping. We fill him in on the latest from Sag e.

"What did he say after you turned him down?" Jay asks.

As if to respond to Jay, I get one last text from the Sage.

"You will fail. I have seen it.
They all die."

Tess, the city on the coast of the Black Sea, is a city like any other. It's filled with skyscrapers, parks, and homes. But Tess does have two things that separate it from any other place. First, it's covered by a glass dome, making it impossible to get in or out. And second, it looks like a slew of mini tornadoes are surrounding the city. But, as we now know, the "tornadoes" are really the Goumy.

We scout the location before we go charging in. We find the demons hovering over the glass dome. Although the Sage sent only six of them, I'm sure what the demons lack in numbers they make up for in powers.

There are a set of triplets that scan the air, making sure there are no angels near. The other three demons are camped at the base of the glass dome. A redheaded girl with expansive black wings has Rahell tied up with Samson string.

The last two demons work on opening the lock that holds the Goumy prisoner. The lock is exactly like Tony said it would be. The blond demon tries to place the Prim over the lock, but he's having trouble aligning it. The last demon, a tall bald guy, goes over to help him.

"Remember what Tony said. Once they align the Prim and place it over the lock, it will configure. Then the only chance we have to stop the glass from breaking is to stop them from placing Rahell's hand on the lock," I remind them.

"All we have to do is secure Rahell," Ameana replies.

"Yes, but we also want to get the Prim back. If we leave it with them—"

"It's only a matter of time before they hunt down another Para and try to free the Goumy again," Jay finishes.

"Exactly; Jay and Miku, take the triplets. Ameana and Rio, get Rahell back from the redhead. Rage and I will go after the Prim," I order.

Everyone agrees and takes to the air. Jay Glides over to the triplets. He captures one of the three brothers in a choke hold. The other two quickly come to their brother's rescue, but Miku is close enough to them to start singing. Soon, wailing and crying hit the air as the triplets begin to rip apart their own flesh.

Although they are in serious pain, somehow the triplets manage to make contact with each other. The minute they do, a massive power surge emanates from them. The surge turns into a lasso and quickly snares both Miku and Jay by the neck.

The triplets manipulate the lasso so that it now spins the two angels around at inhuman speeds. They then fling them across the sky. The force with which Jay and Miku are being thrown makes them look more like comets than angels.

I call out for Ameana to redirect them towards a safer landing, but Ameana is in no shape to help. She and Rio are being drained of their power by the redhead. She opens both of her palms, and my teammates' powers funnel into her palms. Rio doesn't even have enough strength to put up his shield.

"Rage, can you get Ameana? I'll get Jay and Miku."

"Got it," he replies as he swoops over to his girl and Rio.

Meanwhile, Miku and Jay are about to hit the side of the mountain at a speed that will definitely end their lives. I cut through the air and make it just in time to place myself between them and the mountain. While they still crash, I'm able to slow them down so their crash isn't fatal.

"Are you okay?" I ask.

"I'm alright; Jay?" Miku asks.

"All good, baby. Let's do this!" Jay replies.

They fly back towards the triplets, more determined than ever to take them down.

I look over and find Rage hurling Powerballs at the redhead. She tries to counterattack and drain Rage of his power, but she's having a hard time getting a clear shot.

Rio takes advantage of the distraction Rage has caused. He uses his shield and covers Rahell so that she doesn't get hurt in the cross fire. Ameana sends the redhead flying into the dome. She bangs her head on the way down, leaving smears of blood on the glass.

"I got this, go help Marcus. Don't let them configure the Prim," Ameana tells Rage.

He flies over to me. Together, we head for the lock at the base of the dome. There, we find the two demons trying to align the Prim with the lock. As soon as they see us, they stop what they're doing and charge towards us.

"I'll take baldy. You take the blond guy," I tell Rage.

"Got it."

The bald demon comes after me with great fury. He wields a machete with red trim that glows. I'm not sure what the machete is laced with, but I know it's probably a bad idea to come in contact with it.

"I'm just gonna cut off all your limbs and then I'll feed them to my Fire Swans," he says, his voice dripping with hate.

"I'm right here," I challenge him.

He lunges at me wildly. I manage to dodge him but, I have to admit, his speed is impressive. The machete cuts through the air with the precision of a samurai sword. It's as if the demon and the machete are one.

Chapter Eighteen: I Have Seen It

This is going to be harder than I thought. I can't get close enough to him to tackle him or reflect his fear back to him.

A few yards away, Rage has his hands full with the blond demon. He curses at Rage and calls him a traitor. Then he summons up a red Powerball unlike any we've seen before. Rage goes to hurl a fireball at him, but it's too late. The red Powerball coils around him like a snake and starts to electrocute him.

The volts are so powerful I can smell Rage's wings burning from here. The bald demon is on my tail with the machete, making it impossible to help Rage. I hear him cry out as the Powerball continues to sear into his flesh. Judging by the volts zapping through Rage, he only has a few minutes to live.

For a quick second, I wonder if Rage dying is such a bad thing. He is a demon, after all. But then I think about Ameana. For whatever reason, she's truly in love with him and if he died, she would be inconsolable. I can't let her go through that. And I also refuse to let the blond demon kill anyone I came with; team member or not.

The blond demon is too busy with Rage to pay attention to me or the bald demon chasing me. That's what I'm counting on. I tackle him to the ground. The bald demon, not giving a damn what happens to his teammate, sends the machete slicing through the air, although it could hurt both me and his demon pal.

I flip the blond demon over at the last second and use him as a shield. It works. The machete slices clean through the blond demon's back. His flesh slides off the edge of the blade like slimy meat.

Realizing he's outnumbered, the bald demon rushes back to the lock to align the Prim. I go to stop him but then I hear Rage call out. Although the demon that made the red Powerball is dead, the "red snake" Powerball is still alive and killing him.

I run over to intercept the snake, but there is no way to get it off of Rage. There is no way to do it without touching it. I reach out towards the red coiled "snake" and hope I am strong enough to get it off before it kills us both.

"Hang on," I shout.

I place my hands around the red Powerball's "snake." The second I make contact with it, I jerk out of control. The volts travel through my body, scorching my insides like a marshmallow on an open flame. My teeth feel like they're on fire, and I can practically hear my blood boil.

"You're crazy. It's gonna kill you, Guardian," Rage warns.

"Shut up!"

I use every ounce of strength I have to uncoil the Powerball from Rage's body. I summon up as much will as I can not to let go of the very thing that is trying to kill me.

Finally, I am able to uncoil the "snake" from around Rage's body; I hurl the Powerball away and sink into the ground, too weak to move.

I force myself to turn my head slightly and check on Rage. That's when I see him getting ready to launch a fireball straight at me.

Rage is going to kill me…

"What the—"

I don't get to finish my sentence because Rage throws his fireball directly at me. Or so I thought. The fireball goes flying past me and lands in the center of the bald demon's chest. He would have sliced me in two with his machete, if not for the Akon.

"Ah…thanks," I mutter, not sure what else to say.

Rage shrugs. He's just as uncomfortable with this as I am; maybe even more so.

With no time to waste, I run over to the gate and find the Prim has not only been put in place but it's glowing, meaning it's been configured.

"Damn it! All they need now is Rahell," I rage.

"Never gonna happen," Jay says confidently as he flies down with Rahell in his arms.

"You got her?" I ask in disbelief.

"We switched off. Miku and I took care of the redhead. We tortured her until she agreed to untie Rahell. Then Miku sang an oldie but goodie," Jay replies.

"Yup, and what's left of her is spread all over the mountain," Miku says proudly.

"What about the triplets?" Rage asks.

"Rio and I took care of them. Once he blocked their lasso thingy with his shield, the rest was easy. Or 'cake,' as Jay would say," Ameana replies.

She flies down with Rio by her side. I go over to inspect Rahell.

"Are you okay?" I ask.

"Yeah, just a little shaken, but I'm fine. Thank you for such a timely rescue," she says, hugging me.

"It's okay. We were long overdue for some good news," I reply as I embrace her in return.

"Marcus, you really should have taken my deal," a voice says coldly.

We turn and find the Sage midair, on his Port. Without warning, he swoops down and grabs the machete lying beside the dead demon. He then whizzes by Rahell and heads for the lock.

It happens so quick we don't notice anything is wrong until Rahell cries out in pure anguish. That's when we look and realize her right hand is missing.

The team goes to help Rahell, and I bolt over towards the Sage just in time to watch him place Rahell's severed hand on the lock.

"NO!" I roar.

But it's too late. The glass begins to crack. The shadows seep out from the city under glass. We have failed. The Goumy are out. The end isn't coming; it's here.

"Marcus," Rage calls out to me. I don't answer.

"MARCUS!" Rage shouts.

"WHAT?"

"Elle texted me; the human is awake."

BOOK 2:
EMERSON BAXTER

"Compromise is but the sacrifice of one right or good in the hope of retaining another - too often ending in the loss of both."

—Tryon Edwards

(Submitted by contest winner, Sheila Roth)

CHAPTER NINETEEN:
COMA GIRLS

The first thing I s

"Elle can't kill you; she's on our payroll."

I turn my head and find Marcus standing at the door. He's the most beautiful thing I've seen in a long time. He tells the demon to wait outside and that he'll take care of her payment in a moment. She leaves the two of us alone. Marcus moves so quickly, I don't even see him approaching the bed. All I know is one minute he was at the doorway and the next I'm wrapped in his arms.

"It's a good thing I'm in the hospital; you're holding me so tight, I may need a doctor," I warn him.

He doesn't care. He continues to embrace me tightly. I can feel the relief and joy in his touch. And long after he's supposed to let go, he's still holding on.

"You're gonna have to release me at some point, First Guardian," I inform him gently.

"No," he says stubbornly.

And true to his word, he holds me longer still. When he finally does release me, he won't let me out of his reach.

"What is it?" I ask.

"I just want to look at you," he says, studying me.

"Why? I'm a mess, right?"

"You're perfect. The mixture allowed your hair to grow back, you have color in your cheeks, and your eyes are still stunning."

He holds me once again and swears he'll never forgive me if I die. I promise to do my best.

"The team wanted to see you, but I had to send them to the battlefield."

"It's okay, I understand."

"How are you? I mean, do you feel a hundred percent or do you need to rest? Should I come back?" he asks, fussing over me.

"No, I feel great and I've rested enough. How's Ty?" He flinches slightly at the mention of the boy's name. "He didn't make it," Marcus says with his head down. "I'm sorry," I reply, placing a hand on his shoulder. "Don't worry about that for now. We need to get you new clothes and

something to eat."

"How's the mission?" I ask.

He avoids my eyes.

"Jay says as soon as he can he will cook for you again. And Miku said something about going on a shop-athon."

"Marcus…"

"Also, Rio has a girl. Well, it's not official but she's really—"

"Marcus Cane, talk to me."

He sighs heavily, runs his hands through his hair, and plops down on the bed.

"We won the battle but we're gonna lose the war," he replies with deep reg ret.

I sit down next to him, take his hand, and make him tell me what I missed. After he's done, I try to make all the pieces fit in my head.

"So, the Goumy even scare evil Lucy?"

"Yes, and now they're out in the world."

"Yes, but maybe they're not as horrific as Dalce made them out to be.

I mean, since I've been awake, everything has been normal. Maybe their powers were weakened after all that time under glass."

"No, they weren't," he replies.

He takes the remote on the side of my bed and turns on the TV.

Every station is reporting the same thing: random unexpected

hurricanes, floods, and tornadoes in Southeast Asia. Thousands of people are injured and hundreds are dead. The meteorologists are baffled by the sudden bad change in weather patterns.

One of the TV anchors said, "It's as if Mother Nature wants us off her planet."

"That's not far from the truth," Marcus replies miserably.

"You can't catch them?"

"It's like trying to hold on to a shadow."

"So, what's being done, right now?" I wonder.

"The team is in Southeast Asia, trying to help the survivors. Some of the Foundation soldiers are there as well. It's actually a brilliant plan the Sage had. In order to keep the death toll for the humans as low as possible, I've had to send most of the army to help them. So now, we're losing on the battlefield because we just don't have enough soldiers."

"Do they know about Dalce yet?" I ask.

"No, but sooner or later, they'll start asking questions."

"Why is the Sage killing humans? I thought he wanted us as followers?" I ask.

"He does, but he's willing to kill a billion or so humans and start over."

"How long before they come around here?"

"At this rate, it shouldn't be long. And if by some miracle we were to defeat them, we'd still be out of the time to find the Shoma. So, we're out of luck on both fronts."

I've never seen Marcus so down before. The weight he's carrying shows itself in his shoulders and the furrow of his brow. His wings are practically dragging on the floor. He keeps massaging his neck, as if that will somehow make all the bad things go away.

"I'm sorry this is what you woke up to," he says.

"Me too."

"I guess it's no wonder you didn't want to wake up," he replies, almost to himself.

"What do you mean?"

He tells me what Elle said to him when the mixture turned black and gray.

"I get it, Em, believe me, I do. Who would come back to this?" he asks.

"Me."

"Why did you?"

"I can't say for sure. It's not like I knew what was going on. I was in complete nothingness. But then there were times when I swear I could hear you urging me to wake up."

"I was pretty insistent. But so was your dad."

"Julian was here?" I ask.

"According to Elle, once he learned you were here, he never left your side. He only went away when you started to wake up. He was there for you; unlike me."

"It's not like you went to a frat party. You were trying to stop the Goumy."

"Yes, and I failed. So we have to get you and your family somewhere safe."

"Marcus, they're coming for us all, there is nowhere safe."

"I know, but I have to do something. I can't just let you…"

His words drifted away, and it at that moment I saw just how tired my Guardian had become.

"Mr. Cane, I need you to do something for me," I say, smiling.

"Anything," he vows.

"Come sleep with me."

"Wow, that's the best offer I've had all day, but Bianca still has my Rah. I don't have any Trickk, and you should rest."

"No, I don't mean it like that. I want you to lie down with me."

"The world is ending and you want me to take a nap with you?"

"Yes."

"Why?"

"You don't get to ask why. I'm the 'coma' girl and coma girls get what they want," I inform him.

"Emmy, we have to start clearing out most of the cities and give the humans as much of a chance for survival as we can."

"The team is already working on it, right?"

"Yeah, but—"

"But nothing. Baby, do this for me," I ask softly.

He gently pulls me into him and we lie down on the bed. He lies behind me and places his arms protectively around my waist.

Chapter Nineteen: Coma Girls

I have no desire to nap. In fact, I can't wait to get the hell out of this bed. But I can tell Marcus hasn't Recharged in days. His eyes are worn, his voice is weak, and the natural glow he normally has is fading. First Guardian or not, he needs to Recharge. And knowing him, this is the only way I can guarantee he'll do just that.

"We can't stay like this for too long," he warns me.

"Just a few minutes."

"The whole time you were in a coma, I would have given anything to know what you were thinking," he whispers to me.

"How much I love you," I reply.

"That's all?" he asks.

"That's all."

We stay quiet for a few minutes. Then I slowly turn to face him and am relieved to see my plan worked. He is Recharging. His eyes are closed and he lies perfectly still. His face looks at peace. I whisper his name and he doesn't open his eyes. I hope he can get an hour or two of Recharging. That seems to be enough to get angels back on their feet.

I know the world is in trouble, but he needs to Recharge, and it's my job to make sure that he does. I mean, after all, I am his fiancée.

Well, technically, I'm his mistress.

How did that even happen? How can I, Emerson Hope Baxter, be someone's mistress? Mistresses wear red stilettos and expensive perfume and live in luxury homes paid for by their lovers. All I have are my running shoes, my Kindle Fire, and Ms. Charlotte.

How did I get to be Marcus's mistress? I haven't lost my memory or anything. I remember the events that have led me here, but it's still hard to take in.

I close my eyes and the major events of the last month flash in my head. I relive them as if they are happening right before me.

It's a few weeks earlier and I'm standing in front of Marcus after Dalce dropped the bomb about marrying Bianca. We're alone in the room and Marcus tells me he won't marry her because he loves me. I tell him that he has no choice. And after a while, he agrees with me. Although he is doing exactly what I tell him to do, I want to slap him, hard.

Did this boy just say he was going to marry another girl after I went to Hell for him? Is he out of his freaking mind? Does he think I'm just gonna stand by and watch him be with someone else? Wow, maybe he's still on CP, because he has lost his mind.

I risk my life for him time and time again; we made love just a few hours ago, and now he's gonna marry someone else? This can't be happening. Seriously, this is not happening.

I tried to put on a brave face as I exited the room. I lied to Marcus and said that I understood why he had to go through with it. But I didn't understand; or at least my heart didn't. It kept waiting for him to stand up for us; for him to tell Dalce to go screw himself, because he was marrying me.

Marry me and then what? Watch as an entire race is obliterated?

I don't care. He should never have married her!

The internal conflict raged within me for what seemed like an eternity.

I tried to put myself in his place. What would I do if I had to make that choice? Would I save humanity or be with Marcus? I'd like to think I'd put the world ahead of our love, but it's hard because his love *is* my world. In the end, my head understood why he did it, but my heart wouldn't come around.

So, when Marcus and I met up again a few days later, I was going to break up with him. I loved him too much. And I was paying for it. I didn't know how that conversation was going to happen, but I knew I had to have it.

We gathered on a mountaintop in the Swiss Alps, where he had flown us. I had prepared my speech and was ready to end it, yet again, when I saw him smile.

"What is it?" I asked.

"I'm just enjoying the last few moments I have left with you before you break up with me."

I looked at him, shocked. I hadn't said anything to him about breaking up. In fact, I had forced myself to try and be as supportive about the Bianca situation as possible.

"How did you know?" I asked.

"Em, how can you stand by and watch me make vows to another girl? And yes, I'm being forced to do it, but it doesn't change the fact that I'm doing it. I'm hurting you. What else can you do but walk away?" he asks.

"I tried, but…you and Bianca…I can't…it's so…" I replied, trying to stop my voice from trembling.

He took me in his arms and lifted my chin up with his hand, gently. He made sure I was looking into his eyes.

"Emmy, being loved by you is like watching the perfect sunrise. I'm elated and honored that I get to share in it. But I know it's ephemeral. That's what happens to perfect things: they end. And your love is perfect. So in my heart, I've been saying good-bye to it even as I said hello."

Damn him…

How could I break up with him after that? So, I hung on to "us" and I tried to find the strength to get through it. Strength, as it turns out, comes in the shape of pot brownies. They helped make everything funny.

Hey, did you hear that knock knock joke? It cracked me up!

Hey, is that a poster of an apple? Funny!

Hey, is that my fiancé getting married to another girl? Hilarious!

The problem with pot is the problem with all other drugs—the high will always end. And whatever it is that you were trying to forget is sitting in your living room, awaiting your return. In case no one ever told you, misery is patient as hell.

When Marcus took me to the cabin and said he wasn't going to marry Bianca, I was so relieved, I nearly passed out. I knew it was a major risk on his part, but I loved that he felt I was worth it. And then the team came with the news that Dalce would join the Believers if Marcus didn't take Bianca. I held on to what I knew was his strong and unwavering love for me. Then, he told me about the Exchange clause.

Oh, Omnis, he's gonna have sex with her! He's gonna see her naked and touch her. They're going to be in each other's arms. She'll know what he feels like inside her. Why, Omnis, why?

I was done with Marcus then. Sweet words be damned, I just couldn't take the hurt anymore. I was on the brink of a nervous breakdown. But then he reassured me that we could survive this. We even made a sensible deal: he would never tell me about that night. I broke our deal almost immediately.

When I was in the room and the contract was fulfilled, meaning Marcus had slept with Bianca, I was beside myself with rage and sadness. Even though I had said it was okay, I would have given anything to stop it from happening.

The whole time they were on their honeymoon, I pictured what they were doing. I pictured bottles of Coy and multiple complicated sex positions that would make the Kama Sutra look like the Bible. In my head, they had sex that was so exciting it required props and medical personnel standing by.

What's worse was the way I pictured the pillow talk. In my head, it went something like this:

"So, did you enjoy having sex with me, Marcus?" Bianca would ask.

"Yes, it was so good. Much better than what's her name—Easter, Edith, Emily?"

"I think her name is Emmy."

"Whatever; it's time for round two, Bee. Bring the honey, rope, and blindfold."

When Marcus got back from his honeymoon, he held on to his part of the deal and refused to tell me what took place that night. That only made things worse. Though I'm pretty sure knowing the details would have sucked, too.

It wasn't just Marcus getting married that burned me. It was who he married. I have never actually hated anyone. But I can honestly say that I *hate* Bianca.

You would think that I hate Lucy, and I do. But Lucy is the source of all evil, so…um, yeah, I guess she's doing what's in her nature. Then there's the Sage; he's a raving lunatic who is hell-bent on power and world domination. You really don't expect much out of a guy like that. But Bianca is not evil by nature nor is she insane; she's just an old-fashioned super bitch.

I can't count the number of ways I've killed Bianca in my head. Once, she died a painful and gruesome death thanks to Miku's song. After her death, I danced on top of her bloody remains. Then I thanked Omnis for getting rid of her fake-smiling, lying, angel-stealing, social-climbing ass.

Chapter Nineteen: Coma Girls

Another time, I fantasized that Tony made a mixture to peel her perfect caramel skin right off her bones. Then he'd give it to me, and I'd use her skin as bathroom wallpaper for the house Marcus and I have together. Sometimes, her death is not angel related. Like the time I killed her with a bear. I know it's not very imaginative, but when they found her, her eyeballs were dripping off the trunk of a nearby tree; beautiful.

The worst thing about Bianca is the way she pretends she's innocent in all of this. Like it just so happened that she ended up with my angel. *Bitch.*

I remember seeing her proposition Marcus when we were in the city of Cree. She was shameless and sneaky. She will never blind me to the truth: she's a poisonous, sweet-talking succubus.

Bianca wasn't the only one I killed in my head. I killed Marcus, too. Don't judge me. He married another girl. And while I know he had to do what he did, I still murdered him a few times. But each time I did, I would end up teary-eyed and bring him back to life.

I was getting around to telling Marcus to be careful with her, but I never got the chance because Ty walked in on us holding each other…

Now, I lie on the hospital bed with Marcus Recharging beside me, and a world nearing its end. I think back to how simple things used to be when the Guardians first got here. I remember them sitting me down, telling me all about the balance between good and evil.

"That's it!" I exclaim as I pop my eyes open and leap off the bed.

I shake Marcus excitedly. He wakes up and is immediately on high alert.

"Emmy, what is it?"

"I know how to stop the Goumy."

CHAPTER TWENTY:
FINAL HOURS

my idea. I really didn't need an audience, though. I mean, what if my idea

sucks?

The one bright side to having everyone here is it makes me realize how much I missed them. And yes, that even includes Ameana. Compared to Bianca, Ameana is looking better and better every day.

Miku brings some clothes and food for me. She makes everyone wait until I've had a few bites of my sandwich. It does not go smoothly. That's what happens when people are waiting for you to down your chicken and pesto sandwich so they can hear your plan to save the world. I chew so fast, I'm guessing I'll be the first seventeen-year-old to have heartburn.

I look over at Marcus and whisper in his ear.

"I wish you hadn't gathered them; what if my idea is stupid?" I ask.

"Stupid or not, it's all we have right now," he replies.

"Way to build more pressure," I scold him.

He takes my hand and squeezes it reassuringly. I take a deep breath and tell them my idea; if they laugh, so what? I'll be embarrassed, but it's the end of the world, so I won't be embarrassed for long.

Wow, Emmy, dark much?

I shake my head and make myself focus on the Guardians around me.

"Do you remember when you guys first came to Earth, you sat me down and told me why Omnis created Lucy?"

"Of course, baby girl. I was the one who told you. As we know, I have the best speaking voice," Jay says proudly.

"Yes, Jay, you're a national treasure, now can we continue?" Ameana replies.

"You guys said that Omnis thought the world needed balance. And that for every good, there's bad. That's why, as the source of all good, he needed an opposing source, hence came Lucy," I start.

They agree and wait for me to continue.

"See, that's just it; everything we've encountered has had its opposite. From Guardians to Akons. From the Fire Swans to Tallies. I know the Goumy are an aberration but even so, they have to have an opposing force."

"You mean some aberration of good?" Marcus asks.

"Exactly. What if there is some fanatic embodiment of good out there that could rival the Goumy?" I ask.

"We would have heard about something like that, Emmy," Rio replies.

"Well, we didn't know about the Goumy until now. We didn't know about the Quo. Hell, we didn't even know a city of half angels existed. I hate to be the one to say it, but the council sucked at keeping you guys informed," I remind them.

"If there was such an aberration, the Paras would be the ones to talk to," Miku suggests.

The team quickly makes a call to Wolf and puts him on speaker phone. He says he has never heard of any such thing. Frustrated, I sigh and lay my head back. But as Wolf is about to sign off, he tells us to check in with Rahell, as she might know something.

When Arden puts Rahell on the phone, her voice is weak and worn. We inquire about her hand and she tells us it cannot be repaired by any mixture known to angels. The red tip of the blade Sage attacked her with was poisonous. It ensured that whatever body part it cut off could not be mended.

Rahell tries to sound upbeat but we can hear the stress and worry in her voice. She is so beautiful. I don't think her losing a hand is going to change that. Still, it's got to be devastating for her to look over and find a piece of her is missing.

The team tells her my theory. She thinks on it for a few minutes. In the meantime, I'm feeling like a fool for getting everyone's hopes up for nothing. Finally, Rahell answers us.

"I can't say that I've heard of any such power. But you need to ask an Original Para to be sure. They have been here the longest. They know all there is to know about our history."

"I thought all of the Originals were gone," Marcus replies.

"We've keep the fact that some are still alive hidden. We can't chance them being hunted. They are spread throughout the world. It's not safe to say it on the phone. I will make a Plate and place the info inside. It will reveal itself only in your hands, Marcus."

"That's perfect, thank you, Rahell," Marcus says.

"Can I ask your team for one thing?" Rahell inquires.

"Anything."

"Kill the Sage. Don't just win the war. Wipe him off the face of this Ear th."

We all glance at each other. We've never heard Rahell sound so angry and bitter. We all understand why, it's just hard to hear a once so peaceful angel sound so vengeful. But I understand. In fact, lately, I've had waves of anger wash over me. I'm not really sure how to deal with it.

"Will you do that for me?" Rahell asks again, snapping me out of my thoughts.

"You got it," Marcus replies.

He looks over at the rest of us with doubt. The promise he made is a major one. And everyone in the room knows there's a chance it may not be fulfilled.

While we wait for the Plate to come by Shadow Servant, Miku clears out the room so that I can get dressed in the clothes she picked up for me. Before he leaves, Marcus tries to get me to consider sitting out the rest of the mission. I don't even bother replying. I gently push him out the door so that I can get ready.

"Thanks for the clothes, Miku."

Chapter Twenty: Final Hours

"Any excuse to shop," she replies.

There's sadness in her voice that she's trying to mask with a smile.

"What's wrong?" I ask.

"Nothing; it's crazy and ridiculous."

"I know; 'crazy' and 'ridiculous' are old friends of mine, so try me."

"Emmy, the world is breaking apart. Everyone is dying: Believers, soldiers, humans, angels… And yet, I can't stop thinking about Jay. What's wrong with me?"

"Well, it doesn't help that he's always just like three feet away from you. It's hard to work with the guy you like," I reply.

"I just don't get how I could want him so much, but be so pissed at him."

"I love Marcus, and since the whole Bianca thing, I've wanted to throw him down a flight of stairs. Headfirst." I laugh.

"You two are doing pretty good, considering."

"Yeah, considering I'm his mistress."

"It's different for you, Emmy. You know Marcus loves you. Jay doesn't…I mean he's not…you know."

"Maybe he is, but he's not ready to say it out loud," I offer.

"No, Rio would have picked up on something. My brother can be a little blinded when it comes to me, but if Jay were in love with me, he'd know. No, it's clear; Jay doesn't want me. So help me, how do I stop wanting him?"

I reach over and embrace her tightly. I've never seen Miku lacking in confidence. I know how she feels. The first few months Marcus and I met, all I did was try not to love him. And well, we all know how that worked out.

"Look, when we get back from this mission, we'll have a 'Love Lost Bonfire,'" I inform her.

"What is that?"

"It's where we hang out, eat ice cream, and burn something of Jay's."

"Oh, I like that!"

"We can set his favorite car, Siren, on fire!" I joke.

"Yes!" Miku replies joyfully.

She knows I'm joking, but for a moment, it helps pull her out of her misery. The moment passes quickly. Miku's face is back to being sorrowful. "What is it?" I ask.

"We're looking for a power that may not exist and the Goumy are ripping this planet apart as we speak. All kidding aside, Emmy, we might not make it back…"

Miku and I head out to the waiting room to meet up with the team. On our way, we pass a group of shocked doctors. I can understand their reaction. A few hours ago I was in a coma, on the edge of death, and now, not only am I awake, but my hair has come back and has a new shine to it.

I wonder if I can use the mixture as a shampoo. Seriously, my hair has never looked so healthy…

When Ameana sees Miku coming towards her, she mutters under her breath.

"Did you ladies have enough girl time?" she asks resentfully.

"It was nothing, Mimi, we just talked," Miku replies.

"We used to talk. Now, it's all business."

"It's not like that."

"Yes, Miku, it is. Ever since Thomas and I got together you've been pulling away from me. If you don't want to be friends anymore, just say so."

"I do want to be friends, but I don't know how to be friends with a demon's girlfriend," Miku snaps.

Damn, I was hoping they wouldn't head down the "demon boyfriend" path in their argument. Now things are about to get messy.

"Guys, we need to stay quiet. It's a hospital," Rio reminds them, trying to stop the situation before it gets worse.

"So that's all I am now, some demon's girlfriend?" Ameana asks Miku, ignoring Rio completely.

"Well…yeah."

"How can you say that, Pretty?" Ameana wonders.

"Just because Rage was able to get into your pants doesn't mean he can get into our hearts."

"You're not even giving him a chance!" Ameana snaps, frustrated.

"A chance to do what? Kill more Pawns?"

"He saved Marcus when we were in Tess," she reminds Miku.

"Yes, but only hours before he killed a human," she counters.

"He was a Pawn!" Ameana objects.

"So what? He has a soul, and your boyfriend killed him."

"Why are you being like this?"

"I want you to wake up. You can't date Rage. He has no heart. Literally!" Miku shouts.

"You can't tell me who I should and shouldn't date."

"I'm looking out for you."

"Maybe it's time you started looking out for yourself, because falling for Jay is a bad idea."

"What's wrong with Jay?" Miku replies, offended.

Jay and the rest of the guys are wise enough to remain silent.

"Nothing. He'll make a great boyfriend when—and if—he ever grows up!"

"I would rather date a guy who has a playful side than a guy who sets people on fire."

"He is trying to change," Ameana roars.

"I'm sure that's of great comfort to the Pawn's family," Miku mocks. "Marcus fell for the human and put all of us in danger. You were fine with that. But now, I'm with the guy who saved my life and that's a problem?"

"I never said it was okay for Marcus and Emmy to get together. Marcus did what he wanted," Miku tells her.

"And I'm doing what I want," Ameana challenges.

"You're letting your heart make a fool out of you."

"Me? You're in love with a guy who commits more to cars than he does girlfriends. He's a bad gamble and you know it."

"It doesn't matter what happens with me and Jay because in the end, I'm pretty sure he won't set me on fire!"

"Of course not; he won't stick around long enough to light the match."

Someone interrupts the argument by clearing their throat. We all look towards the direction the sounds came from and find Julian standing a few feet away.

"I hate to interrupt this think tank here, but I need to speak to my daughter—alone," Julian says.

"Now isn't a good time. We're about to leave," I reply. "So, the end is here and I can't get three minutes with my only child?" "The Plate isn't here yet, Em. You have a few minutes," Marcus replies. I shrug, place my hands in my pockets, and follow Julian down the

hallway.

"Are you alright?" he asks.

"Yes, the mixture worked, as you can see."

"I just wanted to make sure."

"Um…thanks," I reply.

I have no idea what to say to him. I've spent years hating him, and now we're supposed to bond or something. I don't know. Sometimes, I want to get along with him, but that gets hard because he's always trying to split me and Marcus up.

Like we need any more help in that area.

"How did you get hurt in the first place?" he asks.

"You know, mission stuff," I reply, avoiding his eyes.

"What happened?" he pushes.

"I got hit by a Powerball," I say, trying to sound nonchalant about it. As if getting hit by a giant ball of energy was an everyday occurrence.

"Marcus let you on the battlefield?" Julian rages.

"No, it was an accident."

"That's crazy, Emmy. You could have died!"

"Yes, but I didn't, so can we move on?"

"Move on? Your boyfriend allowed the Goumy to get out. There is no moving on. There's just the end. And since it's here, I want to spend the final hours with my family."

"Julian, it's not the end. We'll figure something out. That's what we're working on right now."

"The team has an idea?"

"No, I do. But I'm not sure it will work."

Chapter Twenty: Final Hours

"Wow, you're so much like her," he says, studying my face.

"Who?"

"Your mom. Like you, she just didn't know how to give up."

Anytime anyone brings my mom up in conversation I feel a pool of ice form in the bottom of my stomach. It brings with it a dull ache that never goes away. Then, I almost always end up crying because I miss her so much.

I don't want to cry in front of Julian, or anyone else for that matter. I start to walk away, but he calls out after me.

"I just want to get to know you before it all ends," he pleads.

"It's not going to end. We won't let it," I assure him.

"I love you," he says softly.

It turns out the one in tears isn't me; it's Julian.

"I know I should have been there and I wasn't. But please, know I love you more than my life." The tears fall down his face; he looks down at the floor and heads to the elevator.

Damn, what am I supposed to say?

"Julian!" I call out.

He looks up as he walks into the elevator.

"When this is over, maybe we can…talk and stuff."

Talk and stuff? Lame, Emmy.

But it made him smile, a little. And given the events of the past few hours, a little smile is all we can hope for.

When I walk back to the waiting room, the team is silent. The tension between Miku and Ameana is heavy in the air. But it pales compared to the wave of hatred bouncing back and forth between Rage and Miku. Jay is trying not to look at Miku, and Rio is standing as far away as he can from Jay.

"If we survive this, you guys really need some kind of team spirit building or something," I whisper to Marcus.

He sighs heavily and shakes his head.

"How'd it go with your father?" he asks.

"He cried and I feel like crap."

"It's gonna take time."

"You mean the one thing we don't have?"

He smiles sadly and pulls me close to him. Mercifully, the Shadow Servant arrives and brings a Plate for Marcus. It's a flat, round, coin-like object that gathers red specs of light and forms a message. Marcus holds it in the palm of his hand and tells us to get ready; we're headed for La Rinconada, a small city on the outskirts of Peru. Once there, we will find the oldest Original Para, Raphael.

Whatever tension was built back in the hospital waiting room takes a backseat to the sight of the colossal destruction going on down below. People are screaming and running for their lives while trying to protect their loved ones. We have to stop five times to rescue people trapped in collapsed buildings, in fires, or drowning in the flash floods.

Finally, after we help a family of four whose car had been trapped in a sinkhole, Marcus makes the difficult decision not to stop anymore for anyone.

"So, we're not gonna help these people?" Rio asks.

"We can't keep stopping. We have to get to Raphael," Marcus reasons.

"So, we just fly over them like it's nothing?"

"You can stay here and save a few dozen people or you can go with us to save billions. Up to you," Marcus says, clearly losing patience.

Marcus, no longer waiting on Rio, takes off into the sky with me. The rest of the team follows. For a moment, I fear Rio isn't coming with us. But a few minutes later, he takes to the sky.

Things have never been this bleak before. There's the devastation below, the tension with the team, and now the sky itself seems to be against us. We are flying in the midst of severe lightning and thunder. The dark clouds are spitting at us in the form of massive hail. The wind seems to be actively fighting us. More than once the team has had to dive and loop around to avoid being hit or swallowed up by unnaturally high twisters.

From the corner of my eye, I see Jay in full panic mode.

I look over to see what has him so terrified. His wings are disappearing and then reappearing in rapid succession. I turn to Marcus and point to Jay, and by that time, Jay's wings are no longer blinking in and out. They have disappeared altogether. Jay is plummeting at top speed towards certain death.

CHAPTER TWENTY-ONE: THE LYRIS

Marcus can't mak

in the sky and hits Jay in the chest.

Before the lightning hit him, Jay was flailing his arms and legs furiously.
He looked like a bird caught in a wind tunnel. But now he looks more like
a paper bag in the wind. He is at the mercy of the elements.
Ameana tries to redirect Jay again. This time she's successful and sends
him towards the hillside of the town below. Unfortunately, when Jay hits
the side of the hill, he's picked up by one of a dozen cyclones in the area.
The wrathful wind whips him around like fruit in a blender. When it finally
drops him, Jay is motionless on the ground at an unnatural angle. I'm sure
he's broken a few bones, or worse…

When we land, we race to Jay's side. His face is twisted in pain. His
wings are gone and his eyes are closed.

Please, don't let him die, Omnis…

"Rio," Marcus calls out.

Rio reads Jay's Waves at least two or three times. Marcus pushes for
him to tell us what he sees.

"He's not dead, but he will be soon if we don't get him help. His Wave
is fading," Rio continues.

Miku lets out a gasp as if someone has punched her in her chest, hard.
She kneels beside Jay and takes his hand. The worry etched on her face
makes me want to console her. Rio studies his sister carefully. He's taken

off guard by how deeply Jay's condition affects her. Marcus looks around the small town in the valley below us and makes a decision.

"According to the information on the Plate, Raphael's home should be on top of the mountains, just a few miles from here. He might be able to help Jay."

Ameana uses her power to suspend Jay's body in the air. She controls him as we take off into the sky once more. I look over at Miku and give her an encouraging sign. It's hard to do when Jay seems all but dead.

We arrive at a modest house near the top of the mountain. It looks like it has no more than two rooms and is nearly falling apart.

"Raphael is the oldest and most powerful Original Para. It's said that he's the most powerful angel in the universe. He's the closest thing to Omnis on Earth. We need to be careful how we address him," Marcus warns us.

"So, should we bow or something?" I ask nervously.

"No, but we do have to show respect and be gracious," he replies.

"I don't care if he's Omnis himself; can we go in already? Jay's fading," Miku says, marching up to the house.

We exchange worried looks and follow Miku to the house of the almighty Raphael. Much to our surprise, the door is unlocked. Miku slowly pushes it open.

Raphael's home looks more like the inside of the closet of a gadget junkie than the home of a mighty angel. All around the room there are video games, gadgets and, well, just about anything Apple ever created. It's nerd heaven.

At the center of the room sits an Original Para, illuminating brighter than any I have seen before. He sits with his back to us, his wings flapping gracefully in the air. He faces a huge flat-screen plasma TV. I turn to Marcus to see if maybe I missed something.

"Um…is the most powerful Para in the universe playing Grand Theft Auto?" I ask.

"No, he's playing Grand Theft Auto *5*," the Para says, not bothering to turn towards us.

We exchange a look of utter confusion.

"Are you Raphael?" Marcus asks.

"Damn it, where'd that cop come from?!" He screams at the TV.

"Look, are you Raphael or not?" Rio asks.

"I am."

"We need your help," Ameana replies.

"Are we sure it's him and not his dorky teenaged son?" Rage says.

Marcus glares at him for being rude. Rage shrugs his shoulders. Miku shakes her head, signaling she's had enough.

"Hey, 'Big Bang Theory,' our friend is dying, so get off your ass and help him!" she demands.

"I'm starting to like your friend," Rage mumbles to Ameana.

Raphael puts down his remote and hovers above us. He begins to glow even brighter in the air. He studies Miku closely with a stern expression. "Are you Redd?" he asks.

"Not yet, but keep pushing," she warns.

From the look on his face, I'm pretty certain he's going to strike her down or do something equally awful. Rio must feel the same because he steps in front of Miku so that he can block whatever is coming. What comes is something none of us expected.

"Oh my Omnis, you're Redd; you're, like, my idol!!!" Raphael says. Raphael grabs Miku's hands as if he's meeting a rock star and has dreamed of this moment for years. He rushes to the table in the corner where comic books are piled high. He hands her a dozen of them and begs her to sign them.

"They make Redd comic books?" I ask.

"Apparently," Rage replies.

"It's rare, but yes. Ever since you turned, you've been the rage of collectors like me. And now, I have you right here. Man, the guys aren't gonna believe this," Raphael gushes.

"What guys?" Miku asks.

"The ones on Redd's chat room!"

"You guys are celebrating someone who killed humans?" Miku asks, disgusted.

"No, it's more than that. You're the antihero. You didn't want to do what you did but the council pushed you too far," he says, sounding animated and over the top.

"Okay, whatever, can you help our friend please?" she asks.

"Oh yes, sorry, sorry. Para duties come first, unfortunately. What's wrong with him?" he asks.

"We were flying and suddenly his wings began to disappear."

Raphael lifts Jay's body high in the air and effortlessly turns him three hundred and sixty degrees in the air as he studies him.

For several minutes, we hold our breath as Raphael examines Jay in the air. A series of small Powerballs emanate from the Para's fingers. The mini Powerballs enter Jay's eyes, nose, and mouth. They whiz in and out of him. When they are done, they return to the palm of Raphael hands. He studies the mini Powerballs with interest. He then turns his attention back to us.

"So, which one of you is this Guardian he's in love with?"

We all stare at him blankly. He shows us the Powerballs that have now turned bluish gray.

"These are Seekers. They look for foreign objects in angels. And based on the tint of blue, your friend has ingested a fair amount of Gentum."

"What is that?" I ask.

"It's a neat little mixture that makes you think you are no longer in love with the person you're in love with. The only problem is that it's a lie. And sooner or later, you need more Gentum to keep from feeling. And the more you take, the more it affects your body."

"Is he okay?" I ask.

"No, but he'll be fine soon," the Para replies.

"I'm reading his Waves and they are fading. That means he's dying. How can he be fine?" Rio asks.

"Well, Gentum tells your Rah and your soul that you're not in love. When your true feelings start to fight back, Gentum goes into overdrive and tells your body other crazy things, like, 'Hey you're dying.' Or, 'Hey, you have no wings.' It becomes a matter of your mind tricking your body."

"Okay, so how do we help him?" Marcus asks.

"I can wake him up, and fix him. But he has to stop taking Gentum or it will happen again."

"So, he took Gentum because he didn't want to feel what he was feeling," Miku says to herself.

"Yes. Are you the reason he took the mixture?" Raphael asks.

"Yeah, I'm the girl he's trying to not love," she says sadly as she runs out of the house.

We try to go after her but Rio tells us she needs to be alone. Meanwhile, Raphael places Jay on an empty table and prepares the mixture. Relieved that Jay is in the clear, Marcus tries to gather the information we came for.

"Rahell said you were coming to ask about an unexpected force of good," he says as he skillfully mixes colorful liquids together.

"Yes, that's why we're here. Is there any such thing?" I ask.

"As an unexpected force of good, no," he replies.

Damn…

"But there is a force of good that was purposely placed on Earth," the Para tells us.

Just then, Miku enters. Before we can say anything, she tells us she's fine and does not want to talk about Jay. She turns her attention to Raphael and tells him to keep talking.

"Before I tell you about it, who came up with the idea to look for the opposing force to the Goumy?" he asks.

"It was Emmy," Marcus replies.

"A human, of course. You guys come up with the best things. I mean, yeah sure, we gave the world courage, wisdom, blah, blah, blah. But you guys gave us the iPhone. That's true power," he marvels.

"Well, you know, we humans do what we can," I say, not sure what my reply is supposed to be.

"Tell me something, what does a hamburger taste like? It looks so g ood."

"Um…it's okay," I reply, looking at Marcus for some help.

"If you don't mind, we came a long way and we really are pressed for time," Marcus explains to him.

"You won't be able to go anywhere until your friend is healed. That will take another hour or so."

"Fine, but can you finish what you were saying about a force of good?" Marcus asks.

"As I said before, there is no unexpected force. But there is a reserve of perfect power that has been added to by many, many Paras over the past cycles. You see, when Omnis first made this world, we Originals were overjoyed; the humans were engaging and innocent.

"Once that changed, and we had to come to Earth to fight evil, we felt sorry for them. There were times when we wanted to clean up the mess humanity had gotten into, but we weren't allowed to interfere. So, in order to give the humans some extra help, without actually being there, we created the Lyris."

"Lyris, what is that?" I ask.

"The Lyris is a reserve of perfect power that has been gathering over thousands of years. We Paras started it and every time we're on Earth, we would add to it. It's like a savings account, except we didn't deposit money, we deposited power."

"What does the Lyris look like and where is it kept?" Marcus asks.

"The Lyris looks like a stream of plasma, surrounded by beams of light. We placed it in a little hole in the ground. But over time, the Lyris became more and more powerful. Soon, the hole could not contain its power. It expanded and what was once a small unremarkable hole is now the Grand Canyon.

"As you can imagine, it was impossible to hide it from evil now that it had grown so big. Lucy found out about it and she insisted that Omnis get rid of Lyris, because it offset the balance of good and evil. But after having seen what some of the Goumy could do, Omnis was reluctant to comply.

"So, in the end, Lucy agreed to help put the Goumy in prison and Omnis agreed to get rid of the Lyris. But here's a secret about Omnis: he's pretty crafty."

"You mean he didn't get rid of the Lyris?" the twins ask.

Chapter Twenty-One: The Lyris

"Well, yes and no. He did, in the sense that it can't be found in the ground. But he allowed the Lyris to seek out its own home. That is to say, every cycle, the Lyris resides in someone of its choosing."

"So, this great force of good is inside a human being?" I ask.

"Yes. After all, it was our gift to humans. The Lyris places itself inside a being that is pure of heart and deserving."

"Why didn't we know about this?" Miku asks.

"Both sides have secrets from each other. That's just the way the game is played."

"This isn't a game, Raphael," Marcus replies heatedly.

"I have faith in your team. We all do, Marcus."

"Where can we find the Lyris?" I ask, hoping to give Marcus a chance to calm down.

"Every cycle, we are told where the Lyris is and the name of the being it has entered. This cycle, I believe it's in a woman named Bailey Coulter."

"Great, where is she?" I ask.

"She can be found in a monastery in Tibet." He gives us the location and tells us the fastest way to get there.

"I don't get it. You guys had this info and you never told us. Why would you let things get this bad if you could have stopped it?" Marcus snaps.

"Guardian, we saved the world a few times. It's your turn."

"That's what this is about? Whose turn it is? That doesn't seem unfair to you?"

"Yes, it seems unfair and awful. But what is it that makes you think unfair and awful things won't happen? For Omnis' sake, your mother murdered you. Do you still need me to tell you the world is unfair?"

"You could have at least told us about the Lyris before this," Rio replies.

"And then have IM Trouble make it front-page news?" Raphael asks.

"There is hardly a Splash anymore," I counter.

"It doesn't matter, human. There are Believers everywhere. One word about the Lyris and whoever it is that it's inside will be killed. So please, guard this information with your lives."

"You went to all that trouble to give us humans the Lyris, but you hid it. How were we even supposed to know it was there?" I ask.

"I have faith in humans. A great being once said 'Humans are noble, honorable, and some really smart. I have a very optimistic view of these individuals.'"

"Who said that, Omnis?"

"No, Steve Jobs."

I suppress a smile, and Marcus shakes his head.

"Can you at least tell us what this Bailey woman is like?" I ask.

"I have never met her. But rumor has it she is difficult, stubborn, selfish, and unyielding."

"The Lyris went into someone like that?" Rio asks.

"I can't explain why, but it did."

"So, is she being guarded or what?" Marcus asks.

"She is watched by Cravens so that her power can be neutralized. But it takes nearly a hundred of them to subdue her powers, and even then, she can be very dangerous."

"What are her powers?" Miku asks.

"She inhales evil."

"Seriously?" Marcus replies.

"She is the best weapon we have against Lucy. That's why it was important no one know about her. Honestly, we all hoped we would never need to use her. But Sage has lost touch with reality…," Raphael says, lost in thought.

"Once we find her, we just walk up to her?" I wonder.

"She has a built-in shield. If she doesn't like you, you won't be able to touch her. In fact, no one has touched her before because she hates everyone."

"Sounds charming," Rio chimes in.

"Okay, so suppose we get to her and she somehow lets us near her, what then?" Marcus inquires.

"Then you take her and journey to a small fishing town in Greenland. That's one of the places our power is strongest on Earth. There are many different theories as to why that is, but more on that at another time."

"And that's it, we take her to Greenland, she stands there, and sucks in air?" I ask.

"She will be airborne; she'll rotate in a circle of awesome, perfect power. The Goumy will begin to get weak. At that point, they will be drawn to her location and will fight like hell to stop her. But so long as her shields are up, she will be unstoppable. She will kill them all."

"Okay, don't be mad, but I need a human minute to recap," I reply. They all look at each other and permit me to continue.

"Okay, so the Lyris is a reserve of perfect Para power. Every cycle, it enters a human being that it thinks is worthy. And in this cycle, the woman's name is Bailey. She can be found in Tibet. Once we find her, we take her to Greenland, and she will use her power and defeat the Goumy. Right?"

"Right," Raphael assures me.

"Am I crazy or does that sound too simple?" I ask the team.

"Getting Bailey to come with you will be difficult. She has never left the monastery," Raphael tells us.

"Well, she's leaving with us, one way or another. I don't care if we have to use force; we will not let this world end," Marcus vows.

"Glad to hear it, Guardian. One more thing, the Lyris can only be used once. So wait until you get to Greenland, where her powers are greatest. Your friend is now awake."

We look over and Jay's eyes are open. His wings are back.

"What happened?" he asks us.

"The mixture you were taking had side effects," Marcus replies.

"Oh," Jay says, looking away.

"Where did you get it?" I ask.

"Tony-Tone," Jay replies.

"I swear I'm going to kill him. I'm done with that snake," Marcus swears.

"It's my bad, yo. Not Tony's. He said it could have side effects but I didn't listen."

"Because you wanted so badly not to love me?" Miku asks.

We all look at each other and silently wonder if we should leave them alone. But since they continue talking anyway, everyone just stays put.

"It's complicated, Miku," Jay replies.

"No, it's not. I thought the guy I had feeling for was…courageous. Honest. But you're not. You're just a scared little boy and I'm done wanting you, Jaden. I'm done."

She turns to Marcus and tells him she's ready to go whenever he is ready. Then she heads outside to wait for us.

"She's really mad, huh, baby girl?" Jay asks me.

"How could you put yourself in danger like that?" I ask.

"I'm trying to stay focused on this mission. I don't want to be a distraction. I don't want to end up like…"

"Like what?" I push.

"Like you and Marcus."

"What does that mean?" I ask.

"All love has done is hurt you two. It will never end. I don't want to be in love; ever."

"Well, I hate to break it to you, but you're already in it. You're just pretending not to be. I've been there. It doesn't end well."

Jay is good as new but he's being given the cold shoulder by Miku. And frankly, I'm not really a big fan of his right now, either. I can see how much he is hurting Miku by not wanting to admit his feelings.

But we do finally have good news; I was right and there is a power that can combat the Goumy. I'm sure we can convince Bailey to come with us. Even if she isn't the nicest woman in the world, I'm sure she'll help us.

We fly all night in crazy weather. More than once we have to take detours to avoid homes and bodies whizzing by us inside twisters and hurricanes. Rio isn't the only one having a hard time knowing so many people are dying. But like Marcus pointed out, this is the best way to help not just a few people but everyone.

By the time we arrive on top of the mountain where the monastery is located, I'm drenched to the bone; we all are. But we are so taken with meeting this Bailey woman, we don't pay attention to how wet we are.

There are Cravens standing all around the monastery. Marcus told me about them. They have two powers. They can neutralize other demons and they can tell instantly what your desires are. But the thing that gets me about Cravens is how their veins are on the outside. It's almost like they are turned inside out.

"We have come to see the Lyris," Marcus says firmly.

"She is not seeing anyone today," the Craven nearest us replies.

"She will see us," Marcus says with a steely tone.

"The Lyris does what she wants," he replies.

"We will see her. The question is will we have to kill you in order to do so?" Ameana replies with certainty.

"Fine," the Craven says, smiling as if he knows something we don't.

They step aside and allow us inside the monastery.

Once inside, we see the being that the Lyris has chosen to reside in. She is looking out the window. Her beauty is unique and breathtaking. She has albino skin. It's so white it's almost translucent. Her unruly red hair forms a mass of curls atop her head. She turns to face us. Her eyes are an intense gray that makes it nearly impossible to look away from them. The combination of red hair, colorless skin, and deep gray eyes make Bailey an odd and intriguing sight. But it's not her hair, or her even her skin that renders us speechless. What gets us about Bailey Coulter is she's only three years old.

CHAPTER TWENTY-TWO:
INTRODUCTIONS

Bailey is by far th

But Bailey is not happy to see the "gods." In fact, she does her best to show us just how unhappy she is that we are here. She crinkles her button nose and purses her heart-shaped lips with suspicion, folding her arms over her chest. So far, Bailey has the world's best and biggest pout.

The thing about toddlers is that the more upset they try to be, the cuter they get. I learned that with Ben, my neighbor. When he was two, he hated when I was babysitting and would make him go to bed. He would give me his best "I'm mad at you" face.

But the "meaner" he looked, the more adorable he was. Sometimes, I'd pretend it was bedtime just to see his "mean" face. Bailey is no different. Yes, the toddler standing before us wearing jeans and a long sleeve balloon print shirt wants nothing to do with us.

"It's a mistake, right?" Ameana asks.

"This is crazy," Marcus replies.

"No, this is good. This is the first break we've had in a long time. All we have to do is say hello to her and she'll be eating out of our hands," Miku says.

But something in the way Bailey furrows her brows makes me think Miku may be wrong. She walks up to the little girl and says hello.

As soon as Miku gets within reach, Bailey's shield goes up. It's a see through barrier, like Rio's, but a much smaller version. Miku touches the shield and it hurls her to the other side of the room. We run to see if she's okay.

"This may be a job for candy; a lot of it," Miku says as she sits up and massages her bruised shoulder.

"Why would the Lyris go into a kid?" Jay asks.

"Well, it actually makes sense; when I read kids, mostly they're joyous, courageous, pure," Rio informs him.

"Okay, well we need to get her to come with us—so, any ideas?" Marcus asks.

"I could try," I volunteer.

I walk up to Bailey, smiling. When I get within reach, I have to stop myself from reaching out and pinching her puffy cheeks. Or placing my hands on either side of her face and smooching it like a big gooey sweet marshmallow.

"Hi Bailey; I'm Emmy," I say, kneeling down so we are eye level.

She furrows her brow again and looks at the rest of the team with even more uncertainty.

"Bailey, can you say 'hi'?" I ask her.

"NO!" she shouts stubbornly.

"This is great. This is just great," Rage says, irate.

Ameana takes a turn. She goes up to Bailey and asks to see her collection of stuffed animals by the window. Bailey shouts, "No!"

The twins, Jay, and Marcus all try to get the little girl to lower her shields, but she has only one answer to that: No.

"Can you Convince her?" Marcus asks.

"I can't get close enough to whisper to her. And besides, I've never Convinced a little kid. It might really screw with her head." Jay looks concer ned.

"Well, we have to go and we can't leave without her," Marcus reminds us.

"Can you airlift her?" Rage asks Ameana.

"Not with her shields up."

"C'mon, angel, you wanna take a ride with us?" Jay asks in a sticky sweet voice.

"No!" Bailey replies with absolute resolve.

"She's never gonna lower her shields if she doesn't like us," Rio says.

"Jay, why don't you whip up a quick little mixture to make her forget her feelings; you're good at that," Miku says snidely.

"C'mon, yo, let it go!" Jay snaps.

"That *was* reckless, Jay," Marcus agrees.

"Really, Marcus, you're gonna tell me what is and isn't reckless? *You*, of all people?" Jay counters.

"What the hell does that mean?" Marcus asks.

"He means you put your love for a human ahead of your mission. So, you are the last person to judge him," Ameana informs him.

"Someone who's dating Rage shouldn't talk," Miku reminds her.

"Guys, can we focus? She's just a kid, we should be able to get her to lower her shields," I tell them.

"I could fire at it," Rage says casually.

"You would really throw fire at a toddler?" Marcus asks.

"He was kidding," Ameana comes to his defense.

"Or so you hope," Jay mutters.

"Say whatever you want about him, Jay, at least he didn't take the coward's way out by using a mixture because he's too afraid to love," Ameana snipes.

"Yeah right, like Rage can love," Jay counters.

"Maybe I can't love; what I can do is throw a good barbecue. I can make the flames nice and hot for you," Rage says as a fireball starts to form in the palm of his hand.

"Yo, I'm right, boss man, let's do this!" Jay counters, ready to attack.

"WHY IS THE THREE-YEAR-OLD THE MOST GROWN-UP ONE IN THIS ROOM?" I shout.

Everyone turns towards me. I stare back at them with no apologies. I'm getting more than a little sick of the constant bickering.

"Yes, that's right; the human is really pissed off. And from now on, you either say something helpful or shut the hell up. We're on a mission, not on the last season of *Jersey Shore!*" I scold them.

The room is silent. The only sound comes from Bailey, who has grown bored of us and is now playing with her stuffed rabbit. The group doesn't respond to my outburst, but they are no longer arguing. After a few moments of silence, Ameana is the first to speak.

"Maybe it's easier to get her to come to us," she says.

"How?" I ask.

Ameana raises her hand and calls for the stuffed rabbit to come towards her. It flows in the air and away from Bailey. She watches as her rabbit becomes airborne. She's surprised at first and a little dazzled. But when she realizes the rabbit is steadily getting further and further away, she starts to cry. The earth begins to shake.

"Um…is she doing that?" I ask.

"Yeah, I think so," Marcus replies.

"Yo, give her the rabbit back, she's gonna cause an earthquake!" Jay says.

"Come on, Bailey, come get the rabbit," I tell her.

"Boo-Boo," she says, calling out for her cherished toy.

She weeps and tries to reach for Boo-Boo, but it has flown well above her head. We all call out for her to come closer. Finally, she comes close enough for us to touch her. Jay quickly tries to pick her up but before he can, her shields go back up. She sticks her tongue out at us.

Ameana lowers the rabbit down to where Bailey can reach it but she is too smart. She won't lower her shield even to get Boo-Boo back.

"Damn it!" Rage swears.

All of us scold him at nearly the same time.

"What?" Rage asks, clueless.

"Watch your mouth around the kid," Jay says.

"Seriously? Now we're having child-rearing classes? Can't we just scare her into coming with us?" Rage insists.

"You want to scare a girl who can move the earth when she cries?" Miku says in disbelief.

"Miku's right, we don't know what she can do if she's scared," Marcus ag rees.

"So not only do we have to take her with us, we have to get her to go willingly?" Rage complains.

"Something's wrong," Rio says.

"What is it?" Ameana asks.

"The Cravens; they're scared," Rio says, reading their Waves.

Marcus and I exchange a quick worried glance as he dashes to the door. He opens it just in time to see a flock of Fire Swans hurl a river of flames into the room. Marcus shuts the door quickly, but it's too late. The monastery is on fire. Out the window, we can see the hundreds of swans circling above us, getting ready to launch another attack.

"Get down!" Marcus shouts at me.

He leaps into the air and uses his body as a shield to save me. Luckily, Rio's shield prevents Marcus from being burned alive. I look at Bailey and fear springs into my eyes. Marcus reminds me that she can protect herself. And sure enough, Bailey has her shield up. What I'm even more thankful for is that she is not scared; she thinks of the flames as a pretty firework display.

The team races outside to battle the swans, but there are too many of them and the fire is spreading. We still can't get Bailey to let down her shield so she can fly with us. I'm grateful that she thinks the fire is some kind of game because otherwise, she would burst into tears and things would be even worse.

"The Cravens are dead," Rio says as he reads their fading Waves.

"That's what they came to do: kill the Cravens so the demons could get to her," Marcus concludes as he takes flight to kill as many swans as he can.

"How did they even know where she was?" I ask, trying to find a spot away from the blaze.

"Sage probably got a vision," Rio replies as he shields Miku and Jay.

Rage and Ameana take to the sky and tackle two swans at a time. Once Jay and Miku are free from imminent danger, they too take to the sky.

"We have to get her out of here, there's no telling what the demons will do to her," I shout up to Marcus.

"You have to find a way to get her to let you in, Emmy, or else she'll die here," Marcus replies.

I look off into the distance and see a dark cloud, moving too quickly to really be a cloud. The sky has been invaded by *thousands* of demons.

The team turns and sees the demons have taken over every inch of the sky. And for the first time ever, I see fear in their eyes. I don't think it's for their own lives, but for Bailey. There is no way her shield will hold up against thousands of demons.

Once they find her, they will take her to Sage, or worse, to Lucy, since the power she has inside her isn't technically supposed to exist. In order to get rid of the Lyris, they will have to kill Bailey. An action I'm certain Lucy would not only commit to, but enjoy.

I rush back into what's left of the monastery and plead with the little girl to come with me. I offer her candy, tell her we'll play games, anything and everything, but Bailey does not want to go.

What's worse is that the fire display is no longer fun for her. In fact, the sight of the swans spewing fire causes Bailey to cry. At once, the earth begins to shake. What's left of the roof starts to crumble.

The monastery is all but gone now. We are out in the open. The demons all swoop down and flock towards Bailey. Her shield is holding, but she's crying really hard now, causing the ground beneath us to crack open.

I pick up whatever discarded bricks and pieces of wood I can find and bash the demons on the head. Some of them, already hurt from dealing with the Guardians, fall to the ground. Others aren't hurt by my attack, just pissed.

One demon comes after me, his jagged teeth dripping with what must be poison. He tackles me to the ground, grabs me by my neck, and smiles as he moves in to rip a chunk of flesh from my face.

I close my eyes and brace myself for the agony and blood soon to follow. I feel a heavy weight fall down onto my chest. I open my eyes and the demon is on my chest, staring up at me, lifeless. All I feel is a soft wind blow. I breathe a sigh of relief and silently thank Jay for the quick rescue.

"We can't fight this many of them," Ameana shouts to her leader.

"Has she lowered her shield yet?" Marcus replies.

"I'm working on it," I shout.

"Emmy, hurry!"

I run to the center of what used to the monastery, where Bailey is now having a full-blown tantrum. The mountain begins to split apart. Bailey's temper is going to kill us all if we don't calm her down.

"Bailey, it's okay, sweetie, don't cry," I beg.

It does no good at all. I repeat it several times and tell her that everything is going to be okay. It does not help in the least.

"I can't get her to let me in," I shout up to Marcus, who has a swan and a demon in each hand.

"Figure something out. There are more demons coming," Marcus orders.

What am I supposed to do to get this girl to lower her shield? I mean we've tried everything. All of us have approached her and she won't let any of us in.

Actually, we all haven't approached her…

I called out for Rage in the sky. He swoops down beside me.

"You have to try and get her to lower her shield," I tell him.

"What, me?"

"Yes, you, you're the only one who hasn't tried to talk to her," I reply.

"Yeah, that because demons freak the hell out of kids."

"Yes, but we're out of options," I reply.

"This is crazy. She's just gonna cry harder and bring the whole mountain down," Rage objects.

"Look, it's worth a try; just say something to her."

Rage looks over at the weeping child inside the force field-like bubble.

"She's gonna freak out, human," he insists.

"Just do it!" I order.

He shakes his head and swears at me. Then he walks up to Bailey, still very angry, and glares at her.

"Rage, say something," I encourage.

I know it's a long shot, but I am officially out of ideas.

"I don't know what to say!" Rage counters as yet another massive chunk of the mountain crumbles.

"Damn it, Rage, say something!" I roar.

Rage, officially irate and fed up with Bailey, turns to the toddler, grits his teeth, and growls at her. I close my eyes and wait for Bailey to cry even harder.

Damn that Akon. But Bailey doesn't cry harder. In fact, there's no sound at all. I open my eyes and find the corner of Bailey's lips turned up in what looks like the beginning of a smile. Then the smile turns into something I never thought possible: laughter.

She found Rage's growl funny. Rage, taken aback, does it again. This time not only does Bailey laugh, she growls back! To her, this is yet another game. They are competing to see who has the best "fake" evil growl.

Bailey is so engrossed in Rage, she forgets about the demons flying overhead.

"What the hell?" Rage says to me.

"I don't know, I think she likes you," I offer, in disbelief.

"Don't be stupid. No one likes demons. Especially little girls with bunny rabbit dolls," he rages at me.

"Well, you're wrong," I reply.

"She giggled once or twice, that doesn't mean she likes me."

"No, but that does."

Rage turns around and finds Bailey has lowered her shields. She is now standing by his leg, reaching out to him with her chubby little arms, waiting to be picked up.

Rage looks back at me with utter panic; I signal for him to pick her up. He picks her up as if she were a bomb about to go off at any second. He keeps her as far away from his body as possible. He reluctantly looks at her face. She smiles brightly and hands him her rabbit.

"Boo-Boo," she says, making introductions.

I look on in complete astonishment. Around us, the world is collapsing; demons are closing in. The team is outnumbered and overwhelmed. The very ground we stand on is quickly disappearing beneath our feet; but none of that matters to the three-year-old Lyris. For Bailey, this day is a good day; today is the day she befriended the First Akon.

CHAPTER TWENTY-THREE:
WHO DID THIS?

out. Now we're heading to Greenland so Bailey can use her power against the Goumy.

This is imperative because judging from the latest news Rio is getting via cell phone, things have gone from bad to dismal. Only two networks are still broadcasting. In all parts of the world, people are terrified of what they are rightfully calling "The End."

Some small remote islands have already disappeared under water, such as the Galapagos, the Falklands, and Attu Island. In addition, major cities are faced with five-alarm fires, brought on by the downed power lines and the severe weather.

New York City is ravaged by hurricanes and earthquakes. London has lost thousands of people due to a sudden, unnaturally brutal heat wave. Tokyo is reporting a death toll in the tens of thousands.

If people aren't dying from the elements, they are dying from sheer panic. Thousands have taken to the streets in an attempt to head out of the cities. The fear and hysteria causes them to turn on each other. There are reports of people being trampled to death by crazed mobs attempting to flee.

We are on our way to Greenland when Marcus makes us land on a mountaintop somewhere in Hungary. There's a row of small one-room cabins with a pile of wood stacked high alongside each one.

"Why are we stopping?" Ameana asks.

Chapter Twenty-Three: Who Did This?

"Winter texted me. Sage has all the routes to Greenland covered. He knows we're coming," Marcus replies.

"We still have to face them," Rio says.

"Yes, but we'll need a plan. We can't just walk into a mob of demons, not with Bailey. And besides, we've been flying for hours and she needs to rest," Marcus points out.

We turn and look at the toddler. Her eyes are bright and alert. But it has been hours and we have no idea when the last time she ate was.

"Marcus is right. She needs to rest and eat. Um…actually both humans need to eat," I point out bashfully.

Rage puts Bailey down onto the ground. He watches her as if to see if she has come to her senses and is now afraid of him. That is not the case. Bailey looks up at Rage and smiles.

"We go play now?" she asks.

"No," he says, sounding a lot like her when she had her earlier tantrum.

"What's your name?" she asks Rage.

"None of your business," he snaps.

"Uh oh, that's not nice. You gonna be in trouble," she warns him.

"Look, you little super power mouse, I'm not your friend," he informs her.

She bursts into tears immediately. Then the ground under us starts to r umble.

"I swear to Omnis you better say you're sorry, or you will be," Marcus warns Rage.

"I didn't come to babysit," Rage swears.

He and Marcus are about to get into it, with Bailey weeping loudly in the background. But then Ameana calls out to her boyfriend.

"Thomas, you're making her cry," she says.

Rage looks instantly sorry. It's not that Ameana spoke to him with anger or even firmness. The emotion behind her voice was disappointment. Ameana sounded genuinely hurt and disappointed that "Thomas" would neglect the feelings of a child.

"Okay, okay, super mouse. I'm sorry," he mumbles.

"You are sorry?" she asks between sobs.

"Yes, I am."

"Say sorry to Boo-Boo, too," she insists.

Rage is about to say something rude but then thinks better of it and apologizes to the rabbit as well.

"Now, tell her your name," Jay says, enjoying this a little too much.

"My name is Rage," he says, gritting his teeth behind a fake smile.

"Hi Ray," she says.

"No, it's Rage."

She tries to sound out his name, but she seems to have a problem with the ending. No matter what she tries, "Rage" sounds like "Ray."

"Fine, I'm Ray," he says, shaking his head.

"My name is Bailey and I'm this many," she says proudly, sticking out three fingers to show us her age.

"Great, mouse. Glad to hear it," Rage replies.

"You call me mouse," she says, giggling.

"Bailey, are you hungry?" I ask.

"Yes, can we have hot dogs? Boo-Boo loves hot dogs with a lot, a lot, a lot of ketchup," she informs us.

"After flying for hours for the first time, this kid isn't throwing up or anything. Now she wants hot dogs? Yeah, she's got super powers," Rio says.

"Okay, you can have hot dogs," I reply.

"And cookies?"

"Yes, and cookies."

She starts to do a dance-wiggle type thing that lets us know she's happy.

"Is Ray going to eat with me?" she begs.

The team is dying to laugh at how uncomfortable Rage is right now.

"Yeah, sure," he says begrudgingly.

Marcus tells us to each pick a cabin and that after our meeting, the team will Recharge.

"How'd you know this place would be here?" I ask.

"Winter texted me this location. She's gonna join us as soon as she gets more info on the Sage's movement," he replies.

We each pick a cabin. Bailey picks the one with Ameana and "Uncle" Ray. When Jay and Rio encourage Bailey to call Rage that, she does. I laugh so hard my sides hurt.

Chapter Twenty-Three: Who Did This?

Later, Rio and Miku go to town to get food for the humans and warmer clothes for Bailey, since she left without a coat. Thankfully, Rage's wings are like wearing fur; they keep her warm. I would have frozen many times, had it not been for the warmth of the Guardians' wings.

Marcus says the team will be meeting as soon as the twins come back. Meanwhile, we have nothing to do but make fun of "Uncle Ray."

Bailey insists on sitting next to Rage at the only table in the room. We watch as she fills him in on very important information, such as Bailey's favorite color (yellow), Bailey's favorite bedtime story (*The Three Little Pigs*) and Bailey's favorite nursery rhyme ("Itsy Bitsy Spider").

When Ameana and Rage have had enough of us laughing at their expense, they kick us out of their cabin. Once outside, we laugh even harder as we hear Bailey instructing "Uncle Ray" on how to properly hold his hands up while singing "Itsy Bitsy Spider."

Just as we are about to walk away from their cabin, Jay grabs me by the hand to show me something through the window of their cabin.

Oh my Omnis, Rage is on all fours, giving Bailey a pony ride. I think no matter what happens from here, I'm going to die happy. Jay records it on his cell. Marcus can't stop laughing, and I'm pretty sure I'm going to remember this moment forever.

The twins come back and bring the food to Ameana's cabin. The only way Bailey will eat is to have Rage beside her. The two of them have hot dogs, juice, and three cookies. I tell Marcus I didn't know demons could eat. He says food is not necessary for them, but they can if they wish.

The twins bring along a bottle of Coy from a Seller in the area. I eat the hot dog but pass up the Coy, since I don't like the taste. The team is taken with Bailey. She is as engaging as she is energetic. Rio whispers to me that Rage isn't radiating hate or anger; and while he's not blissful, he does not altogether hate being called "Uncle Ray."

Finally, Bailey falls asleep. Rage places her onto the small cot in the corner. He lays her down and she curls up into the fetal position. It's one of the few times we have seen her without her shield up. She wakes up briefly and talks to Rage for over ten minutes.

"What did she say?" Marcus asks.

"The mouse asked questions," Rage replies, shaking his head.

"Questions about what?" Miku asks.

"Everything. Where did the sky come from? Why is an elephant gray? Can you race a butterfly? How do they make up candy? Where is Dora the Explorer's house? Can we go? Why not?" Rage recalls.

"I need someone's jacket," Rage says bashfully.

"Why?" Ameana asks, handing him hers.

Rage mumbles something that we can't make out. Then he folds the jacket into a square, goes over to where Bailey is sleeping, and places it beside her.

"What did you need with the jacket?" she asks again.

"I needed to make a bed for the stupid rabbit, okay?" he snaps.

"You made a bed for her stuffed doll?" Ameana asks.

"I kind of promised her," he says, avoiding eye contact.

Ameana simply says okay. But we can see that she is battling the urge to go "aww" and embrace him. Meanwhile, we are trying not to make jokes; Ameana glares at us as a warning. I look around and, surprisingly enough, everyone is in pretty good spirits, considering.

Later, I ask Ameana if Rage could place a fireball inside the stove so I could heat up some water. Ameana, not my biggest fan, is reluctant to do anything for me. But she reconsiders and has Rage place a small fireball under the stove that would otherwise be useless.

As the pot of water boils, I thank the twins for getting me peppermint tea a few hours before. I remember the last time I had peppermint tea; it was in the Sage's home. Back when I thought he was on our side.

It's amazing how wrong we were.

At the meeting, the team comes up with a plan. Instead of going to the demons, they will have the demons come to us. Once they are in our area, we will use Miku to take out the first wave. Marcus contacts Winter and gets her to spread the info about our location to Sage. She tells us they should be here any minute.

When the demons reach our location, they are baffled that the team isn't out and ready to fight. The only one awaiting them is a small-framed female angel. The demons are so cocky; I can feel their smugness from where I am in the cabin. There are hundreds of them, with more coming every minute to get the Lyris, and the only thing that stands in their way is one girl.

It's only when the demons get close that they see the red tips of her wings and realizes it's Miku. That's when they start to panic. They shout out to the others to retreat because she's going to sing. But it's too late. We all put in our earplugs as Miku begins her serenade.

As she sings, she makes the demons carve into their skin as if it's a turkey for Thanksgiving dinner. It's raining demon blood, and Miku is having the time of her life. She takes off and follows the demons that are far enough away from the song to try and escape. She cuts them off and sings until the black blood flows like a spring. It's demon carnage; beautiful.

Marcus texts Miku and signals to her that she can go help Wolf at the camp. Once she takes off, the demons that remain swoop down on the cabin. They are met by the Guardians, who proceed to attack them without hesitation.

I nervously look on from the window of the cabin. Meanwhile, Rage complains about not being able to take off. I remind him about what will happen if Bailey is unhappy.

"How do you know my leaving will make her cry?" he asks.

"Move away from her, two feet," I tell him.

He does so, and Bailey's eyes begin to fill with tears.

"Dam—darn it," he says, correcting himself midsentence.

The sight of Rage trying not to curse is beyond funny. He shakes his head and looks over at Bailey.

"You're gonna have to learn to be without me. I'm not a babysitter. I'm an Akon," he says to her firmly.

"I Akon," she repeats, equally firm.

She wants so much to be like him that she has taken the same no-nonsense stance Rage does. He shakes his head in disbelief. She shakes her head, too.

"Come on, we need to hide you," the First Akon says as the battle outside rages on.

"Hide-and-seek?" Bailey asks.

"Yeah, something like that."

While he takes her into the back room to hide her, I peek out the window and instantly wish I hadn't. A demon grabs Ameana by the hair, whirls her around, and flings her into the side of the mountain. Ameana crashes and slides down and is about to hit the ground.

Thankfully, Jay appears in time to catch her. I'm glad Rage didn't see it; he would have taken off at top speed to kill the demon. Then Bailey would cry and it would just get worse from there.

But there's no need for Rage to worry, because Ameana soon takes off like a rocket and finds the demon who threw her. She calls for his eyes to come to her. I've never seen her do that before. The demon's eyes pop out of their sockets and float on over to Ameana.

She shakes them in her hands like they are a set of dice. She hurls them down to the ground below. The newly blinded demon is livid. But all the fury in the world doesn't help him to find Ameana. When he gets close to her location, she drop-kicks him and sends him flying to his death below.

Meanwhile, a few yards over, Marcus is at the center of a circle of determined demons, being beaten to death.

"Jay!" I shout desperately.

However, Jay is busy with a mob of demons all his own. I look back at Marcus and curse myself for not having wings.

"Ameana, help him!" I shout at the top of my lungs.

It turns out my panic is unnecessary. One by one, the demons are thrown out of the circle with broken bodies. The First Guardian doesn't need any help. The circle of demons is no match for his brute strength. He rams through them, punching, kicking, and reflecting back their fears. He is a marvel in the air.

I'm so busy admiring how skilled my fiancé is, I don't notice the Believers until Rage pulls on my shirt. He signals for me to look toward the side of the mountain and, dear Omnis, I'm sorry I did.

There is an endless stream of Believers climbing up the side of the mountain. It's as if they are an army of ants and we're the picnic food. As soon as they land at the top, they launch Powerballs our way. We duck; the Powerballs go over our heads and land at the other side of the cabin. The walls begin to collapse.

Chapter Twenty-Three: Who Did This?

Rage and I run to go get Bailey. He had placed her under the bed, where she had gotten comfortable, playing with Boo-Boo. When Rage pulls her out, she takes his hand and invites him to play tea party with Rage says he will play later. He then lets go of her hand, knowing it will make her raise her shield. She does exactly that. Now that she is protected, he tells me to take her out back and keep her calm. Although Bailey trusts no one but Rage, she does know us well enough now that we can get her to follow us. I take her to the opening of a nearby cave we scouted earlier.

Bailey, upset about being separated from Rage, begins to cry. I start to sing her favorite song. She quiets down and the ground beneath us stops shaking. I have never been so happy to sing about a spider.

I take a peek out of the cave at the battle in the sky and on the ground. Bailey peeks out too. She sees Rage fighting numerous Believers with multiple fireballs. Excited, Bailey jumps up and down shouting, "Go, Ray, go!"

As impressive as Rage's skills are, there are far too many Believers for him to take on alone. He is quickly losing the upper hand. I turn to Bailey and ask her a vital question.

"Can you promise to stay here for me?"

"Okay," she says.

Something in her voice tells me she's not sure she can stick to her promise.

"Bailey, if you stay here, Ray will give you candy," I vow.

"Ray give candy?"

"Yes."

"Can I have two candy?" she asks as she sticks out two of her little fingers at me, her eyes wide in anticipation.

"Three candy," I promise.

"Three? Yes!" she says, hardly able to stand still.

"Remember, you have to stay here, okay?"

She says yes now with a renewed resolve. She turns to Boo-Boo and fills him in on the plan.

"Boo-Boo stay, okay?" she says authoritatively to the rabbit. They "both" look back at me with certainty. Staying in the cave is now their only mission in life.

By the time I run out to help Rage, he's being mobbed by a bunch of Believers who have him pinned to the ground. One of them is a woman; she stands over Rage, sucking the life out of him, literally. I look around anxiously for something to attack the Believers with.

Seriously, Emmy, how many times do you have to be in a battle to remember to carry a weapon with you? I mean, really, this is like mission number five hundred and ten; you still walk around with nothing in your hands. Argh!

I shake my head, irritated with myself. Would it have killed me to remember to put a switchblade in my back pocket or something?

Then I have a thought and dash back inside what's left of the cabin. I grab the nearest rag, wrap it around my hands, and pick up the scalding pot of water. I run out and throw the pot of water at the life-sucking Believer.

She doesn't melt like the wicked witch in *The Wizard of Oz*, but she does scream her head off as parts of her skin slide off her body like tender meat sliding off the bone. Shocked, she places her hand on her face to see how much of it is still left: very little.

Rage uses the distraction I've provided him to summon up a fireball and roast the other Believers who had held him down. That is the good part. The bad part is I now have a Believer, who looks like a walking open wound, determined to kill me.

Her left eye drips down the side of her face. She looks like a living, breathing nuclear accident. I can actually see the bones protruding where there once was flesh. It's then I realize that Rage's fireballs aren't just hot, they're supernaturally so.

The Believer's anger far surpasses her pain. She should have been on the ground writhing in agony but her hatred of me keeps her standing. She raises what's left of her palm and starts to pull the life out of me.

It feels like I'm being sucked up inside a giant black hole. The more of me it takes in, the less useful my body is. Only a few seconds under her power and my legs give out. I fall down to my knees. Then my arms, face muscles, and fingers go numb.

There's a coldness invading my body. She's only a few seconds away from rendering me completely without sensation. I try to fight back but her pull is too strong.

Chapter Twenty-Three: Who Did This?

Just when I'm about to black out, I feel the life slowly draining back into my body. I look and Rio is blocking her with his shield. She swears at him and doubles her efforts. But Rage launches another fireball and ends her in one swift motion.

Rio helps me to my feet. I thank him and run back to check on Bailey. Before I can get to the cave, I see Winter pop up on a Port. At the same time, a demon, who we had thought was dead, uses his last breath to launch a Powerball at her.

Rio spots the demon at the same time as I do. Knowing that his shield will not work so long as he is that close to Winter, I shout at him not to block the attack. But Rio doesn't hesitate; he leaps out in front of her.

The Powerball hits him right in his chest. Rio collapses onto the ground. The demon who attacked him grins and dies on the spot. I run over to Rio. Winter gets there first. The Powerball has torn his chest wide open.

The blood rushes out of him quickly. His face is drained of color and his wings lie eerily still. Winter takes off her jacket and tries to stop the bleeding. Within seconds, the jacket is soaked with the Guardian's blood.

"I'm so sorry," Winter says over and over again as she bursts into tears.

Rio shakes his head as if to tell her there's no reason to be sorry.

"Your sister can heal you, right?" she asks desperately.

"I already texted her; she's on her way," Ameana vows.

Rio looks at us with sad eyes.

"She won't make it," he whispers.

"Yes, she will," Marcus replies as he steps closer to examine Rio.

"I'm sorry about Virginia. Virginia is who I never wanted to be," Rio replies.

I think that Rio may be delirious, but Marcus seems to understand what he's saying.

"You can make it up to me later," Marcus replies.

"Forgive me?" Rio asks.

"No, that's something for someone who's about to die, and you're not," Marcus promises him.

"Forgive me," he repeats.

"Don't think about that now," Marcus tells him.

"Yo, you know you can't die, so just stop being dramatic. You're gonna be fine," Jay adds.

"She's gonna need you," he says to Jay.

Jay knows Rio is referring to Miku. He can't bring himself to look at his friend, so he turns away. We all look at each other in silent panic. I call Miku. There's no answer. I'm sure she's too busy trying to get here to pick up.

"Stop acting like this is the end. You've been healed a million times. Miku is on her way. You've hardly broken any bones," Ameana replies.

"Liar," he says.

"Rio, please stop talking like it's the end," I beg him.

"Marcus, forgive me," he asks again.

"No," Marcus replies stubbornly, knowing that forgiving Rio would be like telling him it's okay for him to die.

"Please."

Marcus looks his friend over. The pool of blood is ubiquitous. We're all soaked in it. Marcus looks at me, pained. He silently asks me what he should do. I look at Rio's now completely colorless face and then nod to Marcus with tearstained cheeks.

"Yes, I forgive you," he says sorrowfully.

Rio smiles a little. Then he looks towards Winter. She takes his hand and kisses it.

"I can read you without my powers now. I know what you're feeling. And no, I don't," he whispers.

"Don't what?" she asks.

"Regret my actions."

She cries hard and puts his hand on her heart.

"Rio, don't go," I plead.

"Miku is here! I see her. She's only a few yards out! Hang on!" Ameana says, filled with relief.

We look up at Ameana with regret. She looks down on the ground and sees that Rio is no longer smiling; the boy who never got to really live dies with his eyes open.

"How could I survive a Powerball attack but Rio die from it?" I ask.

Chapter Twenty-Three: Who Did This?

"Powerballs are only as powerful as the person throwing them; demons are stronger than Quo," Marcus replies.

Miku arrives mere seconds later. She flies down, pushes past us, and takes her brother in her arms. She calls out her brother's name but he does not respond. She touches him in hopes of being able to heal him. It does not work. She looks down at Rio and begs him to wake up. The grief in her voice causes everyone that can cry to weep openly.

When Miku looks up at us, it's not what we expect. Miku isn't sad or grieving. She's enraged. Her voice is filled with wrath and fury. Her eyes have turned into black pools of soullessness. She speaks with all the venom of Lucy herself.

"WHO LET HIM DIE?" she screams.

We look at each other in a total state of alarm.

Oh no…

"Winter, get out of here," Marcus orders, never taking his eyes off of Miku.

Winter disappears on the Port just as Miku's wings start to change color. She takes to the air and screeches down at us with rage unlike any we've encountered.

"WHO LET HIM DIE???" she demands.

The blood-soaked wings, the soulless eyes, the words dripping with malice and the promise of violence, this means only one thing: Redd has retur ned…

CHAPTER TWENTY-FOUR: LETTING GO

Redd looms in the air, looking down at us. Her hair flies furiously behind her. Her blood-colored wings have expanded to nearly twice the size of Miku's. Her nails have grown to the length of claws. I look in her face and find darkness swirling where her eyes once were.

"Pretty, you have to fight it. You can't Turn on us now," Marcus orders her.

"Miku, don't do this," I beg.

Jay and Ameana call out to her as well, but she does not respond. She simply looks down at us and awaits an answer.

"Rio died, it's no one's fault," Ameana says, trying to reason with her.

"We need to go up and get her," Jay pleads to Marcus.

"I don't want to make any sudden movements and make her go on the attack," he replies.

"That's great, Guardian, but how are we going to stop them from moving?" Rage says, signaling to the horde of demons headed our way. There are so many we can no longer make out the sky. It's just waves and waves of demons.

"Redd, no one is at fault. Please, we need Miku back," Jay shouts.

The demons get closer and closer to us. Miku does not pay attention to the multitude of evil about to surround her. One demon, eager to attack, hurls a Powerball at her from half a mile away. The Powerball sinks into Redd's skin without causing the slightest damage.

Up until that moment, Redd isn't sure what she wants to do. But when the Powerball hits her, it helps her set a goal—death to everyone.

Calmly, Redd turns to face the slew of demons coming for her.

"Stop," she orders in a whisper of pure malevolence.

Chapter Twenty-Four: Letting Go

Every single demon in the sky stands absolutely still.

"How the… did she…?" I begin.

"She's more powerful than Miku. Miku needed a song, a melody, to make people obey the order given to them by her unnatural sadness. Redd is able to convey enough macabre sadness in a word or two," Marcus concludes in amazement.

Marcus is right; the power of her words far exceeds that of any song.

"Blood," she orders.

And without hesitation, every demon in the sky begins to mutilate themselves in order to send blood to Redd. Some of them bite off chunks of flesh from their forearms. Some use blades to fillet themselves. One demon claws at the side of his neck until a vein pops in order to obey. The demons are wailing and groaning as they are forced to torture themselves.

Redd has even more power than Marcus first assumed. Not only can she cause damage in a word, she can control the very elements that make up her victim.

"Come," she says to the blood as it oozes from the demons.

We stand in awe as the river of blood flows from each demon and into the air, moving towards Redd. She drains demon after demon of blood. They fall from the sky and smash, lifeless, onto the ground.

On the ground, the Believers cower, fearing Redd's wrath, but she does not allow them to get away. She looks down at the masses running for their lives, and she speaks again.

"Hear ts."

The massacre is unlike any I've ever seen. The Believers impale themselves on sharp rock edges, hurl themselves down the mountain, and use their powers to slice into their skin. The screams coming from the air and the ground form a spine-chilling chorus of terror.

"She's killing them for us, that's good, right?" I ask as I flinch at the sight.

"No, it's not," Marcus says.

"Why?"

"Because now, she's coming for us."

And sure enough, Redd swoops down and aims for us. She doesn't want to speak and cause our death. Judging from the look on her face, she wants to personally dismantle us using her bare hands.

"Take Bailey and go!" Marcus shouts to Rage. Rage picks Bailey up in his arms and takes off at record speed.

The team takes to the air, and Marcus tells me to hide. Every single demon and Believer has been killed. It's only us and Redd on the mountain.

Redd sees Marcus flying near her. She is about to speak and end his life with a single word. But Jay flies behind her and tries to get her attention. Jay begs and pleads with Redd to try and remember who she was before. It's not working. Redd goes after Jay, now determined to feel his flesh between her fingers.

"Jay, she's not gonna change," Marcus shouts out to him.

"Miku's in there, we have to find her," Jay replies, dodging Redd in the air.

"It's not working," Ameana says, filled with regret.

"Ameana's right. We have to take her down!" Marcus calls out.

"You touch her, I'll kill you," Jay vows.

Redd has had enough. She opens her mouth and calls for Jay to come to her. His body does as she asks; it cuts through the sky and stands, helpless, in front of Redd.

"Miku, you have to fight it," he begs.

"She is gone," Redd replies coldly.

"No, she's in there. Miku, please, please, don't do this," Jay cries out.

"Blood," Redd demands.

Without the slightest pause, Jay digs into his chest and blood spews out. He groans as he is dissected by his own hands.

Marcus moves to tackle Redd. Jay shouts at him to stay back in between screams.

Redd looks on as Jay continues to murder himself.

"We have to take her," Ameana says to Marcus.

"No!" Jay roars as he uses both hands to split his chest open. He calls out for Omnis as the agony causes him to shiver. Jay's blood drips down on us like rain. He's starting to lose consciousness.

"We can't just let her kill you!" Marcus says, flying fast towards them.

Chapter Twenty-Four: Letting Go

"She's in there," Jay counters softly as he can no longer shout.

"She is gone," Redd reminds him again.

"No…she can't be gone," Jay says as his hands fall helplessly to his sides.

He's not carving into himself anymore. The only thing he can do at this point is wait for death.

"But she is gone and I'm all that's left," Redd replies with a bloodlust that rivals Lucy's.

"No…she's there…Miku…please…," Jay mumbles as his eyes close.

"I told you she's gone!" Redd says, getting more and more enraged.

"She can't be…I need her," he says as his head hangs to the side.

"Why?" Redd demands.

"I love her."

That's the last thing Jay says. The blood loss causes him to black out.

Marcus goes to tackle Redd.

"Marcus, no!" I scream.

He looks down at me, confused. I signal for him to take a closer look at what's happening. Redd is studying Jay's ravaged body. She gets this look on her face as if a memory has just flashed before her. She lightly touches his face with her fingers.

"Jay?" she says with the weak voice of a little girl.

The crimson in her wings slowly changes back to white, though still with their red tips. Her wingspan is decreasing back to its normal size. Her claws retract and are replaced by her natural nails. Her eyes are a beautiful gray again.

She looks like someone who has just been pulled out of a deep sleep. She looks around, fully aware for the first time of what has just taken place. She places her hand over her mouth in horror.

Marcus takes Jay down to the ground. Miku looks on helplessly as the angel she loves clings to life. By the time Marcus lands, Jay's wings have stopped moving completely.

"Oh no, please, no," Miku cries. Ameana embraces her tightly as they look down on what could be the third Guardian death.

Marcus is the first to see her. She stands on the edge of the mountain. The wind blows through her hair. Her beautiful white dress makes her look elegant and ethereal. Missing a hand doesn't diminish from Rahell's beauty in the least.

She looks upon us with grave sadness and regret. Even though we already know Rio is dead, there's something about Rahell's presence that makes it official. I flash back to Reese's Passing. Rahell took his body to the house of fire and we stood by helplessly and watched. The grief and hurt that came with Reese's death has returned.

"I thought you didn't take angels anymore because there are too many of us dying at once?" Marcus says in a voice dripping with sorrow.

"He's not just an angel; he's a Guardian. He deserves a Taker," she replies.

"Where are the others?" Ameana asks in a pained whisper.

"Normally, the Para would show up, but with the war…"

She is trying to say that she's the only one coming to say goodbye to Rio. Everyone else is either fighting, dead, or in hiding. It's not fair. Rio risked his life so many times for us; he should be sent off by millions of Paras.

Warm tears make their way down my face. The all-too-familiar ache of loss wraps itself around me, yet again.

"We have to take Jay to a Healer," Marcus replies.

"No…gonna say goodbye," Jay whispers.

We turn to him, shocked that he's awake. He lifts his head and says he will not go until the Passing is over. He's hurt really badly and can't keep his head up without help. I go over to him and help him prop his head against me.

Miku goes over to Rahell and kneels at her feet, begging in a voice that sounds more human than angel.

"Please, don't take him. He's all I have."

She moans like a wounded child. She begs and begs Rahell to take her instead. She vows to give anything, everything, if Rahell doesn't take him.

I bite down on the bottom of my lip to keep from crying even more. I want to take her pain away. I want so much to make Rio come back. But there's nothing I can do. There's nothing anyone can do. Rahell kneels down and takes Miku's face in her hand.

"I'll guide him. He won't be alone. I promise," she vows.

"He's half of me."

"I won't take him until you're ready to let go," she says.

"Jay needs to get help," Miku replies.

"You're in love with Jay?" Rahell asks, studying Miku.

"Yes."

"Then go take care of him. And I'll take care of Rio."

Miku's lips quiver as she nods and stands up.

She signals to Rahell that she's ready. Rahell stands up and waves her hands, and feathers from her third coat gather in the air and form a Reef: a bed of feathers that carry the body to the house of fire. She uses her power to place Rio on the Reef.

From the corner of my eye, I see a bright light. I turn and find a Para standing along the mountain range. Rahell was wrong; they do show up. In fact, in the minutes to follow, the mountain is graced with the presence of a few dozen Paras.

It's not like Reese's Passing, with hundreds of angels in attendance. But any angel who could come, did. Wounded Ground Walkers, and Travelers too. In addition, the Original Paras stand on the tallest peak of the range to pay their respects.

Rio's body floats by us. We each whisper our goodbyes. Miku thanks him for taking care of her their whole lives. Jay thanks him for his friendship. I do the same. Ameana thanks him for his love.

Winter, who has quietly joined us, thanks him for saving her life and for the best kiss she's ever had. Marcus passes up the chance to say goodbye. He shakes his head and walks away from the group.

The Original Paras begin to sing. The others join in. It's a sad but beautiful melody just like the one they sang at Reese's Passing.

Rahell stands beside Rio's body and prepares to travel alongside it. However, the Reef does not move. That means someone is not ready to let him go. And until then, the Reef will stay where it is. Unfortunately, Lucy will come get what is rightfully hers if Rahell doesn't bring it to her.

"I'm trying to let go," Miku begs Rahell.

But Rahell tells her she's not the one keeping the Reef from moving. The Taker looks around the mountain to find the source that loves Rio too much to accept his end.

"Marcus, it's time," Rahell says.

He is facing away from us. He shakes his head "no." He won't let Rio go. Miku goes over to him and takes his hand. Marcus bows his head and whispers something to her. She answers him in a whisper. He nods his head in agreement, but the Reef doesn't move.

"Marcus," Rahell warns gently.

Suddenly, the Reef begins to move. Rahell guides it gently across the mountain range. The angels and Paras slowly start flying away.

I flash back to a memory I had with Rio. I was at home and I was supposed to be staying away from Marcus. Back then, he and Ameana were together. But I just couldn't stay away from him. So, I rushed out of the house to go tell Marcus that I loved him and wanted to be with him. Rio was waiting for me at my door.

"I read your Wave. It told me you were about to do something very brave and very stupid," he said.

"You gonna try and talk me out of it?" I asked.

"Could I?" he questioned.

"No."

"Then no," he replied warmly.

I smile at the memory of his wit and sarcasm. The smile fades quickly when I realize I will never again see his face. He will never sit beside me and offer me ice cream because I'm hurting.

Looking around, I know I'm not the only one lost in memories. The team is silent and pensive. Winter is crying softly as I take her hand in mine. We look on as Rio and Rahell move further away. Then, all too soon, the Guardian whose love has always been eluded disappears forever from our view.

CHAPTER TWENTY-FIVE: REMEMBER

Jay loses consciousness as soon as the Passing is over. We take him back to Raphael, in the hope he can fix him once again. Raphael tells us what we already know: Jay is severely hurt and may not recover. Hearing the harsh reality of the situation, Miku runs from the room. Raphael assures us that he will try everything he can and says it's okay to check on our friend.

She sits on the edge of the mountain, her wings hanging low and her head bowed. It's hard to believe that just a few hours ago she was this massive force of nature. Now she looks like a lost kid. I so want to help her, but like the others, I have no idea how.

We all sit on the edge of the mountain with her. That's nothing for the beings with wings but as a human, I have to tell you, sitting on the edge takes a little getting used to. I try not to look down and remember that if I should fall, there are angels to catch me.

"It's gonna be okay, Pretty," Marcus assures her.

"How? Everyone I love is being taken away. And worse, one of them could die because of me."

"You couldn't control yourself. You had no choice," Ameana tells her.

"It doesn't matter. If Jay dies, his death will still be on me. And Rio, he's really…"

She whimpers, and Marcus pulls her into his embrace.

"Why did he do that? Why didn't he just let you guys kill me?" Miku asks.

"Jay knew you could fight against Redd. That's why he risked his life, because he believed in you," I reply.

"Yeah, and look what that got him. He's half dead," she replies.

"He did it because he loves you. That's what brought you back, and I know he doesn't regret the risk he took," Marcus adds.

"How do you know that?"

"You never regret saving people you love. When you save them, you save yourself." He takes my hand in his.

"I know you guys are trying to help, but the fact is, Rio was my only brother and he's gone. And now the only guy I have ever loved could be gone too. I don't want to feel better. I just want to be alone. I'm sorry," she says as she takes off into the sky.

The team and I agree it's best to give her some time alone.

Marcus signals for us to look in the sky; Rage and Bailey are coming in to land. Ameana tells us she told him our location.

Ameana runs to Rage, wraps her arms around him and buries her face in his broad chest. He embraces her, his face filled with concern.

"Me, me," Bailey says, reaching her little arms out to be picked up too. Surprised, Ameana picks her up and cradles her in her arms.

We've never seen Bailey lower her shields for anyone besides Rage. Seeing her in Ameana's arms, unprotected, catches us all off guard.

"No cry, be happy, like this," Bailey says to Ameana.

She then displays her best grin so that Ameana has a visual of what happiness is supposed to be. Bailey waits for her to smile. Ameana tries her best to do as she's told. Strangely enough, while the smile is sad, it is g enuine.

Rage tells Bailey to go inside. Her face falls and she is about to cry. Rage looks at her sternly.

"Are you gonna cry?" he asks.

She shakes her head. "No."

"That's right, because what did I tell you about crying?" he asks her.

"Crying is for punks," she says, sounding very well trained.

"That's right. Go inside and I'll be there in a minute."

Ameana puts her down and she runs inside.

"Where did you take her?" Marcus asks.

"We laid low until Ameana called and said it was okay to come back. The mouse ate and asked about three thousand questions," Rage replies.

Chapter Twenty-Five: Remember

"Good; as soon as Raphael treats Jay, we'll head to Greenland. Redd was able to take out a large portion of demons; the journey should be easier," Marcus concludes.

"So is Speedy gonna die or what?" Rage asks.

"Are you fucking kidding me?" Ameana snaps, pulling away from Rage.

"What? I'm just asking," he replies, surprised by her reaction.

"I could lose two friends today. Two members of my team and that's how you…I swear, sometimes you're just such an Akon!" She shakes her head in utter disgust and flies off.

Rage looks at us, bewildered. But he remains where he is. He makes no attempt at all to go after Ameana. I roll my eyes and address the clueless demon.

"I know you're new to the whole 'good' guy thing, but when you say something reckless and awful to your girlfriend, you should probably go after her," I advise him.

He turns to Marcus and he agrees.

"She's right. That's usually the next move," he tells the Akon.

"I was just asking a question," Rage argues.

"Look, we don't have time to teach you how to be decent. Just think of it this way, every minute you stand here with us is a minute she's rethinking her relationship with you," Marcus warns him.

Rage walks towards the edge of the mountain but he doesn't take off. Instead he turns back to look at us. The tone in his voice is strange. It lacks confidence. In fact, I'd say his tone borders on quiet desperation.

"What do I say to her?" he asks.

"How should I know?" Marcus replies.

"She needs like…angel words…give me some."

"If she wanted angel words, she should have got with an angel," Marcus replies.

"If I say the wrong thing…"

"Rage, just go get her," I push.

"She's sad and stuff. I'm not good with sad."

"I guess you're gonna get some practice then," I reply.

He looks down at the ground, and then takes off after the girl he loves.

For the next few hours, very little changes. Jay's wounds are so bad that Raphael says he needs to apply layers of different mixtures, each one more potent than the next.

The longer we stay here, the worse things get with the world. All the networks and the emergency response systems are gone. The cell phone connections are spotty at best and the death toll reaches hundreds of thousands. The Goumy have laid waste to three continents and they have showed no sign of stopping.

On the battlefield, Miku's help has given the Foundation soldiers a much needed push, but the fact of the matter is, they are spread thin. There just aren't enough of them to win the war and help the humans. That is exactly what the Sage was counting on.

The Guardians are going to lose this war; or at least we will if we don't get Bailey to Greenland. Marcus knows all of this but he refuses to leave a Guardian behind. I try to talk him into going but it does no good.

I can't imagine what Jay's death would do to the team; especially to Marcus. I can practically hear his internal dialogue. He's blaming himself for Rio's death. If another member of this team dies…Marcus will lose Raphael had no idea how old Bailey was. Once he sees her, he is fascinated that the Lyris has chosen her. As we wait to see if the mixtures help Jay, Bailey and Raphael become fast friends. I think it has to do with the fact that Raphael lets her play video games with him. While Bailey can't really play, she presses each and every button on the controller and gets excited when it causes something to happen on the screen.

"How do you have electricity?" I ask.

"I'm a Para, we come fully loaded," he brags.

"How long do you think it will be before Jay wakes up?" I ask.

"He may not."

"Raphael, please don't say that."

"I'm sorry, Emmy. I just want to prepare you. I think the rest of the team should go take Bailey to Greenland. Staying here is ill advised."

"I know, but Marcus won't leave him."

Chapter Twenty-Five: Remember

"You only have a day or two to find the Shoma," he reminds me. "Maybe we'll get lucky and all three pieces will be down the street at a Fed Ex or something. Then all we'd have to do is show ID to get it," I joke lamely.

He laughs. I shake my head and slump down on my chair. He studies me.

"You and the team have been through a lot. I'm sorry," Raphael offers.

"Me too."

I turn and see Marcus out the window, looking out into the sky. I check on Bailey; she's as engrossed in the video game as Raphael. I head outside so I can talk to the First Guardian.

"Hey," I say.

"I should go get Miku. It's been a few hours," he replies.

"We should get her when we have news about Jay," I suggest.

"I guess."

"Has Ameana come back?" I ask.

"No, her and Rage are still somewhere, arguing or screwing. I don't know which."

"Maybe both," I joke.

"Yeah, maybe," he says with a serious, pensive voice.

"Marcus, maybe the team should go to—"

"I'm not leaving here without him," he snaps.

"Okay." I nod as I get closer to him.

We are silent for a few minutes. The sky gets darker and clouds roll in. I'm hoping he'll talk to me without me having to push him. It takes nearly twenty minutes but he finally says something.

"I didn't think I'd have to worry about the twins," he confesses.

"Yeah, me either."

"I thought with them being self-healing, I could relax and focus on the rest of the team. And now he's gone and it's my fault."

"No, it's not. You didn't blast him with a Powerball, Marcus."

"I SHOULD HAVE SAVED HIM!!!" he shouts, pulling away from me.

"You had to send Miku to help on the battlefield. You did what was best for the team. You're a good leader," I remind him.

"No, a good leader would have been smart enough to realize the Sage was evil. A good leader wouldn't miss something like that."

"Baby, it doesn't help to keep tearing yourself up like this," I say, taking his hand in mine.

"I just want to understand how it happened," he says, lost in thought.

"How what happened?" I ask.

"How did I lose two Guardians? How did I let my friends die? *Why* can't I save the people I love?"

"You save me. You always save me."

I wrap my arms around him. He holds me tightly. I can feel the stress and tension in his body. I look into his eyes; the worry etched inside them breaks my heart.

"Everything is gonna be okay. I really believe that. We'll get Bailey where she needs to be and we'll save the world—again," I promise him.

"We have less than a few hours to find the Shoma; that won't be enough time. So in the end, we may save your world, but we won't save mine."

Not long after Marcus and I talk, Ameana and Rage return. They're holding hands, so I guess they've made up. Bailey greets them eagerly.

"Mimi, look!" she says, pointing to the video game. Ameana pretends she has never even seen a video game. She acts surprised and delighted. Rage kisses her on her temple and whispers something in her ear that causes Ameana to smile.

"Has anyone seen Miku? It's time she was back. She shouldn't be out there on her own for this long," Marcus says.

"I'm here," she whispers from the front door.

She looks smaller somehow. It's as if the weight of her grief has taken five pounds off her already small frame. Her eyes are worn looking and droopy. I suggest she rests, but naturally she refuses to Recharge until Jay wakes up.

"Can I do it now?" Bailey asks Rage.

"Do what?" Marcus says suspiciously.

"Yeah, Mimi will help you," Rage replies.

Chapter Twenty-Five: Remember

Bailey and Ameana disappear into the back. We all look on curiously. A few minutes later, Ameana comes back and makes an announcement.

"Ladies and gentlemen, welcome to the Bailey fashion show!"

"Can I come out now?" she asks from behind Ameana.

"Yup, we're all ready."

"Wait!" Rage says as he goes over to Raphael and tells him something. Raphael goes over to the table with the mountains of gadgets. He presses a button and music fills the room. Rage tells Bailey to start the show.

Bailey leaps out in front of Ameana and shows off her new outfit. She has on a black leather jacket with dark jeans and a pink shirt that proclaims *"I'm as awesome as they say."*

Everyone in the room laughs at her unbridled enthusiasm. Even Miku smiles a little as Bailey works the room and throws kisses to us. When the show is over, we clap and tell her what a great job she did.

"Can I have candy now?" she asks Rage.

"No, nap time, candy later," he says, sounding like he has had years of experience.

Bailey pouts but agrees. Raphael points to a small armchair where Ameana can lay her down. Ameana walks her over to the chair and starts to sing "Itsy Bitsy Spider."

"What happens to her, after the Lyris is used?" Rage asks, concerned.

"She'll be a normal human," Raphael replies.

"Where's her family?" I ask.

"The Lyris usually chooses people without families. That way they don't have to separate them from their loved ones."

"So, Bailey doesn't have anyone?" Ameana asks.

"No, but we will see to it she's taken care of," Raphael assures her.

"What if we take her?" Rage says.

The room goes silent. We all turn to Rage, including Ameana. Rage looks over at her to gauge her reaction. Slowly, she smiles and nods in ag reement.

Marcus and I exchange looks of confusion and uncertainty. Miku is about to ask what I'm sure will be one of many questions but then we hear Jay mumble.

Miku rushes over to him. Raphael warns him not to get up because he is still too weak. Jay looks awful. His skin is ashen and his eyes are dull.

"Are you okay? How do you feel? I'm so sorry, Jay. I'm so, so sorry," Miku says, taking his hand.

He looks up at her and blacks out again. Miku begs him to wake up but Jay doesn't. Miku's face falls as Jay's hand goes limp inside hers. Raphael tells her it's natural for Jay to go in and out of consciousness, but it does little to cheer Miku up.

I turn to Marcus and ask him for a favor. He looks at me curiously.

"You really want me to do that?" he asks.

"Yeah, please," I reply.

He flies me to New York City, or what's left of it. We land on the block his favorite bar is on. We find him sitting in an alley not far away. He has his head down and a beer in his hand. When he looks up and sees us, he's on high alert.

"Hi, Julian," I say, not sure what I'm expecting to happen.

"What's wrong? What happened? Are you hurt?" he asks, looking me over.

"She's fine," Marcus replies.

"Yeah, no thanks to you," Julian counters.

"Can you two please knock it off?" I bark.

They both fall silent.

The alley, like most of New York, has been ravaged by the weather. Very little remains standing in the area.

"Can we go somewhere and talk?" I ask Julian.

"You wanna talk to me?" he asks, shocked.

"Um, yeah…kind of."

He looks around to see what's still standing. We head for an abandoned gas station across the street. I tell Marcus I want to talk to Julian alone.

"Are you sure about this?" he asks.

I kiss Marcus's forehead and walk across the street with the original First Guardian.

Chapter Twenty-Five: Remember

We enter the small convenience store attached to the gas station. The wall is cracked, the windows are smashed, and everything has been thrown to the floor. There's about a foot of water under our feet and all the lights are out.

Wanting to talk to Julian was a spur of the moment thing, and now that he is right in front of me, I'm not sure what to say or even where to start.

"What is it?" he asks.

"Um…nothing. How's the end of the world thing going for you?"

WTF???

"Emmy, what's happening?" he asks, filled with worry.

I shrug my shoulders.

"I don't know," I reply, staring at the floor.

Damn it, Emmy, why did you want to meet him if you weren't gonna say anything?

"Tell me what happened," Julian insists.

"Nothing, really. I mean, we found a source that could help save the world, so that's good. She's only like, three years old, but she can help."

"That's great, what's the problem?"

The tears run from my eyes even before I realize they were coming.

"He's dead," I sob.

"Who's dead?"

Suddenly, it all comes pouring out of me. I become a volcano of pent-up emotion. I'm erupting in the form of uncontrollable sobs and shaking. In a moment of utter weakness, I bare my soul to the man I worked so hard to ignore.

"Rio's dead. He got hit with a Powerball and he died. He died with his eyes open and he was my friend and that's not fair. It's not fair! He never got a chance to find love and he deserved it. And Miku's so broken…I can't fix her. And Jay's hurt; Redd cut him open. And I want to help Marcus but I don't know what to say. And I know he loves me but I'm still pissed he married Bianca. And I just…I just…I miss my mom, I miss her so much… I can't take it anymore, I can't…"

I don't remember if he came to me or if I went to him. All I know is that Julian is holding me as I blubber on his shoulder. I didn't think I could break down like that, but I did. I cry into his chest and he strokes my hair and tells me things will work out.

"No, they won't," I sob.

"Yes, they will, Piglet."

I pull away from him and look into his eyes.

"How do you…?"

"I used to watch you and your mom all the time. I heard her call you that. It always cheered you up," Julian replies.

"You watched me? I mean you *really* came to see me?"

"There was a kindergarten play with the best queen bee in history. Then, there was the field trip to the zoo where you tried to open the gate and set the bears free."

"They looked really sad. It was like their eyes were begging me," I reply.

"Yeah, well, I was in the crowd and got security to intercept before you could 'rescue' them."

"You did?"

"Yeah; then there was the time you were gonna run away from home, remember?"

"I was like, five. My mom wouldn't let me stay up and watch TV."

"You packed your *Sesame Street* backpack with socks, a coloring book, and a box of ice cream."

"How did you know that?"

"You snuck out of your apartment when your mom wasn't looking. You got all the way down the block, leaking vanilla ice cream with every step."

"I remember that! I ran into a man who asked me where I was going. I told him I was running away. He laughed and looked down at the trail of vanilla drops. He said I better eat the ice cream before it all melted. We sat down on the sidewalk and 'drank' the ice cream together. Then he said maybe I shouldn't run away because there may not be ice cream where I'm g oing."

"Then he took your sticky hands and walked you back home."

"Julian…?"

"After you were back safe in your apartment, I stood outside that door for hours. I would have given anything to be able to walk in and tell you and your mother who I was. I wanted to be with my family, but after that day, I stopped watching over you; it hurt too much," he says with a catch in his voice.

He's close to crying; too close.

"I should go," I reply, clearing my throat.

"Yeah, okay," he says, avoiding eye contact.

"Thanks for…listening," I say as I head out.

"Emmy, you've done an amazing job at keeping it together. These aren't normal circumstances. It's okay to lose it."

"Yeah, I guess. Thanks again," I reply, heading for the door.

He calls out after me in a voice filled with pride.

"Femi was strong, courageous and, most of all, unbreakable. And you, Emerson Hope, you are your mother's child."

CHAPTER TWENTY-SIX: DARKEST OF THE DARK

She takes my hand and drags me to Jay's bed.

"How do you feel?" I ask.

"Like a good engine in the hands of a bad driver; I'm being tortured," Jay says, obviously referencing his caregiver, Raphael.

"I'm running tests to make sure he is safe to go to Greenland with you. He's better but he should recuperate for at least a few weeks," Raphael replies.

"Yo, I'm good, son. I can handle mine," Jay says confidently.

"Maybe you should stay back, Jay," Miku says, concerned.

"Yo, we only been together a minute and you already try'n to control all this right here?" he says, shaking his head.

"Are you two together?" Ameana asks.

Miku looks at Jay.

"Girl, you know you been had me. Your man just needed some time, that's all," he replies with a half-smile.

"Um…I think you mean my man was scared," Miku corrects him.

"See, all that ain't even necessary. You 'posed build your man up. Say good things 'bout him."

"Oh really? Like what?" Miku asks.

"You 'pose to say 'Jay you is fineeeeeee and the way you drive…turns me on,' real talk." He instructs her.

"Actually, you're ugly and your turns need work," Miku replies.

Chapter Twenty-Six: Darkest Of The Dark

"Oh, so it's like that? You just gonna pick on an angel when he's lying here on his death bed? That's cold, yo," he says, shaking his head dramatically.

"Okay, okay, I guess you're kind of okay looking," Miku says as she leans in and gives him a quick kiss.

"That's right, girl, put it on me!" he replies.

"I'm sure you two can get back to that later. Right now, we need to make sure you are good enough to battle," Marcus insists.

"Yo, I'm good, right, man?" Jay asks Raphael.

Raphael raises Jay's shirt and reveals a gash that runs from his chest down to his lower stomach. There's a trail of silver stitches that runs along his wound and helps keep it closed.

"I did everything I could do to get the bleeding to stop. But there's only so much a mixture can do. And there's also the matter of your inflicting the pain on yourself."

"I had to," Jay replies.

"I know, but mixtures can detect self-inflicted wounds, and they are less likely to heal them," Raphael replies.

"It wasn't his fault. I made him do it. I mean, Redd did," Miku says, bowing her head in shame. Jay reaches out and takes her hand in his.

"So, I'm always going to have this scar?" Jay asks, serious for the first time.

"Yes."

He looks away.

"It's okay. I think scars are hot," Miku says.

"Really?" Jay says, not convinced in the least.

"Yes. And when we have time, I'll show you just how hot I think they are," Miku promises. The smile returns to his face, but it's short lived. He turns serious again.

"I was in and out a lot. Is Rio really gone?" he asks.

We all look at each other in great dismay.

"Yeah, he is," Marcus replies.

"You okay?" he asks Miku.

"Don't worry about that now. You should let Raphael finish examining you." She lets go of his hand.

"Hey, don't go too far. Seeing your face helps a brother get better faster."

She beams and promises not to go too far away.

In the next few hours, Jay's strength begins to return. Miku stays by his side the whole time, as promised. Raphael suggests we start training Bailey so she knows what to do when she gets to the top of the mountain.

"We can guide her when she gets to the top," Rage says.

"She has to be up there by herself. She'll be too powerful for you to be that close to her, especially given that you're a demon."

"Fine, what should we do to prepare her?" Ameana asks.

"Get her to practice inhaling as deeply as she can. That's how the Lyris gets activated. After a short while it will take over and give her inhuman breath control. That's when the Lyris will be at its strongest and will take over her body completely," Raphael replies.

We take Raphael's advice and show Bailey what she needs to do. She listens to instruction well enough, so long as she gets a cookie and playtime with Uncle Ray.

It's nearly dawn when we set off for Greenland. Marcus makes Jay promise to take it easy. Miku assures Marcus she'll stay on top of him. Jay makes a silly joke about her being "on top"; we laugh and take off into the sky.

Redd did some good when she was here. On the way to Greenland, we do not encounter any demons. That is until we get to the town of Nuuk. Here, we find what may be the most heavily guarded place on Earth.

The clouds here are dark and moody. The sky swears at us with thunder and spits at us with lightning. There is an unnatural frost in the air. It's the kind that goes right through to your bones and makes you feel like you will never be warm again.

Demons swarm around every inch of the sky, waiting to attack. There are so many, Marcus makes us walk the last mile so we will not be spotted. We hide behind an unguarded hill and hope we can surprise the demons and gain the upper hand.

Rage quickly goes over the plan with Bailey.

"Mouse, do you remember what you have to do when you get to the top?"

"Yeah…go like this." She mimics sucking air in and out.

"Good job, and remember to keep your shield up," Rage says.

"Okay. Can Boo-Boo come with me?"

"No, but he's gonna wait for you, for when you get off the mountain."

"Are you coming to get me?"

"After you make the bad guys fall asleep, okay?"

She nods in agreement. She surprises him and hugs him tightly. He pauses, taken aback, and hugs her back.

"It's time," Marcus announces.

"Bailey, sit on the floor and raise your shields up, okay, angel?" Marcus instr ucts.

She nods and sits on the ground. Rage gives her a reassuring smile. She raises her shield around her. Everyone is in place.

Rage holds the bubble containing Bailey in the palm of his hand and hurls it towards the top of the mountain. Bailey makes it halfway but then she starts to descend. Ameana uses her powers to guide her through the air, past the multitude of Powerballs and demons.

Suddenly the bubble is no longer under Ameana's control. It plunges towards the ground and Bailey screams for dear life. I turn and see Ameana being held down by a demon. He has her pinned to the ground. I rush over to her but I fear I will not get there in time to enable her to help Bailey.

Thankfully, as I head for Ameana, Marcus dashes off towards Bailey. He gets there in time to stop her fall. Bailey looks up at him through her shield with wide eyes. She's not sure if she should be excited or scared. Marcus smiles at her and that helps her decide. She's excited and having the time of her life.

"Are you up to trying again?" Marcus asks her.

"I got this, yo!" she replies with more attitude than a little girl should have.

That's when I realize she's spent way too much time with Jay. Marcus laughs, despite himself, and signals for Jay to Glide to the top of the mountain to catch her.

It's like they are playing a football with demons and using a child as the ball. I hold my breath when Bailey is tossed into the air in the middle of an onslaught of Powerballs. I'm weak with relief when I see that her shield holds up. She is headed for the top of the mountain, where dozens of demons await her. Fortunately, they don't see Jay Glide behind them.

Bailey is only a few yards out when Jay takes to the sky and catches her. Furious that Jay got by them, the demons attack. But Jay is too quick for them to get a good shot, even with Bailey in his hand.

Rage, pissed that Bailey is in danger, throws a slew of fireballs at the demons. They are being taken out left and right until finally, the only ones left standing are Jay and Bailey.

Meanwhile, the demon who's pinning Ameana down is getting ready to blast a Powerball into her face when all of a sudden, his body stops working. He opens his mouth and blood gushes out. He falls to the side. Ameana looks up from the ground, confused.

"Guess who finally remembered to carry a knife?" I ask her proudly.

"Thanks," she says quickly.

Ha, I saved Ameana and not by some random stroke of luck. I had a weapon and used it. What does that mean? It means I'm a bad chick; or at least "bad-er" than when we first met.

Marcus shouts out to Jay to get off the mountain before Bailey uses her power. Jay looks into Bailey's eyes and tells her something that makes her happy. He then Glides away from the top of the mountain.

Although Bailey is alone at the top, the team has her covered. Miku sings softly to dozens of demons. They beg for mercy as they meet their death. Marcus and Jay battle in hand-to-hand combat with several demons and get the upper hand.

Rage and Ameana make a great team because while Rage is blasting the demons that dare get close to Bailey on the mountain, Ameana is redirecting all the demons' Powerballs. I'm at the base of the mountain and call out when I see a demon try to sneak up on them.

I was so busy watching for the team, I didn't notice the demon behind me. He knocks me to the ground and bashes me in the face. He stands over me and tells me that he won't even waste a Powerball on me. Then he covers my face with his hand and tries to suffocate me.

Chapter Twenty-Six: Darkest Of The Dark

I panic, kick my arms and legs in the air, but it does no good. I'm not getting any air. My lungs start to burn, and the pressure builds in my chest. I feel like I'm going to implode at any second. Everything in front of me starts to blur. All I hear is the demon laughing as my life is draining from me.

"That's why most demons are single; they have no idea how to treat a girl," I hear Ameana say.

The next thing I know, the demon is being thrown to the other side of the city, hitting a power line along the way. Right before he fades from our sight, his body twists in agony.

"Thanks," I say, trying to catch my breath.

"Look," she says.

I follow her gaze to the top of the mountain. It has begun. Bailey places her hands around her little mouth and pretends like she's inhaling juice through a straw.

The change is almost immediate. The tornadoes and earthquakes that surround us begin to lose ferocity. The gray winds of madness are being sucked in by Bailey. The team encourages her to keep going. She takes a deep breath and inhales again. The earth slowly begins to come back tog ether.

Just as soon as the weather begins to settle down, the team and I behold the Goumy. After everything I've heard about them, I thought I was prepared for how frightening they would look. I was wrong.

They don't have bodies anymore. There's only a shadow of what was once a face. They are swirls of destruction, rooted in the earth, and reach well beyond the sky: a mushroom cloud of all-consuming death.

We are frozen in awe at the sheer size of the Goumy. There are dozens of them and they are coming for one thing: to stop the little girl who is getting in their way.

The Goumy do not discriminate. They destroy. They lift up demons, Believers, and angels alike. Inside the giant swirls of torture, I spot severed body parts and debris.

Rage tells Bailey to keep going. She inhales again, and the Goumy whip around and head straight for her. Rage bolts off to help Bailey. Marcus stops him and reminds him that she was chosen to do this. Rage is about to argue when Miku signals for us to look towards the mountains.

Bailey is sucking away the furious funnels of evil. She is working harder now because her face is turning red. The Goumy get so close to her, I also want to run and help. But then something remarkable begins to happen.

Bailey somehow no longer needs air. She inhales as if it's natural to do it without end. She raises her arms, and suddenly she is airborne, shield and all.

The Goumy lose power with each passing second. They are unraveling like thread from a spool.

Bailey continues to levitate high above the mountains. The Lyris turns her around in circles. Each time she turns, the Lyris gains more power while the Goumy's powers diminish. She is now so high up and so powerful, she is a magnificent supernova.

The Goumy, now drained, are more like windy days than forces of nature. But Bailey isn't just killing off the Goumy. The demons nearby fall out of the sky, drained of power too. Seeing this, Ameana tells Rage to get clear of the area. Rage reluctantly takes off.

The deep cracks in the earth begin to reassemble themselves. The lightning is fewer and further away, and soon disappears altogether.

"Oh my Omnis, it's working!" I shout at the top of my lungs.

By the time the Lyris allows Bailey to descend slowly back down to the mountain, the Goumy are reduced to decrepit, shadow-like beings. Their bodies melt into a sticky black substance and seep into the earth.

Evil is dead.

YES! YES! YES!

I leap into Marcus's arms. Miku and Jay scream their heads off with excitement. Bailey is on top of the mountain, jumping up and down too. We clap for her like she just saved the world because, well...

"We did it!" I shout to Marcus as I wrap myself once again around my angel.

I can feel his body finally, *finally*, begin to relax. He holds me tight and whispers in my ear that he loves me.

"I love you too; I can't believe we did it!!!" I say, placing his face between my hands.

Chapter Twenty-Six: Darkest Of The Dark

I wish I could kiss him.

Damn Bianca!

Whatever, she's not going to ruin this moment for me. We faced the darkest of the dark forces and we won! We won!

We look out into the sky and see Rage heading toward Bailey. Ameana is right behind him. I turn to Marcus with tears in my eyes.

"What is it?" he asks.

"Happiness; I know it's a new emotion for you and me, but here it is," I reply, grinning like a fool.

"Okay, well good tears or not, don't cry," he says, embracing me.

"The world is not going to end. Do you know what this means?" I shout, playfully punching his chest.

"You should start going back to school?" he says in a parental tone.

"No, it means that all of this was for a reason. And we're gonna be okay."

"Well we don't have the Shoma yet and—"

"Don't you dare add any negative thoughts to this moment, Marcus Cane. We won, we beat the bad guys. That's all that matters. We won!" I bellow.

"Hell yeah, baby girl, you *know* how we do!" Jay says behind me. I turn and leap into his arms. Miku kisses Marcus on the cheek, and the two of them embrace.

"Rio would have been so excited," she says.

"I think he knows we won, hell, Lucy knows we won," Marcus replies.

The team is elated. All our work and effort is finally paying off. And the Sage couldn't destroy us. We held on to each other and not only did we survive, we prevailed.

YES! YES! YES!

Marcus laughs, takes me up in the sky, and whirls me around. I can't remember being this free, this happy. I'm practically glowing.

"I've never seen you like this; it's nice. And a little scary," Marcus tells me.

"We've been through so much and even though everything has not been straightened out, we saved the world—again. We. Are. Awesome!" I yell to the whole world.

The glow of victory shines on all our faces. This was long overdue. After all the death and horror we've witnessed, victory is not only welcomed, it's well deserved.

I look up and find the sun is breaking through the clouds. Light bursts through and shines down where once only darkness lived. Even though we struggled and lost a great deal, we accomplished our mission. And thanks to us and Bailey, millions of people will see tomorrow.

I no longer feel the exhaustion of the past couple of weeks. I even get a break from the grief of losing the ones I love. All I focus on is this moment: right now.

And right now, Marcus and Emmy are happy.

Write it down, make a note of it.

Marcus Cane and Emerson Baxter are happy.

And to make it even sweeter, the team is triumphant and for once, all is right.

CHAPTER TWENTY-SEVEN:
A MESSAGE

turn to face Bailey on top of the mountain. I marvel at the enjoyment on her face. I know to her this was just a fun game, with good guys and bad guys. I'm thankful for her innocence. She is not only excited, she's being a good girl by keeping her shields up like we instructed, just in case there are demons hiding somewhere.

I look into Marcus's face eagerly, because I'm certain for the first time in a long time, it will be stress free. But when we make eye contact, his are filled with panic.

He's in such a hurry, he accidently knocks me down. He leaps into the air and crosses the length of the mountain range in a few swift flaps of his wings. He tackles a demon that had dedicated his last breath to sneaking up the side of the mountain to attack us.

The demon hurls a Powerball at Marcus with full force. Marcus dodges it and breaks the demon's back; his death is instantaneous. Marcus looks at me to see if I'm alright. I look back at him with shock and dread.

"I'm sorry, Em, are you hurt?" he asks.

"No, not me…," I reply, turning my attention to the three figures at the top of the mountain.

The stray Powerball missed Marcus but hit another highly desirable target: Bailey.

She was told to keep her shield up and she did. But then she must have seen Rage and lifted up her shield. The Powerball hits her in the neck. I watch the events unfold in utter disbelief. Rage runs and catches her before she hits the ground. She falls into his arms. Ameana kneels down beside her, too shocked to understand what is taking place.

Jay and Miku take me up to the top of the mountain with them. The whole time I'm begging Omnis not to let Bailey's injuries be too bad. Marcus gets there about the same time we do. Rage places his hand by her blood-soaked neck and tries to stop the bleeding.

"Mouse, we're gonna get you help. It's gonna be okay. It's gonna be okay," he repeats over and over until the words have no meaning.
Ameana takes Bailey's pulse and looks up at us. Her face is grave and pained. She shakes her head slightly, indicating there is no pulse to be found.
Rage carries her in his arms and begs us to take her to the hospital or, better yet, a Healer. We all look at each other, and dread and sadness is etched on all our faces.

"COME ON!!! HELP HER!" Rage roars at us.

But Rage knows the same thing we do: Bailey is gone.

He turns his focus to Marcus.

"You, Guardian, we can take her to the Para, right? He can fix her," Rage pushes.

"She's not fighting for her life, Rage, she's…" Marcus can't bring himself to finish.
"One of you angels can fix her," he begs us.
We don't answer.
"So…that's it? She dies?"
We all remain quiet, not sure what to say.
Suddenly Rage attacks Marcus. The team takes to the air to defend their leader. Rage fights the whole team, including Ameana, but Rage's attack lacks focus. He's too emotional to aim at anything. He takes a swing at everything and everyone. He punches the mountainside and tries to take it down with his bare hands.
"Fuck you, Omnis, fuck you!!! ARGH!!!"
He screams so loud it echoes throughout the mountain range. When he's done, he crawls over to Bailey's body, takes his jacket off, and places it on top of her.

"This'll keep you warm, Mouse," Rage says.

He pauses like he's waiting for an answer. It doesn't come. Rage is learning what I've long since known. Death doesn't negotiate or compromise; death just takes.

It takes incredible moms who don't deserve to die.

It takes Guardians who are secretly in love with you.

It takes brothers who died for you.

And yes, it even takes beautiful little girls who love cookies and worm their way into the hearts of Akons…

Rage won't let us take the body. He just lies there beside it. Ameana asks us to leave the two of them alone. We fly back down to the ground.

Miku buries her head on Jay's chest. I just sit on the ground and cry. There's really nothing else to do. I hear her giggle in my head. I recall, in a flash, her brilliant smile and her perfected pout. Then I cry harder. She was only three, and it was our job to make sure she didn't get hurt; we failed. *Just once, why can't the people we love be spared?*

"Something's wrong," Marcus says.

"She was just a baby, why would Omnis let this happen?" I scream at him.

Only seconds ago we were insanely happy. Now I can't remember what that feels like. I'm back to the soul-crushing reality of death and loss.

"The Sage wasn't here," Marcus says.

"Who cares? Bailey is dead because she helped us and all you can think about is the Sage?" Miku snaps.

"I cared about Bailey, like all of you did. But I don't want her death to be for nothing. We have to get the Sage. Or he'll come after us and the humans again. Then Bailey's death would have been in vain," Marcus explains.

"This was the final battle. Why wasn't he here?" Jay asks.

"He must know he's lost by now," I reply as I wipe my tears.

We try our cells and the connection, while not perfect, is better than it was before. We call Wolf and he tells us they have won the battle at their end. Since the weather madness ceased, they could focus on the Believers. They were able to kill many and imprison the rest.

"That's great. Is Winter there?" Marcus asks him.

Marcus speaks to Winter for a few minutes and then hangs up. We look at him eagerly and wait to be updated.

"Winter says Sage knew exactly when Bailey reached the top of the mountain because the weather got better, not just here, but all around the world. He was livid. He took off on his Port," Marcus relays.

"Did he say anything? Do we know where he is?" Miku asks.

"He said he should have started from the beginning and that would lead to the end."

"What the hell does that mean?" I ask.

"I don't know, but the Sage is an evil bastard. He wouldn't take losing very well," Marcus gathers.

"No, he would want to retaliate," I add.

"What else can he possibly do to us?" Jay asks.

Anger flashes in Marcus's eyes. His hands ball up in fists and he sneers.

"Argh, that delusional lunatic!" Marcus rants.

"What is it?" I ask.

"He's planning to destroy us," Marcus says.

"Yeah, we know that already," Miku counters.

"No, he tried to take us out but it didn't work. So now he's going to do the next best thing to ensure he never has an angel problem," Marcus informs us.

"How could he guarantee he never has to worry about angels?" I ask, clueless.

"By making sure we're the last generation."

"He's going to Noni. To destroy it," Jay replies, fear in his voice.

"He would destroy thousands of babies?" I ask, dumbfounded.

"If it means the angel race would die with us, hell yeah," Miku says.

"Let's go find him," Marcus replies in a deadly tone.

We fly back up to the mountain. Rage watches over Bailey as if she were just sleeping, while Ameana watches over him protectively. She signals to us that she is unable to get Rage to move away from Bailey's body.

Chapter Twenty-Seven: A Message

Jay looks at Rage, and for the first time, it's not a look of contempt. He studies Rage as the demon lovingly strokes Bailey's cheeks and feels sorry for him. Jay asks Rage a simple question. But that question would do what Ameana could not: get him to snap back to reality.

"Hey, Akon, we're gonna kill a Sage, you down?"

Rage looks up from Bailey's body for the first time. A light flashes in his eyes. His anger is mixed with a lust for vengeance.

"It has to hurt," Rage says.

Marcus and Jay nod in agreement.

Marcus calls Rahell to plan a human funeral for Bailey. She is happy to help and rushes to our location. We say our goodbyes. Rage and Ameana kiss her forehead before Rahell carries her away.

Rage and the team take off. For the first time, I'm afraid of them. I'm not afraid for my safety. I'm afraid because I've never felt this much rage and fury among angels before. There is nothing peaceful about them in this moment.

I don't get the feeling of grace or calm, like I normally do around them. Right now, the Guardians aren't angels; they are powerful, pissed-off beings with one goal: to kill.

The entrance to Noni is at the edge of a clearing in a forest in South America. It's a circular platform that's hidden by trees. According to Marcus, once you get on the platform, it illuminates and takes you to the front gate of Noni. Not only is Noni the only place a Sib can grow, it's the only light left.

Normally, the Sage, using a Port, would get here before us. Today, however, the speed of enraged angels and a bloodthirsty Akon, wins over the Port. Marcus has us put a plan in place that has three stages. The first stage is to take out the demons that have come ahead of the Sage.

The second stage is to find the Sage's demon, since he would never come alone. We find the first demon by accident. Marcus reflects his fear back to him until he gives up the location of the other demons. Jay Glides behind several of them and snaps their necks before they even realize he is there. I've never seen Jay this singularly focused on inflicting pain.

Ameana gets the jump on the demons with her fight training. But the part she loves is impaling them onto tree branches—calling for stray vines and wrapping them around the demons' necks until their eyeballs pop out. Her actions are not just those of an angry angel, they are those of a girl who's had someone she loves taken away. Ameana is in pain, and she wants to spread it around to demons everywhere.

Miku and I work together. She uses me as bait to lure the demons out; when we were going over the plan, Miku and I wisely left this part out, or Marcus would have freaked. But our plan works well. I lie on the forest floor like some spacey chick in a horror movie who suddenly can't remember how to put one foot in front of the other and run.

I call out for help; they hear me and figure they can kill a silly little human while they wait for their boss to show up. When they get close enough, Miku tackles them and hums a murderous little melody in their ears, causing a trail of carnage far and wide.

Marcus is really thrown by Bailey's death too. I can tell, because instead of reflecting his power to the demons, he beats them to death. The beatings are slow, merciless, and brutal. Like everything else, I'm sure he has Bailey's death on his conscience.

As savage and vicious as the Guardians are in taking out the Sage's demons, no one is more cruel and wicked than Rage. He grabs a demon by his neck, forces him to open his mouth, and drops a fireball inside it. The demon is cooked from the inside out.

Rage is tackled by three demons and we rush to help, but he refuses it. Seconds later, he has summoned a dark blue-colored Powerball. He sets the demons on fire, but they are dying so slowly, they beg and beg him to kill them quicker. He does not. The demons are left roasting over open flames for another hour.

Presently, we move on to part three of the plan: we hide and wait for the Sage. Soon, a young boy, who looks to be no more than six years old, pops up on a Port. He leaps off of it and heads for the platform. Marcus jumps out at him. The Sage is taken aback.

"What, you weren't expecting us?" Marcus asks.

"I told you, Guardian, I don't see everything," he says, only mildly annoyed to be found out.

"I knew you'd be here," Marcus says.

"Really? And why is that?"

"Because you're a coward. Only cowards go after defenseless babies."

"The 'defenseless' babies you speak of will grow to be powerful angels who screw up the world. I am helping to make sure that doesn't happen."

"Wow, every time I think you can't get more deluded, you prove me wrong."

"Why can't you understand the reason behind my actions? Your kind has had the chance to rule humanity for thousands of cycles. And look how they have turned out. Let me take over. Let me lead them."

"Lead by force?"

"Lead them with a kind yet firm hand."

"You want slaves, Sage," Marcus accuses.

"I want Believers."

"So you're willing to kill every soul in Noni to ensure that we are the last angels?"

"Well you see, Marcus, that's what makes me a better leader than you; I do what needs to be done."

"You know, I'm learning that same lesson right now. And what I need to do is make sure this is your last day on Earth."

"Did you really think I would come here alone?" the Sage says, laughing cr udely.

"No, actually I was betting you'd come with a ton of demons," Marcus replies with a smile.

The Sage follows Marcus's gaze. The team and I come from the trees. All of us are bloody from having battled and defeated his guards.

"Where are my demons?" the Sage asks, showing emotion for the first time.

"Well, the thing about being a demon is that you never get any time off. You never get to relax and you know…listen to some music," Rage says.

Miku laughs, and the Sage's face twists with anger.

"It was a great concert. I sang beautifully. You should have been there," Miku says, smiling.

"She could do a repeat performance, just for you," Ameana offers the Sage.

"You dismembered my team; clever, Marcus, you knew I would send them ahead," the Sage replies.

"I knew you would let other people fight for you. That's your weakness: you're always scared to fight your own battles."

Jay Glides up to the Sage and takes the box he holds in his hand. It's filled with a blue-black powder. Rage tells us it's from the black market. It's called Loop. It's a highly explosive powder that goes off once it makes contact with the light.

"So that was your plan? Blow it all up?" Rage asks the Sage.

"You're a disgrace to your—" Sage begins.

Rage decks him and he falls to the ground.

"Oh, so *that's* your plan, to beat a little boy to death?" the Sage asks.

I shake my head. How dare he pretend like he's a normal kid?

"No, Sage. We are not going to beat you. You wanted to blow something up, go right ahead," Marcus says.

He looks at us, confused. Jay moves faster than the light, and before the Sage knows what's happening, he has been tied to the platform with Samson string along with the box of explosives.

"Once it makes contact with the light…boom," Rage says.

"You're willing to destroy Noni, just to kill me?" the Sage asks.

"We had a plan with three stages. The first stage: protect Noni. Every inch of the gate has an Alexi standing in front of it. They are immortal. Nothing you do can harm them. And since they now stand between you and the gate, the Sibs are safe," Marcus informs him.

"You wanted to blow something up; you should get your wish," Rage says.

"Goodbye, Sage," Marcus says coldly as the platform begins to ascend. For the first time since I've known him, the Sage starts to panic. He tries in vain to free himself as the platform goes up. He begs us to try and understand the vision behind his master plan.

Marcus tells us it's time to go. As we walk away, the platform continues to rise. We hear the Sage begging for us to help him. Then, just as he is about to disappear into the light and meet a painful death, he calls out after me.

"Emerson, you can't let them do this. This is murder. You're too good to let this happen," he says frantically.

"You've misjudged me," I reply.

He starts to laugh as the platform nears the light.

"Your end is coming soon, Emerson. You killed Lucy's son, and she will gut you open and feed your organs to her Death Stalkers. You can't run from her!" he screams.

I turn and walk back to the Sage. I hear Marcus yelling at me because the platform is about to blow up. I don't care; I need to say something, and I need the Sage to hear it.

Unfortunately, Marcus does care. He flies down and snatches me up into his arms just as the platform and the Sage blow up. The explosion is ear piercing and causes a blinding light and kills nearly every living thing in the forest.

As Marcus cuts through the sky to avoid the debris, I look down at what remains of the Sage and I scream with such hatred and rage, I'm sure he can hear me in whatever hell he ends up in.

"When you get to hell, take this message to that bitch, Lucy: tell her I'm here. I'm waiting. Bring it!"

CHAPTER TWENTY-EIGHT:
THE HACKER

We are waiting in

few hours. Communications are back up, and people all over the world can now speak to each other over the phone and online.

The Original Paras have been holding a meeting for the last thirty minutes. We were not invited to join, of course, because it's Paras only. But among the Paras in the room is our friend Wolf. As he walked by us, he and Ameana exchanged an intense glance. Rage is not happy about it. Something tells me that Wolf isn't ready to give up on her.

It's amazing how quickly Earth is recovering with the help of the Paras and angels. The Foundation soldiers are also lending a hand. But the thing that impresses me the most is how humans are banding together. People everywhere are taking part in rebuilding their communities. Despite the loss of both lives and property, there's hope in the air.

It's nearly an hour before Raphael comes out and greets us. We all stand and follow him to a conference room, as per his instructions. The room has large windows with breathtaking views of Scotland. He asks us all to be seated.

"The Originals wanted me to thank you for your service to both our race and that of humanity," Raphael says, sounding far more formal than when we first met him.

"It was our duty; we were happy to do it," Marcus replies.

"Yes, but it came at a high price, did it not?" Miku and Rage bow their heads. "Marcus, your team has done the impossible. We should be celebrating your victory and honoring you with everything we have to offer."

"Raphael, thank you, but the truth is while we have succeeded in killing the Goumy and the Sage, we have failed to get the Shoma back together. We now only have a few hours. We can try, but we don't even know where to start," Marcus admits sadly.

"You see, given the sacrifices that you and your team have made, you have more than earned our help. You should get the members of your team back and the Lyris."

"Wait, can you do that?" I ask.

"No, we cannot," Raphael says with regret.

"Oh," I reply, feeling a pit of ice form in my stomach.

"But what we can do is give you the one thing you always seem to be lacking," Raphael replies.

"What's that?" Miku asks.

"Time."

"I don't understand," Jay says.

Phew, I thought it was just me.

"What you and your team did was courageous and selfless. You should be rewarded, and what better gift than the gift of time. So the Originals 'unofficially' hired a hacker to reset the Shoma and give your team the time you were lacking."

"How would a hacker do that?" Rage asks.

"Well, the Shoma is programmed just like most things by the council. And like most things that can be programmed, they can be hacked." He flashes a sneaky smile.

"You hacked the Shoma?" Marcus asks in disbelief.

"Well, there's no evidence of that. All we know is that *someone* somehow was able to program the Shoma remotely so that it reset."

"Is that allowed?" Ameana asks.

"That's a violation of the council rules, but since there is no council at this time…I think the rules are suspended," he says slyly.

"Okay, so you—"

"Hey, hey, there's no evidence it was me," Raphael reminds him.

"Okay, so *someone* hacked the Shoma and reset it to start the clock again? And as a reward, the Originals are letting that stand, so we now have sixty days to find it?" Marcus says, weak with relief.

"No, you have sixty-three days."

"Wait, why?" Miku wonders.

"This hacker person must have thought you and your team deserved a break: three days to have some fun."

"Fun?" Marcus replies.

"This hacker may have seen you and your team struggle. He may have seen the weight the mission has burdened you all with and thought you would greatly benefit from a three-day weekend."

"Why couldn't he give us a year, or more than that?" Jay asks.

"The Shoma can only be reset once. Even the best hacker will not be able to give you more than sixty days. In fact, it took all his strength and power to trick the Shoma into 'forgetting' to start the timer for seventy-two hours. I am afraid that is all the time you get."

"That's all we need. Don't worry, we'll get the Shoma back together and a new council will arise," Marcus assures him.

"We hope you do; if you don't, the souls of humans that should have gone to the light will linger in limbo forever. As for us, we'll never get back home. We're losing power every day we are away from the light. If you don't succeed, we'll die here."

"We won't fail," Jay promises.

"We're so honored to be given another chance. How can we thank you—I mean this hacker?" Ameana asks.

"I heard he might be into video games…?" Raphael offers.

"Okay, do you know which—"

"Call of Duty: Modern Warfare, Xbox 360 console with a larger hard drive and ammo crate casing. Or, whatever," he says, catching himself.

The team tries not to laugh out loud as we thank him again and head out the door.

"We can use the three extra days to get a head start on the mission," Marcus says to me.

Raphael overhears and calls Marcus and me back to the conference room.

"What is it?" Marcus asks.

"You cannot start this mission for three days," Raphael replies.

"Why?" I ask.

"Your team is falling apart. The hacker gave you three days to try and fix that. You've lost a teammate and, from what I've heard, Rio was also a good friend. You should have a whole cycle to grieve but you don't. The least you can do is take the three days given to you."

"I don't know how difficult this mission might be. We need all the time we can get," Marcus says.

"There's a private island in the Caribbean, called O-nay. It's very secluded, very beautiful. Arden and Rahell's father bought it for them a few cycles ago. I suggested they give you and your team the use of the island for the next three days; they loved the idea." "I'm not sure now is the time," Marcus replies. "You should take the time now, while you still have a team. The tension

is mounting."

"I think he's right," I add.

Marcus turns to me, surprised.

"Well, why not? We deserve time off. And if we can get it and still get the sixty days…let's do it."

"Emmy, I don't know…"

"Don't you want us to spend some time together before we go running off to another mission?"

"Yeah, of course I do," he replies, signaling to me that he does not want to have this discussion while Raphael is with us.

"Marcus, take my advice," Raphael insists.

"Okay, I guess we can take a few days off," Marcus agrees.

"Trust me, it'll be great, and it will give you a chance to properly welcome your new teammate," Raphael says.

"Who?" Marcus asks.

"Rag e."

"No, he's just along for the ride while Ameana…he's not…he can't…" Marcus is thrown by the very thought that Rage could be on our side.

"We Originals like you and your team because of how open-minded all of you have been; not only that, we admire your open hearts."

"But, Rage—"

"Rage saw a glimpse of what love was when he met the Lyris. He saw what life could have been like, had he been raised by decent humans. It's easy to be a good person when you've been dealt all the right cards. That never happened for Rage. This is the chance he needs. This is the family he's been looking for."

"He hates us. He's only here for Ameana," Marcus counters.

"So, when you two were in battle, he never helped unless she was in danger?" Raphael asks.

Marcus and I exchange a look.

"Yeah, he did help. He saved us a few times. And he got me a Healer when I was attacked," I reply.

"That doesn't sound like an Akon. That sounds like a friend…"

"We can't just add him to the team because he's acting half decent. He's not an angel," Marcus replies.

"Guardian, you take Rage as your friend or suffer him as your enemy."

The news that we have been given more time is intoxicating. The team is hopeful and determined to find the Shoma. Miku and Jay start to brainstorm about where it could be and how they can find it.

Ameana wants to go over battle plans, and Rage just wants to kill people, so he's up for any plan that allows him to do that. Marcus tells them to hold off on the planning because we are taking three days off.

"I thought you told Raphael you didn't want to do that?" Ameana says.

"I know, but I've changed my mind. We need this time to regroup," Marcus says.

"Fine; Ameana and I are taking off," Rage says.

"Actually, I would like it if we all stayed together for the three days. There's an island that Rahell and her family want to loan us," Marcus informs him.

"Yeah, I'm really not into bonding or sharing battle stories over bottles of Coy," Rage counters.

"I don't know what's gonna happen with you and Ameana, but so long as you're with us, you will be with us," Marcus replies.

"And what if I don't do what you say, like a good little dog?" Rage counters.

"Nothing stopping you from going," Marcus informs him.

Rage looks at Ameana and walks away. Ameana goes after him. Marcus signals for me to look at the watch I'm wearing; it allows us to spy on Rage.

"Shouldn't they talk alone?" I venture.

"I don't trust Rage fully," Marcus replies.

So, we all look on from my watch as the couple argues.

"You can't go, Thomas," Ameana says gently.

"We had a deal. We did the mission and now it's done," Rage says.

"Look, it won't be so bad if we hang out with them for a few days. We can make fun of the human," she says playfully.

"What the hell am I doing here?" he snaps at her.

"What do you mean?"

"I'm a demon. Why am I hanging out with angels? Why am I saving a world I don't care about and that never cared about me? And why did I rescue some little girl, who I didn't even know, and start to…" Rage falls silent.

Then he smashes his fist into the glass door of the shop they are standing by. The glass shatters and falls noisily to the ground.

"I'm sorry about Mouse. I really am. I know it's stupid because we just met her, but she became important to me, too," Ameana shares.

"I don't want to talk about her."

"Thomas, it's okay that you loved her. She's—"

"I SAID I DON'T WANT TO TALK ABOUT IT!!!" he says as he hurls what's left of the glass across the street. Luckily, there was no one walking by.

"Okay, I get it. But can you at least come with me to the island?" Ameana asks.

"I'm not sure about this," Rage says quietly, under his breath.

"Look, the island is big enough that we can avoid the team," she offers.

"No, I mean I'm not sure about *us*."

"Oh, okay," she says casually, as if he'd just told her he didn't want another cup of coffee.

"Ameana, you know this thing with us…I want it too…but…" He fails to find the words he needs.

"Thomas, are you breaking up with me?" she says, determined to look him in the eye.

"I need time to think."

Without another word, the Akon takes off.

CHAPTER TWENTY-NINE: CHILLS

O-Nay Island is no

on the island.

The sky-blue, two-story house is lavish, elegant, and right on the
beach. We enter and find ourselves standing in the middle of a spacious
living room with high ceilings, hardwood floors, and panoramic views. The
room is decorated with tasteful, brightly colored sofas and plush pillows.
Just seeing them makes me want to take a nap. There are five bedrooms,
each with its own private bath. It's perfect.

The trip here was fairly quiet. We didn't want to let Ameana know
we heard the conversation between her and Rage. At the same time, she
looks like she really needs to talk. Normally Miku would have been the
one to do that, but I think Rio's death is really starting to hit her. She looks
lost in deep sadness. Jay keeps throwing concerned glances towards her. I
overhear him ask Marcus what he should do to help her.

"That's just it, Jay, we can't do anything. She's grieving. That takes
time," Marcus replies.

"What did you do when Emmy lost her mother?"

"I felt just like you're feeling now: helpless. But all you can do is be
there for her," Marcus replies.

"Okay, who's sleeping where?" Marcus asks.

"Jay and I are taking the room upstairs," Miku says.

"Sounds good. Emmy and I can take the room down the hall," Marcus
tells the team.

"Ameana, which room do you want?" Marcus asks.

"I don't care," she says quietly.

"Is Rage coming?" Marcus dares to ask.

"I don't know," she says, unable to look him in the eye.

"You should take one of the bigger rooms."

"Why?" she asks him.

"Because Rage will be back for you."

"How do you know?"

"You're a hard girl to leave behind."

He gently brushes the hair from her face and she does what she hasn't done since her conversation with Rage—she smiles.

Marcus was right about Rage, he shows up a few hours later. Although he does come back to her, his mood has not improved. He's sullen and closed off, not just to us but to Ameana as well. She is worried about him. I can tell because she looks at him the same way I sometimes look at Marcus when he's facing danger. But that said, just having him with us picks up Ameana's spirit greatly.

Miku's spirit has lifted too. But that's because she's working on her second bottle of Coy. Jay tries to get her to slow down, but she refuses. Marcus cautions her too, but it does no good. She reminds him that they are here to have fun.

In fact, when Jay gets a text from an old Traveler friend about a last-minute game of Runner Ball, Miku insists he go. Jay refuses because he doesn't want to leave her alone.

"That's crazy, just go. Blow off some steam," Miku tells him.

"You should go too, Marcus; we'll be fine here," I assure him.

After going back and forth, they finally agree to go. Ameana signals quietly for Marcus to include Rage. Marcus asks him if he wants to join them. Rage says no and heads out to the beach to be alone.

"I tried," Marcus says to Ameana.

"I know; thanks," she says.

The guys take off leaving us girls in the house, alone.

"I'm so worried about him," Ameana says, not really meaning to share her thoughts out loud.

"He's fine. Demons don't feel anything," Miku says flippantly.

"Come on, seriously, after all this time, after everything he's just been through, you can't give him a break?" Ameana snaps.

"I'm sorry, but giving a break to a demon is really low on my list right now. My brother just died, so that's kind of my first priority."

"He has risked his life over and over again for us; you really can't find one nice thing to say about him? NOT ONE NICE THING?"
Miku looks at her best friend and is unable or unwilling to find one positive thing about Rage. Ameana is on the verge of losing it, judging by her stern expression. The silence in the room is thick and shows no sign of lifting. So, I take a chance and answer Ameana, even though she wasn't talking to me.

"Well…Rage is hot," I reply.

They both turn to look at me with bewilderment.

"What? Well, he is," I offer with a shrug.

Much to my surprise, Ameana bursts out laughing and Miku joins her.

"She's right; he is hot," Miku concurs.

"Really?" Ameana asks her friend bashfully.

"Look, I'm not saying I like him but yeah, he's…yum; if you're into demons, I mean," she clarifies.

Ameana is beaming. I didn't realize how important Miku's opinion is to her. But apparently what Miku thinks of Rage means everything.

"I just don't want him to hurt you," Miku says to her.

"Don't worry, I'd kill him first," Ameana vows.

"Or I would," Miku replies with a grin.

"Okay, if Thomas hurts me, you have my permission to go Redd on him."

"Good; and since we're already on the subject…what's it like with a demon?" Miku says, taking yet another drink.

Oh my Omnis, I have always wanted to know the answer to that question.

"Um…do you guys want me to leave so you two can talk alone?" I ask. *Please say no, please say no…*

Ameana and Miku exchange a quick glance, and Ameana signals it's okay if I stay.

Yes!

"So, what's it like?" Miku asks, plopping on the sofa and placing a throw pillow against her chest.

"Come on, Mimi, spill!" she pushes.

After pausing for a quick moment, Ameana smiles and sits beside Miku on the sofa.

"Well, I don't know what it's like with all demons, but with Thomas… he's passionate and intense."

"Is that your way of saying he gets it in good?" Miku asks.

"So good."

We both burst out laughing. Ameana gets shy and hides her face behind one of the pillows.

"Aren't you afraid he'll accidentally set you on fire with a Powerball?" I ask.

"He doesn't need a Powerball to do that," she confides.

Miku and I squeal with laughter.

"I don't know, I might have to rethink Rage now," she jokes.

"Pretty, he's so nice to be with because he doesn't try to be anyone but himself. Sometimes he'll call me and be rude about it like, 'Come here.' I pretend like I'm pissed that he thinks he can order me around, but the truth is—"

"It turns you on," Miku finishes.

"Every time!" she shouts with glee.

I've never seen Ameana so taken with any guy before. She looks so happy and so…human. She's not the second-in-command; she's a girl in love.

"I totally get it; they're sexy when they're serious. Jay jokes around all the time. But when we get going, and I pull away, just to tease him…that boy does some *serious* begging."

"Shut up! You did not get Jay to beg!" I shout with delight.

"Many, many times," she brags.

"Begging is good," Ameana confirms.

"Don't tell me you have gotten Rage to beg!" Miku says.

"No, but he's gotten me to do it a few times," she whispers as she buries her head on Miku's shoulder.

"That's awesome," Miku replies.

I shake my head as they share a laugh.

"Actually, the guy I could always count on to beg for more was Marcus," Ameana says.

I'm not sure if she did that on purpose or not. On one hand, she's Ameana and she doesn't like me all that much. But on the other hand, I don't think she really remembered I was there until the words came out of her mouth.

"Oh, sorry. I didn't mean to…," she says.

"No, it's cool," I lie.

Damn, it's uncomfortable now. I don't want it to be. We were having fun and Omnis knows we need more of that. I decide to swallow my discomfort and "be easy," as Jay would say. So, after a pause, I confide in them and hope I'm not making a mistake.

"I don't know about begging, but I really would like to get Marcus to be less…" I can't finish.

"Less what, Emmy?" Miku asks.

"Gentle."

They both laugh at me. But it's not mean-spirited, so I'm relieved.

"Why don't you just tell him?" Miku asks.

"Marcus will never be too aggressive. He's afraid he could kill you," Ameana replies.

"At this point, I'd risk it," I confess.

We all laugh together. This is so nice.

"Is it true what Arden said about demons and their wingspan?" I ask.

"Yes," Miku and Ameana reply in sync.

I turn to both of them, shocked. Ameana and I push for Miku to tell us how she knows about demons and their wings. She refuses to tell us. For the next few minutes, our imaginations are running wild.

"No, no. I'm not telling. All I will say is that Arden was right," Miku says smugly.

"Can I ask you something?" Ameana says to me.

Crap.

"Um…sure," I reply, uneasy.

"Did Marcus ever tell you about his night with Bianca?"

"Mimi, don't ask her that!" Miku scolds.

"Sorry, I was just curious," Ameana replies.

"I asked him, but he won't say anything because we had a deal that he would never tell me. But, yeah, I want to know," I share.

"You don't. It'll just break your heart," Miku advises.

"Screw that; I would want details, pictures, and diagrams," Ameana replies.

"It doesn't matter, he'll never tell me," I conclude.

"There would be nothing to tell if you had taken care of her," Ameana says.

"What do you mean?" I ask.

"I mean if she went after someone I loved, I would have driven a stake through that plastic bitch," Ameana assures me.

"I can't do that. That's crazy—right, Pretty?" I ask.

"Yeah, it's definitely not the right thing to do," Miku confirms.

"What if Bianca came after Jay?" Ameana asks her.

"I would end her."

There's something so final about her voice that it causes both Ameana and me to fall silent. Miku is, and always will be, a powerful angel with a close connection to darkness; maybe too close...

"Maybe I'll let Bianca have Marcus and I'll just hook up with the guy Arden was talking about," I joke.

"What guy?" Miku asks. "The one who likes to Soul Dive all night," I reply. "When you're done, can we have him?" Miku begs. The room explodes with laughter from all three of us. Who knew "Soul Diving" would be the thing that bonds us. Although I suspect it's bonded many girls.

The next morning, I get a call from Julian, and for the first time, I don't stress out about it. In fact, I take the call and we talk for nearly half an hour. It's kind of silly, but it feels nice to have someone worry about me the way my mom used to.

Julian asks about the location of the island. He asks if I have enough to eat and if I am wearing a sweater because it gets cold in the Caribbean at night. We make a date to get lunch when the mission to find the Shoma is over.

"Who was that?" Marcus asks as he walks into our room.

"My father."

He looks at me, shocked by what I have just said.

"I just wanted to hear what it sounded like to say 'father,'" I reply.

"And?"

"It sounds kind of nice."

"So, you and Julian are getting closer?"

"He's not gonna make father of the year but…yeah, I guess."

He's about to say something but then he thinks better of it.

"Marcus, what is it?" I ask.

"Has Julian said anything to you about Bianca?"

"Um…he hates you for marrying her and he wants me to stay away from you. So, you know, the usual."

"Oh."

"Is there something I should know?"

"I just…no."

"Okay…"

I'm sure there's more to the story, but right now all I want to do is head to the beach. We never get time together, so I want to enjoy every second of it.

"Okay, what do you think?" I ask.

I spin around showing off my new, and my very first, two-piece purple bathing suit. Normally, I would rather die than have someone see me in a two-piece. But, there's something about being around Marcus that makes me feel desired. It's like I could be dressed in a plastic bag and he would still want me. Plus, the designer managed to somehow give me the illusion of curves.

"Wow," he says as he studies me.

"Yes, I am kind of cute in this," I reply.

He walks up to me and places his hand on the small of my back; our faces are inches apart. I see longing in his eyes. It's quickly followed by a heavy sigh when he remembers we can't kiss. I smile knowing I can change his mood.

"I have a surprise for you," I tell him.

"Really?"

I hold out my hand and in it is a small vial containing a liquid mixture.

"What is that?" he asks.

"Trickk."

"Where did you…how did you?"

"I did some digging and, well, here you go. By the way, Tony made me promise to inform you that he worked very hard to get the mixture, so be nice to him."

"Done."

I drink the Trickk. It tastes like warm Nyquil. But I don't care because it means I get to be with him.

"I think it takes effect immediately," I inform Marcus.

"Well, we can't let all of Tony's hard work go to waste," Marcus replies. He leans against the wall and gently pulls me into him.

"We're supposed to be going to the beach," I remind him.

He kisses my jaw line and nuzzles down my neck. He does it over and over again. Each time it sends sparks up and down my body. I close my eyes and start to lose any sense of time.

The beach can wait…

Marcus continues to shower me with tender kisses as I run my fingers through his hair. Then without warning he turns me around so that I'm up against the wall. He takes my hands and places them behind me as if he's about to arrest me. He holds them together so I won't break free. It's all happening so fast, I'm confused.

"So…you think I'm too gentle?" he whispers in my ear.

Oh my Omnis! He must have come back and overheard my conversation with Ameana and Miku!

"Marcus, I didn't—"

"Shut. Up."

His tone is severe. Serious. Sexy.

Chapter Twenty-Nine: Chills

My heart is pounding inside my chest. My hands are cold with anticipation; I crave him more now than I ever have before.
I feel him standing behind me. He studies every inch of my body. The heat from his gaze makes me dizzy with longing. Without warning, he bites my neck. Not hard enough to leave a mark but hard enough to make me inhale and bite my lower lip to keep from moaning. Just when I get used to the slight pain, he introduces me to a new sensation with his lips and tongue.

I've never felt this good…
"Marcus, it feels—"
"Did I say you could talk?" he scolds.
Best. Moment. Ever.
He unties my top and makes circular patterns on my bare back that make my knees weak.
Omnis, thank you, thank you, thank you for sending Marcus to me.
He is dedicated to kissing me up and down my back until I'm weak with desire. He palms my breasts in his hands possessively. The he whispers that I belong to him as he caresses my nipples.

Then he…stops.
WTF???
I open my eyes and turn to face him. He's looking at a message on his cell.

"I don't care what it is, we should finish. Marcus, we need to finish," I beg shamelessly.

"I'm sorry, I gotta go."

"Go where? Is it Lucy? Is she—"

"It's not Lucy," he replies with regret.

"Then who is it?" I ask.

"Bianca; she's not doing very well with her father's death and she asked to see me."

This can't be happening.

"You can't tell her no?" I ask.

"Emmy, she just lost her dad. She's crying; she says she hasn't eaten in days…and I haven't checked on her since we've been back."

"Are you telling me the few moments of free time you have, you're going to spend it on another girl?"

"Emmy, calm down."

"Don't tell me to calm down. That is fucking ridiculous. How long am I going to come last in your life?"

"Last? Emmy, you've been the first and only thing in my life. I've sacrificed and risked—what is it going to take for you to get that I love you and want to be with you?"

"If you want to be with me, then why are you racing off to be with her?" I shout.

"You know the situation. I have to go. But don't get mad because it's not always gonna be this way. We took care of the Sage and we will take care of Bianca. Until then, please, stop making it so hard."

"I'm making it hard? Did I kiss my ex-girlfriend? Did I marry another girl? Because if memory serves, you did those things, Marcus, not me." I furiously tie my top back on and throw on some jeans. "I don't even know why I'm surprised. This is how it *always* goes," I roar as I zip up.

"How what always goes?" he asks.

"You and me. You do some shit and I have to find a way to suck it up and deal with it."

"I really don't want to argue about this," he replies.

"Fine, then get the hell out," I bark.

"Why are you making a bad situation even worse? Given what we were just about to do, do you really think I'm happy that I have to leave?"

"Stop saying 'have to' like someone has a damn Soul Chaser at your feet. You are going over to be with Bianca because you want to!"

"Whatever. Think what you want," he says as he heads for the door. He opens it and slams it shut. I leap off the bed and follow him down the hallway, where I continue shouting. Miku and the rest of the house have front-row seats to our argument.

"Are you gonna sleep with her again?" I scream.

"Why would I do that?"

"Habit," I reply coldly.

"I'm not doing this with you right now," he warns me.

"You act like you hate this, but you don't. You love this situation. You're a bastard, Marcus Cane, and I hate you!" I shout as I block him from getting to the front door.

Chapter Twenty-Nine: Chills

"Fine, move," he says, like a leader.

"No, I'm not moving until you admit the truth: you like her. You like fucking her and you're just pretending you don't."

"Stop cursing for no reason. I am not going to Bianca's to have sex. I'm just gonna check on her and be back. Damn!"

"I'm so sick of this. No matter what happens, we can never be together because you always put everything before me."

"I'm not the reason we're in this situation!" he replies.

"YOU ARE ABSOLUTELY THE REASON!"

"HOW IS THIS MY FAULT? WHAT THE HELL DID I DO?" Marcus screams.

"It's what you didn't do. You didn't stand up for us. You should have told Dalce to go screw himself because you wanted me and not that two-faced, poisonous bitch, Bianca."

"I needed the army."

"And I needed you. But you weren't there. You're *never* there when I need you."

I can actually feel the words traveling across the room and tearing into Marcus's chest. They shred him from the inside. He looks like I just spat in his face.

"Wow, I didn't know I was such a disappointment to you," he says.

His pain is palpable.

"I'm just saying that you—"

"Excuse me," he says, trying to get past me and open the door. I don't move.

"Look, I just want us to be able to spend—" "Excuse me," he says again, clearly pissed. "No, I want us to talk about this," I insist. "Emerson. Move," he orders. His tone isn't sexy now. It's deadly. And while I know he would never hurt me, a cold chill runs down my spine. Jay studies Marcus's face carefully, and then whispers softly to me.

"Baby girl, let him go," he tells me.

I step aside and Marcus walks out the door.

CHAPTER THIRTY:
FRENZY

run into Miku's arms and burst into tears. Jay asks if I'm going to be okay and Miku says she'll take care of me. From the corner of my tear-filled eyes, I can see Jay and Rage exchange an uncomfortable look: the kind that guys get when they are around a girl who is crying.
Ameana lets the guys off the hook by asking them to help her check the island to make sure it's demon free. I know it's just an excuse to leave me and Miku in the house alone; I'm grateful.

We go into Miku's room and she hands me a box of tissues. She then takes me over to the bed and lets me bawl my eyes out.

"I hate him," I sob.

She strokes my hair and holds me tightly.

"I don't understand any of this. If Omnis won't let us be together, then why doesn't he give me the strength to be apart from him?" I ask her.
"You love him, that makes things…complicated," she reminds me.
"It's not supposed to hurt this much. I can't do this anymore. I can't."
I sob so hard my whole body shakes. I swear the sorrow is going to take me under. But this time, I won't come back to the surface.

"I tried. I really did. I wanted us to get past Bianca. I wanted us to be okay, but I don't know. I don't know how to make it okay," I cry.

"Well, there's no handbook for this, Em. You just do the best you can," she tells me.

"Why is this happening to me and Marcus? Why is it so hard for us to get it right? What did we do to turn the whole universe against us?"

"It's not against you. It's just…relationships are hard for everyone."

"Sometimes I just want it to stop. Sometimes I pray that Omnis will just make it stop," I admit.

Chapter Thirty: Frenzy

"Make what stop, sweetie?" "Love; I want to stop being in love." "It's not that simple. I'm sorry, Em." "I know in my mind the Bianca situation is not his fault, but in my heart…it just hurts so much. I don't want to be in pain anymore. How do I let him go? How do I live without my heart? Please, show me how," I beg.

She holds me even tighter, but it doesn't stop the tidal wave of despair, doubt, and misery from washing over me.

Please, please make this hurt go away. Please…

"I keep turning these questions over in my head. Should I leave Marcus? Does him agreeing to marry her show how little he loves and respects me? Or does it show how much he loves humanity and would do anything to save it? Is he an asshole or a hero?"

"I think it depends on who you ask," she replies.

"Tell me what to do, Miku. What do I do? Do I hold on and hope it gets better? Or do I let go? Please tell me what to do," I beg her.

"Oh, sweetie, I can't tell you what to do. That's something for you two to figure out."

"Our love lives outside of reason and logic. All the times it should have died, it just got stronger. But I think it's stronger than me, now. I think it's stronger than us put together."

"He's hurting too, Em. Rio told me when he was flying away with Bianca to the wedding, he thought Marcus was gonna turn back at any moment because his heart was breaking so badly."

"I try not to picture him and her. But I can't get it out of my head. I can't."

"Well, that's what this all comes down to: are you and Marcus stronger than this situation or not?"

I leave Miku's room because I know she has her own issues and watching me blubbering isn't helping. I miss Rio so much, I can only imagine how she must feel. Before I head to my room, I call Jay on his cell; I tell him to come back and be with Miku because I don't want her to be alone.

He enters the house and asks how I am.

"I don't know, Jay. Everything is falling apart."

"Come here, baby girl," he says.

His embrace is warm and comfy. I hope he can help Miku. I hope their relationship isn't cursed, like mine and Marcus's seems to be.

"How is Miku doing?" I ask.

"She's trying but it's hard, yo, like... they were tight. I want to make it okay but I don't know how," he says sadly.

"Well if anyone can get her to smile, it's you. She really loves you."

"Yo, how did that even happen?" he jokes.

I laugh, despite myself. He wipes a tear from my eye.

"I'll be fine. Go check on your girl."

He kisses me on the cheek and goes upstairs.

Once in my room, I don't see the need to turn the light on. Sitting in the dark somehow seems fitting. I check my cell. Marcus hasn't called me. But then I haven't called him, so...I guess neither of us wants to talk.

I look out my window and see two figures out on the beach: Rage and Ameana. They are too far away for me to really make out.

I look inside my watch and there they are. I wonder if they are doing better than Marcus and I. Who am I kidding? Right now, Kim Kardashian and Kanye are doing better than Marcus and I.

I know I shouldn't look but there's something fascinating about the two of them. It's like they see a side of each other none of us really ever get to see. I confess to watching their scene play out on the watch.

They are sitting on a hammock slung between two palms trees. Rage looks out at the waves and Ameana stares at him. I'm guessing he's been silent for some time.

"I can get you some Coy if you're thirsty," she offers.

He shakes his head "no." She sighs and looks out at the ocean.

"If being here makes you feel this bad, it's okay if you want to go," she offers.

"I'd be like this no matter where I am," he replies.

"Thomas, talk to me."

"What do you want me to say?"

"Whatever, your...feelings."

"That's an angel thing, feelings."

She lowers her head to her knees and wraps her arms around herself.

"I never told you to love me back," he says.

"What?"

"You're upset because I don't want to play pretend therapist session. And you're mad at me, but it's on you. You fell for a demon. Now you regret it."

"I never said I regret it."

"No, but you do."

"No, I don't," she counters.

"Bullshit."

"What is wrong with you?"

"I LET HER DIE!!!"

Ameana is taken aback by the outburst.

"She was…so little. She didn't deserve to…"

Ameana reaches out for his hand, but he pulls away.

"Why won't you let me get close to you? What's wrong with letting someone in? Damn it, Thomas, what do I have to do?"

"It's not you, okay? I just think maybe you'd be better with someone else. Maybe that Wolf guy."

"You don't love me anymore? If that's the case, then just—" Ameana begins.

"I can't let people start to matter to me. When it's time for them to… there's nothing I can do about it."

"Nothing is going to happen to me," she assures him.

"Nothing was supposed to happen to Mouse. We had an eye on her every moment and she still ended up…Ameana, her neck was split open… she looked so shocked…so small."

"It's okay to mourn her."

"No, I don't want to. I just need to figure out how to…forget about her. That way it doesn't feel this fucking bad."

"She's always going to be with you; you loved her," Ameana replies.

"Then I was right about love; waste of time."

"Love doesn't always end badly."

"Your mother murdered you and you still think that? Man, you angels are so…delusional," Rage counters.

"So that's your plan, Thomas, to stop loving me so when I'm gone, it doesn't hurt?"

"I don't know," he says, shrugging his shoulders.

"There are millions of Baileys out there and you helped save them," she pleads.

"I DON'T GIVE A DAMN ABOUT MILLIONS; I ONLY CARED ABOUT HER. AND THAT OMNIS BASTARD TOOK HER AWAY!"
She looks at him and says nothing.
"But then again, what did I expect? Omnis didn't give a damn about me when I was human, why would he care now? I just thought maybe he'd spare Mouse. She was so…"

"Mouse dying wasn't a punishment, Thomas. There was a war; we lost people and evil lost people," Ameana counters.

"Yeah well, if I didn't care about her, I wouldn't feel like shit. So, I'm thinking this whole loving and caring thing isn't for me," Rage barks.
"Are you breaking up with me?" she asks plainly.
"We can't; I don't remember what it's like to be without you."
He pulls her over to him and kisses her feverishly. His actions are passionate, frenzied, and reckless. He tears off her blouse and her bra in a swift, graceful movement. He's aching to touch as much of her as he can in as short a time as possible.

He's possessive, eager, and seeking. He pulls on her hair. She bites her lower lip and moans. He grabs her by her throat and sucks on her bottom lip until it's bruised and raw. He groans and she closes her eyes, leans her head back, and sighs.

She opens her eyes and studies him as he kisses down her bare, perfect breasts. There's something about the frenzy of his pace that she finds odd, judging by her expression. Rage doesn't look like an Akon who is having sex. He looks like a guy who's looking for an escape.

The fury in his movements as he explores her body reminds me of someone who's desperately in search of something valuable he lost. Rage searches for it in Ameana's thighs, her breasts, and her lips. He can't find it. She takes his head in her hands and stops him.

Chapter Thirty: Frenzy

"What is it?" he asks breathlessly, making eye contact for the first time.

"I don't want to do it like this," she replies.

"But we always—"

"I know. But tonight I want to do something different," she says.

"What do you wanna do?"

"I want to show you why love isn't worthless."

He's about to say something but she stops him by placing her finger on his lips. She takes him by the hands and walks him over to a palm tree. She leans him against it. He studies her, not sure what's coming next.

She reaches up on the tips of her toes and bathes him with sensual, soft kisses that judging from Rage's reaction, leave a trail of delicious sensations.

She kisses his temple, eyes, collarbone, and then makes her way down his chest. She takes the long and slow route to her destination. The ecstasy of her touch is too much for Rage. He groans and holds on to the trunk of the tree.

Once she grazes his belly button and works her way a few inches further south, Rage loses control. He forms Powerballs in both of his hands. He swears as she continues the whispered conversation with his body.

No longer able to stop himself, Rage drops the Powerballs. The trees around them are set on fire. I start to panic until I realize it's the same blue-colored Powerball he had thrown at the demon earlier. The flames on the trees are burning slowly and with control. They give off a magnificent soft glow.

By the time Ameana is done kissing him all over, he's shaking and yes, begging. He longs for more of her. But it's not like before. There's no frenzy. There's only longing.

When Rage picks her up and places her in the hammock, I can tell they are about to experience the inner Arc soon. Rage is no longer a lost demon in search of something valuable. He's a guy who's finally found it. I'm sure Rage has had plenty of sex. But judging by his reaction, this is the first time the demon has ever made love.

"Hey," he says in a low voice.

I turn over on the bed and find him standing in the doorway.

"Hey," I reply, slightly hoarse from all the crying.

I sit up and look at him directly. He looks worn-out, and sad. His eyes are pensive and dark. He has his hands in his pockets and is looking down at the floor.

"So…how is she?" I ask.

"Bianca? I didn't see her. I texted her that I'd come by later."

"Oh, so where have you been?"

"Green Mountains; thinking," he replies.

"Listen, about earlier—" I begin.

"You wanted to know what happened the night I honeymooned with Bianca. The truth is I don't know what happened because the whole time I was there, I didn't see her. All I saw was your face. When I reached for her, I felt you, and when I kissed her, it was your lips I tasted. Emmy, you consume me."

"Marcus, I—"

He raises his hand to stop me from continuing.

"Please, let me finish, okay?" he asks.

"Okay."

"I thought that I could make you happy, but you're always crying. And more often than not, it's because of me."

"That's not true. There's been a lot of death and horror in our lives, that's not your fault," I promise him.

"The council put your name as the clue to the Triplex. They are responsible for dragging you into that *one* mission. But I brought you into this world, and I'm the one keeping you here."

"I'm here because I want to be," I reply.

"Do you? Because you don't seem happy. And the only thing I want more than to love you, is for you to be happy. And so far, every decision I have made has brought you further and further away from happiness."

I get out of the bed and walk towards him. He steps back.

"Marcus, what are you saying?"

"I've asked you to endure things that no human should have to endure. I did it because I couldn't take being without you. But today, standing at the door with you screaming at me that I'm never there for you, I realized something: I'm not strong enough to be with you."

"What—wait—don't say that. That's not true; you're the strongest being I know!"

"Then why can't I get this right?"

"We just need to figure this Bianca thing out."

"No, it's not her. It's us. We keep crashing and colliding. We keep dismantling each other, piece by piece. And no matter how much we struggle, it never works. I think it's because no matter what, I'm always gonna be the guy that tries to save the world, even if it means hurting the girl he loves."

My eyes fill with tears. I look down at the floor because I can't bear to look at his face. He comes closer to me and takes my face in his hands. "You don't want me anymore?" I ask as the tears fall.

"I will *always* want you. I just don't know how to keep you."

"But I'm here; I'm with you, Marcus," I reply, taking hold of his shirt.

"I always think that, but then we go back to the same thing: you doubt our love. And I can't blame you, because so much has happened. But throughout everything, I have *never* wavered. I have always loved you. But I don't think it's enough. I don't think my love will ever be enough."

"Marcus, your love is enough. We can get past this."

"Until the next thing and the next thing… Baby, I'm so tired…"

I cry hard against his chest.

"Marcus, I don't want to do this. We can't break up."

"I'm never gonna be the guy who puts you before the whole world. And you deserve that guy."

"No, no, no." I put my arms around him and tell him I'm sorry for what I said before.

"Stop, you don't have to be sorry. I asked you to be okay with me marrying another girl. That was too much to ask of anyone."

"But we love each other," I sob.

"I don't think it's enough."

The endless days and nights I spent without Marcus when we broke up before flash in my head. The flashes come with a sea of panic that drives me to the depths of desperation.

I can't lose him again. I can't. I can't.

I force myself to breathe deeply and stay focused. I wipe my eyes and tuck my hair behind my ears.

"Okay, okay, I know we're both exhausted and trying really hard to make things work, but we just need to keep trying, okay? Okay? When you love someone, you don't give up on them."

He looks at me with these sad eyes that tell me this is goodbye.

No! No! No!

I pull him towards me violently and kiss him. He tries to pull away but I won't let him. I rip his shirt off and kiss him with the frenzy of a thousand tornadoes.

"We shouldn't do this," he says between labored breaths.

"Shut up," I reply as I take off the rest of his clothes and drag him down onto the floor.

He removes my clothes quickly. He objects again, but I can feel the lust and longing in his touch. He doesn't want to leave me. He just wants the pain to go away.

He objects again but I don't stop. I straddle him and bring him to a feverish climax by touching all the places I know he's most sensitive. Once I get to his inner thigh, he groans loudly and holds onto me.

'Baby, we shouldn't...," he says, fearing it's a mistake.

I don't care if it is a mistake. I want him. I need him. I will have him.

I insert him inside me. I look him in the eye and dare him to pull out of me. This is the moment. This is his chance to either make love or run away. Both of us are breathing heavily. Lust and need drip down our foreheads in the form of salty sweat.

"If you want to stop, you'll have to pull out of me," I dare him.

"Fuck," he says, cursing himself for not having the strength to stop. In fact, once inside me, he thrusts harder and deeper. So much so, I gasp and I cut into his perfect flesh with my nails. He inserts himself into me over and over until I shudder.

The Inner Arc is the most powerful I've ever felt. And when the Outer Arc happens, and the Exchange occurs, it leaves us so weak we never make it onto the bed.

I wake up and look at the clock by the bed. It's four in the morning. I don't remember how I got onto the bed; Marcus must have carried me there. I turn, but he's not next to me. I head to the kitchen to get some water and think maybe I will find him there; I was right. He's sitting at the island counter, drinking Coy.

"It is okay to do that with the whole CP Tic thing?" I ask hesitantly.

"I don't think it'll drive me back to being a Tic."

"Okay. I woke and you weren't there," I tell him as I pour myself a glass of water.

"Couldn't Recharge. I think I'm gonna go back to the Green Mountains for a while."

"You should come back to bed," I offer. "Can you sit down next to me?" he asks. "Sure." I take a seat beside him. "I should have had more control. I'm sorry," he says. "Don't say that. You make it sound like us making love was a mistake." He looks at me with regret in his eyes. "Marcus, was it a mistake?" "Being inside you could never be a mistake. But it was…makes this

even harder than it was before."

"Makes what harder?" I ask.

"Saying goodbye."

"What? Wait, Marcus…"

He gets up from the counter, kisses my forehead, and whispers in my ear.

"I love you. And I hope the next guy is a guy who doesn't make you cry as much as I did."

CHAPTER THIRTY-ONE: R.I.P. EMMY

remain seated at the counter because I can't bring myself to watch him go. And as much as I want to run after him, I know there's only so far I can get.

It's over, again.

I'm out of tears. I didn't think that could ever happen. But it has and now I'm empty; hollow. I place my head in my hands and think back.

Where did we go wrong? How could two people, so willing to die for each other, end up like this? How did we get here?

The night offers no answers. The refrigerator hums softy and says it doesn't have any answers either. I sigh and take it out of my pocket: the ring he gave me. The one I carry every moment of every day, although he doesn't know it.

I remember us making love for the first time. He placed the universe at my feet. He gave me the heavens and all the stars that come along with it. He even placed the light in my ring. But now he's gone and he took my world with him.

Could I have loved him better? Could I have been stronger? Was there something I didn't do? How did I lose him? How did I lose my Guardian?

I can't take the silence anymore. I head up to Miku and Jay's room. When I get there, the door is closed and I can hear them making love.

I smile to myself. I'm so happy they found each other. I remember how amazing Marcus was when my mom died. Miku deserves that kind of love. I quietly head back downstairs. I get my jacket and head outside for some air. I don't really know what to do with myself. Where do you go when your gravity is taken away?

Chapter Thirty-One: R.I.P. Emmy

I make my way down the beach and watch the tide rolling in. I've never been so alone in my life. I zip up my jacket and pretend the reason I'm cold is because of the wind and not because of his sudden absence.

While I feel alone, I just now realize, I am not. A few yards away from me is an Akon, about to escape off into the sky.

"Did you at least leave her a letter?" I ask.

He turns and finds me looking at him with my hands on my hips, pissed.

"Mind your own business," he snaps.

"She loves you and you're taking off on her. Coward."

"Screw you; you don't know anything about me or us."

"Maybe not, but I know a lot about running away. I'm good at it," I reply.

"She wants me to be someone I'm not."

"Bull. She loves you for who you are. You're just in denial because you never thought Thomas would be worthy of being loved. But she did it. She loved you. And this is how you thank her."

"Human, you don't understand the pressure of being…"

"Being in love with a Guardian? Please, I could write a blog."

"It's hard," he confesses.

"Yeah it's damn near impossible; I've tried," I mumble.

"She's so…intense. She believes in me. *Me,*" he says incredulously.

"Look, we shared a laugh today, Ameana and I. That's never happened before. Rage, you're not the only one changing; she is, too."

"You've been with them longer, are things always this…complicated and messy?" he asks.

"Always."

"Human, you ever want out?"

"Yeah, but the exits aren't clearly marked."

"I don't want to hurt Ameana," he shares.

"She's in love; what other outcome could there possibly be?"

"Wow, dark. I'm impressed."

"If only you knew just how dark my thoughts have been lately."

"I figured you were, you know, goody-good girl."

"I'm sure I was, somewhere along the way."

"Please, how dark can you get? You're like a Girl Scout with rainbow cookies and a smile," he jokes.

"You wanna see a Girl Scout lose it?" I ask.

"What do you mean?"

"If you're done running from the only person who loves you, I could use a ride."

"Okay, where to?"

"Rome."

"Why?"

"I'm going to see Bianca. She took something from me; I'm going to get it back."

Rage and I land somewhere outside of Rome, where the new Foundation headquarters is located. The city, much like the rest of the world, is still recovering from the Goumy. However, they have made great progress. Most of the streets are clean and free of debris.

Rage waits for me outside while I go inside the apartment building that houses the Foundation members. According to the roster on the door, her apartment is the first one.

I take a deep breath and knock. She comes to the door a few moments later, looking gorgeous as usual.

"Human, what can I do for you?" she asks with fake politeness.

"I need to talk to you, can I come in?"

She lets me inside her ever-so-fancy apartment.

"What can I do for you?" she asks.

"Actually I came to do you a favor."

"Really, and what is that?" she wonders.

"I thought I'd give you a fair warning."

"A warning about what?"

"Marcus."

"What about my husband?"

"I've decided he's the last guy on Earth I'm ever going to love. He's not perfect. In fact, he can really get under my skin. But you see, Bianca, I love him. I mean ridiculous beyond reason kind of love."

"Why are you telling me this?" she asks.

"Because sometimes people die and no one knows," I explain.

"Excuse me, who died?"

"Emmy."

She looks at me as if I'm crazy.

"You see, Bianca, Emmy was so nice and sweet. She worried about who did and didn't like her. And she spent a lot of time caring about the consequences of her actions. Another thing Emmy used to do a lot, is lose people she loved. But that Emmy is dead. I want you to meet Emerson."

"Really, and what is the diff—"

She didn't even see the blade until it was pressed against her throat.

"I want you to know I *see* you, Bianca. *I see you and your sixteen faces.* Marcus isn't a stepping stone to power. He's my heart, and I would sooner carve into your pretty face than lose him."

"You're just posturing. Do you really think you can frighten me?" she replies, looking down at the blade.

The blood runs down her neck, quickly. Shock spreads on her face. I smile. I only nicked her, yet the fear in her eyes would suggest I stabbed her repeatedly.

"You're just a human. You have no power," she says, glaring at me.

"That's what Kairo thought before I sent him back to his mommy in pieces," I reply as I pull the knife away from her neck and head out the door.

She comes after me and shouts down the hallway.

"I'll give him back when I'm done with him; if the mood strikes me. Or maybe I'll keep him around as a pet."

"Bianca, test me."

She sighs and shakes her head as if I just said something funny.

"The reason you're 'having a moment' is because I slept with your guy. And we had lots and lots and lots of orgasms. But the truth is, I can't take credit for that. The person who insisted we put an Exchange clause in the contract, the person who made this all possible, is Julian."

I can't feel my legs, and my blood runs cold.

"What the hell are you taking about?" I ask.

She laughs.

"Silly, stupid human. Your father ensured that Marcus would have to spend the night with me. That way you would break up with him."

As I storm out of the apartment building, Rage follows me.

"What happened?" he asks.

"Nothing, let's go."

I can't find words to truly express the rage coursing through me. The worst moment of my life, second only to my mom's death, was because of Julian. I replay the agony I felt the night of Marcus and Bianca's honeymoon. I'm so livid I press the knife into my skin without realizing it. I only stop when I notice I'm bleeding.

By the time we get back to the beach house, it's lights are out. Everyone in the house is out and about except Marcus. He stays up in one of the rooms upstairs, alone. I do the same thing. Alone is exactly what I need right now.

For the rest of the day, the team hangs out together. Rage even joined them for a game of Runner Ball with a few angels from the next island over.

Me, I stay in my room. I don't eat. I don't drink. I just sit and reflect. I go over the events of my life. And I find that the worst moments I face are often brought on by Julian.

The next morning, the team packs to go back to New York City and prepare for the Shoma mission. Once again, my mind is on other things. The others check in on me, but I don't really say much. I let them believe Marcus is the reason I'm so deep in thought and distant.

At around noon, I spot Rage in the kitchen, getting ready to join the others outside. Not knowing when I'll get a chance to speak to him alone again, I quickly pull him aside.

"What's up?" he asks.

"I needed you to get me a mixture from the black market."

"A mixture to do what?'

"Kill someone."

"Ah…okay, who do you want to kill?"

"My father."

Just as Rage is about to speak, Jay calls for us to come out to the front porch. Not knowing what or how bad the emergency there could be, both Rage and I rush out of the house.

When we get to the front porch, we find the guys along with Ameana and Miku, standing there, frozen in shock. I follow their gaze and that's when I see it, headed straight for the beach house.

"Alexi."

END OF BOOK FIVE, PART TWO

OTHER BOOKS BY LOLA STVIL

THE GUARDIANS SERIES
Book 1: The Girl
Book 2: The Fallout
Book 3: The Turn
Book 4: The Triplex
Book 5, Part 1: The Quo
Book 5, Part 2: The Lyris
Book 6, Part 1: The Shoma
Book 6, Part 2: The Nycren

The Noru Series
Book 1: Blue Rose
Book 2: The Last Akon
Book 3: Fall of the Chosen
Book 4: When Angels Break
Book 5: Ways of the Wicked
Book 6: Rise of the Alago

ABOUT THE AUTHOR

Lola StVil is a *New York Times* and *USA Today* bestselling author living in California. She enjoys spending time with her family and staying in touch with her readers.